J.-K. Huysma

Certain Artists
(*Certains*)

Translated with an introduction and notes by
Brendan King

Dedalus

This book is supported by the Arts Council England and by the Institut français (Royaume Uni) as part of the Burgess programme (www.frenchbooknews.com)

Supported using public funding by ARTS COUNCIL ENGLAND

INSTITUT FRANÇAIS ROYAUME-UNI

Published in the UK by Dedalus Limited
24-26, St Judith's Lane, Sawtry, Cambs, PE28 5XE
email: info@dedalusbooks.com
www.dedalusbooks.com

ISBN printed book 978 1 912868 61 2
ISBN ebook 978 1 912868 67 4

Dedalus is distributed in the USA & Canada by SCB Distributors
15608 South New Century Drive, Gardena, CA 90248
email: info@scbdistributors.com www.scbdistributors.com

Dedalus is distributed in Australia by Peribo Pty Ltd
58, Beaumont Road, Mount Kuring-gai, N.S.W 2080
email: info@peribo.com.au www.peribo.com.au

First published in France in 1889
First published by Dedalus in 2021

Printed by Clays Ltd, Elcograf S.p.A.
Typeset by Brendan King

A CIP Catalogue record for this book is available on request.

About the Translator

Brendan King is a freelance writer, reviewer and translator with a special interest in late nineteenth-century French fiction. His Ph.D. was on the life and work of J.-K. Huysmans.

His previous translations of Huysmans' work for Dedalus include *Là-Bas: A Journey into the Self, Parisian Sketches, Marthe, Against Nature, Stranded, The Cathedral* (a revised and updated edition of Clara Bell's 1898 translation), *The Vatard Sisters, Drifting,* and *Modern Art.*

He also edited Robert Baldick's definitive biography *The Life of J.-K. Huysmans,* which was published in paperback by Dedalus in 2005.

Contents

Introduction 7

Translator's Note 29

Certain Artists (*Certains*)

i. Dilettantism – Puvis de Chavannes – Gustave Moreau – Degas 35

ii. Bartholomé – Raffaëlli – Stevens – Tissot – Wagner – Cézanne – Forain 55

iii. Chéret – Whistler 73

iv. Félicien Rops 93

v. Prices – Jan Luyken – The Monster 137

vi. The Museum of Decorative Arts and Well-Cooked Architecture 167

vii. Iron – Millet 177

viii. Goya and Turner – The State Hall at the Louvre – Bianchi 201

Notes 211

Glossary of Artists 241

Introduction

Published in 1889, *Certains* (*Certain Artists*) was J.-K. Huysmans' second collection of art criticism. In many ways it can be seen as a companion volume to the first, *L'Art moderne* (*Modern Art*), which appeared six years before, and Huysmans himself described it as 'completing' his earlier book. Like *L'Art moderne, Certains* comprises a mixture of previously published reviews and specially written pieces, with many of the artists whose work Huysmans found particularly compelling, such as Gustave Moreau, Edgar Degas, Jean-Louis Forain, Jean-François Raffaëlli and Odilon Redon, featuring prominently in both volumes.

Despite these surface resemblances, however, the two collections are strikingly different in tone and intent. *L'Art moderne* established a clear dichotomy between the official, effectively State-sponsored art of the annual Salon and the new group of Independent artists who would come to be known as the Impressionists, with Huysmans unequivocally condemning the former and giving his aesthetic support – albeit not always unqualified – to the latter. By contrast, *Certains* makes little reference to Academic art, and Huysmans' artistic *bêtes noirs,* William Bouguereau, Antonin Cabanel and Jean-Léon Gérôme, barely even merit a passing insult. Part of the reason for this was that by the end of the 1880s the battle between the Academic art institution and Independent artists had been all but won. When he came to prepare his previously published reviews of the Salon for inclusion in *Certains,* Huysmans saw no need to reprint his attacks on painters such as Bouguereau and Gérôme, who he had not spared in *L'Art moderne,* and instead concentrated on the artists whose work truly fascinated him. The death of Cabanel – a frequent target of Huysmans' abuse over the years – in the same year as the publication of *Certains* seems symbolic in this regard: for Huysmans to have spent his time berating the stalwarts of the Salon with the same venom he had in *L'Art moderne* would have been to flog a dead horse.

But the differences between the two books go beyond the polemic about Academicism in art, and reflect not just the broader social, cultural and economic developments of the 1880s – the impact of entrepreneurial, privately-owned art galleries on the art market for example, or the *fin-de-siècle* fascination with spiritualism and the occult – but also, on a more personal level, the progressive change in Huysmans' political and existential outlook on life.

Huysmans' estrangement from Zola's materialist-based conception of Naturalism was marked by a corresponding drift rightwards in political terms. He came to see democratic reform as a pollution of social and cultural values, a prostration to the gaudy, commercialised tastes of the masses. Turning his back on Zola's progressive, albeit bourgeois, brand of Republicanism, Huysmans' views became increasingly reactionary, something reflected in his choice of literary friends during this period: Léon Bloy, Auguste Villiers de l'Isle Adam, and Jules Barbey d'Aurevilly, all three of whom were Catholics and whose political views, if unorthodox, could be described as anti-progressive and illiberal.

While in *L'Art moderne*, Huysmans had claimed that the vast field of contemporary reality was open for modern artists to explore and represent, there is no such optimism in *Certains*. Instead, he inverts Hippolyte Taine's theory of the social milieu and its influence on an artist's work, and his contention is not that artists represent their period, but rather that the best artists work in reaction against the detestable times in which they live. Here, revulsion and hatred are the keywords that animate an artist's vision, more than truthfulness or verisimilitude. In

Certains, the vein of pessimism and misanthropy that can be traced in Huysmans' fictional work across the decade, from *À vau-l'eau* (*Drifting*) of 1882, to *En rade* (*Stranded*) of 1887, found a corresponding expression in the work of the artists he admired – or perhaps it would be more accurate to say that he interpreted their work in the light of his own increasingly negative and reactionary feelings.

Comparing the analyses of works by Degas in the two books, for example, there seems to be a world of difference in approach. In *L'Art moderne,* Huysmans praised Degas' truthfulness to life in his depiction of music hall singers and ballet dancers, vaunting the artist's refusal to prettify or romanticise his images of women, as Academic artists tended to do. But in *Certains,* this kind of verisimilitude in terms of external representation is no longer sufficient. Instead, Huysmans sees in Degas' portraits of women at their toilette images that reflect his increasingly misogynistic vision of women as irredeemably degenerate – not to say demonic – creatures.

The longest essay in the book, an extended analysis of the work of Félicien Rops, is a case in point. Rops had a certain vogue among a particular class of bourgeois male, partly because he produced a significant quantity of erotica which could be accessed via a hermetic network of 'bibliophiles' who dealt in privately-printed limited editions of his more risqué work. In 1882, at a period when his renown in Paris was at its highest, Rops produced a series of five engravings issued under the title *Les Sataniques* (*Satanics*). The theme of the plates was the infernal coupling of Satan and Woman, in which Satan represented the principle of Lust, and Woman represented human perversity, the intermediary between the Devil and mankind. It was through Woman that man became possessed by the spirit of Lust, and as Woman was the servant of the Devil she contaminated every man she touched. In such a symbolic schema it is easy to see a link between moral or spiritual contamination and contemporary social issues – the economic and social threat to bourgeois values posed by the rise of feminism and the 'New Woman', for example, or the spectre of syphilis, which at the time was popularly assumed to be transmitted by women, together with the allied problem of prostitution, which attained record levels during the Belle Époque.

Through images like those in *Les Sataniques*, Rops provided Huysmans with a potent icon of Woman, that of the succubus, who attacks men's minds as they sleep and saps their bodily strength through illicit sexual intercourse. Although Huysmans' dissatisfaction with Naturalism was obviously part of a larger cultural and political reaction, the readiness with which he adopted the iconic image of the succubus in his work – it would become a central motif in his 1891 novel *Là-bas*, for example – clearly shows that this discontent was linked to the literary and artistic movement's failure to provide an adequate symbolic representation of women. Indeed, Huysmans makes the point explicitly himself:

> At a time when materialist art sees nothing but hysterics consumed by their ovaries, or nymphomaniacs whose brains beat in the region of their loins, [Rops] celebrated not the contemporary woman, not the Parisienne, whose affected graces and dubious adornments eluded his dexterity, but the timeless, Essential Woman, the poisonous and naked Beast, the mercenary of Darkness, the absolute servant of the Devil.

Like his study of Degas, Huysmans' analysis of Rops is as much a product of his own state of mind as it is an objective account of the artist's work. Rops himself recalled how, when Huysmans came to see him in his studio in Belgium, despite the fact that *Les Sataniques* represented a very small percentage of his total output, it was only this series of engravings that Huysmans was interested in looking at, and which he would later make the cornerstone of his essay.

Introduction

Although today *Certains* is one of the least well-known of Huysmans' books, it remains a significant one in terms of his development as a writer. It sheds light on a decisive period in Huysmans' literary career, and can be seen as a bridge between two phases of his stylistic evolution: a shift from the Decadent iconography that had permeated *À rebours* and which gave it its distinctive appeal, to a darker, more extreme spiritual vision that would reach its culmination in *Là-bas*, which delved into the controversial theme of contemporary Satanism in Paris. Huysmans' descent into the occult world, and his subsequent conversion to Catholicism, are both prefigured in the subject matter and iconography of *Certains*.

If *L'Art moderne* was the high-water mark of Huysmans' progressive modernity, *Certains* embodies the reaction against it. Again, the example of female representation is instructive: while *L'Art moderne* featured generally positive assessments of work by Mary Cassatt, Berthe Morisot, Eva Gonzales and Kate Greenaway, not a single female artist is mentioned by name in *Certains*.

In hindsight, the book effectively represents Huysmans' farewell to modern art. With the exception perhaps of his enthusiasm for the work of the young Catholic painter Charles-Marie Dulac, on whom he pinned his hopes for a renewal of mystical art until the painter's untimely death in 1898, Huysmans would progressively turn away from contemporary art. After 1889, he would concentrate instead on the religiously-inspired works of the Primitives. This would eventually culminate in the publication of *Trois primitifs* ('Three Primitive Painters'), his studies on Matthias Grünewald, the 'Master of Flémalle' (now generally considered to be Robert Campin), and the unknown artist of a painting in the Frankfort Museum. Published in 1905, this would be the last volume in Huysmans' 'trilogy' of books on art.

The Writing of *Certains*

Certains concentrates more on individual artists than on exhibitions, and includes a more diverse range of subjects than *L'Art moderne*. Alongside extracts from Huysmans' reviews of the 1884, 1885 and 1887 Salons – notably pieces on Puvis de Chavannes, Bartholomé, Raffaëlli and Whistler – and a number of short articles that had appeared in *La Revue indépendante*, *La Cravache Parisienne,* and *La Revue illustrée* between 1880 and 1888, *Certains* also contains a series of more in-depth essays, the most significant of which – those on Moreau, Degas, Chéret, Rops, Redon and Jan Luyken – were written between 1888-89, and amount to over half the book.

Huysmans first reference to the idea of a new collection of art criticism was in the spring of 1888. For the past year he had been working on a novel set on 'the fringe of the clerical world', about Karl-Wilhelm Naundorff's claim to be the legitimate heir to the French throne. In the course of his researches into this Monarchist conspiracy which, as Robert Baldick puts it in *The Life of J-K Huysmans,* 'owed much to supernatural revelation, and which had attracted a considerable following of prophets, spiritualists and miracle workers', Huysmans would encounter an assorted collection of mystics, spiritualists, conspiracy theorists, unfrocked priests, and those on the margins of the occult – a portent of things to come.

By March of 1888, however, the book had stalled. Possibly Huysmans' interest in Naundorff's political intrigues paled in comparison to the stories of contemporary occultism he was now beginning to uncover, but whatever the reason for his writing block, he decided to use the occasion to take out his frustrations with his new publisher, Pierre-Victor Stock. In Huysmans' eyes Stock's lacklustre promotion of his recently-published novella, *Un dilemme* ('A Dilemma'), had resulted in abysmal sales. As he complained to his Dutch friend, Arij Prins:

> As for me – I'm fed up. Stock is a complete imbecile. He's done nothing in the way of promotion. I'm irritated with him – I've almost a mind to break our contract. For this reason, and to annoy him – as he hasn't kept his promises and to stick a couple of fingers up at him – I'm going to do a book on art – reprint a few good articles from *La Revue independante,* then write some studies on Rops, Chéret, Wisthler [*sic*] – rework one on Moreau – and a few notes on some other painters. It will complete my book on modern art. That's tempting enough for me, even though it'll delay my novel – but I was only on the second chapter anyway.
>
> (Huysmans to Arij Prins, 10 March 1888)

But no sooner had he started working again there were more problems. During periods when he was writing Huysmans frequently suffered from bouts of ill health – throughout his life references to insomnia, indigestion, neuralgia, rheumatism, toothache and problems with his eyes appear like a refrain in his correspondence – and *Certains* was no exception, as he told the Belgian writer Jules Destrée:

> I was working on this [book of art criticism], but another two-week interruption – my left eye is ill. Forbidden to work in the evening, ordered to read as little as possible during the day… I've got a sort of conjuntivitis which at the moment is resistant to eye-drops and ointments.
>
> (Huysmans to Jules Destrée, April 1888)

The degree to which these ailments were psychosomatic is difficult to say, but certainly Huysmans' sense of well-being was affected by events around him, and during this period he felt that death, disease and misery were afflicting everyone he knew. In another letter to Destrée written shortly afterwards, he returned to the same theme, this time elaborating on the various problems plaguing his literary friends – Léon Bloy, who seemed to be in a continual state of poverty and misfortune, Villiers de l'Isle Adam, who had been diagnosed with cancer and was living in a precarious state, Paul Verlaine, who was lapsing into alcoholism, and Barbey d'Aurevilly, who was ill and who would die from a haemorrage less than a year later:

> I told you about the horror of my existence at the moment, my distressing state of spirit, my distaste for work, everything. Others here are doing little better. Bloy works, but is not what you'd call happy. Villiers passes his time prostrate in bars, amid idiots and piles of beer glasses, poor Verlaine is sick in mind and spirit, d'Aurevilly is subsiding into old-age after the illness that recently struck him. I see nothing but misfortune and ruin in all the people around me who I love...
>
> I'm still, not being able to work on account of my eyes and my problems with a long-standing work [*Là-bas*], in the middle of a book on art [*Certains*] – but everything's at a standstill. I've got stuff to do for a book on Raffaëlli, and for an English magazine, but nothing comes out, and I'm suffering.
>
> (Huysmans to Jules Destrée, 19 June 1888)

But it wasn't just his own health and that of his literary friends that contributed to Huysmans' depressed state of mind during the composition of both *Là-bas* and *Certains*. His long-standing mistress, Anna Meunier, was suffering from a degenerative disease that progressively incapacitated her and disturbed her mind. The psychological effect this had on Huysmans is reflected in the gloomy forebodings of *En rade* (1887), in which the notion of general paralysis became a literal metaphor, with the crumbling Chateau de Lourps serving as a symbol of Meunier's deleterious mental and physical state. Two years after the publication of *Certains,* Meunier was committed to the Saint Anne asylum in Paris, where she died in 1895.

Such painful experiences could not but have an impact on Huysmans' emotional state and on his writing. Léon Bloy, who was a close friend at the time but who would shortly fall out with him, gives a revealing portrait of the writer during this period:

> If you only knew what sad events were occurring only two steps from me. Poor Huysmans, who has shown himself to be the most admirable friend, came and spent Sunday evening with me. We ate and talked together, *tête-à-tête*, for several hours. The unfortunate man had just left poor Anna, who seems to be on the point of dying. You can imagine how happy our conversation was…I was suffering like one of the damned. I saw, Henriette, what I've never, ever seen, something that very few people would even believe possible… I saw the author of *À rebours* cry. Oh, he must have such a weight of sorrow pressing on his heart, because he's not like me and tears don't come easy to him. In truth, it is too sad…
>
> (Léon Bloy to Henriette L'Huillier, 27 October 1887)

Although Huysmans had mapped out the major pieces he planned to write as early as March 1888, in the event he did not get around to writing them for almost a year. Nevertheless, he completed some short pieces on Tissot, Wagner and Cézanne, and one on auction prices, as well as preparing pieces previously published in *La Revue independante*, on Bianchi, Millet, Goya and Turner, and two additional pieces on architecture.

Huysmans' annual summer leave was taken up with a trip to Germany, which would also have its influence on the new book. 'I have a good friend in Hamburg,' he told Zola in July, 'and I shall go and see the paintings of the Primitives in Cologne, Berlin and Dresden.' The good friend was Arij Prins, and in between sampling the brothels of Hamburg, the two men took in the art museums. It was during a visit to Cassel with Prins that Huysmans saw Matthias Grünewald's *Crucifixion*. Grünewald's depiction of Christ gripped his imagination and formed the inspiration for his conception of 'supernatural realism' or 'mystical Naturalism', which he later expounded in *Là-bas*. 'The Primitives are art in its highest form,' he told Destrée on his return, 'and supernatural realism is the only formula, the only true formula, which can exist for me.'

At the beginning of 1889, Huysmans turned his attention to the studies that would form the nucleus of the book, those on Redon, Degas, Chéret, Whistler and Rops. But as he began to write again, Huysmans' familiar complaints about illness returned:

> The truth is that I've been slowed down for the last fortnight, with a horrible mucal inflammation, all of which is complicated by a rheumatism in my right leg. In the end, my doctor ordered me to rest completely, regular baths, poultices and mineral water. To the extent that I am now shut up in my bedroom [...] And my belly is irritable too, to add to all that.
>
> (Huysmans to Bloy or Gustave Guiches, 15 February 1889)

Nevertheless, Huysmans still managed to complete a succession of pieces during this period. His essay on Redon and the monstrous in art was written during April and May:

> I've finished an interesting piece on the monstrous in art – about the gargoyles of Notre-Dame, Christian symbolism, and Odilon Redon [...] I've still got work to do on the Eiffel Tower and the Machine Hall at the Universal Exhibition – a piece on Wisthler [sic], a piece on Degas, and perhaps one on English painting – after which I'll have practically finished my book of art criticism. I'm thinking therefore that it'll be published towards the end of the year.
>
> (Huysmans to Arij Prins, 14 May 1889)

Although the essay on English painting was ultimately abandoned – in the event Turner was the only representative of the

English artists to appear in *Certains* – the other pieces were either newly written or, in the case of Whistler, adapted from previously published articles. During June, Huysmans worked on pieces about the Eiffel Tower and the Universal Exhibition – which had just opened the previous month – before turning to what would become the book's *tour de force*, his study of Félicien Rops:

> I've plunged into an infernal – and that's the appropriate word – work on Rops. I've seen his etchings, of which *Les Sataniques* are admirable. But it's a hell of a business to convey the complete obscenity and diabolism of his work.
>
> But enough! Once that's done my book on art will be finished. In the next issue of *La Revue independente* you'll find a piece on the Eiffel Tower. I'm pleased with it because all the newspapers have been bought off to promote this piece of pig-iron – no other article in the press has appeared against it.
>
> (Huysmans to Arij Prins, 21 June 1889)

The in-depth study of Rops' work would take a further two months to complete, delayed no doubt by the on-going saga of Villiers' terminal illness:

> At the moment, I'm overwhelmed with sadness and problems. Villiers is in a hopeless state and is dying [...] So, there you have it my friend, I'm running backwards and forwards between my place and the Maison de Santé, all the while expecting to come across Villiers in his death agony – you can imagine how pleasant that is...
>
> I am still working, despite all these problems. I hope to have finished my book of art by the end of the month. Phew! I could do with a holiday – and with not having to go in to work at the office.
>
> (Huysmans to Prins, 8 August 1889)

Less than two weeks later, Huysmans again wrote to Prins, to inform him of Villiers' death and, coincidentally, the completion of his book:

> My dear friend, poor Villiers is dead, and Mallarmé and I buried him yesterday. [...] I've finished my book of art. I've only a few retouches to do, I'm hoping it'll be done and come out in the shops in October or November. I'm exhausted, worn out, sick of all these goings on with Villiers – I'm off to bed at 8 for a couple of days...
>
> (Huysmans to Prins, 22 August 1889)

Fortunately for Huysmans, the process of proofing and printing was infinitely quicker and smoother with Stock than it had been with his previous publisher, Charpentier, who had held up the publication of *L'Art moderne* with continual requests to suppress material he felt was injurious to his artistic friends. During the manuscript stage, the new book's provisional title, *Plusieurs* ('Several'), was changed to *Certains* (literally 'a few'), and on 15 September, less than a month after it was finished, Huysmans wrote to Odilon Redon to say that the proofed book was 'now at the printer'.

Critical response

Certains was published by Tresse & Stock at the beginning of November 1889. After the somewhat dissappointing sales of both *En rade* – the first book to appear under the new imprint two years before in 1887 – and *Un dilemme,* Huysmans was pleased with the initial reaction to *Certains,* even before the press reviews had kicked in:

> *Certains* – in the absence of any mention in the press – has caused a violent reaction in the art world, and sold 1200 copies up to the present moment. Which is unheard of for a book of art criticism.
>
> (Huysmans to Arij Prins, 26 November 1889)

What Huysmans left out of this account is just how active he'd been in organising the book's launch. Although his name was still relatively unfamiliar to ordinary readers, Huysmans' literary reputation had grown sufficiently in the 1880s that he was now well-known to many influential writers, artists and journalists. Consequently, he used his impressive network of contacts to promote the book, and Stock sent out a large number of complimentary copies to various movers and shakers in the Parisian literary and artistic world, including writers such as Stéphane Mallarmé, Paul Verlaine, Émile Zola, Edmond Goncourt, Alphonse Daudet, Paul Bourget and Guy de Maupassant; artists such as Jules Chéret, Albert Bartholomé, Jean-François Raffaëlli, Odilon Redon and Félicien Rops; and art critics such as Théodore Duret, Jean Dolent and Octave Mirbeau – as well as a similar number of prominent writers and artists in Belgium. This advance campaign had the effect of creating a buzz around the book, not least among some of the artists Huysmans either knew or had previously written about, as they searched to see if they'd been mentioned or not. Sometimes, being included was worse than being excluded: Odilon Redon was one artist unhappy about the way in which Huysmans 'appropriated' his work in *Certains* and elsewhere.

Unsurprisingly, given Huysmans' confrontational style, his unconventional choice of artists (which at the time would have been seen as unrepresentative of the canon accepted by the art establishment), and his sideswipes at fellow art critics – most notably in his opening attack on dilettantism – many reviewers highlighted the book's controversial aspects:

> A book has just been published which is destined to cause a stir in the world of art and artists; it will be much talked about; the author is J.-K. Huysmans, to whom we already owe a very interesting book of art criticism, *L'Art moderne*, a

> work of passion and conviction, which had a very big impact on its appearance.
>
> Huysmans is a writer who cannot be read with indifference; he either grips you or revolts you, there is no middle ground; he's not some eclectic that everyone is interested in; on the contrary, he violently rebels against the promiscuity of admiration, which is one of the most disconcerting symptoms of our era [...] As I said at the start, Huysmans' book will undoubtedly raise storms. But it should be read by anyone with a passion for art.
>
> (*Le Moniteur des Arts*, 29 November 1889)

Despite the controversial nature of Huysmans' opinions and the uncompromising style in which he expressed them, many critics nevertheless reacted positively to the book, even when they actively disagreed with him. The reviewer of *L'Estafette* (a paper whose banner motto read 'Order and Progress'), for example, took issue with Huysmans' diatribe against dilettantism, arguing that it was perfectly possible to like both Delacroix and Bastien-Lepage, but such disagreements didn't prevent him from recommending the book to the paper's readers:

> Here is yet more literature about art! In front of a painting, an engraving or a watercolour, what does it matter to know what any man – even a critic – thinks about it? In this case, however, our interest is a bit keener, as there may be a legitimate curiosity in knowing what J.-K. Huysmans' preferences are, in accompanying him on the highly original walk he takes through art, and in listening to what a 'certain writer' is going to tell us about 'certain artists'.
>
> Reading this book is very entertaining: at the beginning the author launches a full charge against the dilettanti and the eclectic: he recognises in them nothing but imbecility or cowardice; he disapproves of promiscuity in admiration. If

> you like Delacroix's *Entry of the Crusaders into Constantinople,* then you cannot tolerate 'those operetta-milkmaids dressed up by that Grévin of the cabaret, by that Siraudin of the suburbs, the late Jules Bastien-Lepage'. This is the theory of J.-K. Huysmans, which he takes to its extreme with a violence, an exaggeration, and an excess that is, at times, amusing. Personally, I believe one can very sincerely be ecstatic in front of Delacroix while also admiring Bastien-Lepage, about whom the author is too severe....
>
> Here and there a few amusing reflections, a few well-crafted paradoxes, a few curious theories, a few original insights. [...] And what's more, all this is said in a language that enchants me, whatever one thinks about how strange it is; his lively, colourful descriptions alone make *Certains* worth reading; it is, without a doubt, one of the most interesting books of art criticism.
>
> (*L'Estafette*, 17 November 1889)

The reviewer of *La Revue des Deux Mondes*, a politically conservative journal that saw itself as the guardian of 'high culture', was more grudging, taking Huysmans to task over his book's somewhat arch, enigmatic title, and its stylistic 'faults':

> Under cover of this bizarre title – a little pretentious, moreover, and above all obscure – Huysmans has quite simply gathered 'certain' articles on 'certain' painters that he has published in 'certain' magazines: on Gustave Moreau, on Degas, on Wisthler [sic], on Félicien Rops, etc. We find here all of Huysmans' usual faults, which we are careful not to reproach him with, since they constitute almost all his originality: a coldly furious style, more drole than truly humorous, and paradoxes that are, in general, more amusing than risqué. However, amid all this, a few just ideas surprise one or strike one, and you ask yourself, a little anxiously, if Huysmans, who was born with an innate capacity for reason, has not deliberately destroyed

> his own natural common sense – assuming at least that he's not concealing it for fun, in order to exasperate the 'bourgeois' even more, or to amuse a few dilettantes.
>
> (*La Revue des Deux Mondes*, 1 December 1889)

Émile de Molènes in *La Liberté* – whose masthead carried the portentous tag, 'All social institutions must have as their goal the amelioration of the moral, intellectual and physical destinty of the poorest and more populous class' – took a more moralistic view. De Molènes' criticisms of the book, the subject matter of which he saw as having a deleterious effect on the reader's state of mind, recalled the moralistic outrage that had generally greeted Huysmans' Naturalist novels. De Molènes also attacked Huysmans pretension to have 'discovered' certain artists whose talents he felt were already recognised. De Molènes might have been on stronger ground here if *La Liberté* had itself done anything in the way of promoting new artists, but the review of *Certains* was practically the first time Odilon Redon's name had even appeared in the paper. Likewise, de Molènes repetition of Huysmans' erroneous spelling of Whistler's name implies that the artist and his work was unfamiliar to him, despite his protestations to the contrary:

> M. Huysmans has just devoted a book, entitled *Certains*, to several artists of our time, those he prefers, it goes without saying, or at least those whose talent corresponds most directly to his preoccupations as a thinker and to his aesthetics as a writer. Because M. Huysmans is both a thinker and a writer. I could also add that he is a painter, so great is his obsession with a particular form and his search for the right image applied to thought [...].
>
> That said, I feel obliged to note, first of all, that M. Huysmans seems to be striking a great blow in order to force open doors that are already open – open in the sense that this

armed and helmeted champion had no need of any of these trappings. However contemptible it may be in the eyes of M. Huysmans – who does not allow any eclecticism in matters of art – critics have not been waiting for the book entitled *Certains* in order to render full and complete justice to the merits of artists who make up Huysmans' gallery.

Who are these artists? Gustave Moreau, Degas, Wisthler (*sic*), Rops, Redon, Chéret, all painters and engravers to whom, for years, we have always lavished praise and encouragement. M. Huysmans, therefore, has no basis in posing as Christopher Columbus *vis-à-vis* these talents, who have been variously appreciated, it is true, but always recognised, each at his proper level, with perfect sincerity. [...]

Coming too late to this party, M. Huysmans was therefore only able to distinguish himself by the particularly studied and brilliant form with which he invested his admiration for the artists of his choice. In this respect, his book is extremely curious, not so much for the whole as for certain chapters – among others, the one devoted to Félicien Rops, and the one entitled 'The Monster' – chapters in which the author has appropriated the works he exalts, and has transformed the material into new pen paintings, as vibrant as masterpiece etchings themselves.

Unfortunately, I cannot insist on this point, because Satanism and Lust enter directly into these works, and I do not wish to encourage readers with an art whose main idealism is to be demonic. I even believe that those with too much of a taste for such research and for such evocations are to be pitied. Living in good health and in a balanced mental state with obsessions like these is a problem that it is not always safe to resolve. In any case, it is much wiser to choose healthier and more refreshing food for your mind.

(Émile de Molènes, *La Liberté*, 17 November 1889)

Despite de Molènes' criticism, it is indisputable that Huysmans' constant promotion of artists such as Moreau, Redon, Degas and Forain, both in his fiction and his art criticism, was at least part of the reason they had become so well-known in the first place.

Proof of this can be seen in a review of an exhihibition of Jules Chéret's work shortly after the appearance of *Certains*. Writing in *Art et Critique*, Jules Antoine noted that 'Chéret has seen his reputation growing day by day', and referenced 'the remarkable study that J.-K. Huysmans devoted to him in *Certains*'.

A few months earlier, a generally positive review of *Certains* also appeared in *Art et Critique*, a 'literary, dramatic, musical and artistic review', which had been founded just six months before the book was published. The review was entrusted to the art critic Felix Fenéon, who had made a name for himself as an enthusiastic supporter of Impressionism. Fenéon also happened to be an enthusiastic admirer of Huysmans – in 1886 he dedicated a copy of his own book on the Impressionists to the author of *L'Art moderne* with the words, 'To the "inventor" of Impressionism, J.-K Huysmans'.

> No one more than Huysmans is as perceptive at discovering among the crowd a painter of new and forceful talent. Théodore Duret had celebrated the nascent Impressionist movement before him, but he used grey ink to evoke their polychrome works...he tried to convert the masses, and was aggrieved when they didn't gather in front of his chosen masters. Huysmans presented his chosen artists to a smaller audience, and in order to impose them he equipped himself with a colourful, tumultuous and magnificent style [...] If young writers today are curious about the plastic arts, and if one can, without scandal, align Degas alongside the most glorious of the old painters, it is to Huysmans that we owe that fact.
>
> [...] Huysmans was the historiographer of the first

> Impressionist campaigns; he appropriately celebrated Delacroix, Goya, Turner, Chéret, Whistler, Redon, Bartholomé; he has covered the official artists in a sticky contempt. His two critical books are, in their certainty of verdict and their firm execution, the only books that have been written on modern art.
>
> (Félix Fenéon, *Art et Critique*, 14 December 1889)

Writing in *L'Événement*, Jean Lorrain, a fervent admirer who had arranged for Huysmans to meet Gustave Moreau in his spectacular house-cum-studio in Rue de la Rochefoucauld in June 1885, lauded the older writer's style in similarly flattering terms:

> There is still, it seems, some comforting reading to be had.
>
> In the midst of the appalling famine of ideas that is ravaging the publishing market, almost in proportion to the ever-growing mass of volumes, a rare happiness has just been given to me – that of finally being able to read a book! The book is one written, thought out, and worked on by a sincere and curious mind, a work the personal force of which, breaking the mould of convention and accepted cliché, opens you up to horizons of aesthetics, of philosophy and of literature that have been seen a hundred times but never yet described.
>
> I'm talking about *Certains* by Joris-Karl Huysmans.
>
> *Certains*, these are the favourite painters of the author of *En rade,* those to whom his almost painful and exasperated apprehensions of a refined scholar attracted and compelled him, and here they are evoked in a prestigious and precise style, engraved as if with a chisel, with an artist's incisive and barbed quill [...]
>
> I have given the genesis of the book, but what I cannot convey through the ordinary style of a review is the curious research, the deliberate profundity and justice, the vengeful equity of word and thought, the spirit of combativeness

> imbued like a breath of fever between the pages and between the lines, which sets you alight when reading this volume.
>
> (Jean Lorrain, *L'Événement*, 1 December 1889)

Another of Huysmans' influential friends, Octave Uzanne, the editor of the periodical *Le Livre moderne*, also gave the book a good review, though a passing remark about Huysmans 'bringing to his arguments the fine and nimble wit of his dilettanisme', implies that Uzanne had skimmed only the titles of the chapters, rather than actually reading Huysmans' scathing dismissal of the dilettante:

> J.-K. Huysmans presents us with his latest essays, which form a rare work by virtue of his talent and the high quality of his artistic views. [...] This work, supremely contemptuous of all the mercantile coteries of this publicity-ridden epoch, finds room only for the strong, for the seekers of new formulas, for the solitary talents spurned by useless art academies. His judgments on the painter Degas, on Forain and on Félicien Rops are better than delicately crafted literary works, a fierce and superb truth emerges from them; the critic's voice remains intact and uncorrupted [...] *Certains* deserves to be read carefully, savoured slowly. It is one of those books, all too rare, that we must take pride in preserving, elegantly bound, and that one opens often, like a bottle filled with an invigorating quintessence.
>
> (Octave Uzanne, *Le Livre moderne*, January 1890)

It was perhaps to be expected, given Huysmans' long-standing contacts with Belgium, that his book would receive a good press there, and Arnold Goffin's enthusiastic review gives a flavour of how warmly Huysmans was regarded in the Belgian literary and artistic world:

> *Certains* logically completes *L'Art moderne*; and since that last-named book, Huysmans' beautifully uncompromising theories, far from weakening, have, on the contrary, become even sharper.

> He salutes his favourite artists with unforgettable pages of precise and fair praise; he analyses and comments on their work, transposing it into a style that is incisive and subtle; as for the artists he abhors, he dooms them to the expiatory torments of the Inquisition, desires to see their sentimental entrails ingeniously unravelled, or have them impaled by slow and clumsy executioners, flayed alive with delicious and novel refinements [...].
>
> The book opens with an execution of dilettantism of a delectable ferocity. [...] There then follow some studies on the Impressionists; on Whistler; on Puvis de Chavannes, Alfred Stevens and Millet, who are expertly restored to the rank they deserve; on Gustave Moreau and Félicien Rops – two exceptional studies – and then, after a piece on the exhausting masterpiece of modern Industry [the Universal Exhibition], a few prestigious pages about a Bianchi in the Louvre, which is of an enigmatic and shimmering beauty.
>
> (Arnold Goffin, *La Jeune Belgique,* November, 1889)

Despite the generally favourable reception that *Certains* received in France and Belgium, the book did little to expand Huysmans' name among English-speakers, either at home or abroad. This was no doubt partly due to the ambiguity of the book's untranslatable title, and partly because many of the artists included were little known in England at the time. It is difficult to know what ex-pats in Paris would have made of this gnomic announcement in *Galignani's Messenger*:

> M. Huysmans is a critic with a very pronounced style, which he has brought to bear on a variety of singular subjects. His book contains a series of cleverly-written articles, which must be read to be understood.
>
> (*Galignani's Messenger,* 11 November 1889)

Elsewhere, the *Saturday Review* published an arch piece on 7 December 1889, asserting that the list of artists 'will suggest that the book is not a Christmas present for young ladies'. The reviewer then took issue with Huysmans' pronouncement on dilettantism and the impossibility of admiring both Delacroix and Bastien-Lepage: '…it so happens that we who talk (so gently) to M. Huysmans can do these very two things most sincerely. But what we admit that we cannot sincerely extasiate ourselves before or admire is M. Huysmans's idea of style.'

At the end of December 1889, Huysmans updated Prins on the press reaction to the book with some degree of satisfaction:

> *Certains* is still attracting notices, either on it or about it […] The book is selling, though New Year will slow sales. All in all, for a book of art criticism, it's been amazing, both in terms of public reaction and sales.
>
> (Huysmans to Arij Prins, 31 December 1889)

In the wake of the publication of *Certains,* Huysmans' reputation as a critic of contemporary art probably reached its highest standing in the 1890s. The respected critic, Roger Marx, provided a fulsome assessment of Huysmans' qualities as an art critic:

> […] almost all modern criticism today descends from him [Huysmans]. Since Thoré, we have not encountered a diagnosis so little fallible, or since Baudelaire the double gift of divination and expression, which makes the aesthetic writings of J.-K. Huysmans definitive pages, and their author not just a judge among judges, but a unique personality: *the* critic of modern art.
>
> (Roger Marx, *Portraits du prochain siècle,* 1894)

Translator's note

As with most of Huysmans' books, the title presents some difficulties for the translator. Although *Certains* can be translated as 'some' or 'a few [things]', I have chosen a slightly more explicit title, *Certain Artists*, partly because it retains the dual-meaning of 'certain', as something sure and established, but also in its use to define something in a vague or offhanded fashion.

To make navigating the book slightly easier, I have added the name of the artist dealt with at the head of each relevant section, and as many of the artists cited by Huysmans are now unfamiliar I have occasionally given their name in full to make identification easier, and dropped the conventional 'M.' for 'Monsieur' that Huysmans sporadically affixed to the artist's name. Every artist whose name is mentioned is given in a Glossary at the back of the book which also serves as an index.

I have relied for this translation on the edition of *Certains* contained in Volume IV of Huysmans' *Oeuvres complètes* (Classiques Garnier, 2019). This incredibly detailed and comprehensive critical edition edited by Jean-Marie Seillan is a model of academic rigour, and proved invaluable in tracking down certain references and allusions in the text, though a few instances where the edition's notes seemed to be lacking or inaccurate are detailed in my notes at the back of the book.

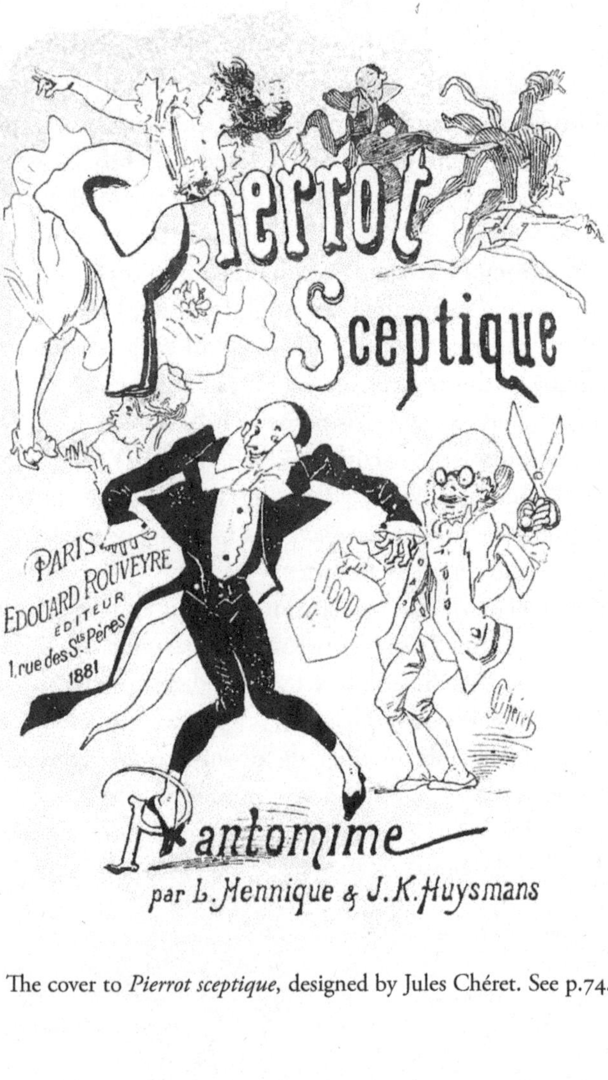

The cover to *Pierrot sceptique*, designed by Jules Chéret. See p.74.

Certain Artists
(*Certains*)

I

Dilettantism – Puvis de Chavannes – Gustave Moreau – Degas

DILETTANTISM

One of the most disconcerting symptoms of the present time is a general promiscuity of admiration. Art having become, like sport, one of those activities pursued by the rich, exhibitions now follow one another with equal success, regardless of the work being shown – provided, of course, that the press is there and the show is held in a well-known gallery, in a room deemed by all to be trendy.

The vogue for such distractions is easily explained.

First, the arid brains bestowed on the fashionable find in this regular parade of drawings and canvases a fanciful resource that is perfect to alternate with their threadbare discussions about politics and their well-worn gossip about the theatre; added to which, platitudes about painting can sometimes supplement an evening of high-society tittle-tattle, or conjure up languid reflections during games of poker[1] or the diplomatic silences of whist players.

Finally – and this reason alone would suffice – visiting, and supposedly admiring, the most dissimilar and antithetical works implies a broadmindedness, a flexibility of artistic taste, that is very flattering.

In literature, especially, these connoisseurs without prejudice abound. Everyone it seems – and who can doubt it? – is an expert at judging sentences. Sometimes you can find the odd fossil, a prehistoric throwback, a naive provincial who admits to not being absolutely certain of the accuracy of his assessments about painting; others, at a push, might acknowledge that the musical sensibility eludes them, or even go so far as to claim that the works of Wagner are not perhaps *completely* mad; but no one has ever confessed to a complete ineptitude when it comes to understanding a page of prose or verse. Take, from among the hordes of Paris, the most noble prince or the most dishonest local greengrocer; choose, from this mass of people, the most empty-headed whore or the most eminent baroness, and straightaway they will fire off an opinion, settled, determined, reasoned, unbending, about a book. Never, and I mean never, will anyone admit that they are absolutely unfit to appreciate an art which is actually the most complicated, the most intricate, the most elevated of them all.

What's more, who amongst us hasn't noticed, amid the bundles of bound paper the middle classes and the fashionable refer to as 'their library', the indecent promiscuity of a Georges Ohnet next to a Flaubert, of an Albert Delpit next to a Goncourt?[2] Who hasn't felt that delightful frisson when a connoisseur tosses off in a nonchalant tone: "You know, me, I'm an eclectic. I'm interested in everything, I have here, untrammelled by the strictures of a particular school, the most diverse specimens of art…" A young gentleman who said he most sincerely admired Émile Zola's *The Drinking Den*,[3] did he not also recently express his ardent desire – right to my face – that Francisque Sarcey[4] – that senile nincompoop, that lacrymose prig who writes for *Le Temps* – should collect his weekly effusions on the theatre into book form!

Well, these individuals, these refined dabblers,[5] are the open-minded, the *dilettanti*!

Ah, all the same, this word 'dilettante' has perhaps been misused in recent times. Basically, leaving aside the conceitedly false meaning that has been attributed to it, we can, by squeezing it hard, break it down, split it into the two parts it is really composed of: imbecility on the one hand, cowardice on the other.

Imbecility on the part of the fashionable; cowardice on the part of the press that directs them.

I. Dilettantism – Chavannes – Moreau – Degas

Imbecility, which is to say – from the artistic point of view that concerns us here – the complete misunderstanding of art, equivocal words of praise pulled out at random like lotto balls from a sack, a perfect ignorance translated into banal eulogies.

The most conclusive example of what I'm saying was demonstrated, from a pictorial point of view, a few years ago. The exhibitions of Delacroix and Bastien-Lepage coincided; women, who as everyone knows take a very lively interest in painting, and who understand it as thoroughly as they do literature – which is not saying much – would, without batting an eyelid, go from the show at the Beaux-Arts to the exhibition at the Hôtel de Chimay,[6] and behold with equal admiration Delacroix's *Entry of the Crusaders in Constantinople* and those operetta-milkmaids dressed up by that Grévin of the cabaret, by that Siraudin[7] of the suburbs, the late Jules Bastien-Lepage. The platitudes raged: "We admire beauty wherever it can be found. Just because Delacroix was a great painter, is that a reason why Bastien-Lepage can't be another?" And no one, no, not a single person winced at this ridiculous intermingling of a fashionable soirée and a sanctuary, at this incredible shoving together of a lackey and a master!

But these sorts of people are unthinking. They would walk around, coolly judging the works of these two painters, which, in their need to praise, they no doubt confounded with that of Miss Timoléon Lobrichon and Miss Adrien Marie[8] – in truth, only death will finally put an end to the torrent of sentimental vignettes that these two industrious individuals inundate us with!

Cowardice, that's the word that applies to the art critic. Like the literary critic who writes reviews for a living, the art critic is generally a man of letters who couldn't produce a real work of his own. Among them, there are some whose brains are as vacuous as those of the fashionable people they envy and mimic; their opinions are therefore predictable. But there are others, more open, more cunning, who, under the guise of dilettantism, profess a need to distrust everything, a desire to not state anything, in other words, a cowardice as regards thought, and a hypocrisy as regards form.

For art critics, this fluctuating terrain over which they move is a profitable piece of real-estate. To praise or denigrate dead artists; to avoid compromising oneself when speaking of those who are alive; to flatter with gift-inducing phrases the old, prize-winning academic milch-cows; to prostitute themselves with 'licensed' ideas and 'regulated' opinions;[9] to utter, under the pretext of analysis, the most noxious commonplaces in a stilted language, to feign profundity under the obscurity of incidental detail; those are their tricks. The equivocating and self-satisfied critic, insensitive and spineless, who masters these techniques will immediately be considered a man of taste, a well-bred man, perceptive and charming, delicate and refined – oh, above all delicate and refined! It's all honour and profit for him… and what's more, I imagine that's all he's looking for.

But no, the truth is you can't understand art and truly love it if you are an eclectic, a dilettante. You can't sincerely go into ecstacies in front of a Delacroix if you admire Bastien-Lepage; you don't truly like Gustave Moreau if you can endure Léon Bonnat, or Degas if you can tolerate Henri Gervex.

Fortunately, the profitable state of the dilettante has a downside; fatally, through such excesses of pusillanimity, such debaucheries of prudence, their language has become debilitated, it sinks and harks back to the dreary, leaden style of the Academies, it liquefies into the wet verbiage of an Ernest Renan;[10] because if you don't love with passion, or if you don't hate with equal force, you haven't got any talent; enthusiasm and contempt are indispensable in creating a work of art; talent belongs to the sincere and to the fervent, not to the indifferent and the cowardly.

And how many painters are there these days who toil, who rage, who suffer over their work?

*

PUVIS DE CHAVANNES

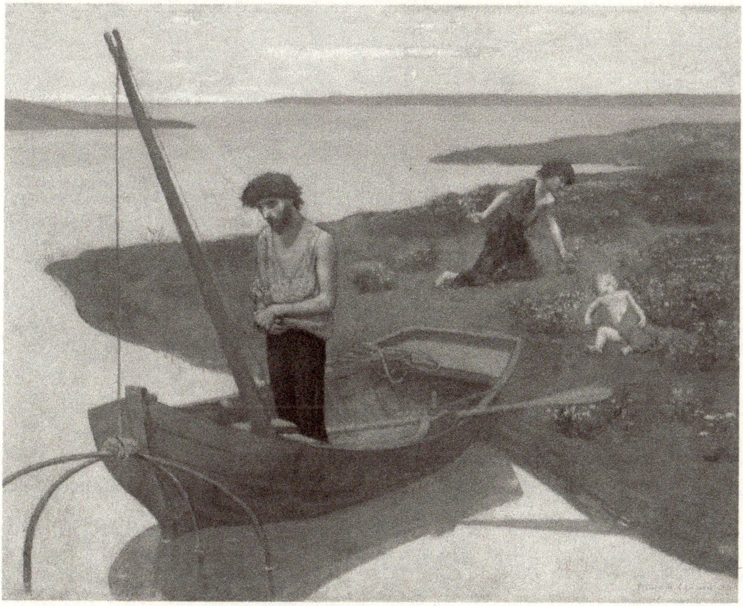

The Poor Fisherman by Puvis de Chavannes.

Another curious *rapprochement* also worthy of note. A tentative coupling, attempted this time by young writers whose good faith is not in doubt: the association, 'among the refined', of the names of Puvis de Chavannes and Gustave Moreau.

Puvis de Chavannes is a regular on the top deck of the art omnibus, because every year he never fails to install himself, among very bad company, on the lofty picture rails of the Salon. Compared to his neighbours in the lower seats – the Boulangers, the Cabanels, the Gérômes, the Tony-Robert Fleurys and the

Henners, those faithful stewards charged with guarding the outdated conventions of art, those vigilant curators of the museum of human cliché – he looks like an extraordinary painter, almost like a bolt of lightning. Indeed, his fresco of Saint Genevieve[II] explodes in the middle of the Panthéon, packed as it is with paintings the benign colour of shop signs daubed by respectable sign-painters; it is an honorable attempt at least, and those that cover the walls of the Amiens Museum are also worth mentioning. I will add that when he deigns not to unfurl his three-masted canvases in the annual Salon he can occasionally be pleasing.

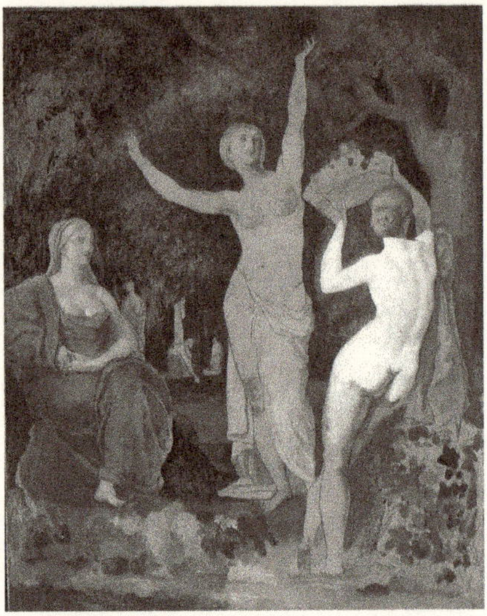

Autumn by Pierre Puvis de Chavannes.

As with his *The Poor Fisherman*, and above all with his little canvas *Autumn*, the subject of which is as follows: a woman standing in a wood picks bunches of grapes and places them in a basket which another woman holds out to her; a third woman, seated, smiles and looks at them. Within the sickly pallor of this picture, the folds of a dress cascade in a charming lilac tone, and the combination of the milky green of the leaves and the floral whiteness of the flesh caresses the eye irritated by the gaudy mediocrity of the works that surround it.

These women, with their slender poses and the blue eyes of an astonished dolls, seem so strange, so vague, in the midst of that flock of females who have escaped from the studios of their peers and been rounded up into the sheep pen of the Champs-Elysées to the sound of a shepherd's horn.

But if Puvis de Chavannes has occasionally exhibited a few canvases that aren't too threadbare, a few panels that are almost fresh, it should not, however, be claimed that he has brought a new note to art.

In 1887, he attempted a ponderous undertaking which sums up his work, when he exhibited a huge contrivance destined for the lecture hall at the Sorbonne.

This interminable cartoon seemed to me to be the presumptuous gala of a lacklustre antiquity, a plodding and stilted work, laborious and false. It was the work of a cunning academic copyist, an ascetic gourmand, a sleepwalker roused from his slumber; it was also the work of an indefatigable labourer who, painting to the formulas entrusted to the elder statesmen of art, could have gained a reputation as a skilled craftsman and a wise master – if the foolishness of popular criticism hadn't striven to proclaim him a great original artist and a great poet. To compare Puvis and Gustave Moreau, to marry them, as it were, in terms of refinement, to conflate them within the frame of a single admiration, is truly to commit one of the most obsequious heresies one could wish to see. Gustave Moreau has

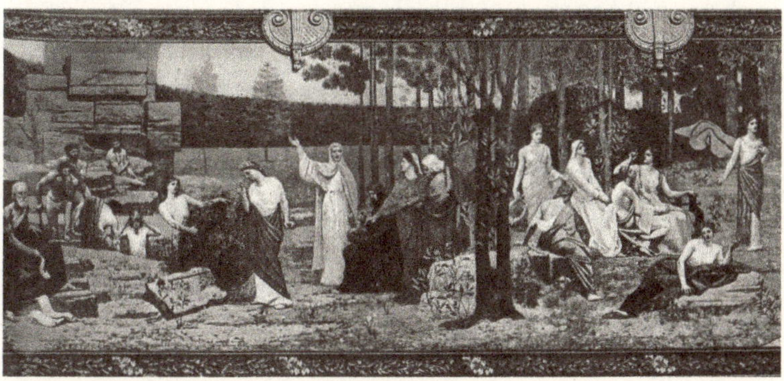

The Sacred Grove by Pierre Puvis de Chavannes.

rejuvenated hoary old subjects through a talent that is at once subtle and broad; he has taken up myths worn out by centuries of cliché and has expressed them in a language that is persuasive and magnificent, mysterious and new. He knew how to create a style that is uniquely his own from scattered elements. Puvis de Chavannes didn't know how to create anything. He didn't refrain, as Moreau did, from employing the academician's box of tricks, their venerable artifices; he stole from the Italian Primitives, pastiching them even, sometimes completely; but where the people of the Middle Ages were believers and innocent, he has brought an imitation faith, a perverted simplicity; in short, he's a *bon vivant* whose malnourished painting dupes us, he's an old two-step having a go at a Requiem.

*

MOREAU

Far removed from the crowds vomited up each month of May by the spiritual emetic of Great Art, Gustave Moreau has for many years now ceased to pin up his canvases beneath the muslin roof blinds that flutter, like pathetic canopies, in the glazed hangar of the Palais d'Industrie.[12]

He has also refrained from fashionable exhibitions. The sight of his work – which is confided to just a handful of dealers – is therefore rare; in 1886, however, a series of his watercolours was exhibited by Goupil & Cie[13] in their gallery on the Rue Chaptal.

In the room that contained them it was like a bonfire of immense firmaments in conflagration; of crushed globes of bloody suns, a haemorrhage of stars streaming in purple cataracts over tumbling tufts of clouds.

Against the backdrop of these terrible flare-ups, silent women pass by, either naked or clothed in fabrics set with cabochons

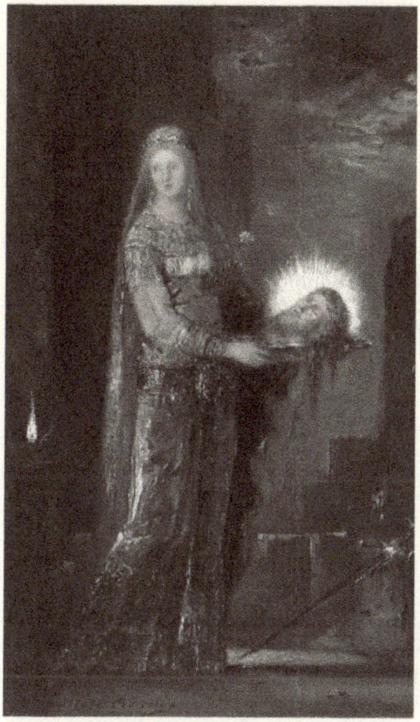

Salomé Carrying the Head of John the Baptist by Gustave Moreau.

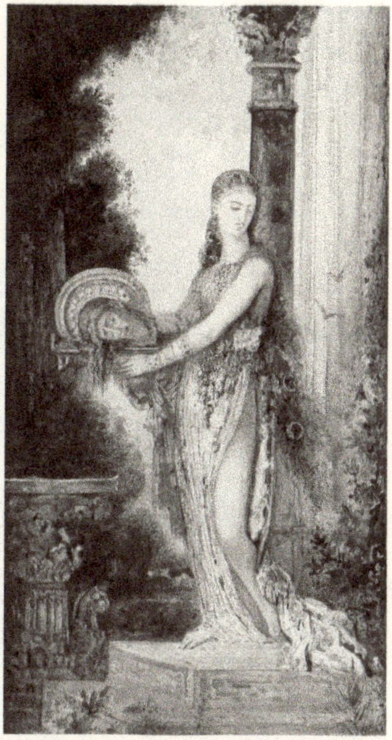

Salomé at the Column (watercolour) by Gustave Moreau.

like the bindings of old bibles: women with hair like silk tassels, with cold, staring, pale-blue eyes, with flesh as white and cool as milt; motionless Salomés bearing on a platter the head of John the Baptist, which shimmers, steeped in phosphorus, beneath a line of trees with clipped leaves of greeny black; and goddesses straddling hippogriffs that scratch the dying clouds with the lapis lazuli of their wings; and female idols, tiara'd, standing before thrones whose steps are submerged beneath extraordinary flowers, or seated in rigid poses, on elephants with foreheads mantled in green and breastbones cloaked in gold embroidery seamed with small bells, like a cavalry harness, or with large pearls; elephants that are trampling their own ponderous image, reflected in a sheet of water agitated by the columns of their legs, encircled by metal bands.

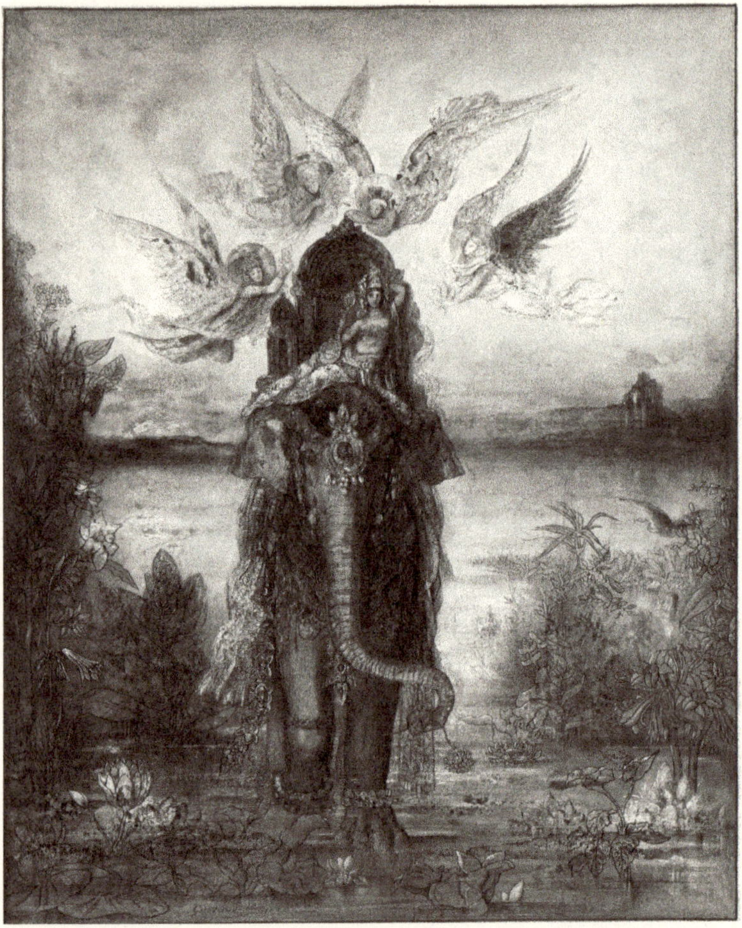

The Sacred Elephant by Gustave Moreau.

An identical impression arises from these diverse scenes, the impression of a spiritual onanism repeated in chaste flesh; the impression of a virgin, endowed, in a solemn graceful body, with a soul exhausted by solitary dreams, by the secret thoughts of a woman sovereign to herself and repeating to herself, in the sacramental rhetoric of obscure prayers, insidious appeals to sacrilege and debauchery, torture and murder.

Outside the gallery, in the gloomy street, the dazzling memory of these works persisted, but the scenes no longer appeared in their entirety; in memory, they dissolved into their indefatigable details, into the minutiae of their strange embellishments. The rendering of those jewels, with their contours engraved into the watercolour as if with the nib of a quill pen, the delicacy of those plants with their intertwining stalks, stems patiently enlaced, embroidered like the lace surplices that were once made for prelates; the surge of those flowers, embracing in their forms religious vessels and aquatic flora, pyxes and water-lilies, chalices and algae, all that astonishing chemistry of super-shrill colours that have achieved their furthest degree, goes to your head and intoxicates your sight, as, stupefied, you stagger past a line of new houses, not even seeing them.

On reflection, as one walks, as the reassured eye watches and observes that shameful embarrassment of modern taste, the street – these boulevards on which languish trees orthopedically corsetted with iron and constricted within wheels of cast-iron[14] by the first-aiders of the Department for Roads and Bridges; these roads shaken by enormous buses and carts sporting vulgar advertising; these pavements filled with a hideous crowd in search of money, with women degraded by successive childbirths and brutalised by horrible compromises, with men reading vile newspapers or dreaming about fornication or deceitful schemes as they walk past shops, from which the officially-sanctioned crooks of business and banking spy on them in order to fleece them – one comprehends better still Gustave Moreau's work, independent of its time, fleeing into the realm of the beyond, floating in dreams, far from the excremental ideas exuded by an entire people.

And indeed, when the moment has definitively come, when money is the Holy of Holies before which all of humanity, sprawled on its stomach, drools with lust and prays; when a country, corrupted by a political system open to anyone, festers with all the abscesses of its government assemblies and its press; when despised art lowers itself to the level of the buyer; when a pure work of art is universally considered as a crime of *lèse-majesté* against an old world drunk on cliché and obscenity, it inevitably comes about that a few individuals, wandering through the horrors of their time, dream in isolation, and from the compost of their reveries spring inconceivable flowers of a vibrant brilliance, of a feverish, proud and melancholy perfume! – The theory of the influence of social milieu, adapted by Monsieur Taine[15] to art is true – but when it's a question of great artists it's true in reverse, because the social milieu acts on them through revulsion, through the hatred it inspires in them; instead of modelling or shaping the soul in its own image, it creates in the immensity of Boston, a solitary Edgar Allan Poe; it acts in an inverse fashion, creating in a disgraced France, a Baudelaire, a Flaubert, a Goncourt, a Villiers de l'Isle Adam, a Gustave Moreau, a Redon and a Rops, exceptional beings who have retraced the footsteps of the centuries and thrown themselves, in disgust at the promiscuities they've been forced to endure, into the abyss of past ages, into the tumultuous space of nightmares and dreams.

*

DEGAS

You can be certain that artists whose minds have little of the nomad about them, whose domesticated imaginations tie them firmly to the present epoch, don't feel any less abhorrence, any less contempt – if they are superior spirits – than those subordinate souls to whom the theory introduced by M. Taine alone applies.

Because their art evolves in a different way; it concentrates itself, it holds its ground, and, in mocking, ferocious works, they paint this social milieu that they detest, this milieu that they scrutinise and whose ugliness and shamefulness they portray.

And this is the case of Edgar Degas.

This painter, the most personal, the most penetrating of all those that this unfortunate country possesses – without it even suspecting the fact – has deliberately exiled himself from official exhibitions and public spaces. At a time when all other painters are wallowing in the public trough, he has, far removed from it all, been quietly putting the finishing touches to incomparable works of art.

Some, as if in a contemptuous farewell, were exhibited in 1886, in a building on the Rue Laffitte.[16]

This was a series of pastels, described as follows in the catalogue: "A suite of female nudes, bathing, washing, drying and wiping themselves, or having their hair combed."

Degas, who previously in some admirable pictures of dancers

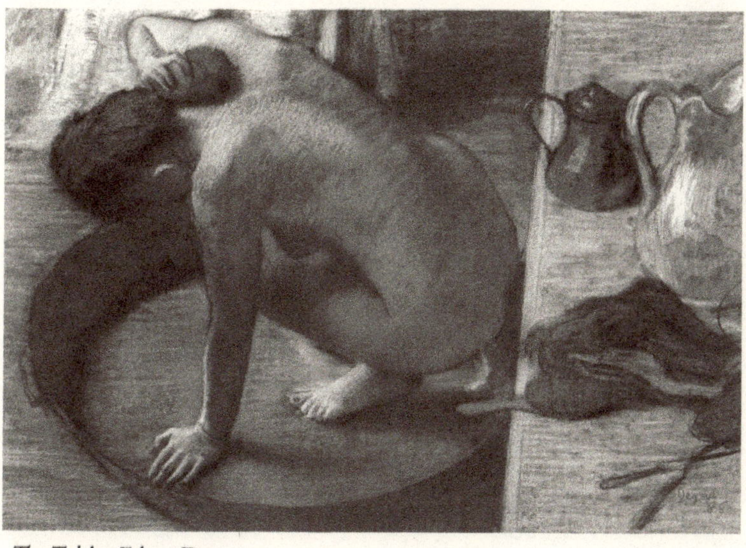

The Tub by Edgar Degas.

had so implacably depicted the degeneracy of the hired dancer brutalised by mechanical frolics and monotonous jumps, this time brought an attentive cruelty, a patient hatred, to his studies of nudes.

It seemed as if, overwhelmed by the baseness of those around him, he'd wanted to retaliate and hurl the most outrageous insult in the face of his century, overthrowing an idol that is invariably treated with kid gloves – Woman – who he degrades by representing her in her bath tub, in the humiliating poses of her intimate *toilette*.

And in order to better sum up his repudiation, he chooses to represent her as fat, pot-bellied and short, in other words drowning her graceful contours under tubular rolls of skin, losing, from the formal point of view, any sense of posture or line, and becoming, whatever class of society she belongs to, a veritable butcher's wife – in a word, a creature whose vulgar size and heavy features, urges continence and inspires disgust.

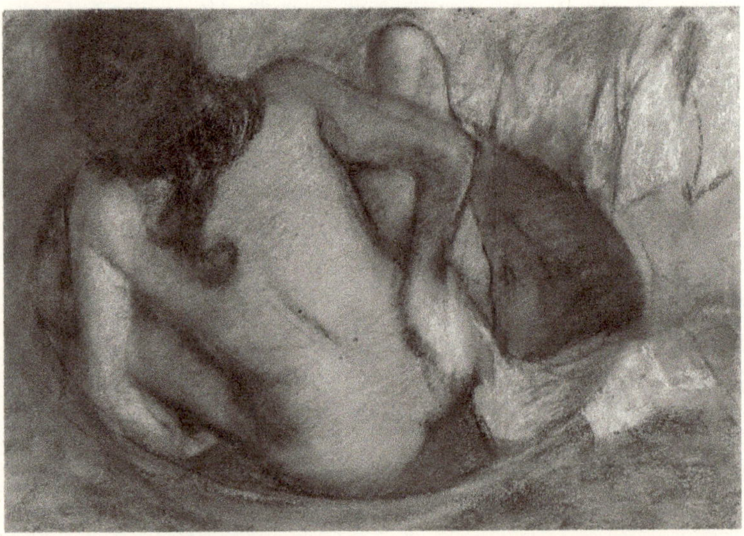

Woman in a Tub by Edgar Degas.

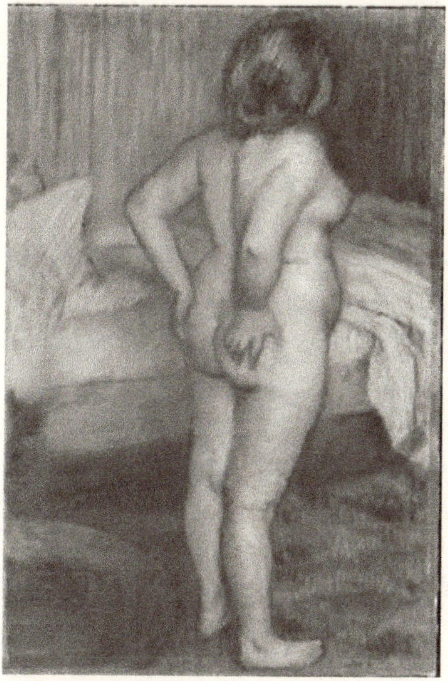

The Morning Bath by Edgar Degas.

Here, it's a redhead, tubby and plump, bending her spine, making the sacral bone stick out beneath the tight curves of her buttocks; she twists, trying to get a hand up to her shoulder blade in order to wipe it with a sponge that drips down her spine and trickles along the small of her back; there, it's a blonde, hunched, thickset and standing, also turning her back to us; this one has finished the job of washing and, resting her hands on her rump, she stretches with the somewhat masculine posture of a man who, lifting the flaps of his jacket, warms himself in front of a fire; or there again, it's a squatting fatty; she leans to one side, raising herself with one leg, an arm crossed behind her back drying herself in the zinc tub; and finally one seen from the front this time, wiping the top of her belly.

Such, briefly noted, are the pitiless poses that this iconoclast assigns to the being lauded by so much inane flattery. In these pastels there's a hint of the cripple's stump, the wrestler's chest,[17] the amputee's waddle,[18] a whole series of attitudes inherent to woman even when young and pretty, adorable whether lying down or standing up, frog-like or simian when she has to bend down like this, in order to mask her filthiness by such grooming.

But in addition to this particular note of contempt and

hatred, what has to be seen in these works is the unforgettable truthfulness of these types, brought out by a rich and deep-rooted sense of design, by a lucid and controlled passion, as well as by a cold fervour; what has to be seen is the fiery, muted colouring, the mysterious and opulent tone of these scenes; it is the supreme beauty of flesh, tinged blue or pink by water, lit by windows covered in muslin, in darkened rooms in which, by the veiled light from a courtyard, one glimpses walls covered with *toile de Jouy* hangings,[19] sinks and bowls, flasks and combs, boxwood hairbrushes and pink copper bedpans.

This is no longer the smooth, shiny, always naked flesh of goddesses, that flesh whose most implacable expression appears in a painting by Regnault in the La Caze Collection,[20] a painting in which one of the three Graces sports a pink backside like oiled percaline lit from inside by a night light; no, this is bare flesh, real, alive, flesh caught in the act of ablution, numbed and goosebumped by cold water.

Among the people who visited this exhibition, some, in the presence of these women who are seen squatting, full frontal, and whose bellies are spared the usual artistic misrepresentation, had protested, indignant at this frankness but were gripped, despite themselves, by the life emanating from these pastels. In the end, they exchanged a few shameful or disgusted reflections, and on their departure unleashed the great word: 'Obscene!'

Ah, if ever works were less so; if ever there were works that, with no hint of cautious hesitation, no hint of trickery, were fully and decisively chaste, it is these. They even glorify a contempt for the flesh which no artist since the Middle Ages has dared to attempt.

And it goes even further still, because this is not the considered disdain of a man, it is rather the certain, penetrating destestation of some women for the devious joys of their own sex, a detestation that overwhelms them with atrocious reasons and leads them

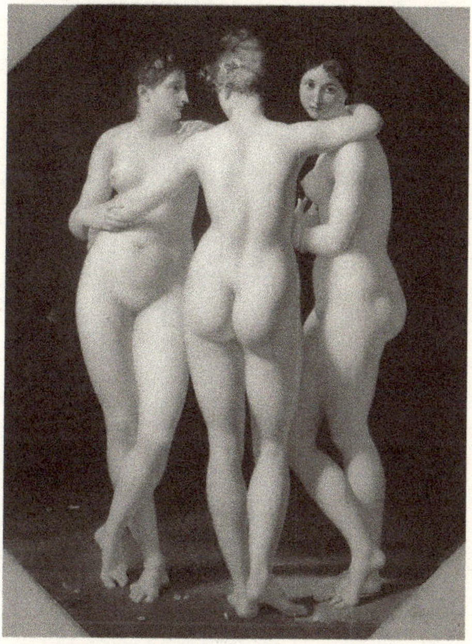

The Three Graces by Jean-Baptiste Regnault.

to defile themselves, openly admitting the moist horror of a body that no lotion can purify.

A powerful and solitary artist, with no recognised antecedents and with no worthy sucessors, Degas continues, in each of his paintings, to arouse a sensation of precise strangeness, of an unseen that is so just you find yourself being astonished and almost blame yourself; his work belongs to a Realism that could not have been understood by that brute Courbet, but which certain of the Primitives rival, that's to say an art expressing an outpouring of the soul – however expansive or fleeting it may be – in living bodies, in perfect harmony with their surroundings.

II

Bartholomé – Raffaëlli – Stevens – Tissot – Wagner – Cézanne – Forain

BARTHOLOMÉ

Amid the solemn infamy of the May Salon, two paintings: one, a playground scene[I] by Albert Bartholomé, is conceived thus: some young girls play in a courtyard around which runs an outbuilding supported by iron pillars and topped with red tiles. In the background, a grown tree leans askew, a section of wall is outlined against a dappled field of sky. A shaft of sunlight divides the courtyard into two parts: one illuminated, the other lost in shadow.

In the foreground, six little girls hold each other's hands and get ready to turn around in a circle. The chain is broken by one of them, who reties the lace of her shoe; further off, others throw and return balls to each other, while, sketching an 'A' upside-down on its point, their feet together and planted on the ground, their bodies thrown back, set to the right and left like the letter's two stems and connected in the middle by a crossbar of arms, two girls, hands intertwined, prepare to spin madly on the spot.

Lastly, some others climb on benches for a game of tick-off-ground, as, in the shadow of the outbuilding, the silent silhouette of a meditating nun passes by.

What must be noted first is the painter's precise observation.

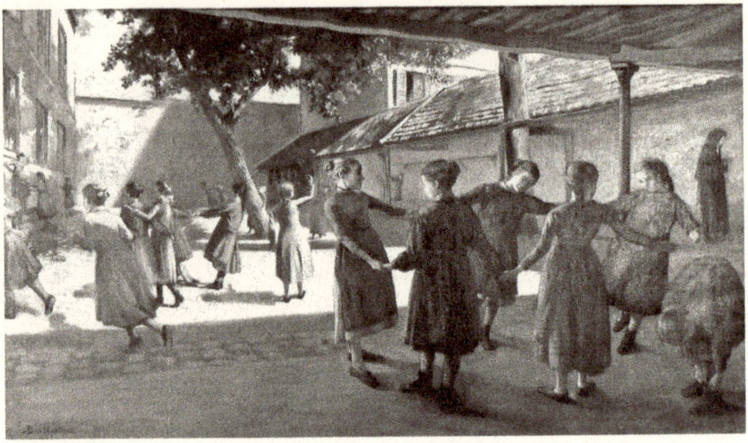

Playtime in a School Courtyard by Albert Bartholomé.

These children are captured, pinned to the canvas, without trick or artifice. From this point of view, the girls who are still holding out their hands to their friend who is so naturally bent over her shoe, are decisive; and then take each of them separately and see how their personalities become even more distinct. Here, a small, lanky girl, anaemic, interesting for her knowing face, almost ennobled by her fragility and her pallor; there, another, stockier, heavier, and marked with freckles; there again, another whose face is already fully-formed: this is what she'll look like at thirty; indeed, this is frequently the case among the children of ordinary people. And, amid this joy of escaping from lessons, in this relaxation of shouts and laughter, in these transports of running and dancing, dormant features awake, worn faces become more marked, even ugly ones become charming. Like puberty itself, this barely covered canvas exudes a simple grace.

Finally, if you add that the painting is luminous and cheerful, that the painter's colouring, at times a little too timid, has become bolder, and that with the neutral tones of the aprons and the blue and lilac of the dresses, with those tufts of hair in plaits falling on a collar or tied in ringlets at the neck, with that blonde hair that will later darken, he has managed to harmonise a melody of exquisite tonal pleasure.

*

RAFFAËLLI

The other is by Raffaëlli, *A Beautiful Morning*. In a padded bed – white lacquered wood, Louis XV style – a woman sleeps; the book she was browsing is there, open, on an empty space of the bed, near the deserted pillow next to her; the gentleman has got up and probably fled; the woman, tired, has gone back to sleep. What is astonishing in this work is the extreme veracity of this woman, who, with her head slightly tilted back, breathes softly, her long hair untied, her neck slightly twisted, her eyelids swollen, her limbs tired; and then the whole ragoût of the bed facing us,

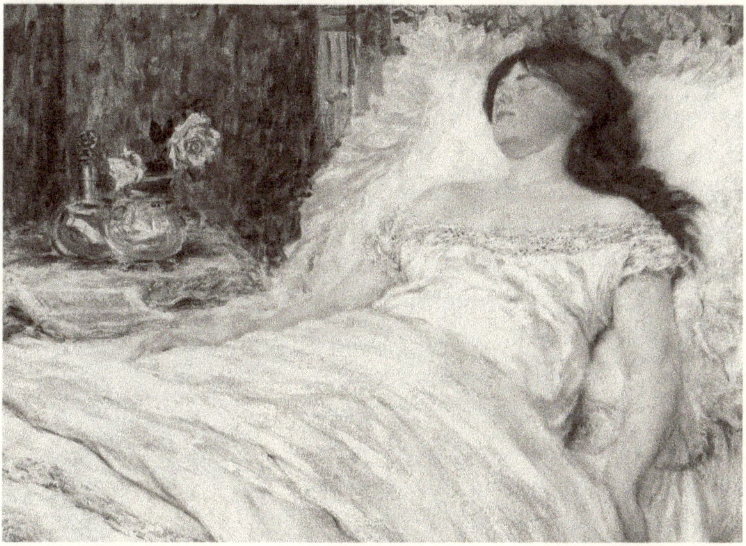

A Beautiful Morning by Jean-François Raffaëlli.

with its pillows and sheets, is very piquant indeed. It is a hymn in white, a hymn in which the painter has betrayed the chaste colour's symbolic meaning, has hystericised its candour,[2] impregnated its cool Communion tones with voluptuousness, aphrodisiacised its evangelical hues, its epithalamic nuances. A work of balanced distinction, a deliberate, precise work of absolute realism, of sharp observation, of intense vigour, this painting sounds a discordant note in the room in which it sings its libertine *hosanna* in white at the top of its voice, amid the multicoloured refrains ground out by the barrel organs of its peers.

*

Also by Raffaëlli, but this time exhibited with landscapes of Jersey in Georges Petit's gallery,[3] are some extraordinary watercolours reproduced in the latest issue of *Paris-Illustré*, 'At the Café-Concert', published by Ludovic Baschet.[4]

One of them shows a quadrille at the Ambassadors: two laundresses who have left aside their 'Gendarme' flat-irons,[5] two washerwomen who have sprawled across every sagging wine-shop banquette, are shaking the sweaty[6] flesh of their wares, kicking the air in a furious ruckus; and the predatory smile of their mouths, the dance of their whalebone corsets, the cancan in the eyes of these three-franc whores, which gleam from the depths of an alleyway, or draw you into the darkness of a bit of wasteland for a quickie, has to be seen!

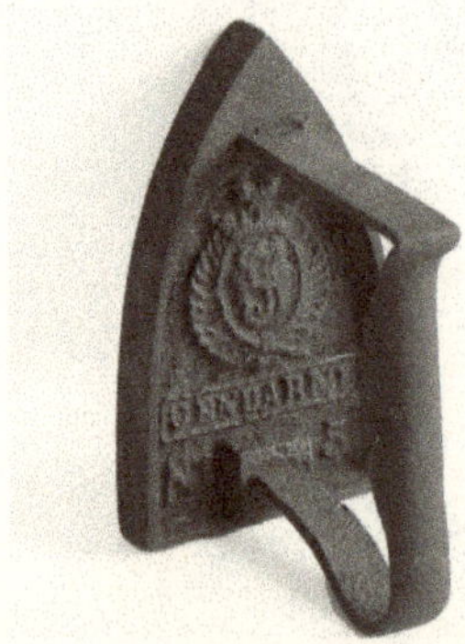

The 'Gendarme' Flat-Iron.

The two men who serve them as dancing partners are even more degenerate; one of them has the leering mouth of a toilet attendant,

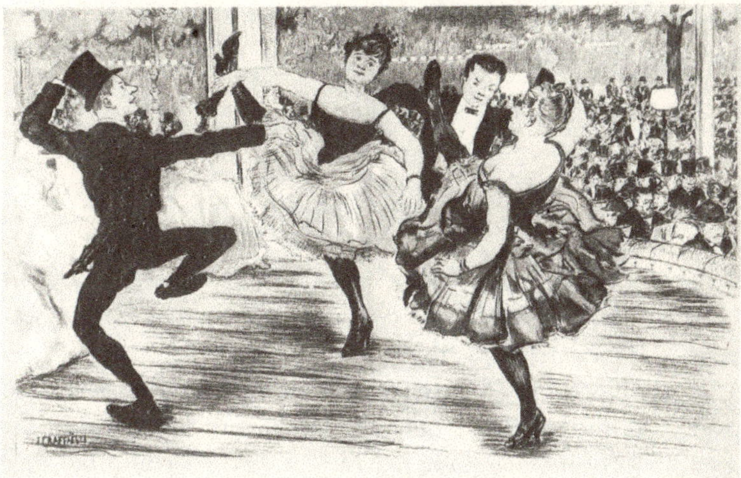

A Quadrille at the Ambassadors by Jean-François Raffaëlli.

and the other the snout of a market-trader or an actor; they, too, dance in a gangling fashion, and beneath the gaslight beat up a remoulade of dust with the whisk of their arms, the suited sleeves of their limbs doing a St. Vitus' dance, as if attacked by a terrible cramp.

It's the elixir of drunkeness, the concentrated extract of a urinal transported to the stage, the quintessence of the dockyards or the underneath of bridges, wrapped up in a music peppered with cymbals and salted with brass.

A painter of suburban landscapes whose mournful abandonment[7] and doleful joys he alone has rendered, Raffaëlli wanted to follow the human creature, escaped from the suburbs and thrown to the lions on a dance floor, amid the visual salaciousness of an affluent quarter of Paris; and beneath the glitter of this carnival, beneath the rouge of these faces, beneath the ostentation of these protruding bellies and jiggling breasts, he has discovered the alcoholic vulgarity of a gesture, the wilful indecency of a glance, and painted them, as if seen through the temperament of an English cartoonist, with a brush that is naive and ferocious, brutal and hard.

*

STEVENS

I really find it hard to justify the presumptuousness of the Belgians over the past few years in describing Alfred Stevens as 'the great painter of modern life'.

Under his clumsy fingers the light chiffons he touches turn to stone, and the ordinary women he illuminates so dully with the icy lantern of his coarse eye may no longer be Flemish but they will never be Parisiennes.

And what a superficial vision of the elegance of Paris it is that he paints! In interiors generally distorted by Japanese porcelains and furnishings, he depicts studio models, who he decks out in stiff ballgowns, in sentimental poses. And this represents the woman of the world, the rich Parisienne.

Amid this series of Belgian affectations, there is, however, an exception. Stevens exhibited a portrait of a girl one time at Georges Petit's gallery: against a striped background a tired face stood out, its flesh bolstered by make-up, fortified by cold creams and greasepaint. Beneath a red wig, watery blue eyes looked weary and mean. It gave off a sense not of consensual nights of lust, but the exhaustion of the solitary act, of unsolicited caresses, of unspoken sin.[8] A little bit of her soul was revealed in the face of this portrait: it was genuine and fascinating. Stevens had suddenly been touched by grace, that grace of art which, more fleeting than divine grace, abandons an artist after a fine painting and puts him back where it got him from: the profitable marketplace of bourgeois success and guaranteed sales.

*

JAMES TISSOT

Despite a vague feeling of rebellion that rises in me at their rigid scenarios, I have for a long time liked Tissot's etchings. Some appealed to me by their firm self-assurance, by their solid grounding as workman-like prints, by their architecture so to speak, by their sepia-like tones, achieved mainly through etching on thick paper. Like his young ladies leaning on the deck of a transatlantic liner, or in the company of soldiers in peaked caps on a sailing ship. These had a particularly modern English sensibility. They were Protestant etchings, a little ponderous, but sometimes conveying a pleasing atmosphere of rigging and sails, with backdrops of the Thames, against which a few tall, silly-looking girls stand out, a few women of limited wit but healthy bodies.

Unfortunately, Tissot thought it a good idea to cross the

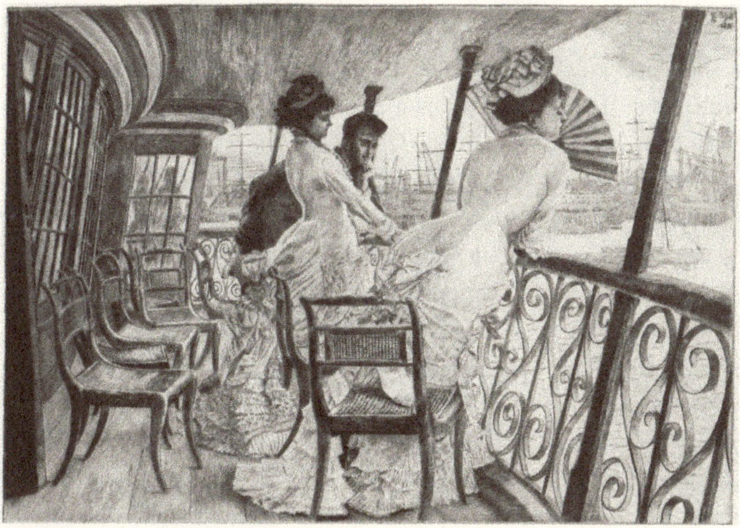

HMS Calcutta by James Tissot.

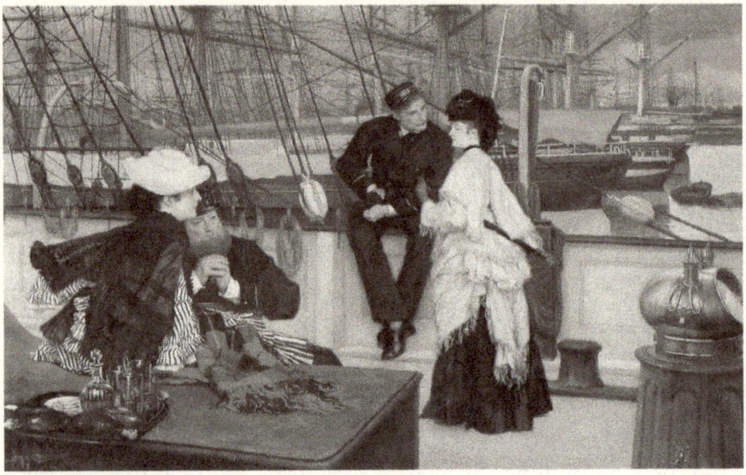

Captain and Mate by James Tissot.

Channel and exhibit his paintings in Paris, and no more than Alfred Stevens – even less so, in fact – was he up to tackling elegant Frenchwomen. His Parisiennes, exhibited at Sedelmeyer's gallery,[9] looked like the offspring of a union between a Savoyard rustic and Jane Bull;[10] the poses were silly and, despite all the posturing, the execution was null and void. I should add that this wasn't an isolated case in his work, because a while ago, in 1883 I believe, in the wasteland of the Museum of Decorative Arts, he exhumed a whole series of watercolours and oils and I never saw anything more excruciating, more funereal or more dreary than the canvases of this man, who had occasionally been so free and colourful in his large prints.

As regards his large pastels which also figured in these rooms – a wet nurse and a child among others – I couldn't help but think of the irritating frivolities of that inconstant handmaid of colour, Giuseppe de Nittis, but a handmaid dulled by age and a savings account, who, by incarnating herself in Tissot, has turned into a crabby matron, a Madame Bossy-Boots,[11] square jawed and big boned.

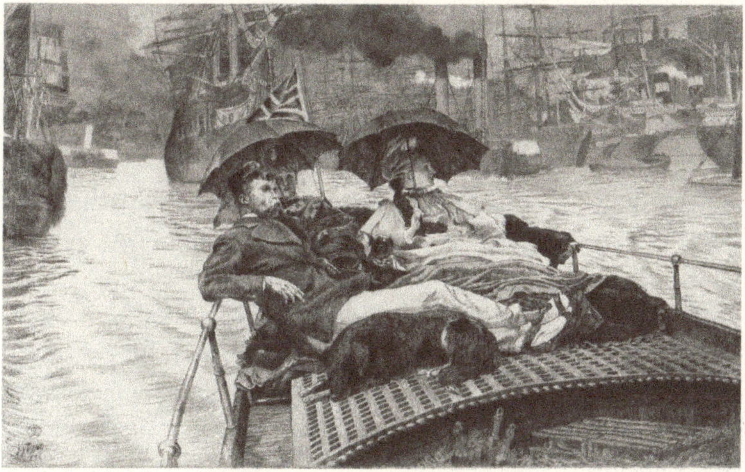

The Thames by James Tissot.

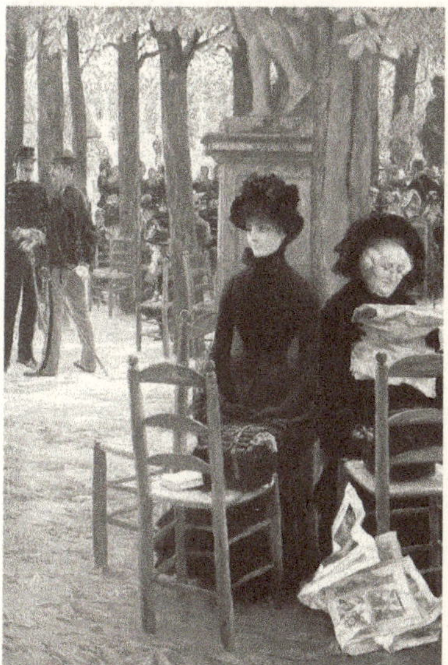

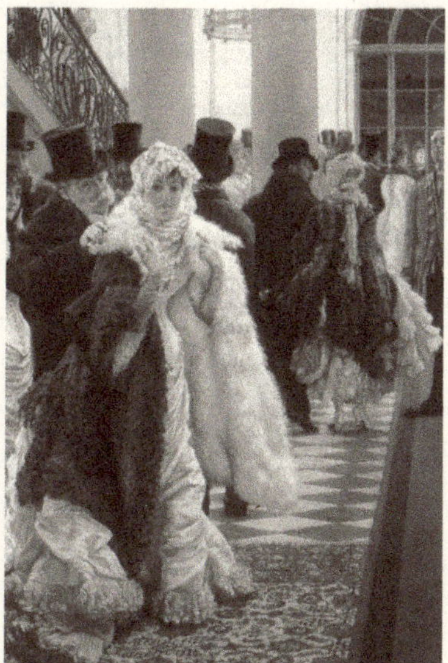

Without Dowry (left) and *Woman of Fashion* (right) by James Tissot, two of fifteen large canvases that comprised the series *La Femme à Paris* ('The Parisian Woman'), exhibited at the Galerie Sedelmeyer in Paris, from 19 April to 15 June 1885.

*

WAGNER

What a strange canvas was revealed to us at the first exhibition by the Society of Independent Artists, which opened in 1884 in those temporary huts erected on the Tuileries.[12]

In a dusky daylight, the sort of daylight that illuminates the nightmare of a bad night's broken and restless sleep, one could make out part of a circus, and shadowy clowns juggling, or holding with outstretched arms those paper hoops that horse riders burst through.

These clowns were living a strange fluid life: they looked like ghosts performing in a dead circus; standing in front of this painting one felt an artistic uneasiness, which only increased as, in contemplating their faces; one saw them come to life and smile with mortally sad eyes.

No details in the catalogue; the painting had no title after this name: 'Wagner'.[13] No first name, no place of birth, no address, nothing.

I've often wondered who this man could be who had never exhibited before and who has never exhibited since. But no one among the writers and painters I know, knew of him. A long time afterwards, I was told one evening in a chance conversation: "By the way, I heard talk of that Wagner whose work you're interested in, by a gentleman whose name I don't even know; well, it seems that this painter is an unfortunate man who was – and still is, I believe – a fairground wrestler and a clown." If only that were true!

But then, how else could one explain the sickly elegance of this painting shrouded in dream, the mournful and delicate murmur of this art created by a clown who lifts weights?

*

CÉZANNE

In full daylight, in porcelain ramekins or on white tablecloths, pears and apples, stark, rough-hewn, plastered on with a trowel, rubbed down by a roll of the thumb. Up close, a furious stucco of vermilion and yellow, of green and blue; at a distance, in focus, fruits destined for Chevet's[14] window displays, abundant and tasty fruit, inviting.

And some hitherto neglected truths become apparent, the strange and realistic tones, the singularly authentic spotting, the nuances of a tablecloth, the blank areas of shadow that spread from the curves of the fruit and scatter into plausible and charming blueish tones, which make these paintings innovatory works, when you compare them to the usual still lifes that stand out against pitch-black backgrounds, or against inscrutable backdrops.

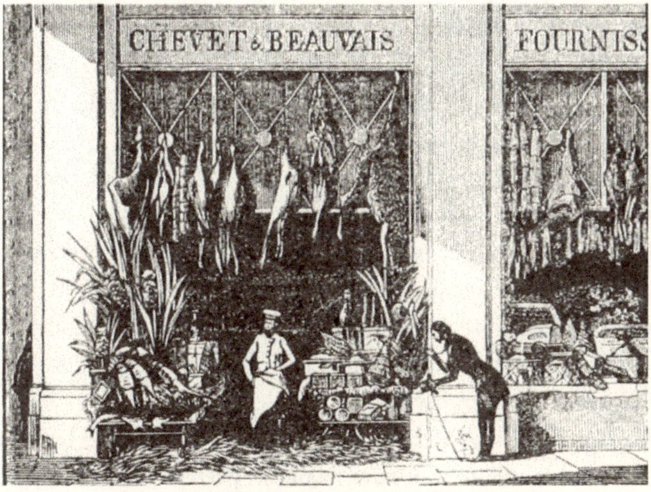

Chévet's, Palais-Royal, Paris.

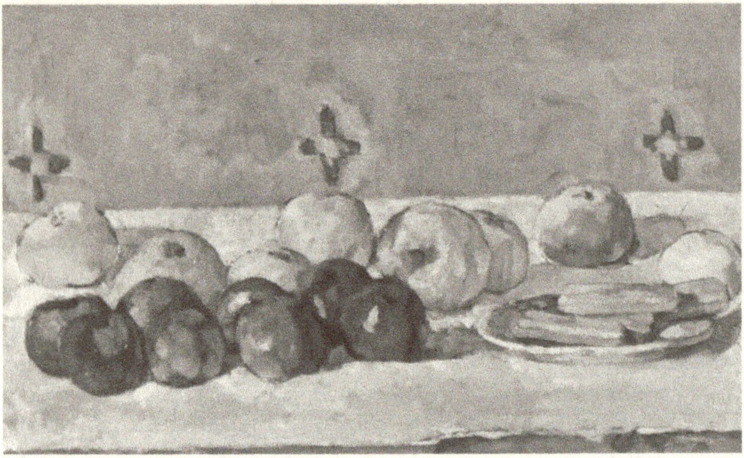

Still Life with Apples and Biscuits by Paul Cézanne.

Then there are the sketches of landscapes done in the open air, attempts left in limbo, studies whose freshness would be spoiled by retouching, the childish and unsophisticated rough drafts with their disorienting imbalances: houses leaning to one side like drunkards; lopsided fruit in tipsy pottery; naked bathers surrounded by crazy lines but, to the greater glory of the eyes, stirred with the fervent enthusiasm of a Delacroix, albeit without his visual refinement or delicacy of touch, and lashed by a frenzy of coloured distemper that screams in bold relief, on a canvas that bends under its own weight!

In short, a revelatory colourist, who contributed more to the Impressionist movement than the late Manet; an artist with diseased retinas,[15] who, through the heightened sensitivity of his vision, discovered the early stages of a new art – this seems to sum up Cézanne, a painter who is too little known.

He has not exhibited since 1877, when, at the Rue Le Peletier, he showed sixteen canvases whose perfect artistic integrity afforded great amusement to the mob.[16]

*

JEAN-LOUIS FORAIN

Forain is now well-known; newspapers promote themselves using his name; his watercolours are bought for stiff prices; there's no longer any need to certify, as I did in the past, the unrecognised contribution of his novel talent; I have only a few notes to add to those I assembled in my book *Modern Art*.

Despite graduating from the École des Beaux-Arts and having even, I believe, passed through the studio of the late Carpeaux, in reality Forain has only had two masters: Manet and Degas. Although the influence of Manet, particularly, can be detected in his early works – which he signed with the now discarded monogram beginning with an 'L' and an 'F' nested in the form of a '4' – it became doubtful almost immediately and was effectively nil. Forain had, in short, the unlooked-for good fortune of not resembling anyone from the beginning.

From this time date some strange watercolours; a few employ a Japanese perspective, lending to nearly all his human creatures a certain ironic stiffness, a bizarre elegance. I remember one of a young mother in a garden; slender, upright, with laconic features, her bust protruding from a cream overcoat, she was leading a child by the hand, whose very simple pose, the body turned at the wrist, was charming; from the same period, a few drawings published in *La République de Lettres*: one, a salon interior with some bald gentlemen chatting together, each looked different and yet also the same; another, a music-hall scene, was full of working men complete with beards and pipes, and a girl passionately sprawled over a cold-hearted lout; another drawing, included in *La Cravache* in 1876, was also wonderful. It was titled *Amanda's Lover* and constituted a parody of Mercié's sculpture, *Glory to the*

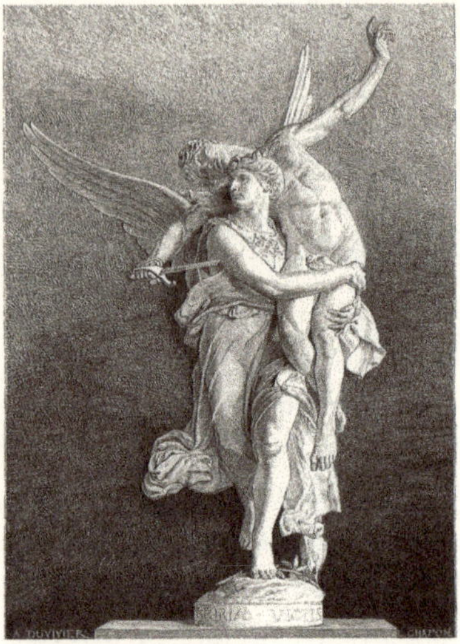

Glory to the Vanquished by Antonin Mercié.

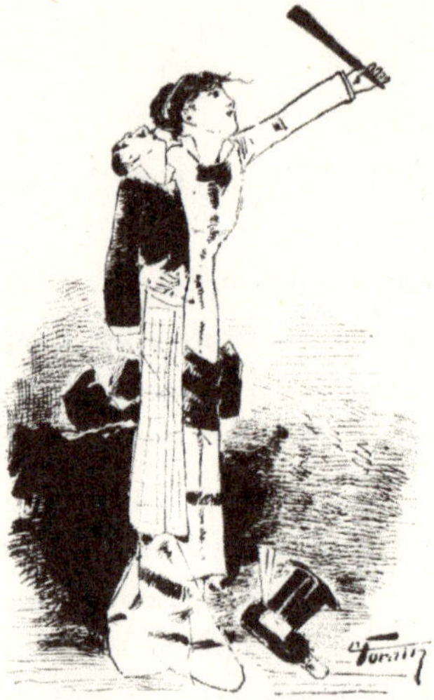

Amanda's Lover by Jean-Louis Forain.

Vanquished,[17] with a rigid dandy, half-dead, head thrown back, held aloft by an exquisite woman who had something of both the shop mannekin and the streetwalker[18] about her!

Then this special flavour, hard, almost naïve – unsophisticated, one could call it – faded away; under the influence of Degas, a whole other style, more complicated, emerged. And so, in extraordinary watercolours heightened with gouache, came scenes of theatres and cafés-concerts, brothels and bars; he prepared his ragoûts of studiously spiced colours, added a delicate sauce to his nudes, obtained incredible effects by the marriage and unexpected clash of tones, achieved just the right shade by a careful observation of reflections and shadows, by a veritable science of additives and compounds.

Thus armed, Forain wanted to do what Constantine Guys, as revealed by Baudelaire, had done for his era: to paint woman wherever she establishes herself, in the places where she works, and naturally he also painted her eternal sidekick in the old farce, a sort of modern-day Baron Hulot[19] or the young dupe in search of worldly fame. Certainly no one has better depicted the whore than him in his unforgettable watercolours; no one has better rendered the lukewarm allure of her vacant eyes, the suave ambush of her smile, the perfumed agitation of her breasts, the glorious sway of her chignon, toned with peroxides and shampoos; finally, no one has more faithfully expressed the exquisite horror of her masked avarice, of her vengeful elegance for past famines endured, of her former poverty veiled under the gaiety of frills and flamboyant make-up.

In addition to his qualities of acute observation, his deliberate, rapid drawing, reducing to the essential, intensifying the merest hint, drilling straight down to the very core, he has brought to art the sagacious irony of the sardonic Parisian.

It is thanks, no doubt, to this predilection for the sharp wit of the humorist pruned of every illusion, that he had the ability to find – for drawings in the newspapers that employ him – the audacious captions, at times cruel, sometimes even almost menacing, that sum up the ridiculous charlatanries of these mad times.

III

Chéret – Whistler

III. Chéret – Whistler

CHÉRET

If I were the man who so formally embodies the taste of the present century, the man who exudes what ordinary people are thinking and who therefore professes an insatiable hatred for art – in other words if I were Monsieur Alphand,[1] the director of public works – I would want to ban the billsticking of Jules Chéret's posters on walls.

They do, indeed, spoil the taciturn dreariness of our streets; at the present period, civil engineers have demolished the few houses, the few alleyways, that could have remained charming; all the intimate nooks and crannies have disappeared, all the vestiges of ancient ages have been knocked down, all the gardens are dead; the Boulevard Saint-Germain and the Avenue de Messine now impose themselves as the model of modern Paris; we will soon see nothing but straight roads, carved out with a spirit level, lined with glacial houses, buildings painted with whitewash, bland and dismal edifices whose facades emanate a dreadful boredom.

What's more, the civil engineers' unadventurous ideal has been ardently followed by the incorrigible stupidity of architects; the public is finally satisfied, because from now on no work of art will ever offend its sight. It is convinced, moreover, that Paris is healthy. In the past, the streets were narrow and the dwellings vast, now the streets are enormous and the rooms microscopic and deprived of air; the space remains the same, but it's been divided up in a different way; it seems that from the point of view of hygiene, this constitutes a benefit that comes at a high price.

Be that as it may, against this widespread, dreary grey hue, Chéret's posters seem out of place and, by the sudden intrusion of their joyfulness, they disturb the unwavering monotony of the prison-like decor lately put in place; this dissonance compromises all the hard work achieved by Monsieur Alphand.

Indeed, in the past, coloured hoardings, whether on railings around houses under construction or along the walls, were so ugly that, despite their crude tones, they harmonised with the look of their surroundings. The dull dreariness of the building and the hawker's cry of the advertisement married well together, almost made a good couple – or at least didn't offend each other by a false harmony. Chéret has changed all that; but one could say that either he or the street, one of the two such as they are now, have no right to exist.

It is, admittedly, impossible to give an account of each and every work by Chéret, who has drawn thousands of posters, who has shown himself, in that day-to-day journalism of painting, to be a true writer, a truly authentic painter. So I can only note, by studying a few of his prints, the very special qualities they reveal.

In the first place, Chéret has a sense of joy, but a joy that makes itself felt without being servile, a frenetic and sardonic joy, as if frozen in pantomime, a joy elevated by its very excess, almost to the point of suffering.

Many of his posters attest to this. Who doesn't remember, among his numerous illustrations, those which celebrate Pierrot, that Pierrot in a black suit,[2] which he was the first to sport and which was subsequently taken up by Willette? Who doesn't remember the irrepressible gaiety of his picture of Henri Agoust[3] conducting the Hanlon-Lees[4] in the pantomime, *Do, mi, sol, do*?

That man, in a bright red costume, shaking his pear-shaped skull topped by two tufts of mountainous hair, his eyes projecting beyond his forehead, twisting his horseshoe-shaped mouth into an asylum grin, jumping into the air and whipping up with all his might the frenzy of the orchestra, beneath which a tiny train, smoking like a rocket, unexpectedly passes by. Agoust has become almost satanic in this drawing, as he leaps up, adorned in red against a greenish background that is picked out in ink and topped by brilliant white letters, outlined in black.

Chéret also gave expression to this demented, almost explosive, joy, on the blue and yellow cover he did for a book by Georges Duval, *Paris Laughs*;[5] here, it's a saraband of people tumbling over each other, rolling about in fits of mad laughter. A stunted Auvergnat[6] practically dislocates his jaw, his muzzle open so wide you can almost see his uvula; a dandy falls over backwards, his hat flying off his head, sticks out his belly and, dizzy with pleasure, beats on it with his fists; a young milliner's assistant,[7] a hatbox in each hand, giggles a sly laugh with her wicked mouth and squinting eyes; a caretaker teeters on tip-toe, guffawing with laughter; a

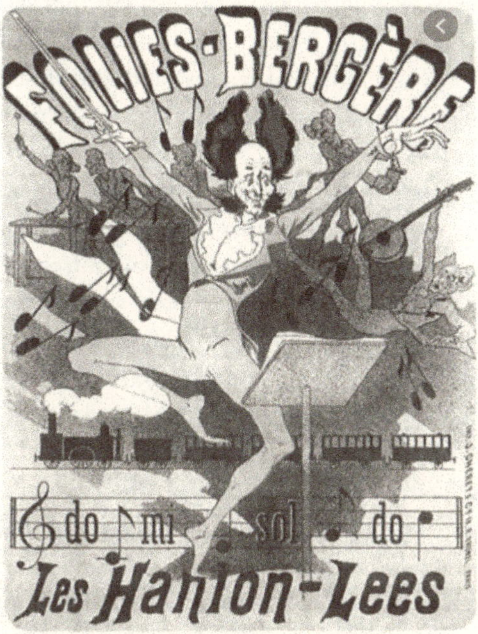

Do, mi, sol, do by Jules Chéret.

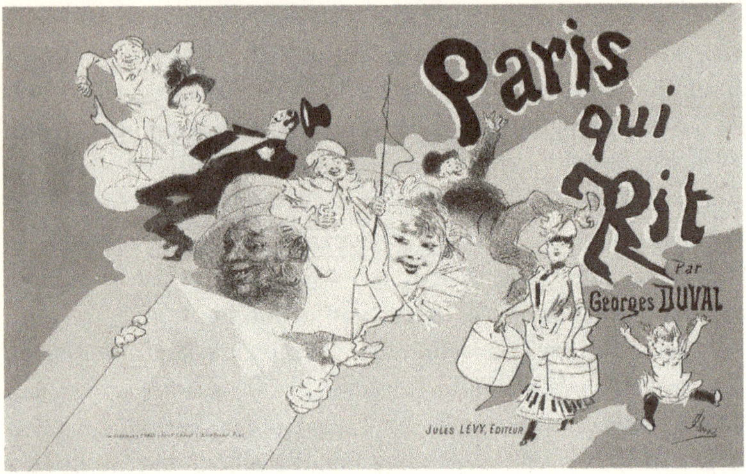

Paris qui rit (*Paris Laughs*) by Jules Chéret.

woman sprawls, one leg in the air, while a little girl sits, her legs spread, arms raised to the sky, and bursts into a jubilant squeal – Chéret has recorded a whole series of laughs, and very finely observed the quality of wit and the particular type of gaiety of each of these people.

But, among the countless posters in which he has depicted laughter, none was more surprising than that huge advertisement he painted for the Hippodrome:[8] a Cadet Rousselle,[9] on horseback, dressed in an incredible costume, fall-front breeches, a canary-yellow waistcoat with a huge turned-up lapel, a black frockcoat, a lace cravat, and yellow-and-red striped stockings; this old man with his mouth grinning from ear to ear, flashing his gums, a ski-slope nose springing from pink cheeks, was aureola'd, as if with a halo of fire, against the backdrop of a purple umbrella; the horse is launching into a headlong gallop, the man, good-natured and jovial, of superb build, is exultant with life!

Also worth mentioning is a small poster that served as an announcement for the Folies-Bergère, bearing this title: *The Music of the Future by 'Les Bozza'*.[10]

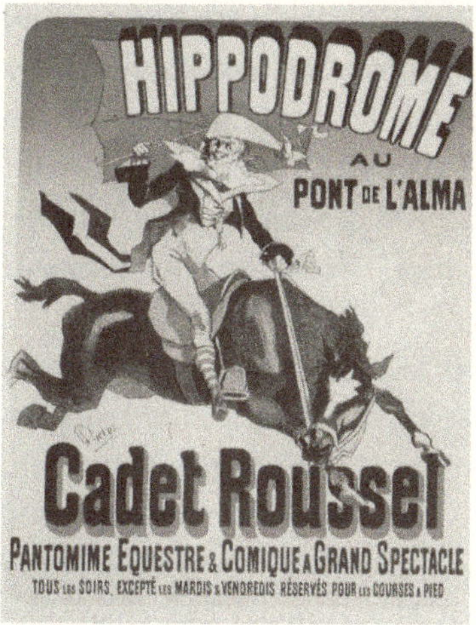

Cadet Roussel by Jules Chéret.

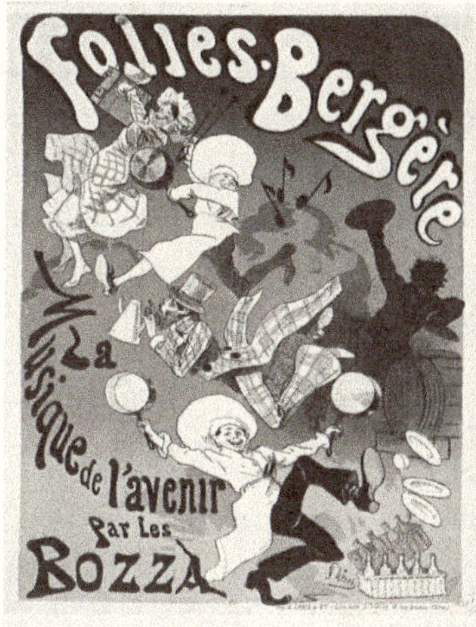

La Musique de l'avenir by Jules Chéret.

This was, of its kind, a true marvel; it staged a cascade of clowns dressed in odd outfits. At the bottom a scullion boy, rocked back by a laugh that splits his face and screws up his eyes, is kicking the air and clashing his saucepans together like cymbals; a little higher up a Yankee-type, floating in bell-bottom trousers and a green and white chequered jacket, sticks out his monkey snout and plays, as if it were a flageolet, the spout of an oil-lamp filler, stopping his fingers on fictitious holes, blowing as if on an imaginary flute; higher up still another kitchen boy prances around uncontrollably, banging his saucepan and tongs, while an old woman in a ruched hat, with a turned-up nose and hair parted down the middle, a good-for-nothing pantomime dame with the look of a quack or a drunken fruit seller, furiously cranks the handle of a coffee grinder, supported in this racket by a layabout from Grenelle, who is beating plates like cymbals over a large barrel that serves as a bass drum.

The torrential gaiety of this poster really did spill out of its light frame, it had the very devil in it, a delirious streak of life, like the chirping of mad birds! These beings, flung headlong into the air, were captured in brief and rapid strokes, with a rare agility of drawing, and its large patches of colour are also conducive to artistic pleasure, with a soft pink starting at the bottom of the page, transforming into flame red behind the man armed with the oil-lamp filler, then jumping, behind the kitchen boy with the tongs, into an opulent pale green, onto which the advertisement bursts out in white letters.

All this gave it a note of hysterical joy, unique in art. But in addition to this dispensation, Chéret has, in less specialised subjects or those that don't adapt themselves to specific personalities – to the Pierrots and the clowns whose character has to be expressed on the poster – revealed a very particular view of the morals and habits of the Parisian.[11] A view that is superficial and charming, adorably false, glimpsed through a theatrical lens, like an extravaganza after a fine dinner.

In this essence of Paris that he distils, he abandons its horrible dregs, ignores the very elixir, so caustic and so bitter, and collects only the fizzy effervescence, the bubbles that sparkle on the surface.

He pours out a light intoxication of sparkling wine, an intoxication that gives off a faint hint of pink; he personifies it, so to speak, in his delightful, scantily-clad women, who stammer and smile without a hint of vulgarity. He takes a girl of the people with a saucy face, sensitive nose, eyes that light up and flutter with desire, he refines her, makes her almost distinguished beneath her old-fashioned finery, turns her into a maid of yesteryear, an elegant scamp whose lapses are discrete; in this regard, one could cite, among numerous others, a print of a masked ball, in which a Mephistopheles in red and black carries off a dancer, whose chiffonned attractions are a delight. From this point of view, he reminds you of the illustrators of a hundred years ago; he is, so to speak, the eighteenth century of today.

And this special corner of art that he's so fond of is also found

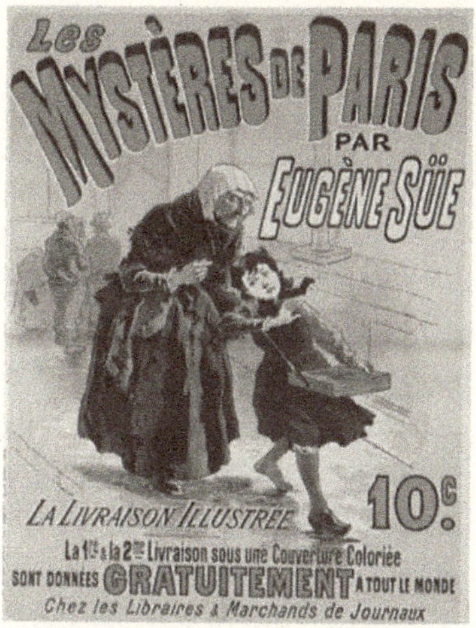

Mystères de Paris by Jules Chéret.

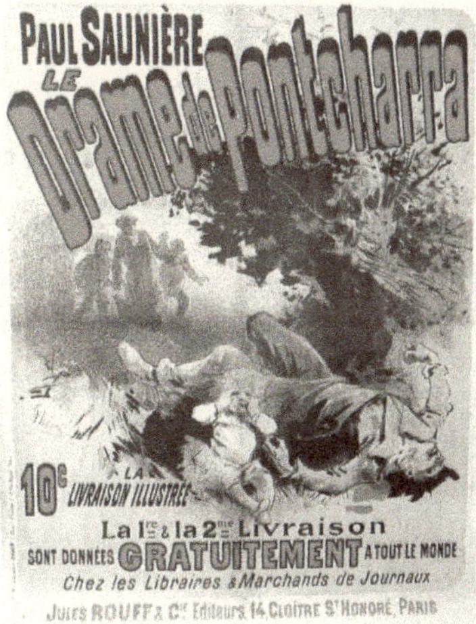

Drame de Pontcharra by Jules Chéret.

in his children, whom he sketches with an incomparable verve, a little chubby, alert, always happy, because they are almost invariably surrounded by toys. The endless posters he has lavished on shops selling novelties proves it. But I like less his large posters for booksellers, such as the ones that advertised *The Mysteries of Paris* and *The Tragedy of Pontcharra*;[12] here, the necessary terror is toned down, the horrible is moderated; in such instances the child he draws so well laughing, cries badly.

To conclude, if we go through the work of this ingenious fantasist, we find in the subjects imposed on him – often against his will, and with a limited number of tones which are boiled down to just a few in some of the prints – an expression of life that is very personal, decorative and comical, a Parisian flavour brought to its supreme acuity and resolving itself into a sort of laughing gas whose effusions delight and intoxicate the people who breathe them.

Simply put, Chéret's work is an exquisite light lunch of art.

*

WHISTLER

The author of keen-eyed and sagacious 'critical essays on the avant-garde', Théodore Duret,[13] who was one of the first to defend Manet, the Impressionists, and all the other escapees from that lucrative artistic prison the Salon, tells us that James MacNeil Whistler[14] was born in Baltimore, to a major in the US Army, that he followed, like Edgar Allan Poe,[15] a course of study at the West Point Military Academy, and that, also like the poet, he hastened to escape a future of barracks and guard duty.

Coming to Paris in 1857, he attends Gleyre's studio, and sends paintings to the official Salons of 1859 and 1860, which the jury reject; in 1863, he figures on the list of the Salon des Refusés, with his portrait of a woman dressed in white, standing out against a white background. Here is the description of this work, which I copied from a now rare brochure by Fernand Desnoyers:

> The most singular and original painting is that by M. Whistler. The title of his picture is *The White Girl.* This is a portrait by a *spiritualist*, a *medium*. The figure, the posture, the face and the colour are strange. It's both simple and fantastical at the same time; the face has a tormented and charming expression that fixes the attention. There is something both vague and profound in the eyes of this young girl, who's beauty is so unusual that the public doesn't know whether to find her ugly or pretty. This portrait is alive, it's a remarkable painting, superb, one of the most original to have passed before the eyes of the jury.[16]

In 1865, the border guards of the Institut de France let his

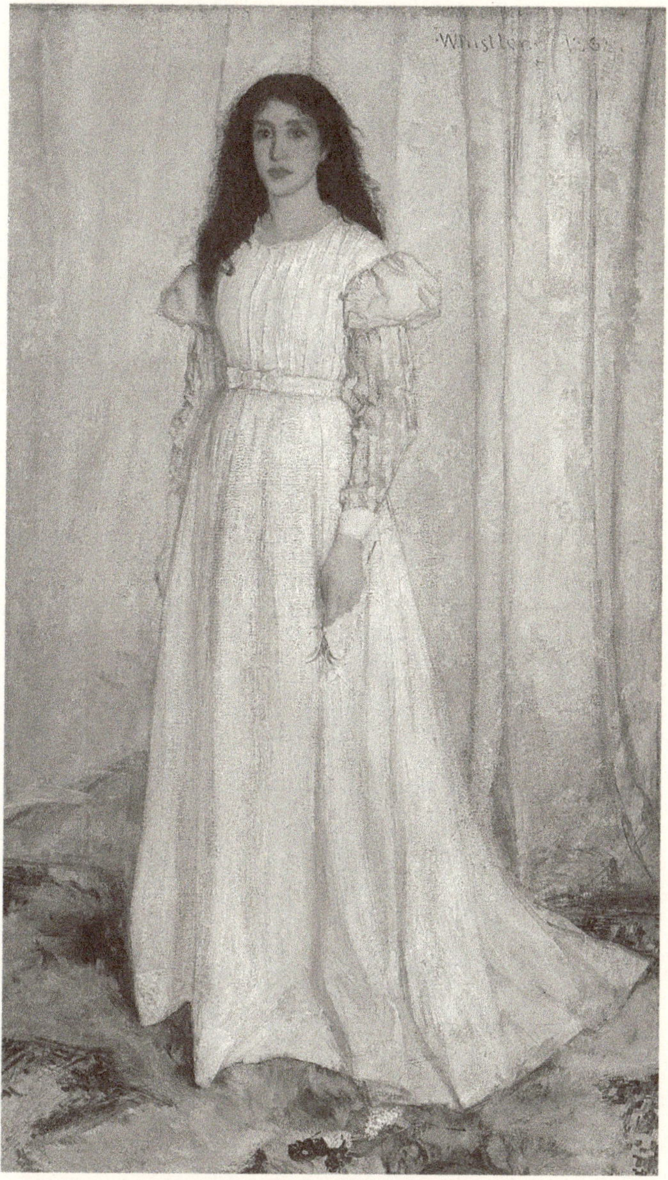

The White Girl by James McNeil Whistler.

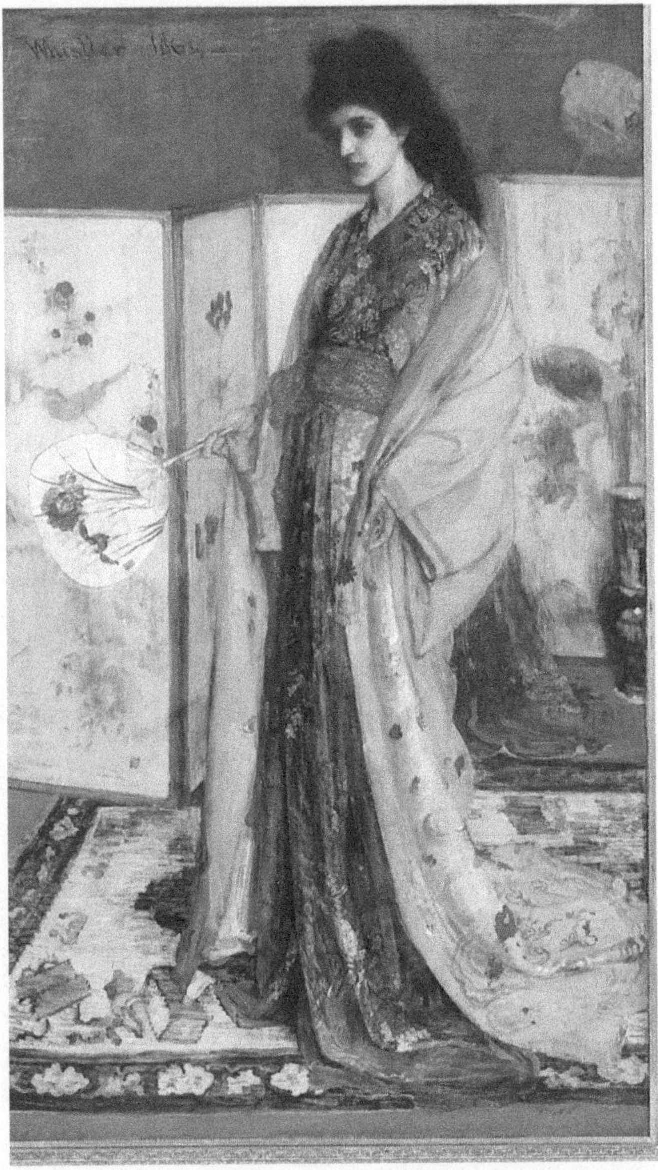

The Princess from the Land of Porcelain by James McNeil Whistler.

Princess from the Land of Porcelain through the doors of the Salon:

> A princess from *One Thousand and One Nights*, as luminous as those forms that the imagination thinks it sees in clouds, stands, her hair tousled, letting her robes trail over a sky-blue patterned rug. I hope that fashion adopts her style; perhaps it will this winter at some court ball, where the princess from the land of porcelain would be a hit: a pearl-grey dress with a floral pattern, a saffron-coloured manteau decorated with tropical flowers, poppy-red sash, and a bird-of-paradise feather fan in her right hand. For backdrop, a pale screen and, above it, whitish panelling. As a colourist fantasy, this princess is provoking. (William Burger,[17] *Salon of 1865*.)

In 1867, Whistler exhibits one painting, *At the Piano*, and, having already settled in England a few years previously, is little talked about in France and no longer exhibits there.

In 1878, however, the rumour of a lawsuit he brings against John Ruskin crosses the Channel. In the review *Fors Clavigera*,[18] Ruskin, the defender of the Pre-Raphaelites, declared à propos of

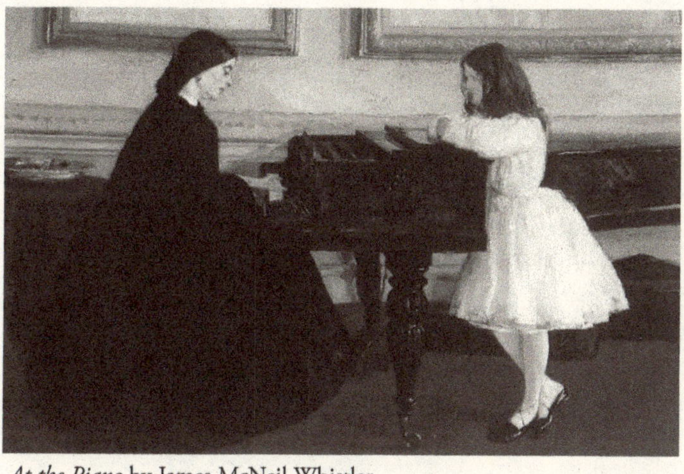

At the Piano by James McNeil Whistler.

certain of Whistler's paintings – his *Harmonies* and his *Nocturnes* among others – that he had 'seen, and heard, much of Cockney impudence before now; but never expected to hear a coxcomb ask two hundred guineas for flinging a pot of paint in the public's face'.[19]

Whistler is indignant and, like any good American would, takes out an action against the critic, for the commercial depreciation of his wares, before the Court of the Exchequer, which orders Ruskin to pay a farthing in damages.

Then Whistler decides to exhibit again in France. He sends a black, phantasmic, particularly bizarre portrait to the Salon of 1882.[20] But in fact it isn't until the following year that we are permitted to admire the extraordinary personality of this painter.

At the official Salon of 1883, he shows the portrait of his mother, an old lady in profile, her black clothes standing out against a grey wall extended by a black curtain dotted with white. It's disturbing,

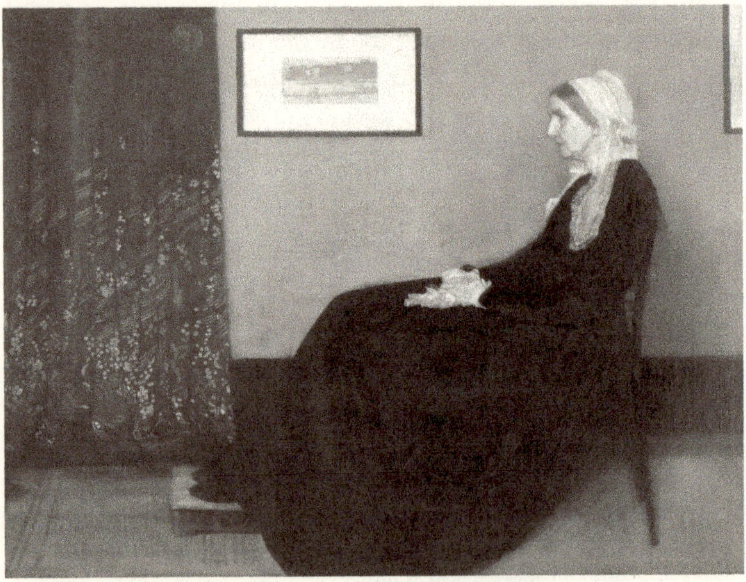

Portrait of the Artist's Mother by James McNeil Whistler.

of a colour different to that which we're accustomed to see. The canvas is, for all that, barely covered in paint, its threads showing through. The harmony between the grey and the Indian ink black was a joy to the eye, taken by surprise at these subtle and profound counterpoints; it's a realistic painting, wholly intimate, but already opening out into the transcendental realm of dreams.

At almost the same time, at the international exhibition in the Rue de Sèze,[21] he exhibits his famous canvases of London, his dream landscapes: his delightful *Nocturne in Silver and Blue*, in which a city built on a riverbank rises up into the azure; his *Nocturne in Black and Gold*, in which fireworks shatter the shadows of a dark night with blood-red rockets and a sprinking of stars; and finally, his *Nocturne in Blue and Gold*, depicting a view of the Thames over which, in a spectral mist, a golden moon illuminates with its pale rays the indistinct forms of ships sleeping at anchor.

Inevitably, one thinks of De Quincey's visions, of those rushing rivers, of those turbulent dreams provoked by opium. In their frames of pale gold, flecked with turquoise blue and spotted with silver, these scenes of air and water stretch out to infinity, suggesting the undulations of the mind, transported by magical means to an indeterminate time, to oblivion. They are far removed from modern life, far from everything, at the very boundaries of a form of painting that seems to evaporate into an invisible haze of colour on these delicate canvases.

In 1884, the artist returns with two portraits, those of Miss Alexander and Thomas Carlyle. The historian – who was honest enough to admit that deep down there was no true history and who somewhere wrote this forceful sentence: 'Altars should be raised today to silence and solitude'[22] – sits in profile, in a black rumpled frock-coat, his hat placed on his knees. This sad, somewhat gruff figure with his greying beard, breathes and meditates, slowly summing things up; it's a portrait that penetrates beneath the

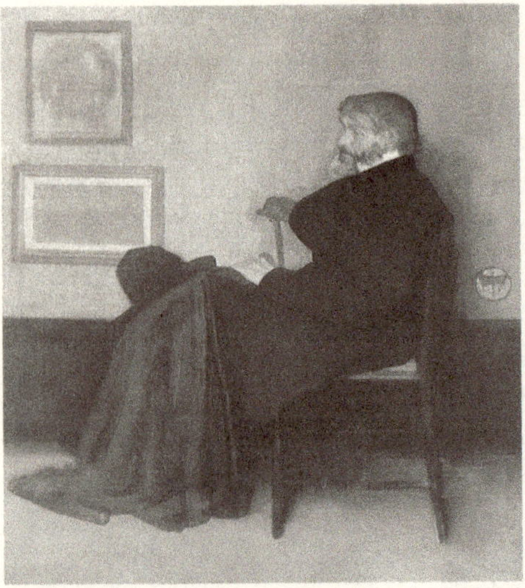
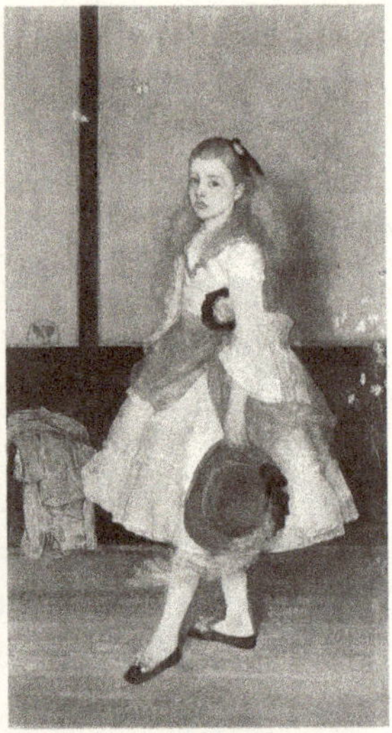

Thomas Carlyle (left) and *Miss Alexander* (right) by James McNeil Whistler.

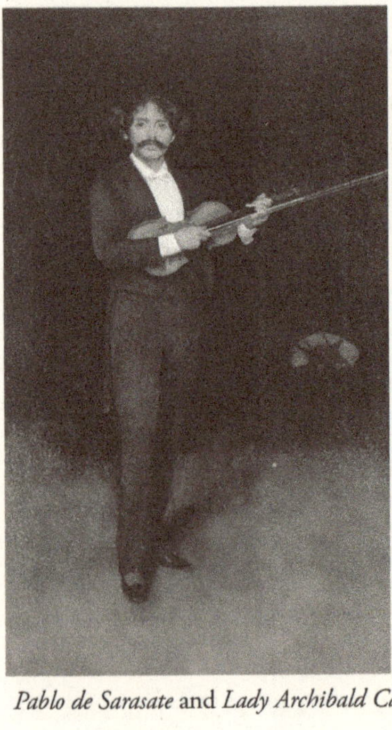
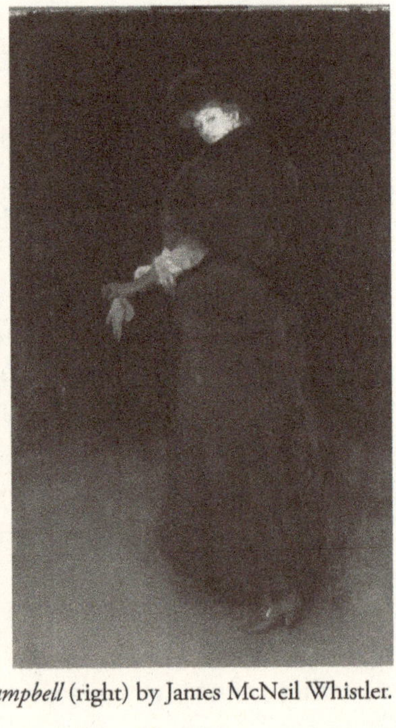

Pablo de Sarasate and *Lady Archibald Campbell* (right) by James McNeil Whistler.

skin, that places on the subject's face a reflection of the thoughts within; it's a portrait of a candid soul, but surprising as it might be, that of Miss Alexander seems to me more admirable still.

Imagine a little girl, with ash-blonde hair, dressed in white, holding in her hand a grey felt hat plumed with a feather, and standing out against an amber-grey panel supported by the pure black of a skirting board; a little blonde, aristocratic and anaemic, nonchalant and calm, an English Infanta moving in a haze of grey, a grey gilded underneath with the faded gold of old vermeil. Again, in its broad finish, barely painted at all, and like a Velasquez, brushed with such a beautiful mix of tones in its range of silver greys, that it lives with an intense life.

As in Whistler's other works, there is in this canvas a supraterrestrial aspect that is disconcerting. Certainly, her image is lifelike, is real, that is sure; certainly there is, in addition to her physical flesh, a little of her character in this painting, but there is also a supernatural aspect emanating from this mysterious, somewhat spectral painter, which to a certain extent justifies Desnoyers' use of the word 'spirititualist'. Indeed, one can't read the more or less truthful revelations by Dr Crookes[23] on the subject of 'Katie', that shade incarnated in the *dopplegänger* form of a palpable yet paranormal woman, without thinking of Whistler's portraits of women, those ghost-portraits that seem to retreat, that seem to want to sink into the wall, with their enigmatic eyes and their ghoulish, icy-red mouths.

These reflections are especially applicable to that portrait of Sarasate, which he loaned in 1886, a mediumistic portrait, elusive and highly-strung, and even to that splendid portrait of Lady Archibald Campbell which was the glory of the official Salon of 1885.

Depicted from the side, almost from the back, showing a figure turning round, she retreats into a dark shadow, deep and warm at the same time, and two spots shoot out, two spots of amadou brown – that of her small boots and that of the long gloves she's

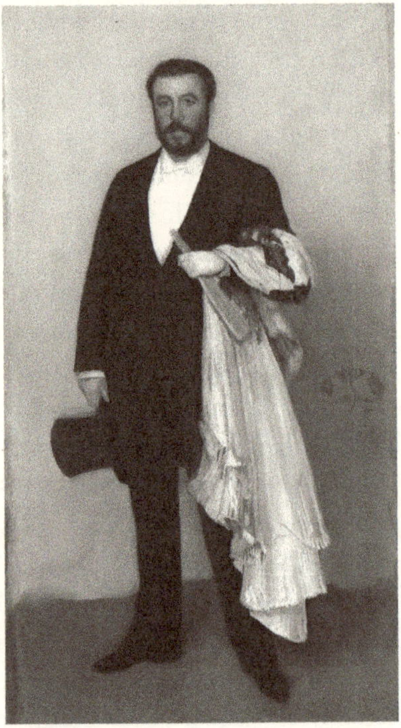

Théodore Duret by James McNeil Whistler.

buttoning – two spots stirring in the night, the darkness of which lifts at the bottom of the canvas; but this is just incidental, a detail amid the ensemble planned by the painter. From her otter-fur cape, from her dark dress, Lady Campbell emerges with supreme elegance, her tightly-laced body palpitating, her mysterious face tilting, with a provocative and haughty eye that invites, and a dull-red mouth that spurns. Once again, the artist has drawn from the flesh an indefinable expression of the soul, and he has also transformed his model into a disturbing Sphinx.

I will now leave aside the portrait of Duret, who is represented in a black suit, holding a pink cloak and a red fan over his arm. It's a curious work, assured, but with less of a transcendental elan, and the colours are sad – one would almost say it was like a smooth and expressionless Manet – and I arrive at that series of paintings, landscapes for the most part, that Whistler exhibited in May 1887 in Georges Petit's gallery, and in May 1888 in the rooms of Durand-Ruel; a whole series of 'harmonies' and 'arrangements': a village with the title *Green and Opal*; a view of Dieppe, *Violet and Grey*; a scene in Holland, *Grey and Gold*; a pastel, *Blue and Pearl*; then duos of *Violet and Rose*, of *Mauve and Silver*, of *Purple and Gold*; and finally a solo, sung by a sweet shop, under this title, *An Orange Note.*[24]

Of unequal value, these paintings, some of which seemed to be only sketched fragments, bear out the revelation of those landscapes exhibited in 1883 in the Rue de Sèze. They were veiled horizons, glimpses into another world, sunsets drenched in warm rain, river mists, clouds of blue fog, a whole spectacle of indeterminate nature, floating cities, languishing estuaries, blurred in the confused daylight of a dream; they were, outside of contemporary art, a painting of convalescence, exquisite, wholly personal, wholly new, a 'fluidic painting' that this visionary has tried to render even in his precious etchings, where, with a few strokes, he disperses buildings and cities, makes space limitless, projects a unique sensation of distance.

A clairvoyant artist, drawing out the suprasensible from the real, Whistler's landscapes make me think of several poems of a murmuring and caressing softness, as confessed, as whispered, by Verlaine. At certain moments he, like Whistler, evokes subtle insinuations, and at others, sways as if in an incantation from which an occult spell emerges. Verlaine has evidently gone to the limits of poetry, to where it evaporates completely and where the art of the musician begins. Whistler, in his harmonies of tones, goes almost beyond the limits of painting; he enters the country of letters, and advances along the melancholy shores on which Verlaine's pale flowers grow.

Whistler, in his 'Ten o'clock' lecture translated by Stéphane Mallarmé, defines art as he conceives it in this way: 'She is,' he says, 'a goddess of dainty thought, reticent of habit.'[25] And this will be his glory, as it will also be of those few artists who have despised the taste of the public, who have aristocratically practised this art contrary to ordinary ideas, this art that retreats from the crowd, this resolutely solitary, haughtily secret art.

IV

Félicien Rops

IV. FÉLICIEN ROPS

The sight of an erotic work, created by an artist of real talent, induces in me obscure descents into the depths of the soul. But far from it being the nudes – which, at first, I had a melancholy pleasure in contemplating – it's their creators I'm dreaming about, and I wonder what impulses, what emotions they yielded to when they executed such works.

Leaving aside the venal aspect, if it's an artist who I know to be honest I must also put aside any suspicion of loose morals, banish the notion that his paintings simply reproduce episodes from his private life, because the moment real debauchery asserts itself the enfeebled artistic impulse falls into a senile coma and dies. Moreover, the artist who gives in to the clamourings of lechery is hardly in a state to translate them onto paper or canvas. I will add that, generally speaking, this latter sort of artist is one who celebrates virtue, proclaims decency and exalts love, who conceals beneath the prudish and frigid outlines of his work the studied turpitudes he dreams up in the expensive secrecy of a private room.

Hypocrisy, which so deliberately veils the licentiousness of Merry Old England currently in the grip of an infantile passion for rape,[1] easily explains the contradictory conduct of these men in their private lives and in their works.

But deep down, when you think about it, just the opposite is true, because there's nothing so truly obscene as people who are chaste. Indeed, everyone knows that sexual continence engenders terrible lewd thoughts, that a man who isn't a Christian – and who is consequently involuntarily pure – becomes overexcited, especially in solitude, gets worked up and gives free rein to his imagination; so, mentally, in his waking fantasies, he goes to the very limits of orgiastic delirium.

Therefore it's very likely that the artist who forcefully treats carnal subjects is, for one reason or another, a chaste man.

But this observation doesn't seem to be sufficient, because looking at it more closely one discovers that, even when one isn't strictly continent, even when one is sated, even when one feels a sincere disgust at sensual pleasure, one is still troubled by lecherous thoughts.

It's then that this bizarre phenomenon appears – a soul that, without the input of physical desire, conjures up lewd visions.

Whether impure or not, artists, whose nerves are stretched to breaking point, have, more than anyone else, constantly endured the unbearable agitations of Lust. I'm not talking here of the act provoked by Lust itself – of the act of fornication – which is merely unclean and which simply testifies to a more or less excitable temperament, a more or less vibrant nervous constitution, a more or less powerful libido. I'm not even talking about the desire that precedes the venereal act and clamours for it, because that only indicates an easy arousal of the senses, or of passive reserves of feeling that have long been reined-in; no, I'm talking exclusively about the Spirit of Lust, of those isolated erotic ideas that have no physical correspondence, that have no need for an animalistic outlet to appease them.

And almost always the scene dreamed up by the artist is identical: images arise, nudes offer themselves; but, in a bound, the natural act fades away, as if deprived of interest, as if it were too brief, as if it provoked nothing but an anticipated agitation, a banal ejaculation; and, in a flash, the impulsion of a preternatural obscenity manifests itself, an exhortation to a climax that has escaped the constraints of the flesh and leaped into the orgasmic beyond. The soul's ignominy is worse, one could say, but it is refined and ennobled by the thought that's mixed up with it – an ideal of superhuman vices, of sins that one would like to think are original.

In spiritualising the obscene in this way, a real dissipation of phosphorus takes place in the brain, and if, during this disquieting state of the mind, which suggests to itself, and for itself alone, these overheated sensual visions, if chance has it that an element of reality gets mixed in, that a woman of flesh and blood appears, then the man, forced out of his dream, is left embarrassed, becomes almost frigid, feels – as in all cases after a real emission – an atrocious sense of disillusionment and sadness.

This strange attraction to the convolutions of carnal desire, this obsession with the obscene for obscenity's sake, this animalistic sexual urge that occurs entirely in the soul, without the body being consulted or mixed up in it, this frenzied but constrained impulse which has, in short, only the most distant connection to the reproductive instinct, remains singularly mysterious when you thinks about it.

'Etrethism of the brain', says science; and if this state persists and gets worse, leading to certain disorders in the body, it pronounces the words 'psychological hysteria', it recommends palliatives, sedatives and painkillers,[2] potassium bromide, and cold showers.

As for the causes that produce these same disturbances, science remains necessarily cautious; as with terrible nervous illnesses, it doesn't know the motives for such disorders and crises; it merely monitors the progress of these episodes, averting them or retarding them, but either way it can't explain the turbulent nature of these unhealthy thoughts at present.

Here, the Church finds itself in its element; it recognises the wily schemes of the old sin. That 'psychological hysteria' is what the church calls 'morose delectation'[3] and defines it thus: 'The acquiesence in a sinful thing presented as if real by the imagination, but without the desire to carry it out.'[4] And, from the point of view of personal responsibility, the Church considers it as dangerous as the act itself, classifying it unhesitatingly on its list of mortal sins.

It sees in this mental masturbation the insidious entreaty of the Devil. In terms of a remedy, it can only offer supplications and prayer; if necessary, it can still resort to the use of holy relics or brandish the rusty sword of exorcism; but, persuaded by the virtue of the Sacraments, those great doctors of the soul limit themselves to compelling people afflicted with this evil to go to communion, expecting the patient's deliverance to come from their approach to the Holy Altar.

In short, this phenomenon is clear to Catholics, but profoundly obscure to materialists, who are incapable of discovering in the brain the mechanism of that soul which they consider to be merely a function of a nervous system that acts on its own.

In art, this psychological hysteria, or this notion of morose delectation, was bound to translate itself into an artist's work and fix the images it had itself created. It found in art, therefore, its spiritual outlet, the only one possible, because a corporeal outlet is, as I have already said, the most certain destroyer of art.

So it is to this special state of the soul that one can attribute the carnal ejaculations[5] – whether written or painted – of true artists.

In the hands of inferior artists, or parasites in love with debauchery, this arid

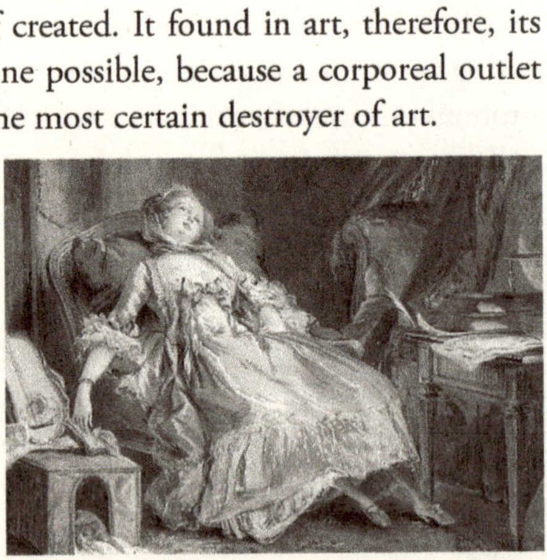

The Reader (detail) by Pierre Antoin Baudouin.

erethism, as one might call it, has produced abject and stupid works of art. Directed or regulated by a master, it is the foundation of those great licentious works that sleep in the 'Restricted' section of public libraries,[6] in clandestine boxes and hidden files.

I want to speak only of these latter works. Some, and among them the most famous – the secret museums of antiquity, the candid works of Gulio Romano, Marcantonio Raimondi, and Agostino Carracci,[7] for example – are, it has to be admitted, very mediocre; and, even if one accepts that the sixteenth-century Dutch painter, Torrentius,[8] was a genius, how can one prove it since all his pictures were publicly burned,[9] while he himself, after having been tortured, was exiled as an Adamite heretic?[10]

On the other hand, Rembrandt's prints are heavy, lacking that keen savour which more priapic artists exude, so I will not stop to discuss them. I will also ignore the depraved gentility of eighteenth-century art. Basically, this period eroticised furniture in a charming fashion, it turned the work of upholsterers and cabinet makers into an aphrodisiac, and triumphed in the lesser branches of art, but in the actual district of painting it revealed only a dubious affectation, the refinement of a *cabinet de toilette*, the cloying decor of a bidet infused with ambergris. Leaving aside the frills and furbelows painted by Fragonard and Boucher, if we let ourselves go down this path we would arrive at the senile frivolities of Baudouin and Caresme,[11] whose works were licentious and pretty, but who, by the baseness of their innuendos and the smallness of their vision, dishonoured the great Biblical vice of Lust.

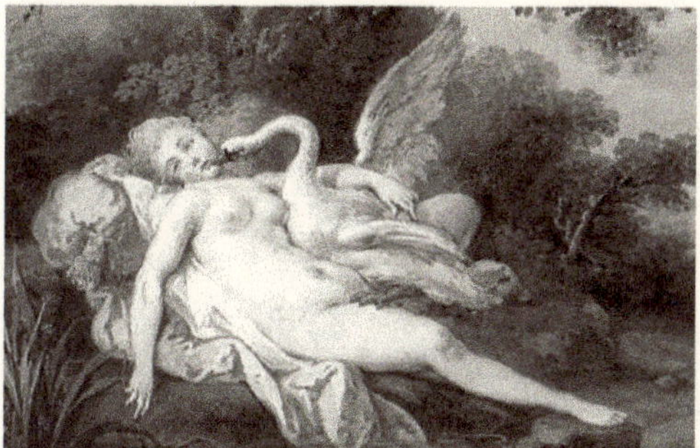

Leda and the Swan (detail) by Jacques Caresme.

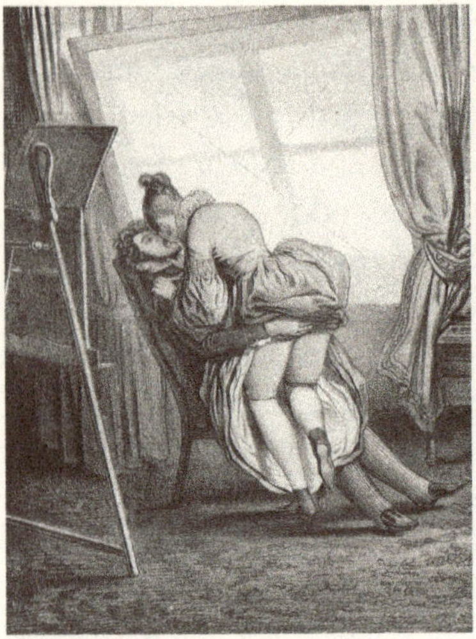
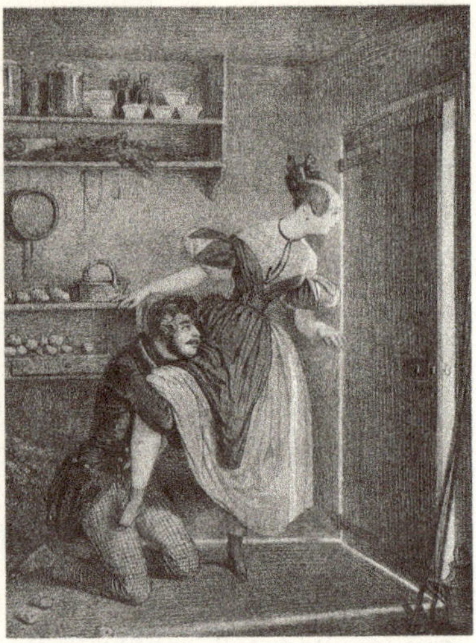

The Landscape Lesson (left) and *The Dark Room,* from *Scenes from Private Life* (c.1837) by Paul Gavarni.

Neglecting also the ridiculous *Scenes from Private Life* by Gavarni, the libertinages of Devéria, and the narrow-minded vignettes of gentle Tassaert, I will pause only in front of Rowlandson and some Japanese prints, before stopping definitively at Rops, whose work I will try to characterise.

Rowlandson treated these subjects with a ferocious humour, an overactive sense of mockery, and a mad gaiety. His heroes

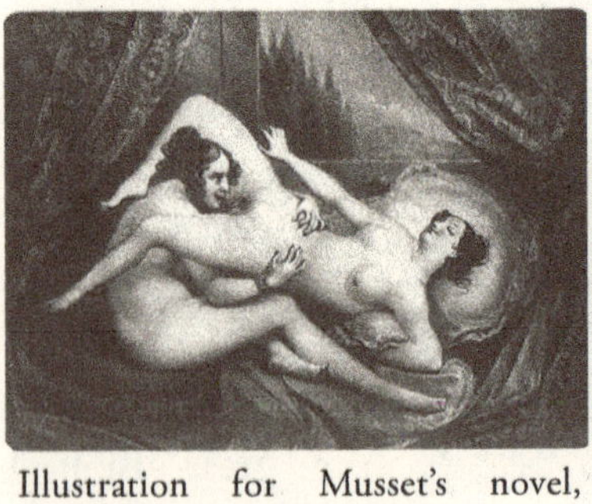

Illustration for Musset's novel, *Gamiani* by Achille Déveria.

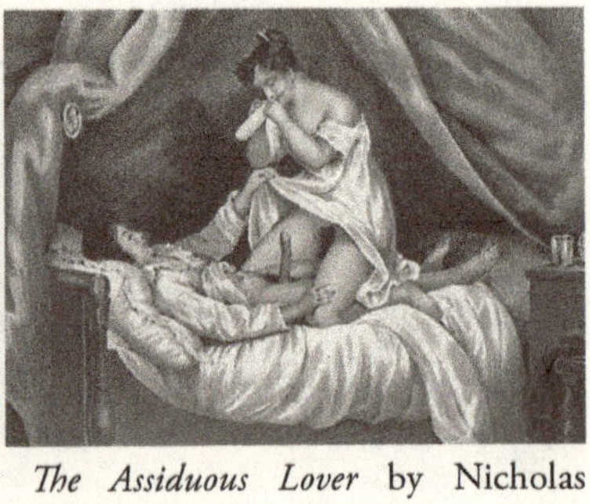

The Assiduous Lover by Nicholas Tassaert

are for the most part hussars who, trouserless, thrash away, and in good-natured fashion ravish girls who are astonished at this godsend and writhe about in frenzied joy. One of his colour plates is an astonishing melee of a rutting crowd: in a public square,[12] a naked female acrobat, her belly like a pumpkin, bends over backwards into a hoop, to the sound of an organ grinder. Sash windows are open; at one, a Turk, sitting cross-legged like a tailor, smokes his pipe, bears his belly and nonchalantly pees; an old marquis grips his épee between his naked thighs, its hilt mirroring the contour of his scarlet rod, while above him a hussar in the act of coupling finishes off, a doctor from the Sorbonne looks astounded and stands motionless, and a woman is hoisted up to a man in a window blowing a horn, her skirts hitching up above her waist as she climbs. It is, in its incoherent realism, like the unbridled gaiety of an enormous sailors' binge, a raucous laugh accentuated by the comical appearance of the old savant,

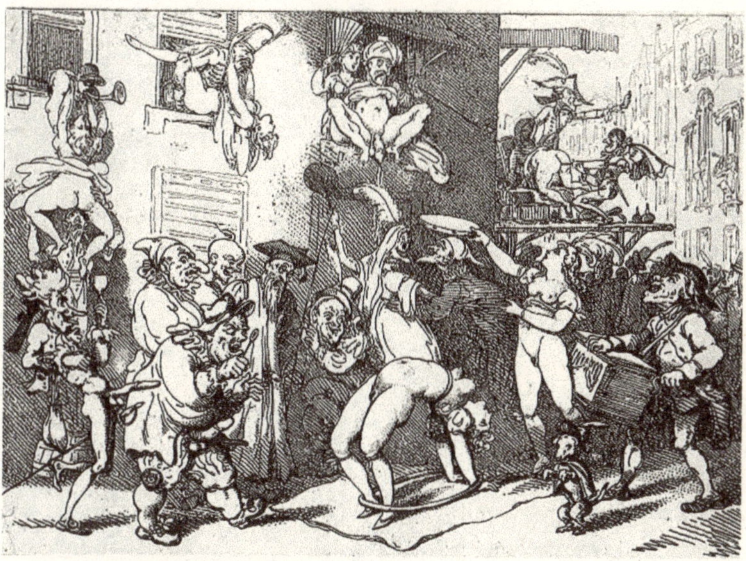

Carnival at Venice by Thomas Rowlandson

stripped of his dignity and watching it all with an outraged pout and indignant eyes that plead for calm relief.

This monstrous, big-bellied joyfulness nevertheless tempers itself, refines itself in Rowlandson's work and, as in Hogarth's wry prints, often turns to a precisely observed scene in his ridiculous episodes, in his comical asides. As in another of his colour prints, *The Miser*:

In a small room, an old miser, wearing a red cap, sits next to a strongbox. Two whores, one, at the head of the bed, her nightdress raised, is fingering herself; the other, is striving to arouse the old man whose trousers are pulled down. In one hand he holds a sack of coins; the other scratches his forehead as he calculates, with a moaning smile on his face, the price demanded by the two whores, vacillating between the entreaties of his miserliness and the baying of his lust.

The man's hesitation, and the sly, sarcastic looks of the women who, fascinated by the bulging and clinking of his money bag, almost neglect to pay attention to the libertine feast they are serving up to the old man, are truly rendered with a mocking good humour, with the finesse of a comedian, with such understanding and verve that the obscene

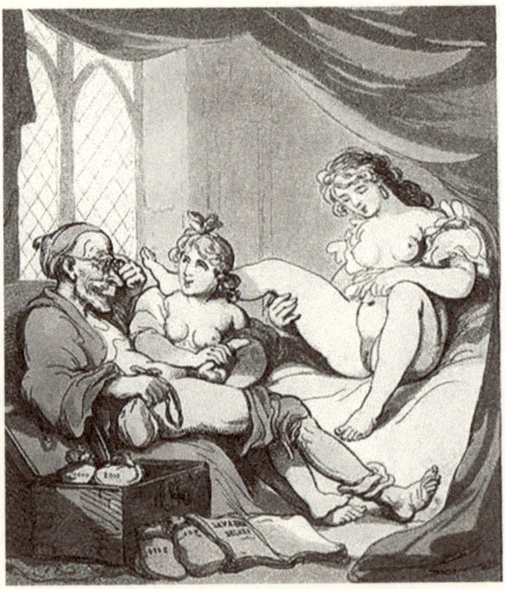

The Miser (c.1810) by Thomas Rowlandson

element disappears, that only the comedy of manners remains, captured in the detail of the physiognomies over which pass the ardent reflections of competing vices.

The fat and pretty woman that Rowlandson captures so well, with her rustic seductiveness of healthy flesh, the woman with a face that is both serious and sly at the same time, and with glowing skin, appears in these prints, as in others of the same genre, in which hussars fornicate, monks have their way with nuns, and musicians, half-naked, their bows in the air, beat out a lubricious rhythm like a metronome, and blow, red-faced, into their brass horns.

But it has to be said, however desirable she might be, Rowlandson's type of woman is all animal, with none of the complications of meaning that would make her interesting. In short, he has depicted more the fornicating machine, the hale and hearty beast, than the terrible goddess of Lust. His men are louts, with a porter's strapping loins, his whores are camp followers with the rumps of a carthorse; they are the sort of creature that Rubens occasionally painted, who, driven by need, lets herself go. And that's all.

With the Japanese, the point of view changes; that somewhat contemptible appreciation of overflowing and comical flesh, that absurd gaiety which, if you ask me, diminishes Rowlandson's libertine work in these subjects, has disappeared, and the opposite is revealed. Suffering asserts itself in their illustrated albums.

With them, sexual commerce seems to shatter the nervous system, to send searing pains through fraught limbs strained to breaking point; it tortures couples, clenches their fists, bends their legs back, contracts them as if from an electric current, their toes curling on their feet.

Their women, with sluggish flesh as white as that of emphysemics, expire on their backs, eyes closed, teeth biting their bloodied lips; private parts, horribly cleft open, gape beneath small tufts of hair, like a wound surrounded by wattles; their groaning men sprawl, sporting inconceivable phalluses with mushroom heads and swollen shafts lined with veins. Coupled in impossible positions, they all lie around like corpses whose bones have been broken by some powerful machine of torture.

The most beautiful print I know in this genre is horrifying. It's a Japanese woman being ravaged by an octopus; with its tentacles, the terrible beast presses the tips of her breasts and probes her mouth, while its head feeds on her lower parts. The almost superhuman expression of anguish and pain that convulses her elongated Pierrot-like face with its aquiline nose, and the hysterical joy that simultaneously seeps from her forehead, from those eyes closed as if in death, are admirable.

The Japanese have thus rehabilitated through suffering the Lust that clinks glasses with such good cheer in the galloping debaucheries of the English painter; but here again, these prints are merely anecdotes, in no way are they works of art elevated by a general idea that inspires them, or furnished with a spiritual backbone that supports them.

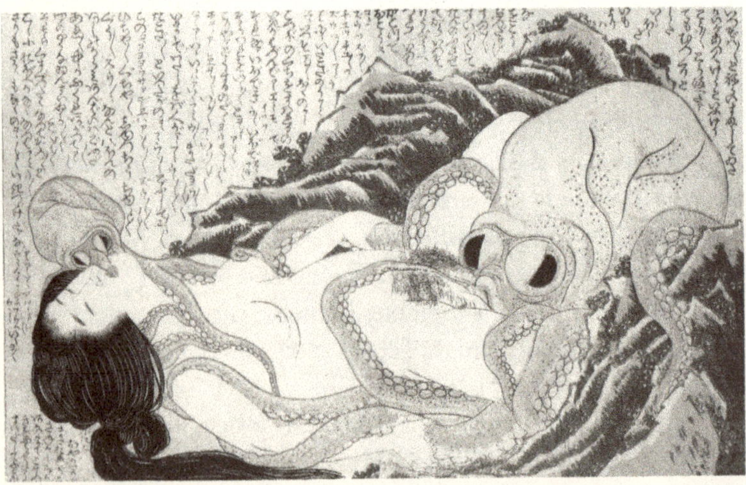

The Dream of the Fishermans's Wife by Hokusai.

IV. Félicien Rops

In these prints there is no concept unifying or condensing that selfsame figure of Lust which fills the Bible, which, from its very first pages, stands beneath the tree of Eden, and which emerges again at the end of the book, when, evoked by the angel with seven vials, the sovereign Whore seen by Saint John rises up, adorned in gold and purple.

Deified by a Paganism that worshipped her under various incarnations – as Venus and as Priapus – Lust, later to become a Christian sin, was symbolised in Salomé's 'Dance of the Seven Veils'. Then, out of this fertile soil, she rendered up to the Grim Reaper of sins the souls of infatuated saints, tormented hermits living alone in their solitary Thebaids, and, over the centuries, led astray the chaste resolve of the cloisters.

It was she, too, who was responsible for tribal migrations, the crushing of populations, who erected on phallic pillars a tottering history; she who, at the present moment, rules the world, who alone can contend against that other power of the age, against money, which, even in the hands of the most miserly, falters when the flesh burns!

It is worth our while, therefore, to reveal the mechanism of this hoister of libidos, this leverager of souls, to dissect her methods and divulge her workings, that we sum her up in Catholic terms, so to speak, in passionate and disreputable images, and that, from the point of view of art, we should substitute the allegorical deities of Paganism with a new figure of demonic femininity, a new Sataness.

Held back in its infancy from various poses revealing that which a centuries-old prudery forbade one to see, incompetently and stupidly delighting in ingenious and vulgar details, painting did not take into account that it had to steer its course – like humanity who gives it birth, or like the earth itself that carries it – between these two poles: Purity and Lust, between the heaven and the hell of art. It could not comprehend that, to be extraordinary, every work has to be either satanic or mystical, that outside these extreme points, there were only works of a temperate spirit that were neither one thing or another, works that issued from human concerns that were more or less craven.

As for Purity, it had inspired some incomparable painting; it had sublimated the talent of some of the great Christians painters, such as Fra Angelico, Grünewald, Roger Van der Weyden, and Memling. But this virtue died after the Middle Ages; it is now, like the divine sentiment from which it emanates, inaccessible in art to those generations deprived of faith.

Lust, for its part, has not produced a single work of art that is truly powerful. And we have had to wait until our present era to find an artist who dreamed of really exploring those Antarctic regions unknown to art. Adopting an old concept from the Middle Ages – that man hovers between Good and Evil, struggles between God and the Devil, between Purity, which is of divine essence, and Lust, which is the very Demon itself – Félicien Rops, with the soul of a Primitive painter in reverse, has achieved a body of work that is the opposite of Memling's; he has penetrated Satanism, summed it up in his admirable etchings, which, as inventions, as symbols, as art that is incisive and vigorous, savage and upsetting, are truly unique.

But, it has be said, Rops didn't achieve this synthesis of Evil at a single stroke. In the deft frontispieces which, in the past, he engraved for the libertine works reprinted in Brussels by Poulet-Malassis,[13] he simply revealed a mocking and impious vitality, a bizarre and lively imagination.

With an often pointed wit, he perfects his prints, sometimes elegant and beribonned like those of the eighteenth century – such as the etchings that precede *Bawdy Plays*[14] and *No Tomorrow* by Vivant Denon[15] – sometimes summed up in wholly personal allegories, with seemingly absolute liberty. Among these are his etchings for *The Satirical Parnassus*,[16] in one of which flights of

IV. Félicien Rops

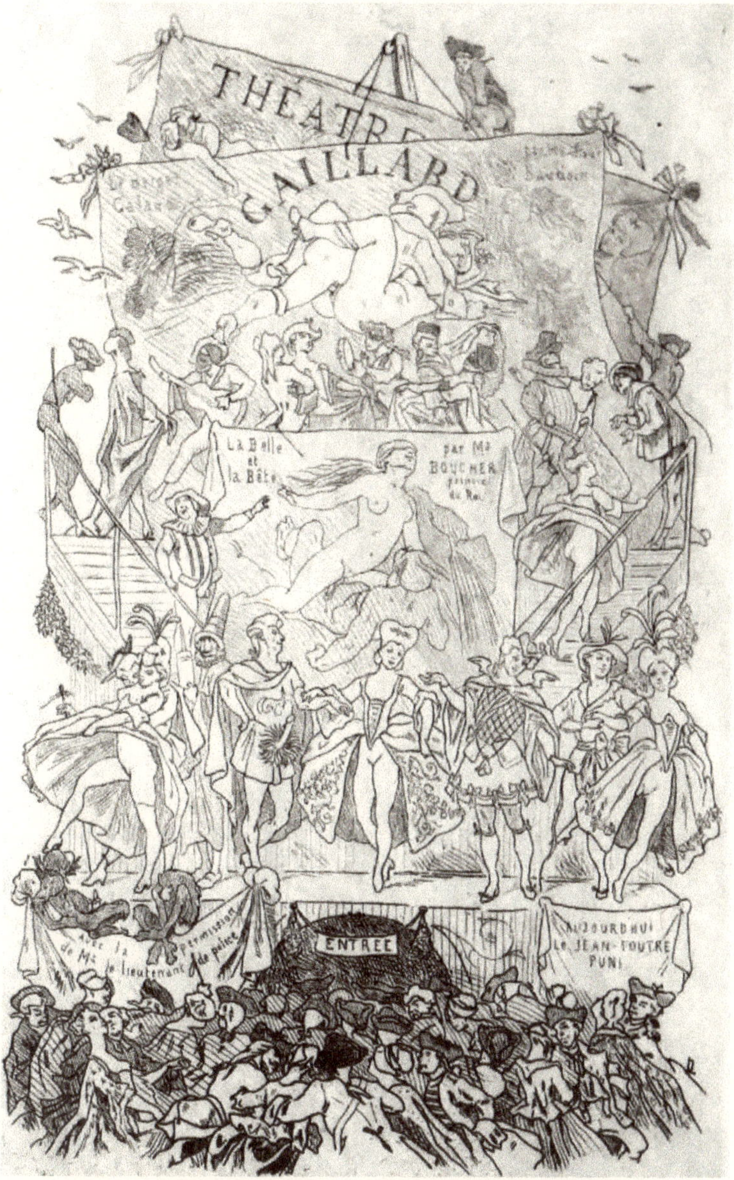

Frontispiece for *Théâtre gaillard* (*Bawdy Plays*) by Félicien Rops.

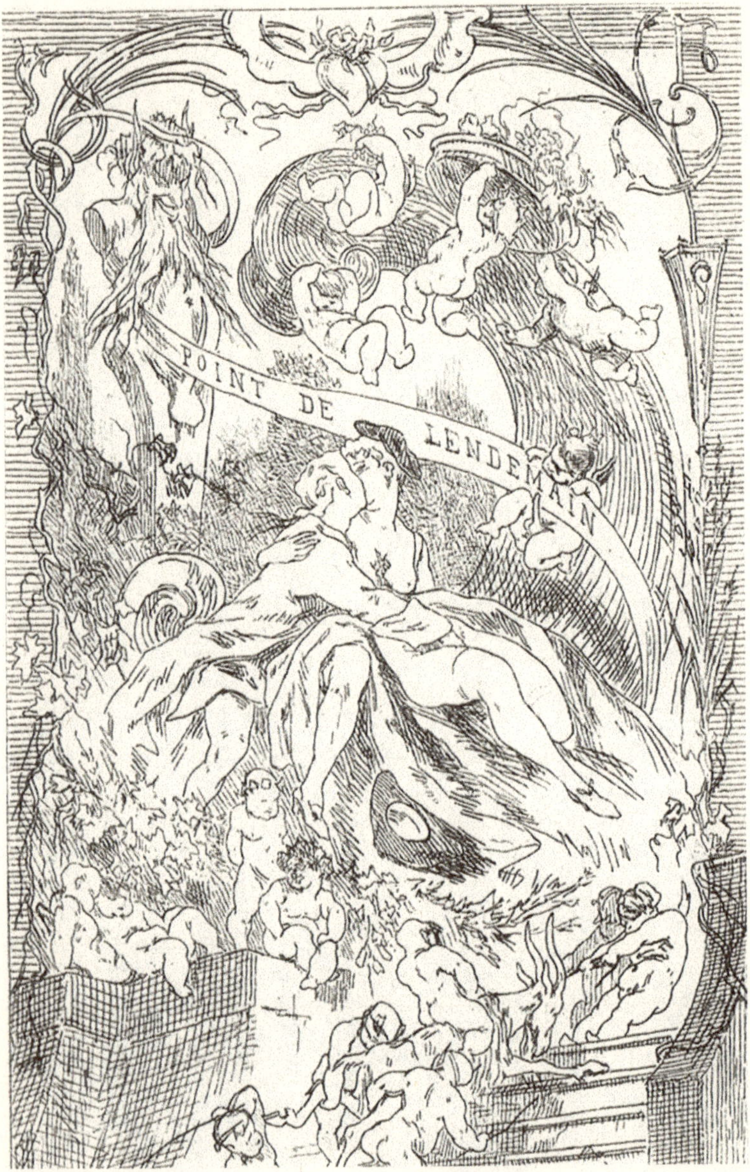

Frontispiece for *No Tomorrow* (1867) by Félicien Rops.

tiny women and small bacchantes[17] climb up the rigid joystick of a pagan statue whose goat's beard splays out in delight, while, with his fatherly eyes, he contemplates one of the women who, in raptures, straddles the tip of his formidable member and who holds out her arms in a swoon and cries for mercy, as her companions hang, howling, on to the spheres of his massive balls; while in another, representing the reverse image of this scene, a troop of small fauns mount an assault on an armless Satyress, crowned by vines, with pointed ears and sturdy breasts. She, too, is in raptures, and smiles, maternal and lascivious, at the little satyrs who suck her breasts, crawl over her large belly, forage the pit of her navel, and slip, as if through a cat-flap, into the half-open eyelet of her sex. But one of the most ingenious, most vehement works in this series remains the one that served as frontispiece for the small volume, *Galant Joys and Other Pleasures,* by poor Albert Glatigny.[18]

Imagine a good-old Flemish wag sitting down, baring his belly, holding open the flaps of his fall-front breeches; he is almost crying with laughter, exuberant and breathless, as a swarm of delightful little creatures launch themselves on his prodigious nudity, which rises up like a lighthouse, the base of which plunges into thick undergrowth.

And they are incredible, these dwarf nymphomaniacs! Never before has the mania of bitches on heat been rendered with such enthusiasm, with such a sense of aroused flesh! Straining, they cling to clumps of hair with their fists, climb his mast, drape themselves round his ball-bag, dragging themselves over each other, devouring each other, and toppling into expiring heaps. All this captured in a lively and natural, penetrating and confident sketch. But then, in his engravings, the phallus often exhibits the strangest, the most unexpected forms. At rest, as in the frontispiece of Delvau's *Dictionary of Modern Erotica,*[19] it hangs down, simulating a butterfly with a human face: the nose traced by the flaccid stem, the eyes at the base of the shaft beneath a

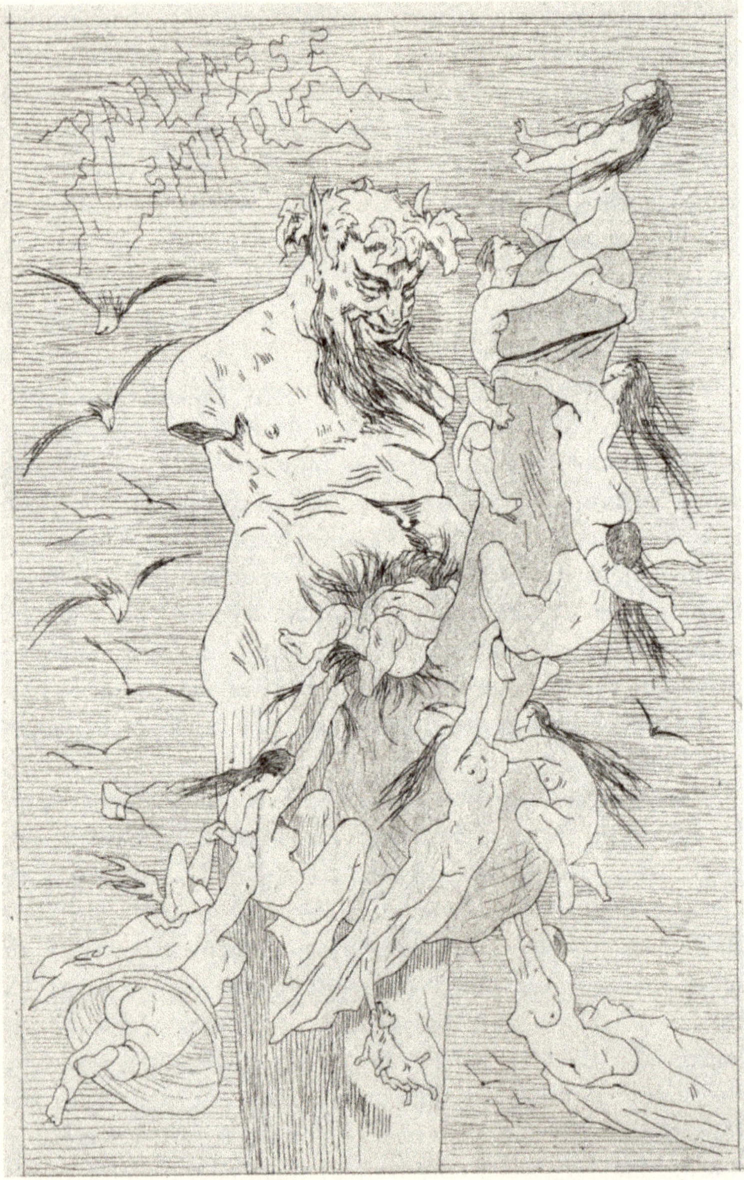

Frontispiece for *The Satirical Parnassus* by Félicien Rops.

IV. Félicien Rops

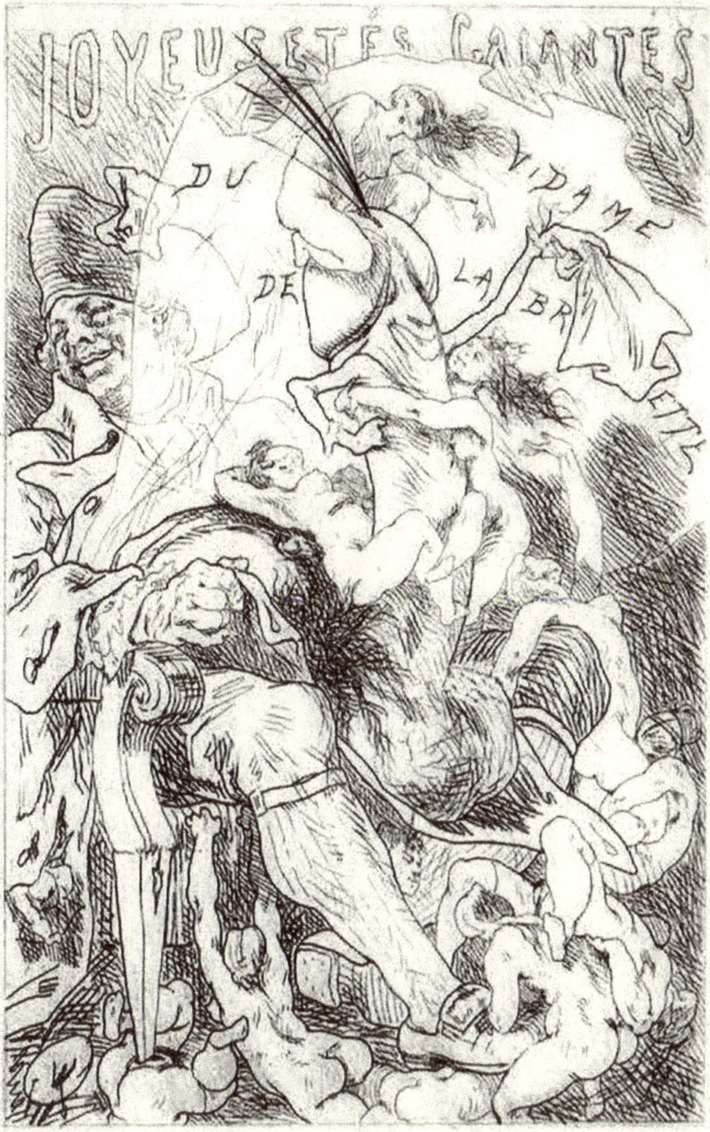

Frontispiece for *Galant Joys* by Félicien Rops.

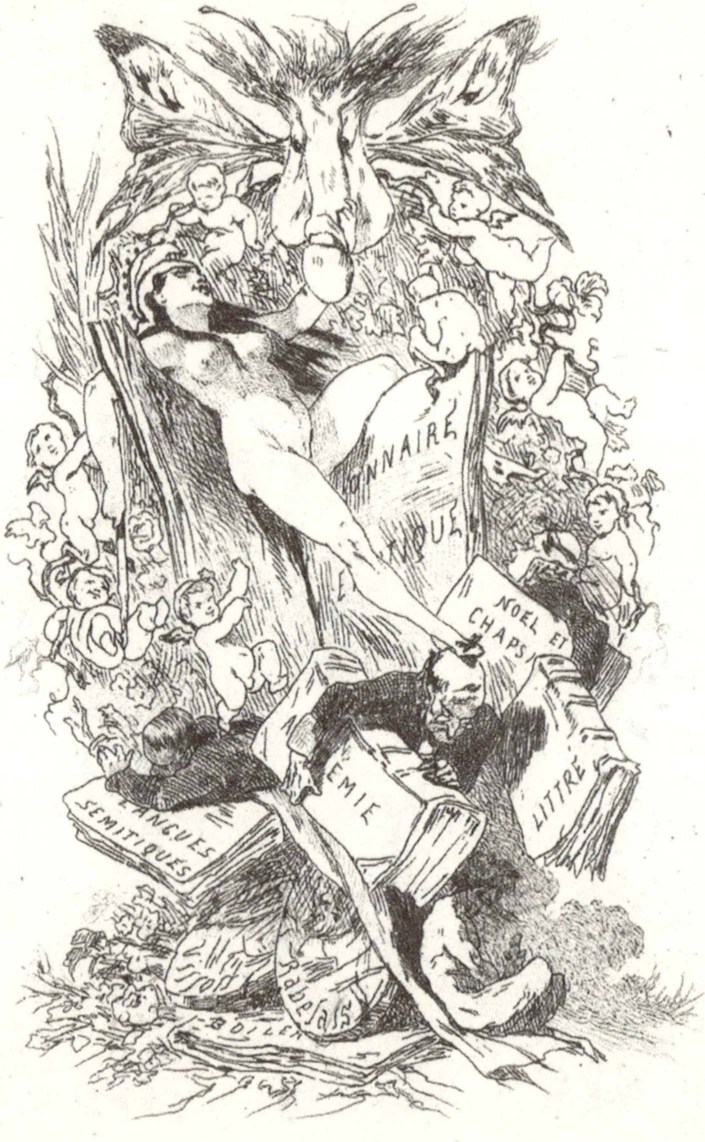

Frontispiece for *Dictionary of Modern Erotica* (1864) by Félicien Rops.

tuft of hair, the cheeks imitated by the two balls. At work, as in the *Galant Joys* etching, it transforms itself into a figurine, the retracted foreskin sculpts itself into a nose and mouth, and the glans becomes a Turk's turban, topped by a plume of semen.

At the same time as he was illustrating a series of published volumes – the publication details of which were variously disguised as 'Everywhere and Nowhere', 'S.P.Q.R.', 'At Eleuthéropolis' and 'At Lampsaque'[20] – and enlivening the dull prose of the late Delvau with his engraved frontispieces, Rops created a type of a woman who we will see again, revised and adapted throughout his work, the type featured in *The Absinthe Drinker* who, world-weary and ravenous, becomes even more menacing and more voracious, with her cold, blank face, malicious and severe, her limpid eyes with the lesbian's fixed and cruel stare, with her open, slightly fullish mouth, and her symmetrical snub nose.

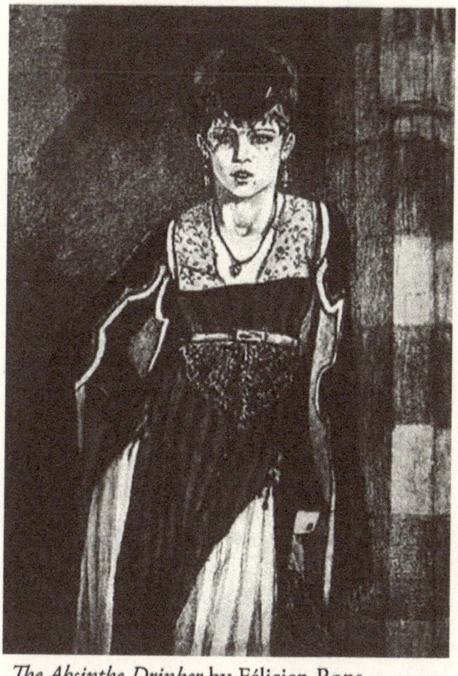

The Absinthe Drinker by Félicien Rops.

This archetype of the insatiable, rapacious nympho appears, modified, in several of his prints; to cite just one, for example, in *Woman Sitting on a Lion-Skin Rug*, which he chose not to insert in the volume for which it was intended, *Rhymes of Joy*, by Théodore Hannon,[21] a poet of talent swallowed up in

Brussels, without the excuse of poverty, in the cloaca of *fin-de-siècle* magazines and the nauseous tirades of the gutter press.

As with those works that Rodin sometimes transposes into his sculptures, when Rops represents actual, unadorned reality, I like him less; indeed, Millet's influence can be felt beneath his peasants, and when he takes on the smart, modern woman, that contemporary being, the veritable whore, he seems old-fashioned and doesn't achieve that powerfulness of reality, that burst of life, that wicked cry of the prodigious Degas; I have to say I also prefer Forain, whose Parisian sensibility is more certain; on the other hand, as soon as Rops allegorises and synthesises his women, as soon as he abstracts her from her real environment, he immediately becomes inimitable.

In this genre, we can point to the adorable creature that – with a few variations – he has portrayed three times: in the appendix to *The Doctor's Sonnets*,[22] in the menu of Mlle Henriette Doucé,[23] and in that of Madame Duluc.[24]

She stands in profile, a little plump, wearing a hat with flowers, a chemise that reveals her bare breasts, long black gloves up to her biceps, and striped silk stockings. With her square jaw line,

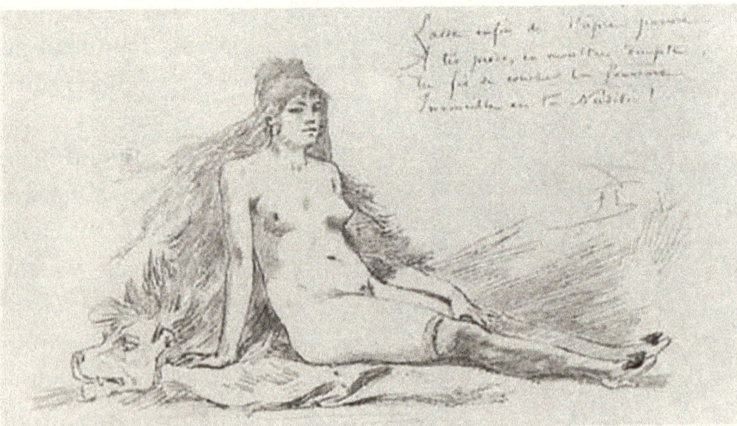

Woman Sitting on a Lion-Skin Rug by Félicien Rops.

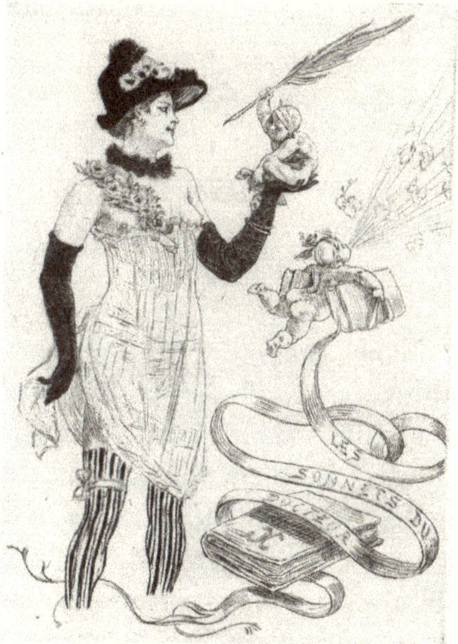

The Doctor's Sonnets by Félicien Rops.

a little common, her eyes sparkling with a lively hint of debauchery, and her wicked pursed mouth, she is irresistible. In the prints in which flying cupids are blowing on vine leaves, she has the aspect of a sentinel placed at the entrance to a camp of libertines. To a man, she evokes the idea of illicit caresses and ungodly kisses; to herself, she suggests the thought of her climactic and capricious fancies.

But in fact this etching, to which many others

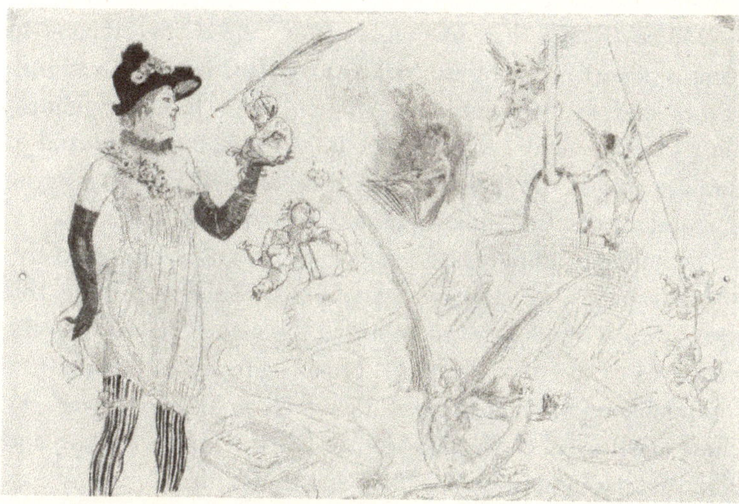
Menu for Henriette Doucé by Félicien Rops.

could be added, is, in Rops' engraved work, merely a portent, a *jeu d'esprit*. All the ones I've reviewed here are simply ironic or salubrious, others almost ostentatious in their vivacity.

We are now going to look at his work proper, in which woman will emerge demonic and terrible, handled by a talent which amplifies and concentrates itself in proportion to the appearance – in a return to Catholic ideas – of that concept of Satanism I spoke about earlier.

Obviously, Rops had to embody demonic possession as a woman. And in doing so he was in accord with the Fathers of the Church, with the whole of the Middle Ages, even with antiquity – because Quintilian, in his observations on couples accused of magic, had already written: 'the presumption is greater that the woman be a witch'. What's more, it suffices simply that the woman be bewitched in order for the man who associates with her to become infected; 'Satan, by means of women, attracts men into his net', as Bodin attested, paraphrasing the Middle Ages, which in all the declarations of its exorcists affirmed that there were fifty witches or demonic women to every man.

Moreover, whether one accepts or rejects the theory of Satanism, isn't it exactly the same today? Isn't man induced into crimes and misdemeanors by woman, who is herself almost always led astray by her kind? She is, in short, the great vessel of iniquity and crime, the sepulchre of misery and shame, the true inaugurator of every embassy of vice appointed to our souls.

Remaining within the circle drawn by Catholics, one could also add that the Devil eagerly incarnated himself in her and, under this form, would couple with men during the night. He was then the Succubus or the night demon.[25] Rops has therefore followed the immutable tradition of the centuries when, in his satanic work, he chose as principal character a woman bewitched by the Devil and empoisoning in her turn the man who touches her.

Elsewhere, he had to bring the very Devil himself into the

fearful scenes that he was contemplating.

During the Middle Ages one fact to note is that all painters represented Evil in horrible or grotesque forms, but never in the form revealed by the typical proceedings of a witches' sabbath.

Here, the documents abound and corroborate each other. Apart from certain instances in which the Dealer in Souls appeared in unusual forms or in unexpected attire – as a vulture for example, to Saint Romuald; as a shepherd to Saint Robert; as a breathless monk to Evagrius the Solitary, and under various disguises or the appearance of a fantastic animal to others still – he always reveals himself either in bestial form as a goat, a dog, or a soot-black cat, or in human form, with certain features that are clearly defined:

> 'He was a tall, very dark man, dressed all in black, always booted and spurred.' (Bodin, *On Demonmania*)[26]

> 'When he takes human form, the Devil is dark, grimy, smelly, and formidable-looking, or at least his face is a dark and dirty brown; his nose is abnormally short or immensely aquiline, his mouth open and deep, his eyes sunken and gleaming brightly…' (Delrio, *Magical Investigations*)[27]

> 'He is lanky, dark, with a cracked, inarticulate voice, but loud and terrible…his hair is spiky…he has a little goatee beard…' (Gorres, *Diabolical Mysticism*)[28]

Here, Rops has resolutely broken with tradition. His Lord of Darkness is no longer that black knight, or that ram, which terrified naive souls in the olden days; if he appeared now in such paraphernalia, or in such a disguise, he'd look as if he'd come from a theatrical costumiers. As for Rops, his Satan is truly modern: he's a gentleman, dressed in a black suit, or a peasant, or a disreputable town councillor, and while he retains his hieratic form, he borrows most of it from Priapus or from Terminus, from satyrs and fauns, who, in the opinion of all the learned doctors of diabolism – Lancre, Bodin, Sinistrari, Delrio, Sprenger, and Gorres – were none other than troops of demons or evil spirits.

Such is the form he assumes in Rops' *Satanics*.[29] This series, which remains incomplete, comprises five prints that utilise the soft varnish method; but to these one could also append, as they draw from the same order of ideas, some of the etchings that illustrate Barbey d'Aurévilly's *The She-Devils*,[30] and a few others that serve as frontispieces to the ramblings of Sâr Péladan.[31]

The first of his *Satanics*, 'Satan sowing tares', is conceived in this fashion:

At night, over a sleeping Paris, an immense sower fills the sky; his feet, encumbered with heavy clogs, tread on the roofs of buildings on the right bank and on the top of the towers of Notre-Dame. Beneath the arch formed by his thin legs, the Seine flows like rice water, frozen by a moon whose disk seems to have been eaten away by clouds of smoke. With one arm, Satan lifts his overall in which larvae of women writhe and, with the other, he scythes

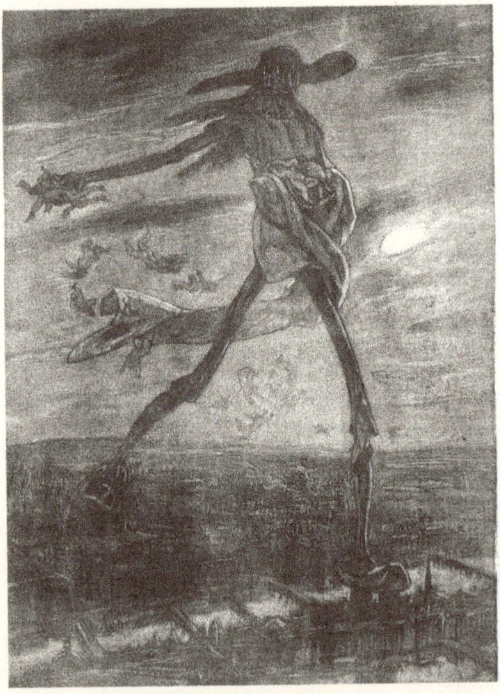

Satan sowing tares by Félicien Rops.

the firmament with a gesture that hurls, with all his force, these seeds of evil onto the silent city.

Dressed as a peasant, wearing a broad-brimmed hat, his smouldering eyes shooting piercing glances from his bony face, he grimaces with a horrifying, sardonic smile. His hair streams behind him, his long beard reveals, by its cut, an American origin, confirmed by the shape of his hat, which recalls in certain details of its brim and certain of its creases, the almost Breton-like headgear of the Quaker.

It seems that he has passed through the New World and, reinvigorated and rejuvenated, washed in its greedy hypocrisy the vices of old Europe.

Scrutinising his horrible face, one can discern the cold, determined jubilation of the Devil, who knows what kind of odious qualities the larvae he scatters are endowed with. He knows, too, that the crop is certain, and his hideous lips whisper a Rogationtide prayer[32] in reverse, mockingly inviting his inert rival to bless these evils of the earth, to consecrate the formidable

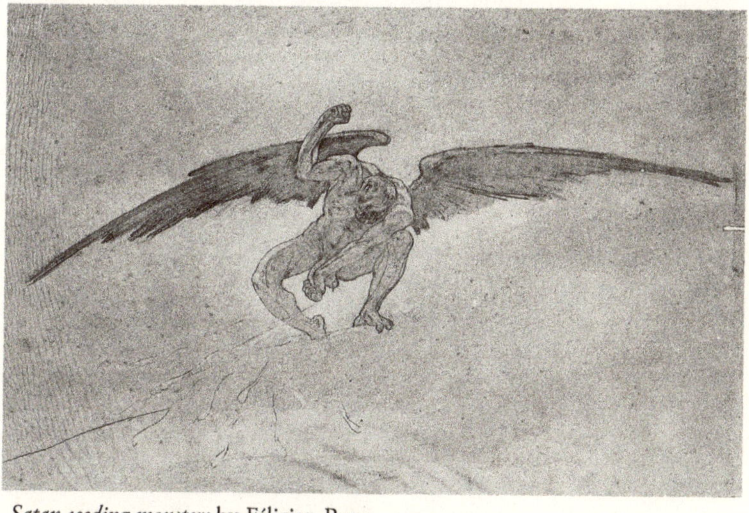

Satan seeding monsters by Félicien Rops.

harvest of crimes this seed is incubating.

This print is truly eloquent, truly beautiful. This enormous Landworker, the heel of whose clog fills the entire surface area of the top of a tower, whose skeletal legs form an immense ogive above the minuscule city spreading out beneath it and fading into the infinity of night, is framed in a drawing that is substantial and yet also compact in itself, concise and elegant.

As an idea, we can compare this print to the one entitled 'Satan seeding monsters', a Satan raising a fist into the night, and with the other inundating space with his seed.

The second print in *Satanics*, 'The Abduction', represents a naked witch, carried up into the air on a broomstick handle held by the Devil. Thrown backwards onto his back, she hurtles, sprawling, into space, until such time as he deposits her in one of those solitary places where Sabbaths are held.

And this print gives rise to long reveries, evokes monstrous recollections of what demonographers have written.

One thinks of the preparations for the Sabbath, of the ointments extracted from mandrake root, of henbane, of deadly nightshade, with which the women smeared their bodies; one thinks of the philtres with which they were

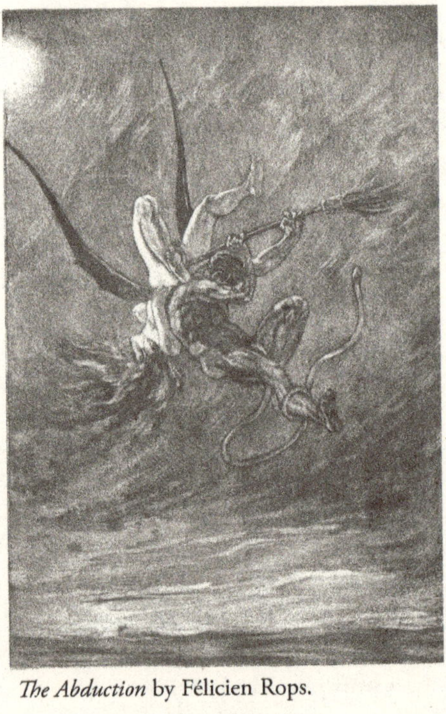

The Abduction by Félicien Rops.

intoxicated, philtres composed, according to Delrio, 'of menstrual blood, sperm, the brains of a cat or a little donkey, hyena intestines, wolves' genitals, and above all *hippomane*, the flux of a horse's vulva when in heat'. Then, after the straddling ride through the clouds, follows the descent into the clearing where the Devil, in the form of a satyr or a goat, proffers his black, hairy buttocks, which they kiss; all around, children carry toads back to their ponds, because, as Lancre says, 'Satan keeps them at a distance, for fear of disgusting them forever at the sight of so many terrible things.' And then the black mass is celebrated on the bare rump of a woman; they feast, they devour human stew, the flesh of children, whose blood they suck through the navel and at the neck; they chew their bones which, cooked for a year in certain herbs, have become soft like turnips. Instead of using salt, which prevents rotting, the bread is made with ears of wheat attacked by fungal rust in which ferment the germs of disease, the seeds of death; the wine is a heady wine whose vines have grown in the warm ash of a volcano; the blasphemies increase, they take communion with black hosts, stamped with the image of a ram, the torches are extinguished, men and women writhe and couple; everyone thrusts into illicit orifices, tries to pair with their daughter or their mother so as to commit incest, strives to get them pregnant in order to slit the throat and eat the child born of these hideous practices during a subsequent Sabbath.

In such acts there were passionate pleasures that have now been lost, and sufferings that are impossible to experience at the present day. Rops understands this, and in some of his prints he has expressed these excesses of pleasure and pain in a disturbing way.

One, 'The Sacrifice', does so to an appalling degree. On an altar, a naked woman is stretched out, her legs apart; above her is an ineffable being whose back is composed of a horse's skull pierced by two empty eye sockets and with a muzzle which stretches down to where the loins should be and at the end of

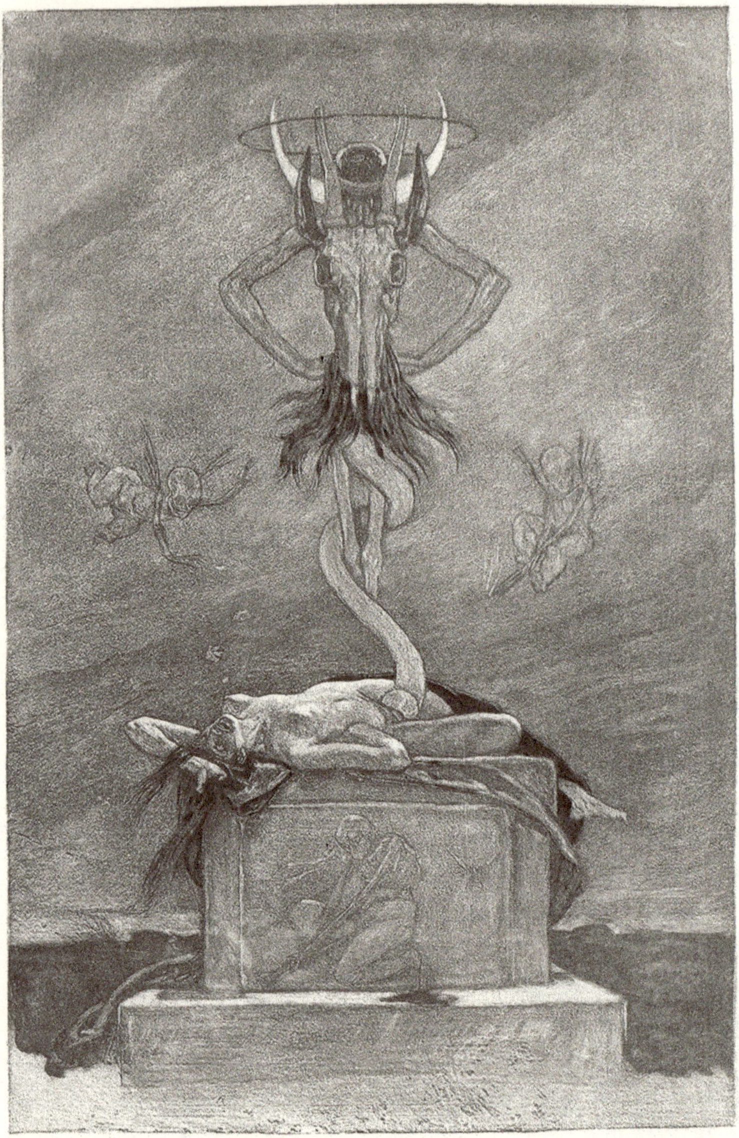

The Sacrifice by Félicien Rops.

which are two long teeth, and topped by a dark head which stands out against a turbulent sky and a crescent moon. Its thin arms form triangles, like jug handles, on either side of this body without a rump, which terminates in a kind of rod that in a double twist plunges into the woman's lower abdomen, pinning her to the stone while she calls out, overcome with horror and joy.

What is unique is the fearful impression this print gives off. This demon, so bizarrely represented, is there, immobile, pitiless, encamped, so to speak, in his victim, whose groans he doesn't even hear. His head, crossed by the lunar horn and of which one sees only the cloudy neck, is lost in thought, far from the earth, while the snaking shaft of his genitals bathes in streams of blood. It is awful and grandiose in its pointed symbolism of Lust stranded in death, of a Possession that is desperately desired, but – like every wish that is fulfilled – immediately atoned for.

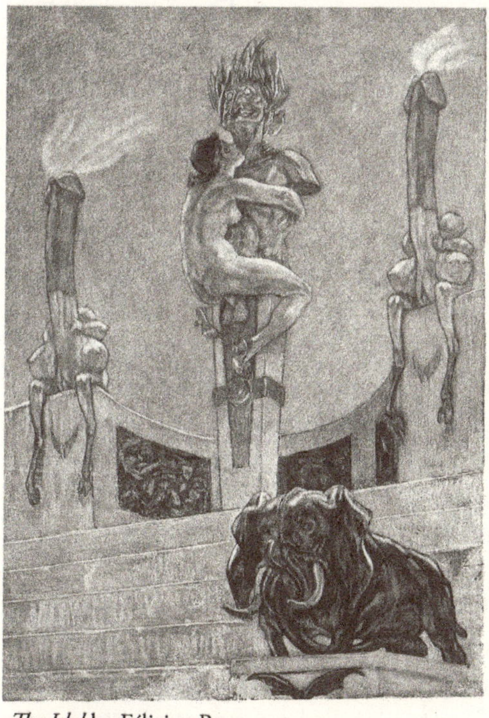

The Idol by Félicien Rops.

In the next print, 'The Idol', another woman possesses her God, an equally horrifying Satan, a kind of Hermes on a plinth of stone, a smiling and lascivious head, despicable with his low forehead, his broken nose, his goatee beard, and his hairy salivating lip. He is there, upright, in a marble hemicycle, flanked by two phalluses, the bases of which hermaphrodise between two goat legs; on the right, an elephant autofellates itself with its trunk.

And the woman has leaped onto the monster; she embraces him in a passionate, ferocious movement, remains suspended on the belly that penetrates her, staring at her abominable lover, with piercing eyes whose look of delight is frightening.

This face is truly magnificent; never has the flesh's violence emerged from an artwork like this; never has an expression of the infinite, of ecstasy, distorted a face like this and made it so sublime. There's something of a diabolical Theresa of Avila, a satanised saint at prayer, in this creature in the act of coupling, waiting for the supreme moment which will be transformed into an unforgettable deception, because all the documents affirm that the woman who makes a pact with the Devil experiences, at the final moment, the unspeakable horror of an icy ejaculation, and falls immediately into an inexpressible fatigue, into an intense exhaustion.

Finally, the last plate is entitled 'Calvary', and it is the Evil One who stands in the place of Christ on the infamous gallows, the Evil One, sneering with a face that blends the vicious peasant, the yankee, and above all the faun, a bestial Satan, drunken and obscene, with his gaping mouth and walrus teeth. He is smiling, his member erect, and, lifting up his unnailed feet, he reaches round and pulls the mane of a naked woman standing in front of him, and he slowly strangles her with the strands of her hair, while terrified, arms stretched out, she expires in a fraught orgasm of atrocious pleasure.

The blasphemous fiction of this scene, the sacrilege of the cross becoming an instrument of pleasure, the debauchery of this Madeleine in ecstasy before the nakedness of this Christ, the erect penis, all this uterine passion lit by a row of candles whose flames flicker in the darkness like white arched windows, are truly demonic, truly born of those ancient Sabbaths, which, if they no longer exist today in a full and real sense, are still nonetheless celebrated, at certain moments, in the putrefied soul of every one of us.

Here again, Rops, the painter of the female nude, has captured passionate, engorged flesh; he has kneaded it, twisted in frenzied excesses; he has at last revealed the preternatural element of overburdened physiognomies that burst into ecstacies so fervent the expression on their faces haunts you and fills you with anguish.

It is here, in fact, that the character of these prints resides. A talented painter might perhaps have rendered this carnal passion, this ferocious debauchery, have simulated in a lifelike fashion the ardent face of satyriasis and nymphomania, have eventually created a work limited to the aberrations of the sexual impulse and with no transcendental element, but I don't know anyone today who, like Rops, could have brought to explosive life the raging soul of a woman, bewitched, possessed and aroused, in all her obsessions, by the spirit of Evil.

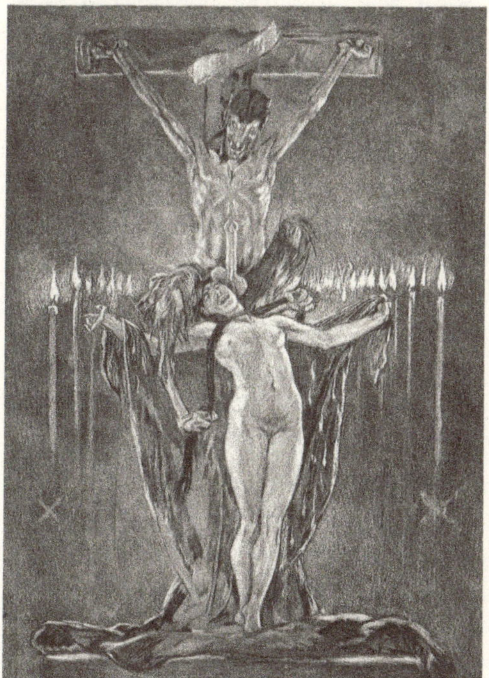

Calvary by Félicien Rops.

One can compare these *Satanics* to other etchings, the frontispiece of Péladan's *A Curious Woman* for example, a woman approaching a pagan sculpture, passing her arms around its neck, looking at it with devouring eyes, scrutinising the smile of its ugly mouth, a woman who seems to be the sister of the one who leaps onto and mounts the sneering Hermes in the *Satanics*. Another admirable one has this inscription: '*Diaboli virtus in lombis*' ('The virtue of the Devil is in his loins'),[33] which represents Love as an image of Death. Seen from behind, her skull crowned with roses, Death raises her wings which flutter on her fleshless back; a black silk corset squeezes her extravagantly thin waist that flares out to enormous buttocks of living flesh; with one hand she grasps the bow of ancient Eros, whose quiver beats against her legs; in the other, she holds up, as if it were the bloody head of John the Baptist, the decapitated head of Hamlet; this Salomé of the sepulchre is frightening, and through the lacing of her corset one can see her spine and a whole vegetation of vertebrae and ribs, sprouting like clumps of dry sticks from the bifurcated vase of her bulging rump, while, glimpsed from

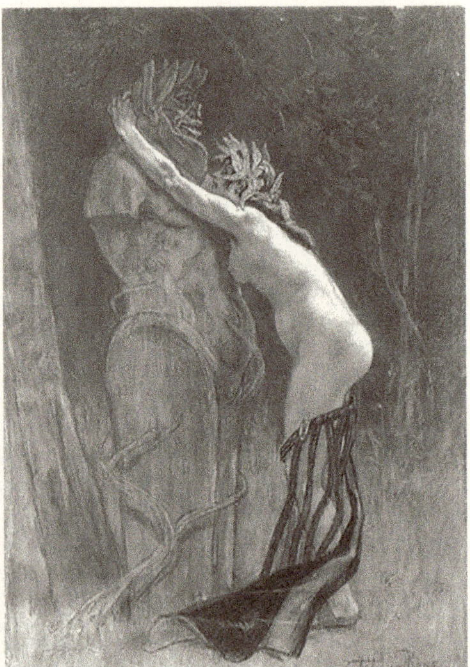

Frontispiece for Joséphin Péladan's *A Curious Woman* (1885).

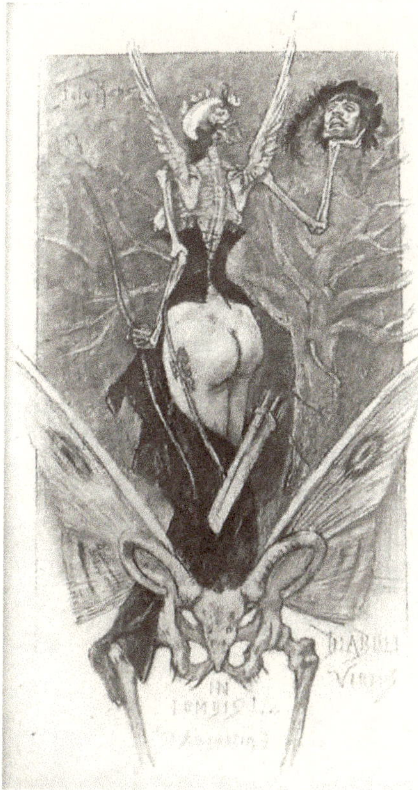

Diabolus virtus by Félicien Rops.

the side, the globe of a powerful breast blooms on the disinterred front of her hollowed-out carcass.

Underneath, to complete the symbolic image, the pelvis-like bone structure of rings and loops stripped of flesh, and the skeleton of the renal regions, to which the artist has added long wings, evoke the idea of a huge moth or the muzzle of an unknown beast, of a volatile and feline animal whose head is topped by two looping ears outlined by the fleshless bones of the hips.

This Death, on which only the significant parts are alive, those places favourable to the follies of man, we find scattered here and there throughout Rops' work; in some prints, where he associates her, as always, with Lust, he has tiny snub-nosed Cupids flying around and playing with each other, or else he reproduces her in her actual form and shows her as a skeleton coming out of a coffin alive, as in the etching combined with aquatint that figures as the frontispiece of *The Supreme Vice*.[34] There, she is more hideous still. Dressed in frills, lifting the train of her gown with her boney, gloved hand, she fans herself and

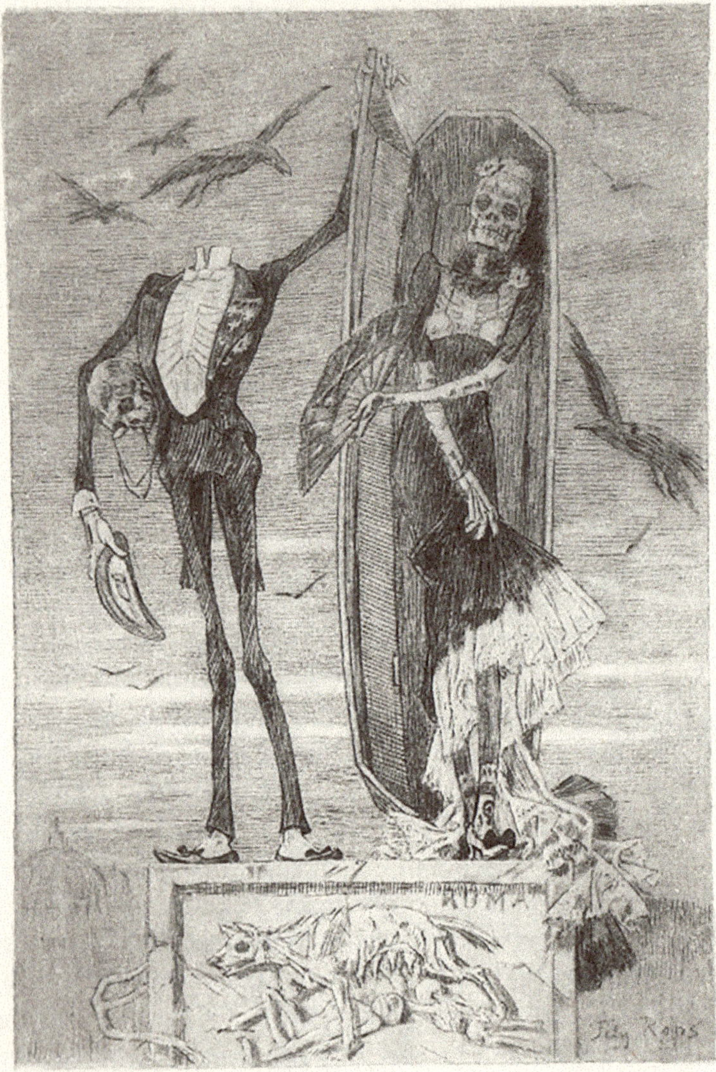

Frontispiece for Joséphin Péladan's *The Supreme Vice* (1884) by Félicien Rops.

simpers hideously next to a decapitated man, who holds his death's head under his arm and struts about in his ballroom suit adorned with medals.

Like the painters of the Middle Ages who were obsessed by the figure of Death, Rops is drawn to it and, fascinated, he circles round her; his work pampers her, diverts her, adorns her, in that Baudelairian way of thinking that seems to be the ultimate expression of Catholic art among the moderns.

So Rops was really the only person who could illustrate *The She-Devils*, which a fundamentally Christian artist like Barbey d'Aurévllly was, likewise, uniquely capable of writing.

Some of these illustrations are authentic works of synthetic drawing and symbolic form. I'm not speaking here, of course, of those etchings so pitifully reduced in size for the purposes of printing the Lemerre edition, but of the originals, using the soft varnish method, in which the artist, by liberating himself from the minuscule pocketbook format, was able to work on proper sized prints.

To mention just the most interesting, here are two postscripts that deal with the same theme: 'Prostitution and madness dominate the world.'

In one, a woman with goat's feet, standing on one of the earth's poles, is outlined against a night sky strewn with stars. Naked to the thighs, she tilts her ugly and yet pretty face, smiles with the provocative grace of a drunken tomboy, rolls her troublemaker eyes, opens a mouth that screams common obscenities and her contempt of the heavens, while, with a tipsy gesture, she adjusts her chignon with her palm. She reeks of the sidewalk and the prison, evokes the image of the lowest whore who gets into knife fights down dark alleyways. Behind her, a cloven-footed Jester, with the features of an old woman, slips an arm round the other's and exposes her belly, and from beneath a pointy cap and bells, gazes out with the paternal, money-grubbing smile of the brothel madame and the streetwalker.

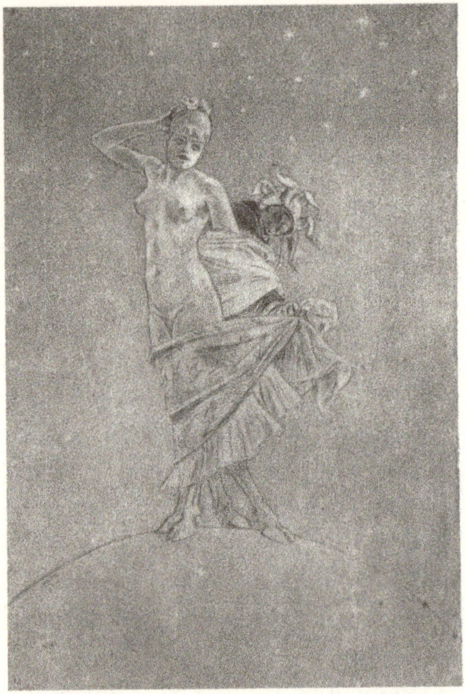

Prostitution and Folly Dominate the World by Félicien Rops.

In the other,[35] on the same pole, but against a brighter sky, a woman is also standing; but it is no longer the head of the blonde slut just described; this time it's a tall, strong brunette who lifts up her flowing hair, laughs insolently with her wide mouth, and pulls taut the chemise that covers her. She is the famed beautiful whore of the brothel; from one of the more central working-class districts, her flesh is healthier, her instincts are less venal and less treacherous. Behind her, likewise, a Jester twists her head and smiles, maternal and devious, planted firmly on her goat's feet.

This brunette isn't trying to seduce God, like the blonde who accosts you in broad daylight, this one at least smiles silently, she's not clamouring for celestial clients, isn't hurling insults at the stars.

This next print, the theme of which is less general, illustrates d'Aurevilly's wild short story, 'Pleasure in Crime'. On a pedestal, on which the pale face of Medusa rests with its mane of serpents, a murderous couple embrace each other, while the disinterred body of their dead victim, still in her shroud, crawls on her

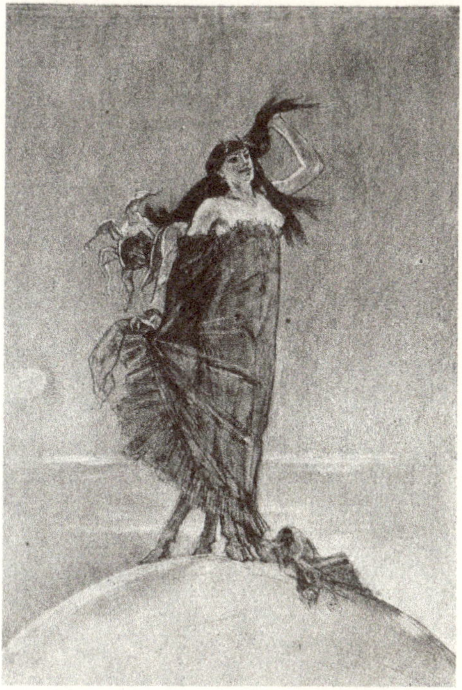

Woman and Folly Dominate the World by Félicien Rops.

knees and screams imprecations, begging the Gorgon, who smiles with impassive lips and white eyes, to avenge her.

One could also note the etching for 'Beneath the Cards in a Game of Whist',[36] with its slim, willowy figure of a woman, standing on a foetus, her eyes staring fixedly out from a head with bony temples, with round, upturned eyes, a head the mouth of which is invisible, barred by ten fingers, held in place by a gag, that imitate the teeth of a corpse, the frightful rictus of the dead.

But the *Sphinx*, which serves as the frontispiece to the book and which is one of the most literate of Rops' pieces, fits especially well into the category of symbolic prints I'm concerned with here. This one is laid out as follows:

On a Sphinx elongated in a meticulous hieratic pose – breasts rigid and hard, legs straight and pointing forward, thighs bent, and head erect – a naked woman slips her arms round the beast's neck, lifting herself up to its ear and, in a whisper, begs her to finally reveal the supernatural secret of undreamed of pleasures and new sins. Unscrupulous and coaxing, she rubs her flesh against the granite monster, tries to seduce it, offers herself to it as if to a man whose money she wants to extract, she's still a whore, despite being transported to this otherworldly scene, seems magnified even, by that uneschewable nudity of a goddess or an Eve.

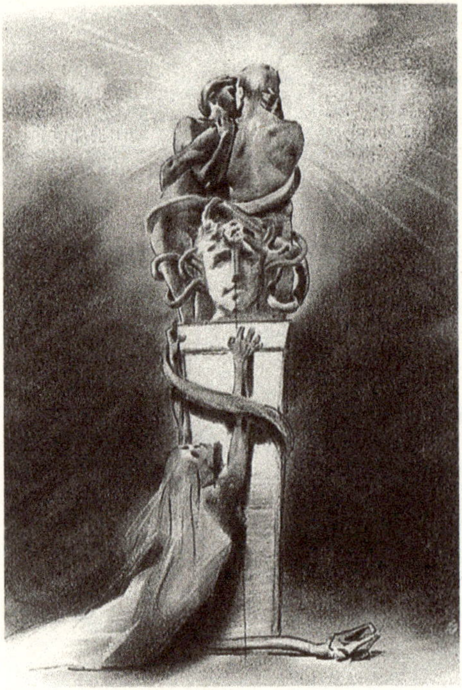

Pleasure in Crime by Félicien Rops.

As, whispering, she clasps the neck of the unmoving Sphinx, Satan, in a black suit, a monocle in his eye, sits between the two wings that rise up like two hollow crescents from the monster's back, and listens attentively to the confession of delirious hope that obsesses this soul, over which his power is not in doubt.

And yet it seems that he himself needs to probe this inscrutable well, the depths of which he has not yet discerned. This is the true tamed Satan of the present *fin-de-siècle*, a gentleman, silent, neat, patient and tenacious; he is imperfect, worn-out, old; obliged now to take stock of himself, he no longer has the colossal attractions of his maturity; he must listen from outside, not hear from within, no longer rely, perhaps, in his hunt for souls, on anything but the limited faculties of man.

One could add numerous prints to this series, because this work, engraved without a care for fashionable glory by an

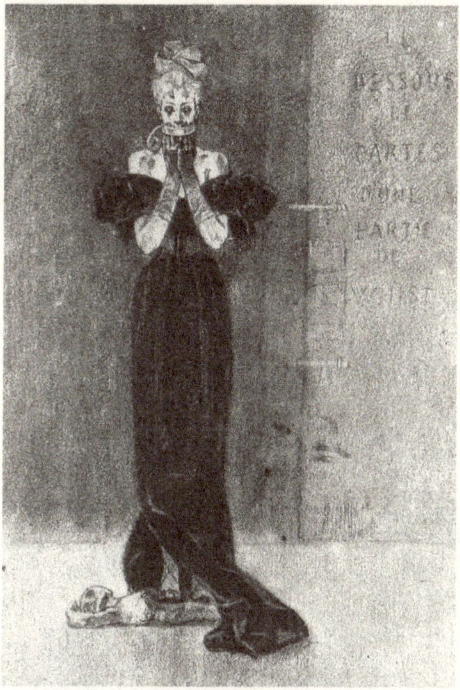

Beneath the Cards in a Game of Whist by Félicien Rops.

artist living apart from the unpredictable clamours of the crowd, is immense. A catalogue published by Ramiro lists, besides the lithographs, more than six-hundred prints, but to detail them would not give us any feelings different from those I've cited and which seem sufficient for us to imagine what the particular temperament of Rops is.

One could, in short, after a few final explanations, sum up in this way, I think, the contribution he has brought to art:

Unlike his contemporaries, who were almost all born in barns and basements and whose education was acquired in rowdy, communal schools, Rops, spared a working-class or peasant origin, and furnished with a wholly literary education, is the only one among the plebian horde of scribblers who is skilled enough to compose the essence of a frontispiece, of which he remains the unique master, the only one, above all, who is strong enough to create a work in which the passive aspect of the eternal Vice is encapsulated.

Initiated in these now neglected matters by Baudelaire, and by Barbey d'Aurévilly who had preceded him in the path of Satanism,

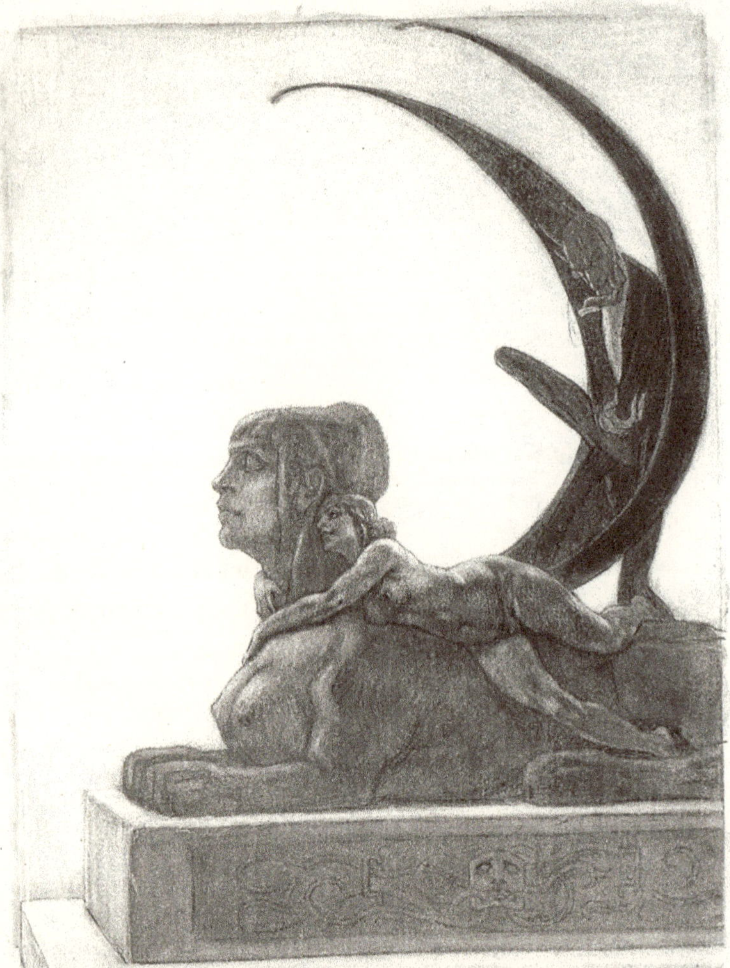

Frontispiece for Barbey d'Aurevilly's *The She-Devils* by Félicien Rops.

Rops has explored it to its limits and, in a different art, it is he who has truly observed the diabolic magnitude of carnal passion.

He has restored to Lust its mysterious omnipotence which had been so stupidly constrained in trivia, so despicably embodied by certain people; he has religiously placed it in the infernal setting where it operates, and by doing that he has not created works that are affirmative and obscene, but rather Catholic works, works that are fiery and terrifying.

He didn't limit himself, as his predecessors did, to rendering the passionate attitudes of the body, but he brought to life the aroused flesh, the suffering of febrile souls, and the pleasures of perverse spirits; he has painted demonic ecstasy as others have painted the mystical impulse. Far removed from his own century, at a time when materialist art sees nothing but hysterics consumed by their ovaries or nymphomaniacs whose brains beat in the region of their loins, he celebrated not the contemporary woman, not the Parisienne, whose affected graces and dubious adornments eluded his dexterity, but the timeless, Essential Woman, the poisonous and naked Beast, the mercenary of Darkness, the absolute servant of the Devil.

He has, in a word, celebrated that spiritualism of Lust which is Satanism, painted in imperfectible pages the supernatural of evil, the transcendence of Evil.

V

Prices – Jan Luyken – The Monster

v. Prices – Jan Luyken – The Monster

PRICES[1]

To be rich, very rich, and establish in Paris, in front of the triumphant Luxembourg hospital, a gallery of contemporary painting for the public.[2]

In short, to gather together works of art. – To buy and exhibit, every day, without charge, in well-lit rooms, Gustave Moreau's *Salomé, Helen of Troy, Galatea,* and *Hercules and the Lernean Hydra*; Manet's *Olympia* and his dead bullfighter; Degas' dancers and his female nudes; James McNeil Whistler's portrait of his mother, his Carlyle, and some of his nocturnes and harmonies; Claude Monet's seascapes from the Durand-Ruel collection; Pissarro's field of cabbages; Caillebotte's café scene and his woman at the window; the first Folies-Bergère series and certain interiors by J.-L. Forain; old Renoir's female portraits; one or two still lifes by Cézanne; Raffaëlli's landscape of Gennevilliers and the Seine in winter; Bartholomé's playground scene and his *Find the Ring*,[3] and a few choice Sisleys.

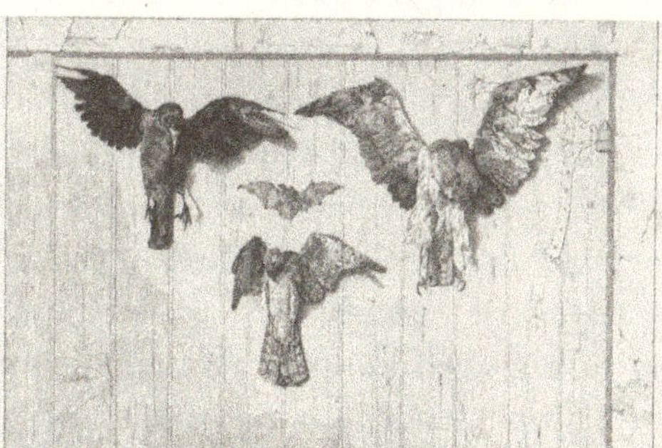

The Top of a Barn Door by Félix Bracquemond.

Then, for the print room, some charcoals by Odilon Redon; Whistler's admirable etchings; some fine lithographs by the unfortunate Rodolphe Bresdin; some old prints by Legros; Rops' *Satanics*; some posters by Chéret; and finally, Félix Bracquemond's *The Top of a Barn Door* and his superb interpretation – in the style of Gustave Moreau – of King David; and François Bonvin's interior scenes, which were exhibited in October 1887 by Georges Petit, and which reveal this plodding, pseudo-Dutch realist, this banal, tiresome painter, to be a talented aquafortist, striking, decisive, almost bizarre.

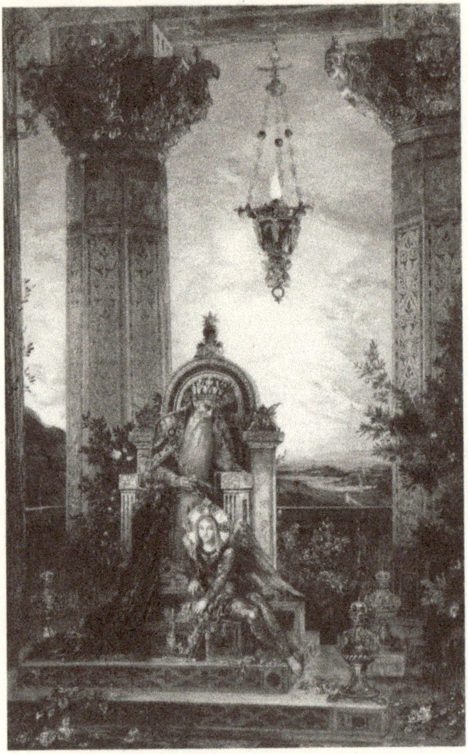

King David by Félix Bracquemond.

But where are the Rothschilds, the Camondos, Judases, or Hirsches,[4] who would even think of alleviating the permanent outrage that their scandalous fortune imposes upon us by a donation of artworks such as these? Needless to say, none of the pictures owners have even thought about it!

It's true that it's in the nature of money to bring to fruition the original bad taste of the people it feeds; so in painting, the wealthy go where their snouts lead them, to Meissonier and Jacquet,

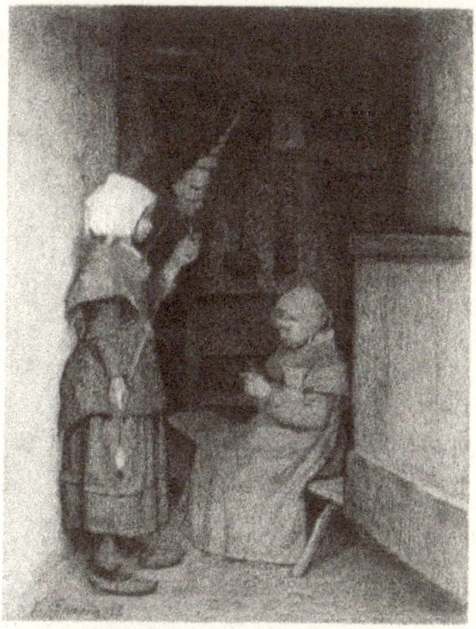

Two Girls Spinning and Knitting by François Bonvin.

to Munkácsy and Henner, to Bouguereau and all the rest!

More so than any execrable bank, the example of a grand American businessman proves it: following the death of a multi-millionaire named Alexander Turney Stewart, who had made his fortune through the sale of silks and skirts, an auction of his paintings was held.

The canvases gathered together by this grand philistine and housed by him in a marble palace in New York, were in no way inferior to the paintings collected by a certain Hon. Edwin Denison Morgan,[5] another parvenu elevated to the status of governor, whose collection – comprising works from Jehan Vibert to Jules Breton, and a pile of other oil merchants – was sold for the exorbitant sum of 4,427,500 francs!

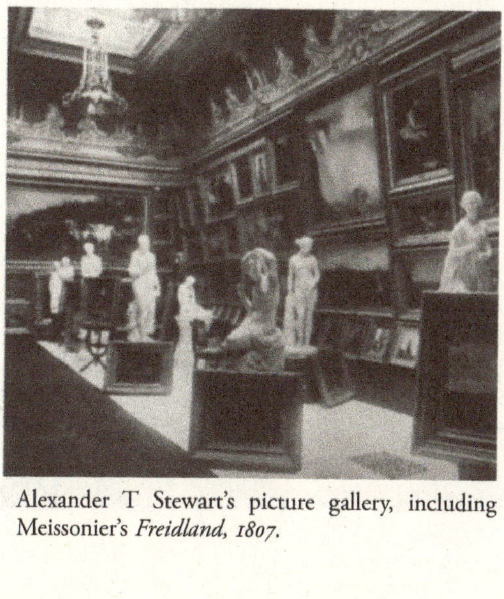

Alexander T Stewart's picture gallery, including Meissonier's *Freidland, 1807*.

Consequently, all the oil-paint potentates, all the high priests of the horse-trading world rushed to the Stewart sales, and, over the course of ten auctions, took away at the following prices:

The Return of the Harvest (William Bouguereau)	40,500 fr.
The Newborn Lamb (ditto)	25,000 fr.
Landscape and Cattle (Constantine Troyon)	55,000 fr.
The Prodigal Son (Édouard Dubufe)	15,200 fr.
A Collaboration (Jean-Léon Gérôme)	50,500 fr.
One Evening on a Terrace (Benjamin Constant)	20,000 fr.
The Rest at Camp St. Maur (Jean-Baptiste Détaille)	18,000 fr.

Three works achieved these sums:

The Horse Fair (Rosa Bonheur)	280,000 fr.
The Children's Party (Ludwig Knaus)	106,500 fr.
and lastly,	
Friedland, 1807 (Ernest Meissonier)	330,000 fr.

That last painting was acquired by the Hon. Henry Hilton,[6] who it seems to me is particularly miserly when I compare him to another American, a Philadelphian sock merchant, a certain John Wanamaker,[7] who a few weeks ago had no qualms about buying

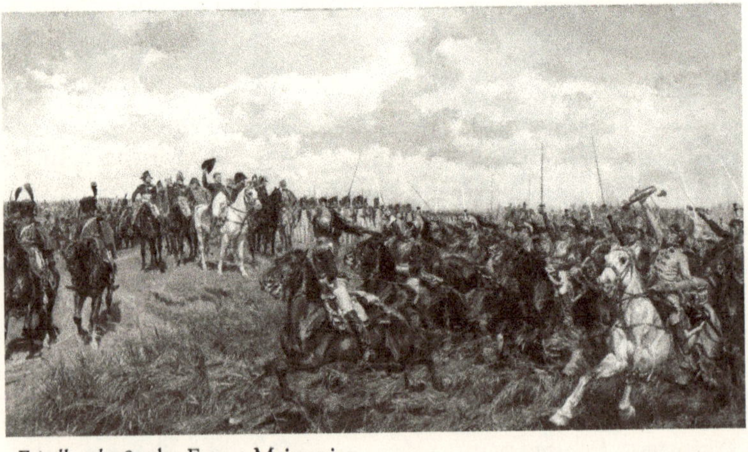

Friedland, 1807 by Ernest Meissonier.

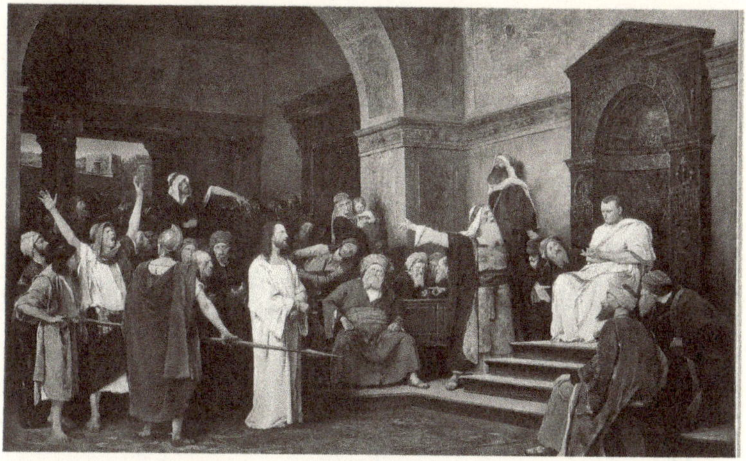

Christ in Front of Pilate by Mihály Munkácsy.

for 600,000 francs *Christ in Front of Pilate*, a paltry decorative piece from the brush of that Brazilian of piety, that foreign upstart of painting, Mihály Munkácsy!

The tortures gleefully thought up by ancient despots have their usefulness perhaps. At least in some instances they could satisfy the need for justice that is in us. Thinking of the prodigious imbecility of the dollars spent and the singular ineptitude of the paintings, I happily imagine myself in front of Jan Luyken's old engravings for *The Martyrs Mirror*. Indeed, the book contains some tortures that, in my imagination, I believe I could apply

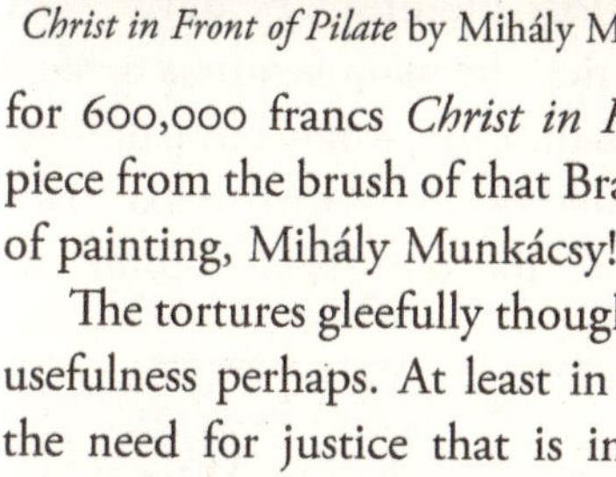

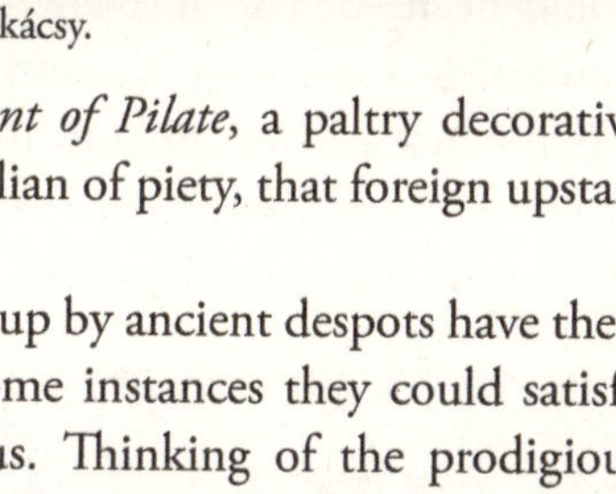

Engravings for *The Martyr's Mirror* by Jan Luyken.

quite easily to most of these purchasers.

Such as these, perhaps: tie them naked to the rim of a wheel fitted with a crank, which rolls and pushes the body as it descends and reaches the ground onto a row of very long, sharp nails; or rather sit these victims on red-hot chairs and gently place white-hot helmets on their heads; or again tie them by a single wrist to a post, after previously binding their legs, and insert into them – gradually and with some difficulty because of the writhing of their bodies which recoil and try to escape – the serrated spiral of a huge drill bit.

But how these necessary reprisals would tire us out! And how many racks, cauldrons of tar, pincers and pliers, axes and saws would be needed to torment the vast multitude of buyers and painters! It would be such as to enrich the manufacturers of steel and iron medical instruments, and as they, too, would buy paintings by Gérôme and Bouguereau, it would be an uninterrupted chain of torture that would extend, over the centuries to come, to

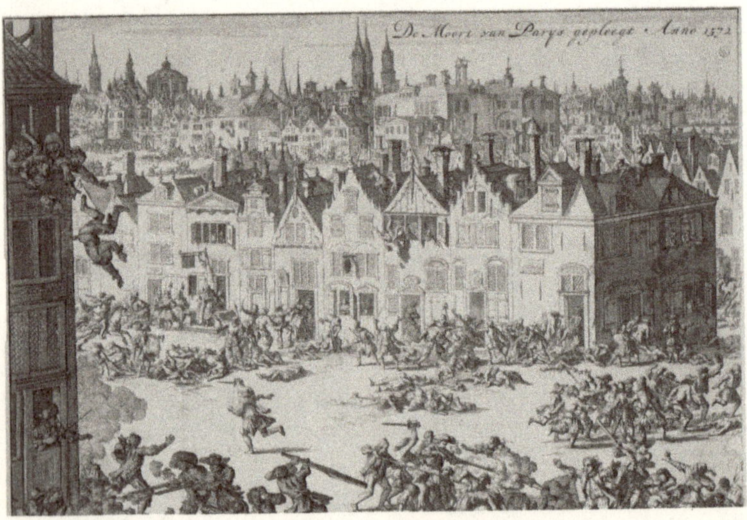

St Bartholomew's Day Massacre (detail), by Jan Luyken.

the generations spawned from their miserable commerce with women, who were themselves born to crooked, over-fed and now-forgotten merchants.

*

JAN LUYKEN
ANOTHER OF OLD LUYKEN'S PRINTS

St. Bartholomew's Day.[8] From a bird's eye view, coming in at a low angle, a strange Paris: the spirals, needles and arrows of church steeples; the quasi-modern domes like those of panoramas and circuses, the almost contemporary pediments with chimney-flues topped by crosses like hospitals and colleges, rise up over houses whose roofs shred the air with their notched crenellations, their stepped and sawtooth gables.

In the streets of this pseudo-Dutch Paris, around a large

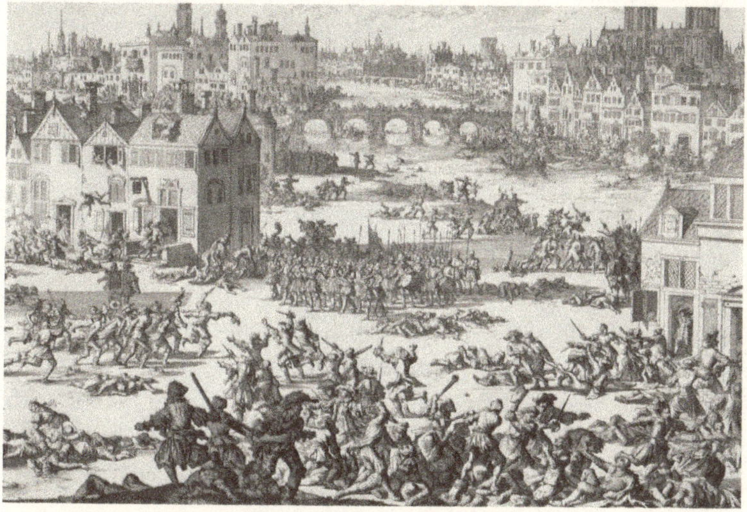

St Bartholomew's Day Massacre (detail), by Jan Luyken.

square, disemboweled, violated buildings, gaping doors, open casement windows, and women and children crushed against the walls, torn from hallways, trampled with boots, beaten senseless with hammers and sticks, stabbed by daggers; hunted men are on the roofs, clinging to chimneys in little groups, sliding down gutters, dislodged by musket shots, hurled headlong out of windows, finished off by troops of boatmen and thuggish soldiers.

A wind of panic blows, accelerated by the roar of alarm bells and the din of trumpets and drums, fleeing families are caught by the murderers; kneeling women clasp their hands together, begging, sheltering their crying children; the dying raise themselves up on one elbow and implore with speechless mouths and limp hands; others, stretched out, are still trying to defend themselves, while pikemen, waving flags and beating drums, advance towards the naked, decapitated Huguenot leader, Gaspard de Coligny, who is being dragged off at full speed by a team of maniacs who are yelling and cheering and waving their hats in the air.

A faint, but sharp whiff of the slaughter-house permeates this engraving in which the Seine, overlooked by an imaginary Notre-Dame, carries away the gestures of defiance, the screams and the blasphemies, the death throes and the twisted limbs, without turning a hair.

Such, set down with notarial precision, is the layout of this engraving. Extraordinary as a whole, because it somehow bustles with the hubbub and the seething of the crowd, this rare print, parcelled out in numerous sections, is astounding in its vivacity of movement, in its elaboration of faces whose furious passions, sometimes heroic, sometimes futile, are alarming. It is both intimate and ferocious at the same time; an honest Dutchman in its scrupulous and fair detail; a wrathful Genevan Calvinist in its unfeeling religious cruelty.

Everything that this man could have had of pity in his soul he certainly put into his work, but beneath this puritanical pity, as if repressed, well up sudden bursts of rage; an enemy by his very temperament of the ritual executions of the Holy See, he laid bare in terrible transcripts, rehashed and condensed into bitter scenes, the studious tortures that the theatrical ferocity of the Catholics inflicted on those tedious Huguenots, whose roots, so badly pulled up by the gardeners of Rome, have sprouted again in their present day offshoots: bourgeois hypocrites and dreary, idiotic pastors.

Obsessed, like Agrippa of Aubigné,[9] by horrific biblical subjects, Luyken illustrated a history of the Jews,[10] and depicted in great detail the blood-filled episodes in the life of this ineradicable people.

Many of these prints are admirable. Among them, a series of the plagues of Egypt in which, beneath tongues of flame that fall from an insane sky, the dying writhe, their forms barely human: heads eaten by gaping wounds, arms bandaged, limbs elephantine and spongy, legs cratered with blisters, bloated with pimples; or other prints in which, beneath skies zigzagged by lightning,

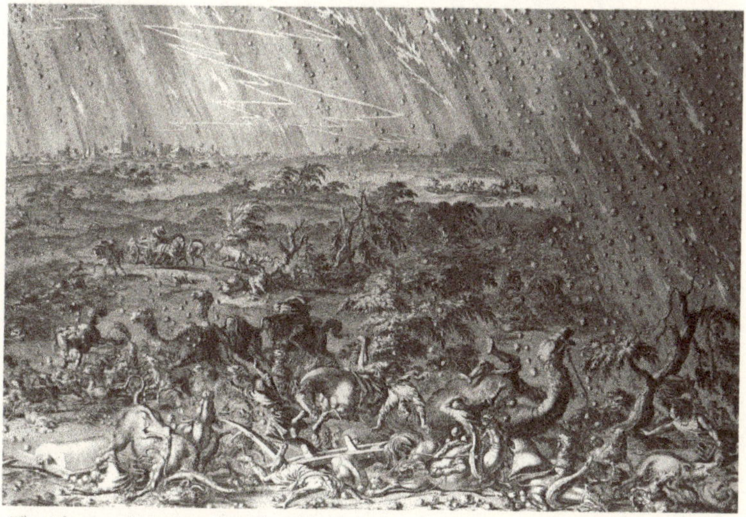

The Plague of Hail and Fire by Jan Luyken.

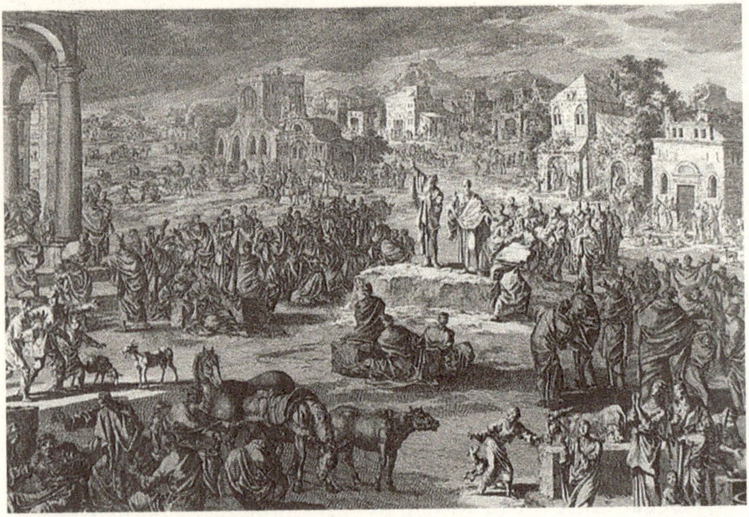

The Plague of Darkness by Jan Luyken.

streaked with hail, blinded horses rear up and panic-stricken herds stampede; finally, others such as *The Plague of Darkness*, in which roaming multitudes stumble around on that black day, screaming in fear, and *The Tower of Babel*, where, under the ominous prodigy of the shuddering edifice, bustling crowds go about their business.

Luyken was a master whose personality remains unassailable. Indeed, no one has been able to render better than him the impassioned swarming of the masses, or more clearly express the talking and shouting of the beings who spring forth, wholly living, from his black drawings. There isn't a single one of his prints that isn't marked by his very special stamp, even when he is depicting bourgeois interiors, as in *The Tutelary Household*, his book of 'instructions on furnishings, with divine aphorisms and edifying verses',[11] or when he amuses himself in drawing battles – which have since been updated by Gustave Doré in his illustrations for Balzac's *Drole Stories* – battles in which a knight slashes Sarrazin on his horse with the back of his sword, in the midst of an explosion of blood that spurts out in a jet from the cleaved body, cut into two slices that are still connected together here and there by a few nerves, like loose shoe laces.

Moreover, he knew how to find just the right nuance, to revitalise, to make precise and familiar poses his own, arms raised to the sky in a moment of distress, groaning heads buried in hands, the lurch and gallop of bodies struggling to run; he knew how to capture that type of young man, elegant and tall, naturally and decoratively dressed, as well as, in *The Resurrection of Lazarus,* typical old Israelites discussing, with mannerisms now mimicked by those from the Midi, the miracle's veracity and the opportunity to be gained from it.

Scattered in books and confined in the old bookshops of Holland, his work, comprising more than 4,500 engravings and one portrait in oil – the only one we know of at least, that of his mother, which belongs to Baron Van Six Hillegom – is almost unknown in France. Jan Luyken, or Johannès Luycken, was born on 16 April 1649, in Amsterdam, to Gaspard Luyken, writer, and Hester Coores, his wife, without profession. He was the pupil of

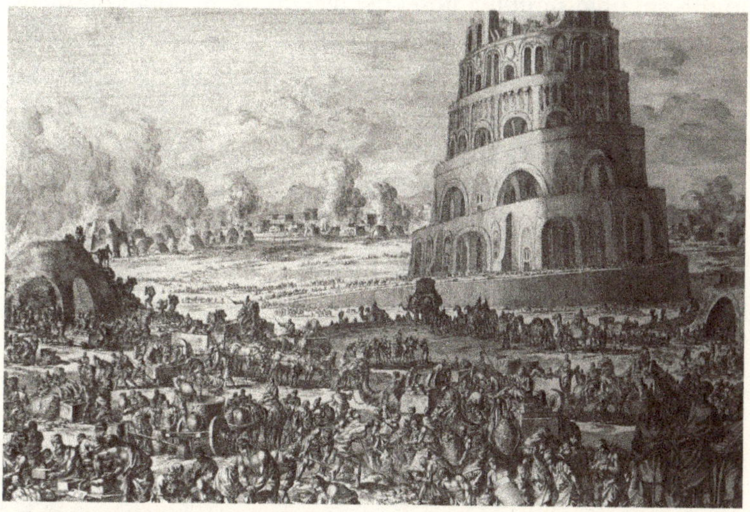

The Tower of Babel by Jan Luyken.

Martinus Zapnolen, and at the age of nineteen married Maria de Oude, had five children, all of whom died young, except one son, Gaspard, whose signature is also on the St. Bartholomew engraving and a few other prints, and who died in 1708, before his father, therefore, who died in Amsterdam on 5 April 1712.

And lastly, as the frontispiece to one of his books entitled *Man's Beginning, Middle and End*,[12] a book which contains psalms on one page and his poems in paraphrase on the other, Jan Luyken engraved his portrait.

It would be difficult, I think, to be uglier. Imagine, above a wide mouth into which the shovel of a locomotive tender would easily fit, a long hooked nose, with dips and humps, ending in open nostrils as big as vats and flaring like the nose of a hunting dog; on each side of this, small sunken eyes, then his hair, dry, parted down the middle and falling flat over his temples. At first sight, he seems mournful and a bit stupid; then, if one examines more closely, the incoherence of his features begins to come together. One discovers in this square, almost brutal forehead, in this sniffing, snuffling nose, the determination of an obstinate and tenacious faculty of observation; in those sunken eyes, lit by dull gleams, in this sickly, bilious head, in his distracted air – contradicted, however, by the certainty of the jaw – one senses a goodness without enthusiasm or tenderness, the narrow exaltation of an apostle, the fanaticism of a mad mystic, an artistic fury haunted by the bloody visions of an obsession. And this is consistent with the episodes of his life I've already recounted in *Against Nature.* During his youth, he was a poet and completed some libertine poems which had great success; then grace came, but the savage and terrible grace of the Protestant; gripped by remorse, he bought all the copies of his books he could find to burn them; but as fast as he would destroy a copy, another would appear, printed afresh by his publisher. He ended up as a complete visionary, gave his possessions to the poor, and, along

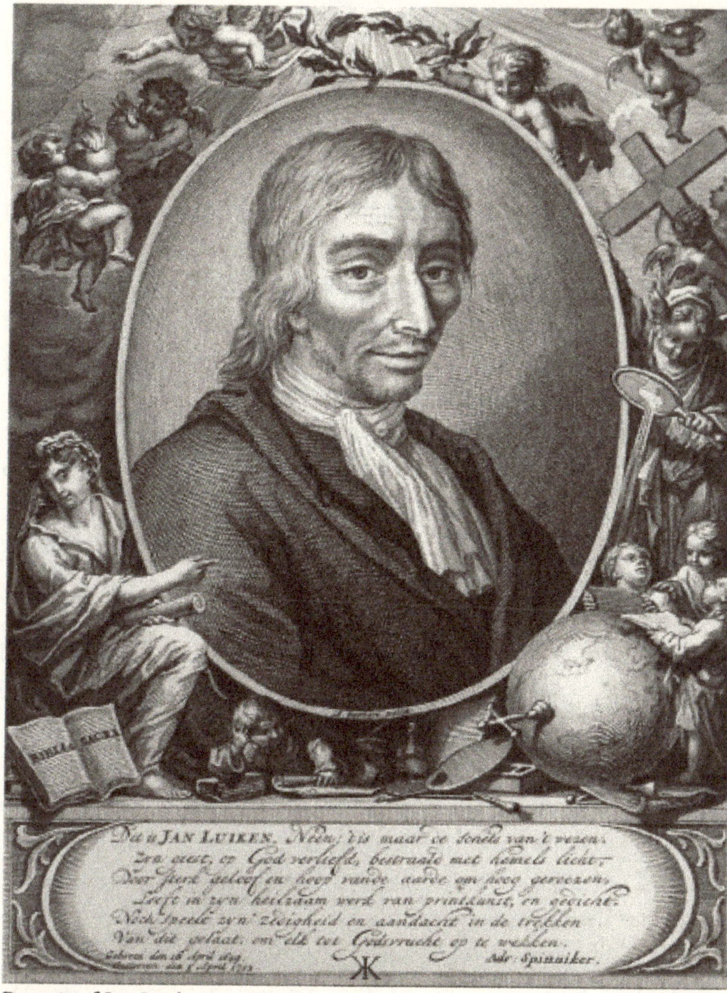

Portrait of Jan Luyken.

with a servant girl he had converted to his cause, he embarked on a boat, refusing food, preaching the good word, singing psalms, and wildly proclaiming his prophecies and threats as he passed through astonished cities.

*

THE MONSTER

The monster in art doesn't really exist, or rather no longer exists for us at the present time. The imagination, which in every period delighted in creating beauty from terror, has changed but little and only arrived at images of monsters by developing and distorting the great carnivors, or by taking some parts from the human body and combining them with others borrowed from the bodies of fearsome beasts.

Because of their completely fictional nature and the incoherence of their forcibly juxtaposed limbs, these monsters no longer seem able today to inspire in us the sensations intended by their artists, who wanted to symbolise evil deities and crimes, and to arouse horror.

Antiquity imagines them as huge but relatively simple in form. In Assyria, they are man-headed bulls with regal headgear and eagle's wings, or flying dragons, or mammals with the jaws of wild beasts. Berossus[13] has conserved a description of these monsters which, according to Chaldean tradition, populated the earth: they were men with the legs and horns of a goat, hermaphrodites with horses' hooves, dogs with fourfold bodies and the tails of fish, centaurs, mares with mole-like snouts, and beasts that were a cross between a sturgeon and a reptile.

In Egypt, canopic jars were topped with the heads of hawks, jackals and humans; amulets that protected pregnant women took the form of a hippopotamus with the belly and breasts of a woman; numerous statuettes displayed the heads of leopards and lionesses grafted onto human bodies. In India, it was gigantic creatures with a thousand heads, armed with the tusks of a wild boar and bristling with innumerable limbs. In Cambodia, Khmer art also conceived of improbable beasts: the *krout*, a bird that turns into a gryphon, the *garudu*, whose male torso is topped by the head of an eagle, and the *yali*, like a cross between a dragon, an ocelot and a cheetah.[14]

In ancient Greece, most of the monsters were born from the coupling of Echidna, half-woman and half-snake, with Typhon,[15] the giant, whose body was intertwined with vipers lurking in clumps of feathers, and whose mouth breathed and spat darts of flame. They gave birth to a celebrated lineage: Orthrus the two-headed dog, the hundred-headed Hesperian Dragon, the hundred-mouthed Python, the Hydra of Lerna, the Chimera, the Gorgon, and the Sphinx, whose combination of bestial and human elements is the most complicated of them all.

In short, if we exclude the terrestrial giants, the Titans and Hecatoncheires – that's to say normal bodies deformed or enlarged and stretching up to the heavens – it is to the glorified snake, to the dragon, that Greek mythology resorts when creating its monsters.

In the Middle Ages, the dragon persists, barely altered from ancient times, surging up in cathedral sculptures and in the lives of saints. It has the appearance of a winged serpent, flexing its spine spiked with barbs, and brandishing in a crocodile's jaw the forked tongue of the python; it branches off into derivative types, such as the Tarasque,[16] but in spite of everything it retains its reptilian, snake-like form. Then, in opposition to the dragon, which in those naive times personified the supreme ferocity of the monster, the demonic and lustful side expressed itself through the pig, the toad or the goat, combined with the haunches of a man. All these hideous beasts were put to good use by the admirable crafters of images who followed the humble brotherhood of 'God's craftsmen'[17] and, under the orders of a master builder, sculpted those prodigious cathedrals whose towers were erected to the singing of psalms.

The circle of monsters that surrounds Notre-Dame in Paris proves it. These are extravagant birds perched on the Saxon flora of stone balconies. The Stymphalian birds[18] of Greek mythology, which borrowed the tough pliability of steel and iron for their feather arrows, their pincer beaks, and their nail-like talons, live again in these sculptures, albeit less threatening and less menacing. Enlivened by the addition of old women's shawls and monks' hoods, they stretch out gullets plated with scales beneath the pincers of their beaks and, without hostility, flutter their tired, retracted wings. Then they deviate from the ancestral type, transforming into gigantic parrots crossed with vultures and roosters, into fabulous flying birds resting on the paws of lions and leopards, bristling with feathers carved into short lamellae like the overlapping plate armour of ancient Gauls or the scales of a fish that one cleans.

These birds alternate with a whole menagerie of animals whose forms have remained unchanged, such as bulls, elephants, pelicans and eagles, next to groups of demons and monsters: hunting dogs with two heads, the teats of a wet-nurse, and the paws of a cat; rams with wrestlers' arms ending in hooked claws like boat hooks; buffalos with hairless breasts on which dangle the dugs of old women; gryphons with sleepy, treacherous eyes, and walrus teeth;

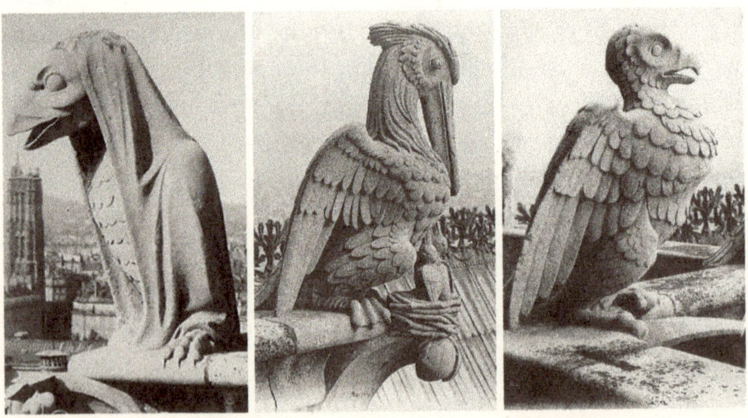

Gargoyles, Notre-Dame, Paris.

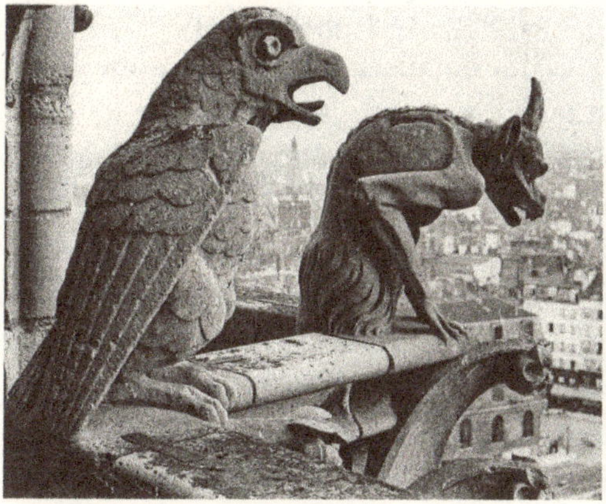

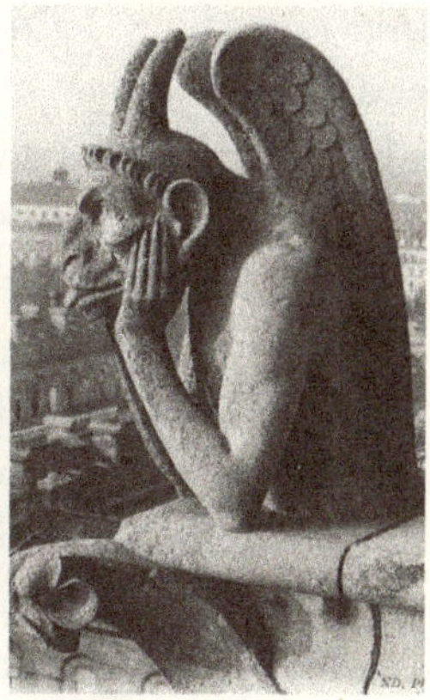

Gargoyles, Notre-Dame, Paris.

wild beasts with the bellies and arms of a man; goats with hairy torsos topped by camel-like faces, elk horns, debauched eyes, and cloven feet like those of a stork or a nanny goat.

Unfortunately, while the signification of these sculptures as individual elements remains relatively clear, the meaning of the sentence they compose in this extraordinary text written around Notre-Dame is forever lost.

Christian symbolism has, indeed, retained an understanding of the words conjured up by these stone animals. It teaches, in addition to the well-known ideas represented by the lion, the ox, and the eagle – the evangelical beasts whose heads serve to make up the Tetramorph – that the cock symbolises savage boldness and vigilance, and that the vulture, once considered by the Egyptians to be the emblem of motherhood, signifies in the Bible the cruel rapacity of the Devil himself. It affirms that the pelican is none other than the Saviour, who feeds his young with his blood, and that in the thirteenth century it was also an image of David meditating on the Passion of Christ; it also attributes to the hare the prudence of the soul fearful of temptation; to the elephant, a symbol of the grievous sinner, the enormous pride that tramples over everything. Lastly, it adjudges that the cat allegorises pillage and cunning, that the lizard simulates idolatry, that the snail, whose body enters and leaves the tomb represented by its shell, designates the long-awaited Resurrection of the dead. It adds that the frog stands for avarice, lust, and the Devil, and that the fish, thanks to the mystical monogram of its Greek name, represents our Lord Jesus himself. It equivocates, however, with other beasts, such as the eagle, which actually accompanies John the apostle but which figures in the Holy Scriptures sometimes as Christ and sometimes as a foul beast; or such as the bull, which on the one hand is used to embody the fury of rape, and on the other merges with the ox, becomes a beast of burden and sacrifice, and ends up lending its name, like the ram, to God.

However, some of the animals lose the attributes that are usually associated them, assembled together as they are and combined into one amid the fantastical statues that surround the towers of Notre-Dame; by combining the symbols that each of them represents and by classifying the whole, one could obviously rediscover the intended meaning of some of these monsters, but we would still be no less inapt at connecting the chain of these significations and deciphering their inexplicable text.

Notre-Dame is now a hieroglyph in which Christian iconographers spell out sad, isolated words, and in which alchemists vainly seek the occult formula of the philosopher's stone from an image carved over a door.

In any event, one can be certain that it is on this cathedral that one of the most wonderful theories about demons and monsters has been erected.

For five hundred years they've been overlooking the enormous city that ignores them, tirelessly contemplating the unwavering assizes of human stupidity. They've followed down the ages the exploits of a sinful mankind obsessed by carnal concerns and the lure of profit; they've sniffed the exhalations of inexpungible vices, watched over the high tide of the old sin, recorded the low-water mark of the eternal obscenities that the hypocritical dung-heap of this overindulgent time cherishes so much.

Sentinels positioned at forgotten posts, on thresholds lost in the airy realm of the winds, they carry out their unknown orders in a dead language. They sneer, screech and growl, feeling no pity for the frightful distresses which, nonetheless, clamour beneath their feet, in the suffering beds of neighbouring hospitals. They embody evil forces on the lookout for souls; they give the lie to the merciful hope of the main sculptures carved further down the portal, they contradict the Virgin and Saint John, whose statues beg the Lord to finally redeem this wretched people who have been deliriously prattling on for the last five centuries!

But this terrible beauty that the nameless carvers of Notre-Dame wished to convey, was lost even on the Middle Ages, which often delights in the facetiousness of its gargoyles; subsequently, the artistic imagination gave up on arousing fear, and veered completely into joy and it was then that farce was born. The temptations of St. Anthony follow one after another, with comical animals mixed up with funny-looking Satans.

In Stefan Lochner's *The Last Judgment* in Cologne Museum, devils push sinners towards a burning fortress simulating the burning region of the old hell. These devils have the bodies of hairy men, and wolves' heads topped by ears like the uncut ears of a bulldog. These heads are, moreover, duplicated on each of their knees; a third, placed at the base of their belly,

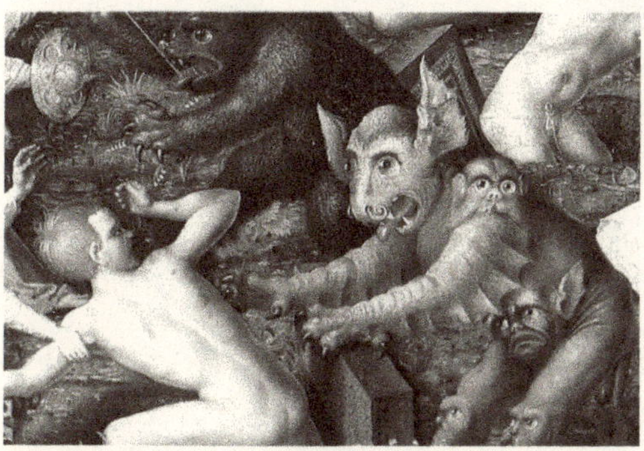

The Last Judgement (detail) by Stephan Lochner.

covers the genitals, symbolising, along with the other two heads, the opposite principle of the Holy Trinity which, being the quintessence of Good, sees the present, the past, and the future at the same time; but these demons are not very terrifying; they are only on the distant fringes of terror; in short, they've turned into a masquerade, been transformed into comic-opera characters.

For his part, Martin Schongauer invents elongated beasts made up of living bones, animals that are half-tiger, half-fish, or bat-winged monkeys whose snouts end with the enlarged proboscis of a fly. Hieronymus Bosch and the Breughels combine vegetables and kitchen utensils with the human body, imagine beings whose skulls are salt cellars or funnels, and who walk on feet in the form of bellows or frying pans. In Breughel's paintings

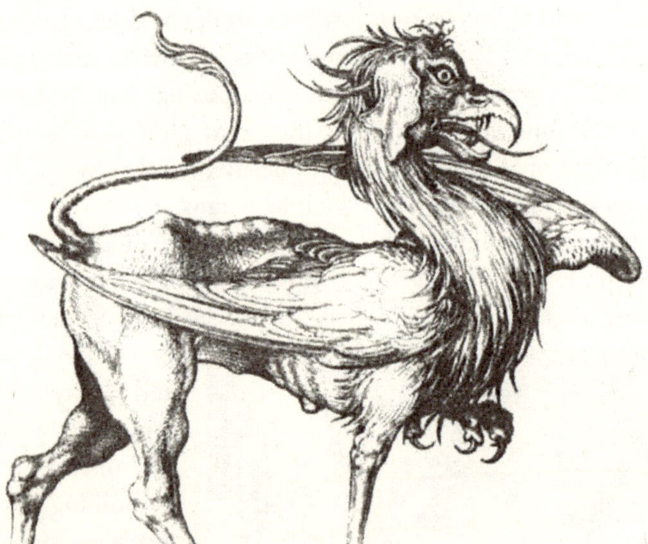

A Griffin by Martin Schongauer.

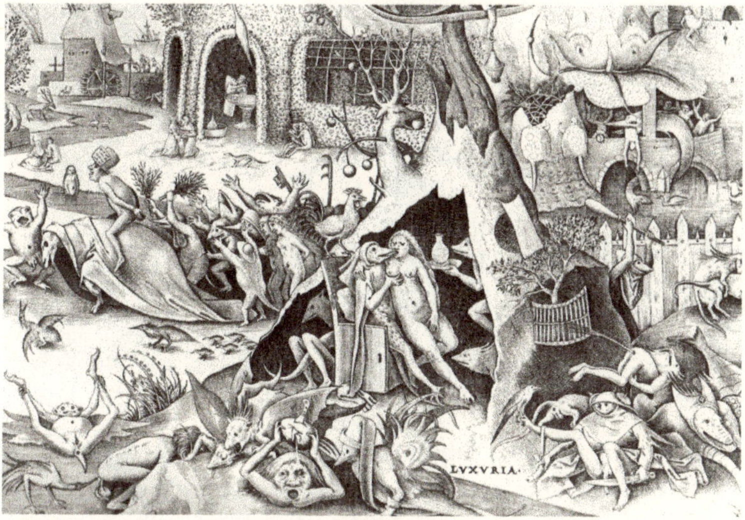

'Lechery' from *Seven Deadly Sins* (1558) by Pieter Breughel the Elder.

of hell, at Brussels, swooning frogs unlace their bellies to release eggs; impossible mammals thrust out pike-like jaws, and dance jigs on tibias stuck into watermelons; in his engravings of the *Seven Deadly Sins* this furious fantasy is accentuated still further: wild boars run on turnip legs and wiggle tails woven from roots and stalks; human faces without bodies brandish lobster claws that serve as arms; birds whose beaks open like mussel shells and whose hindquarters are the tail of a conger eel hop around on two hands, head down, running like wheelbarrows; it's a gathering of hybrid beings, of vegetables and men, a melange of man-made objects and amputees. With the intrusion of household utensils and plants into the structure of their monsters, terror comes to an end; the notion of terrible beauty dies with these burlesquely constructed, overly fictitious creatures.

For his part, Jacques Callot goes back to the old dragon and the old devils, but he conveys neither emotion nor laughter; his invention is banal and the force of his engravings is nil.

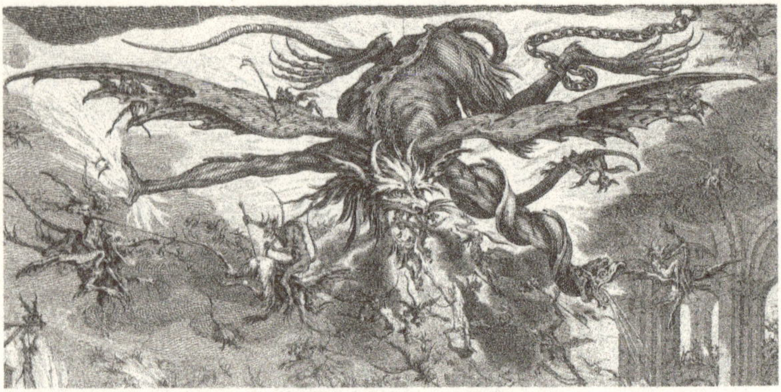

Temptation of St. Antoine (detail) by Jacques Callot.

In the modern era, not a single attempt. At most, from this point of view, one could cite Goya, that caustic and oblique artist, independent and intoxicating. But his *Caprices* turn into lampoons and when he tackles painful subjects, such as the woman trying to tear out the teeth of a hanged man, he simply ends up being macabre. On the other hand, in his *Proverbs* he has often portrayed witches and demons, but his human bodies are given donkeys' ears and goats' feet, so they don't bring any original note to the interrupted monster tradition. Only one of his etchings, in a corner of which rises a being whose jaw is split like a snout and whose forehead sports an eye as big as a headlamp, could now evoke promising reveries.

As for Ingres, he dreamed up a fine nag with wings of tin when he was painting his *Ruggiero Rescuing Angelica*; but since then, Japanese artists are the only ones who have really tried to procreate monsters. Certain figures by Hokusai, especially those of women, who resemble fairies suspended in the mist with their hair falling like a weeping willow over small, pale faces, have a ghostly aspect and succeed in conjuring up an apparition of spectres, but strictly speaking they don't constitute monsters as such, and as regards the Japanese chimera, made in multicoloured ceramic, with their bared teeth, their eyes popping out like those of slugs at the end of stalks, their tails like pagoda roofs, their bodies both carbuncled and smooth at the same time, they have a decorative appearance, an almost heraldic bearing, they can't be taken seriously nor do they arouse any different reflections than the tapestries that set them off, or the pedestals that support them.

So however well-trodden it might seem to have been, the path of the monster is still relatively new. And nature, more ingenious in this instance than man, has moreover created real monsters, not in the world of 'big livestock', but in that of the 'infinitely small', in the world of microorganisms, the infusoria and larvae whose supreme horror is revealed by the microscope.

Indeed, it seems that nothing can equal the anguish and the terror spread by the proliferation of these atrocious species. The idea of the monster was perhaps conceived in man from visions born of nightmare-filled nights, but even these could not have invented more terrible forms.

What artist, even in the fitful hallucinations of a fever, could have dreamed up those living damp spirals that swarm, like filiarsis,[19] in our urine and in our veins; what painter could have created, in his most troubled hours, the fluke worm, that parasitical myrtle leaf that curls, flows, and reshapes itself, teasing its way into the lacerated livers of old sheep; what poet, in search of monsters, could have discovered the *Dracunculus*, 'the little dragon of Medina', which, along the Ganges river, lives in the cellular tissue of

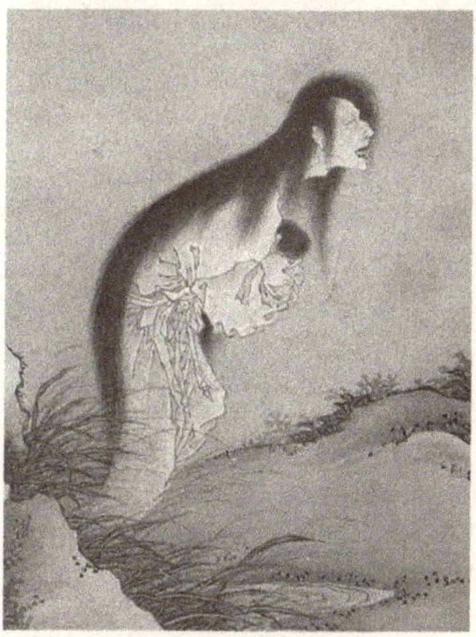

Sleeping Beauty by Hokusai.

feet, and coils itself up in the pus of the abscesses it forms; and finally, what man could imagine that mass of matter that wriggles its domed head, armed with hooks and claws, illuminated by facetted or domed eyes, that sinister and voracious mass of annular wire, of tubular thread – the pinworms, nematodes and maggots that worm their way in and set up camp in the ailing passages of the intestine?

So there is a new starting point, a new way out as it were; and it seems to have been discovered by the only painter now enamoured with the fantastic, by Odilon Redon. Indeed, to fabricate his monsters he was tempted to borrow from the undulating, fluid world, from the realm of the imperceptible, the prodigious terror of their seething swarms, enlarged via projection and therefore more terrifying than the exaggerated wild beasts of the old masters.

This is how, in a recent collection of prints, he sought to translate this sentence from Flaubert's *Temptation of St. Anthony*, 'And all manner of frightful creatures arise':

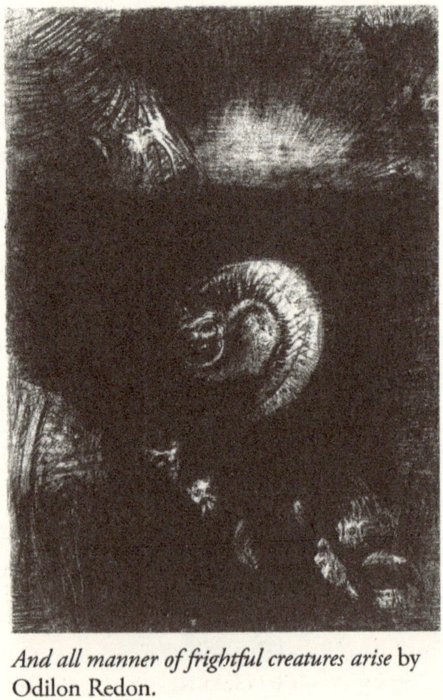

And all manner of frightful creatures arise by Odilon Redon.

In a firmament of everlasting and profound blackness, liquid, phosphorescent beings, vesicles and bacilli, corpuscles ringed by cilia, seedpods lined with eyelashes, hairy, aqueous glands, fly without wings and become entangled in ribbons of roundworms and tapeworms; it seems that all the fauna of nematodes, all the tribes of parasites swarm in the night of this print, in which the human face suddenly looms up, not fully formed, brandished at the end of these living spirals or sunk like a nucleus in the animated jelly of protoplasm.

In effect, Redon had to resort to the old concepts, to marry a horror of the human face with the writhing hideousness of caterpillars, in order to create a new monster.

A wrangler of imaginary infusoria and larvae, he had to interpret certain more precise phrases of the dance of lust and death in the *Temptation*, such as this one for example: 'It's a skull wreathed with roses; it tops a woman's torso of pearly whiteness, and beneath it is a starry shroud like a tail. And the whole body ripples as if it were a gigantic worm rearing up.'

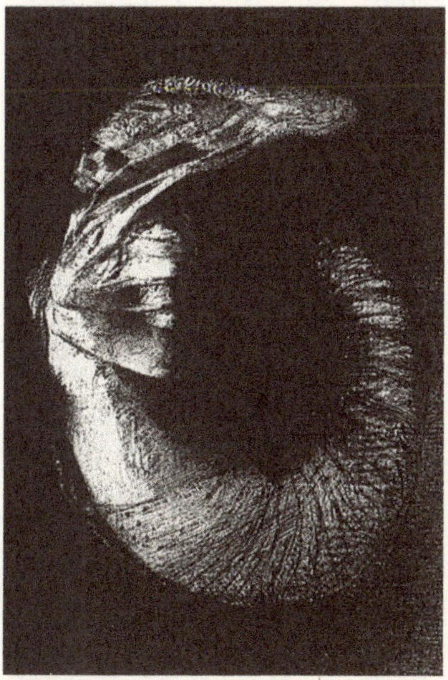

It's a skull wreathed with roses by Odilon Redon.

The lithograph that this inspired in Redon is one of the most formidable this artist has created.

Against an impenetrable dull blackness, as velvety as a black bat, the monster is illuminated in white, stamping the night with the form of a large, rearing 'C'.

The skull, with its wide grimace and big eye sockets like pots of blackness, tilts back over a bust swaddled like a mummy, hands crossed over a throat of hard resin. From this head capped with a long, embroidered wimple, emanates a kind of ice-cold grace, while the monster's diaphanous hindquarters stiffen, lined with oscillating bands standing out beneath its cold skin.

Here and there, stray features, pallid cocoons scattered in the shadows, tremble amidst this frightful image of Lust, which, as the poet intended, blends into an image of Death itself.

In a second album of prints, also dedicated to the glory of Flaubert, as well as in another collection entitled *Origins*, the artist has again produced his monsters using similar combinations.

In one, he has strewn the womb of the world with flying single-celled organisms, sprouting tadpoles, amorphous creatures, tiny disks in which embryonic eyelids and vague mouth-like orifices begin to take shape.

In another, under the title 'A long red chrysalis', in front of the parvis of an improbable temple, curled round a low column, is the body of a thin larva, whose woman's head is resting in the place that should be occupied by the capital at the top of the pillar.

And this face, emaciated, pale, heart-rending with its closed eyes, its painful and pensive mouth, seems to be vainly hoping, like a victim on a chopping block, for the liberating fall of an invisible axe.

In spite of its entirely modern structure, this figure leads you back

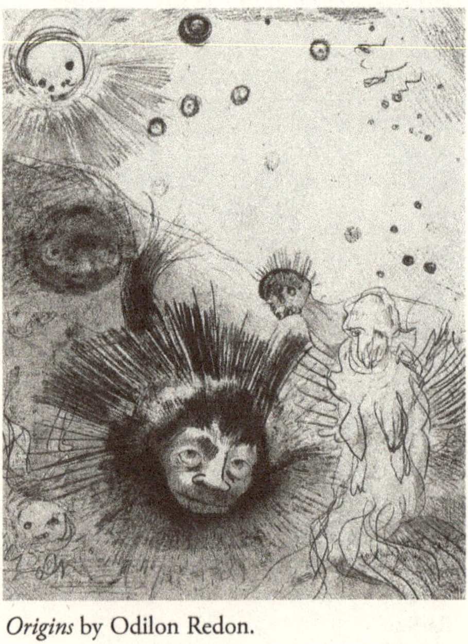

Origins by Odilon Redon.

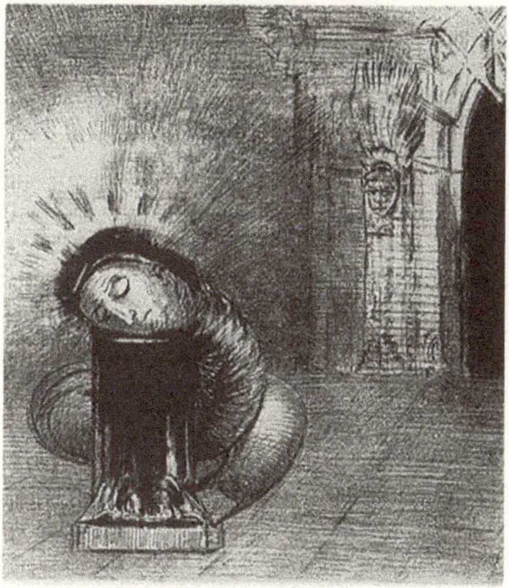

A long red chrysalis by Odilon Redon.

through the centuries, by the profound and unique expression of its features, to the doleful works of the Middle Ages; it connects Redon to the chain – interrupted since the Renaissance – of fantastical bestiaries, of clairvoyants infatuated by the monstrous.

Except that, today, the great science of religious symbolism is no more. In the domain of the dream art remains alone, at this present time when the hunger pangs of the soul seem to be sufficiently assuaged by the ingestion of theories by Moritz Wagner[20] and Charles Darwin.

VI

The Museum of Decorative Arts and Well-Cooked Architecture

VI. The Museum of Decorative Arts

Every month, while the *hors-d'oeuvre* languishes and the *plat du jour* dries out, newspapers demand that they pull down the ruins of the old Council of State[1] and in their place build that Museum of the Decorative Arts they've been deafening our ears with for years.

The platitudes are trotted out: "Those ruins are a constant reminder of the worst period in our history." "Business is not doing well and the construction industry is suffering." "Railways are eradicating distance, but surely in the capital of the world

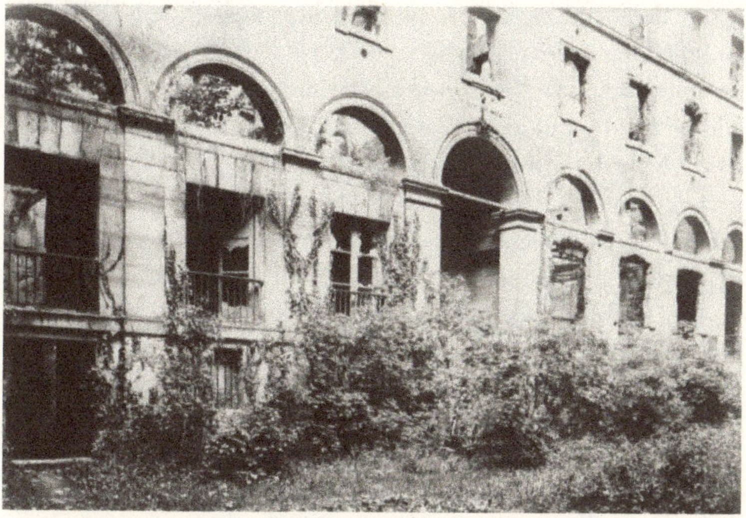

The ruins of the Council of State, destroyed by fire in 1870-71.

we could gather together some examples of French taste that are scattered around our provinces..." etc.

As art exhibitions are lacking at the moment and no important subject is pressing, I thought it might be interesting to talk about these ruins and consider their probable disappearance from two points of view: that of the museum itself, and that of its architecture, strictly speaking.

Without even batting an eye, I will admit straightaway that I don't expect anything useful from the creation of such a museum; firstly, because the objects that compose it will be mostly of dubious authenticity as government regulations will inevitably impose on us the acquisition of a heap of rubbish; and secondly, because the scandalous imitation junk put out by the trade will sully forever the truly artistic models that a benevolent chance would perhaps let slip through the pile of old fakes the purchase of which we are now threatened with.

It will be like those old pieces of wrought iron that an army of second-raters endlessly reproduce, or like those antique bronzes whose deplorable imitations fill the storerooms of the Bon Marché and the Louvre; it will be the export version of Japanese art, printed on terracotta rather than porcelain, on cotton rather than silk; it will be factory-produced Cordoba leather made out of cardboard; it will be luxury on the cheap, mass-produced junk that's an insult to the originals it simulates, just as a barrel organ insults the delicate music it ingests and regorges when its operator turns the handle of his musical enema-pump and its pipes squeeze out entire tunes.

Oh, if this project comes off we'll see some real beauties! It's bad enough that anyone nowadays can mass-produce antique furnishings like those in the Cluny Museum.[2] I know it's true we don't have to buy them, but we have to look at them because all the boulevards and streets are full of them. And these shops are nothing compared to the emporiums of fake Sèvres and fake Saxe porcelain, of which the Boulevard Saint-Germain is crammed.

VI. The Museum of Decorative Arts

All those items of stupid pottery, in washed-out turquoise blue or murky indigo blue, plastered Grecian-style in dull gold, flaunting themselves in the windows; or mounted on copper taps as handles, or emblazoned on the belly of platters, ringed by garlands of myrtle and roses in the centre of which Estelle and Némorin[3] are flirting. The horror of this crockery is incomparable, and whatever you do, even crossing to the other side of the street, you're subjected to it, because the eye, attracted by its crude colour, strays to it and lingers on it; there's a forced impulsion to it, a morbid attraction to the horrible, a weakness for the monstrous, a craving for the ugly! And I'm not even going to mention the dreadful window displays of 'artistic' Louis XIII clocks, made by wholesalers whose slow and elaborate extermination would be a pleasure to me!

Indeed, I've come to miss the hangings and decorations, the scenes of animal lairs and hunting on the walls of butchers' shops; yes, I miss the bust of Hippocrates on its red marble plinth in the old pharmacies; I miss those rivulets of spun glass swaying in pendulum clocks; I miss it all – from the stupid naivete and invariable bad taste of the customer, to the mindless smile of the merchant – because essentially these mediocrities weren't spoiling anything, and above all weren't in any way contaminating, under the pretext of art being applied to industry, the original works in museums which the State should be defending.

I will also add that this project is an insult to 'Our National Industry', which they declare is incapable of inventing any new form whatsoever, and which they formally invite, by way of the press, to come and produce pastiches of the objects they're going to show off in their display cabinets. It's true that our industry, when it does invent something, immediately exhibits the refined tastes of a savage; the most amazing example that can be cited on this subject is displayed in a clock in a Palais-Royal jeweller's shop. It represents the pendulum of the 'Forge-Master' clock and consists of a steam hammer going up and down, beneath a dial with minute and second hands in the form of scalpels. It's certainly difficult to descend further into the depths of the abject and the atrocious, but what collection of decorative art could purify the taste of a man who, without feeling sick, would construct such a thing? Again, from this point of view a Museum of Decorative Arts is useless. An industrialist either has taste or he hasn't; the pretension to inculcate an aesthetic sense in a retailer is laughable. As I said above, the only result we can expect from this artistic force-feeding that they're contemplating is to provoke in the healthy eye a grotesque sense of shame and disgust for the original model it has long been happy to look at.

Putting aside this question of the Museum of Decorative Arts, I now come to that of the ruins of the Council of State building and the Court of Auditors.

Certainly, no uglier monument was ever erected. It was clichéd, pompous, roccoco, obese, patriarchal, a *chaufferette*...[4] whatever you want to call it; this building reeked of Greek, Roman and First Empire styles, all the most nauseating and bland flavours of architecture; OK, so that smell has now evaporated somewhat; the Communards fire has broken up this tiresome pile of stones, disembowelled its ponderous belly, and scalped its old bourgeois head, whose crabby white complexion it has covered in pink and green make-up.

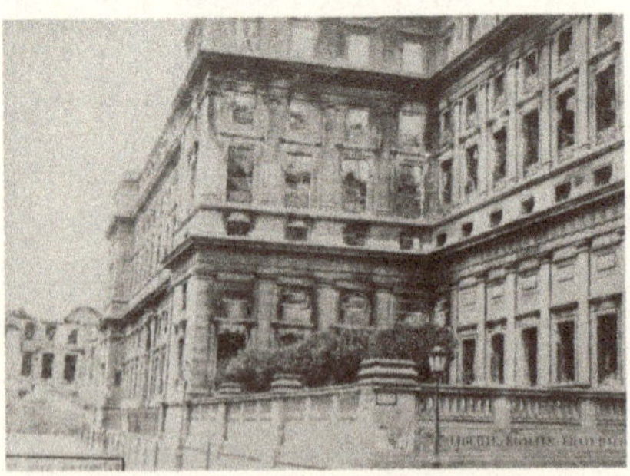

Ruins of the Court of Auditors, Paris.

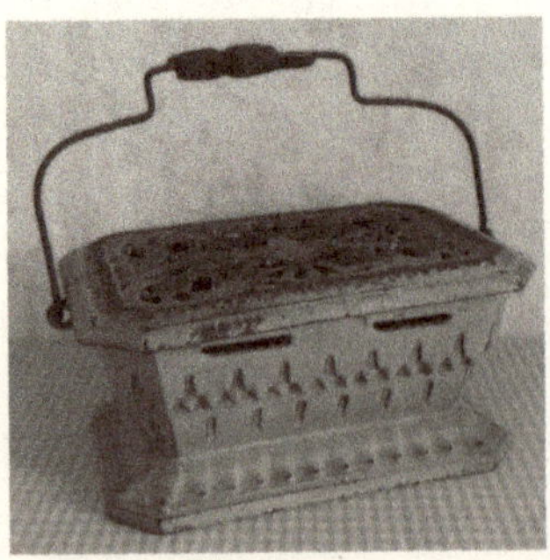

A cast-iron *chaufferette*.

VI. The Museum of Decorative Arts

The carcass of this building suddenly became noble; its columns, so old-fashioned and so heavy, are lighter, and they shoot up almost haughtily into the sky. Through the deserted frames of windows and doors, through gaps in its central structure, through the holes in the dividing walls, the sun enters, illuminating the now cicatriced wounds of the flames, caressing the sooty mass of beams, gliding over the jet-black of calcified rubble, making rusty iron orange and bricks rosy pink, bleaching the plaster, gilding from top to bottom this immense cage in which thousands of crows now circle.

In place of a hideous barracks, we have a crumbling Roman palace, a Tower-of-Babel-like fantasy, a Piranesi engraving with its unfinished vaults, its obscure arches, its galleries running high up in the air, cutting across each other, leaping over the void, its colossal mass of arches intersecting one another, blocking each other's way, freeing themselves and meeting up again in alcoves sculpted in the clouds, a whole dream architecture, a complete nightmare of steep columns, hewn with axes, amid the confusion of a mad night's sleep!

Then a pristine forest in miniature starts to grow beneath the vaults of these ruins; trees rise up on all sides; everywhere shrubs have lifted slabs and saxifrages have broken through the marble terraces; everywhere green mosses emphasise the pink tones encrusted onto the epidermis of certain stones by petrol bombs; everywhere hanging gardens sway above trees, gardens carried away by whirlwinds, minuscule parterres and alleyways cleared by the sparrows that fight each other there, tiny fields left fallow on sections of wall, woods of dwarf plane trees, baskets of wild flowers, from seeds sewn by a gust of wind!

Another ten years, and with the help of a respectful landscape artist, one would have a fragment of a Palmyra or a Sardis, a section of a dead city, a segment of a dwarf Rome, eaten away by greenery and flowers.

At the present moment, and without the scenery planted by Time being completed, this monument is the only one in which the whims of nature, constantly repressed by Parisian city planners, can exist. If only for this reason, we should keep it; and what an instructive lesson this ruin reveals to us.

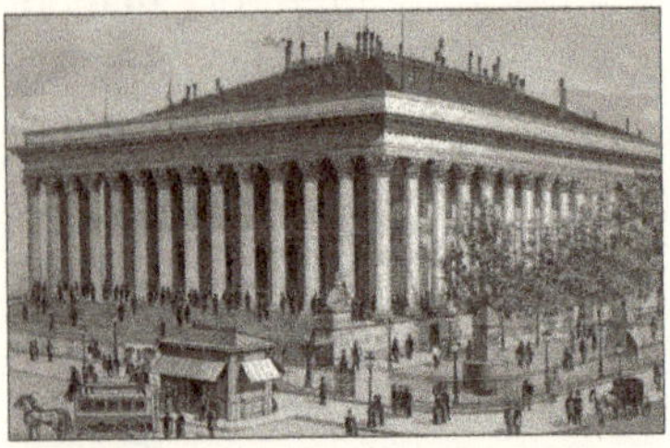

The Stock Exchange, Paris

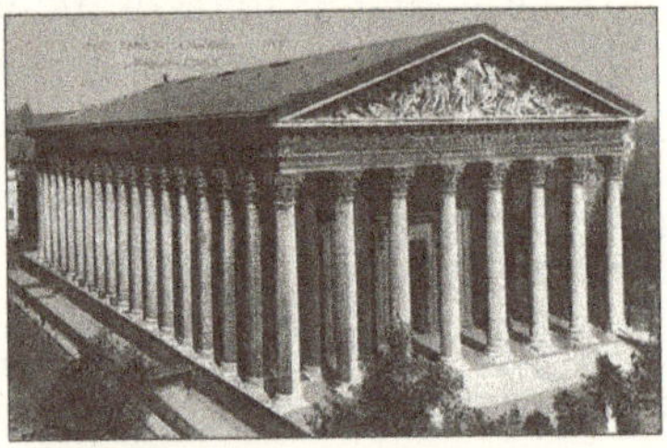

Madeleine, Paris.

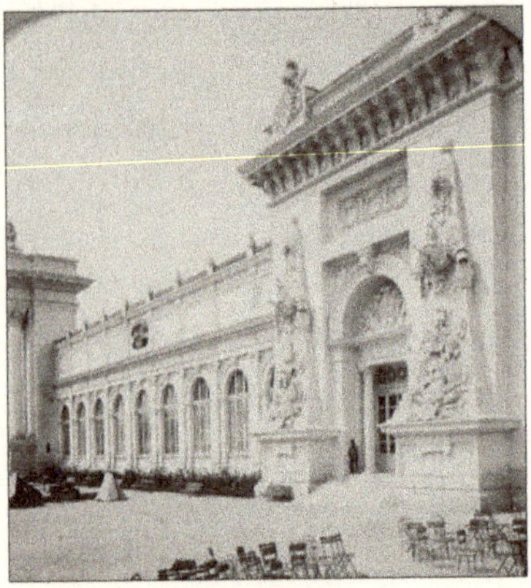

Ministry of War, Paris.

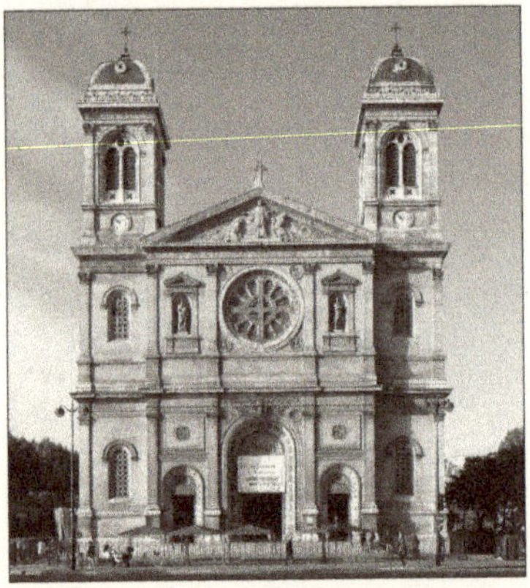

Church of Saint Francis Xavier, Paris.

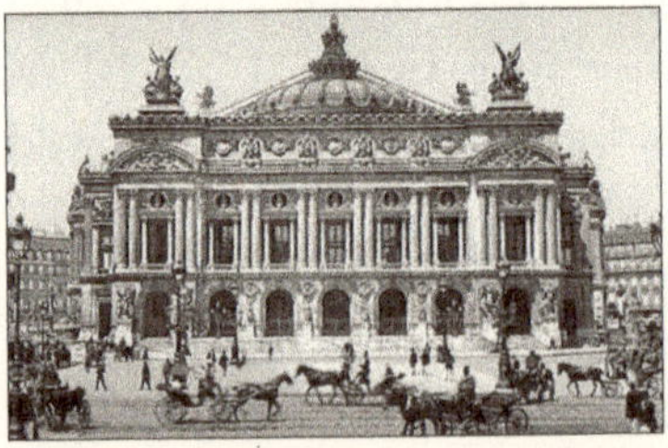

Opéra Garnier, Paris.

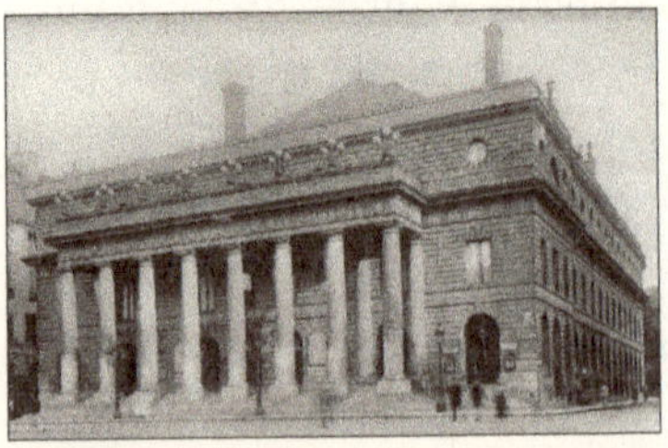

Théâtre de l'Odéon, Paris.

VI. THE MUSEUM OF DECORATIVE ARTS

For a century, architecture has been a crippled art – every building that has been built proves it; formal combinations in stone seem exhausted, and the ironwork structures that have succeeded them haven't yet found their form. So while waiting for this form – which will inevitably reflect the image of an epoch of mercantilism and speed – to blossom, could we not present, as an example to be followed, the beauty that the palace of the Court of Auditors has acquired, ever since an aesthetic chance decided to destroy it and then abandon it?

Instead of giving architects monuments to build, which they construct from odds and ends, taking a piece of antiquity here, a bit of the Middle Ages there, and trying to harmonise the whole thing as best they can, would it not be better to employ them to purify, to ennoble the buildings that remain; would it not be better for a skilled alchemist to replace the professors of the architectural school and teach them the means of printing onto the Commercial Court of Paris, for example, the real stamp of art, by setting it on fire?

To embellish this hideous Paris which we owe to the lamentable generosity of modern builders, could we not – with all precautions taken for people's safety – sow a few ruins here and there, burn the Stock Exchange, the Madeleine, the Ministry of War, the Church of Saint Francis Xavier, the Opéra Garnier and the Théâtre de l'Odeon, all prime examples of a nefarious art? Perhaps we would then realise that fire is the quintessential artist of our time, and that the architecture of this century, so pitiful when raw, becomes imposing, almost superb, when it is well-cooked.

VII

Iron – Millet

IRON

In architecture, the situation is now this: Architects erect ludicrous buildings whose parts, borrowed from every period, when taken together constitute the most servile parodies it's possible to imagine.

It's a mess of platitude and pastiche; contemporary architecture can pretty much be summed up in that miserable pot-pourri that is the Opéra Garnier, and in that nonsensical Trocadéro Palace,[1] which, seen from a distance, with its huge rotunda and its spindly minarets and golden turrets, looks like the belly of a dropsical woman lying on her back, lifting into the air her two skinny legs in their stockings and gold slippers.

One thing is certain; the present era has produced no major architect, nor is it epitomised by any particular style. After the Romanesque, the Gothic and the Renaissance, architecture plodded along, still discovering new combinations in stone, growing fat with tiresome ostentation in the Louis XIV period, losing weight with the Rococo, and then dying of anaemia, once the Revolution was born.

Another thing is certain, which is that stone, hitherto considered to be the fundamental material of a building, is exhausted, drained by constant repetition; it can no longer lend itself to as-yet undiscovered innovations, which would in any case be nothing more than better disguised or more adroitly combined borrowings from ancient forms.

The supreme beauty of the pious epochs of the past created that magnificent, almost superhuman art, the Gothic; the era of debauched commercialism we are currently going through can expect nothing more from stone, which stratified, so to speak, enthusiasm and prayer, but it can incarnate itself in buildings that symbolise its energy and its dreariness, its astuteness and its wealth, in works that are dour and tough, but in any event, new.

And the material used here is obvious, it is iron.

Since the reign of Louis Philippe,[2] ironwork structures have been tried many times, but lacked architects of talent; no new form has been discovered, the metal remains part of a whole, it is linked to stone, remains a subordinate agent, incapable, on its own, of creating a building that isn't a railway station or a greenhouse, a building that can be cited for its aesthetics.

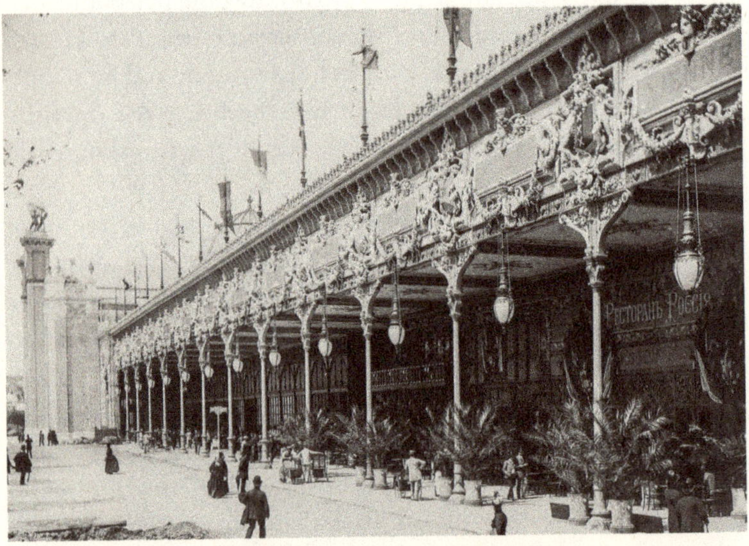

Ironwork veranda at the Universal Exhibition, Paris, 1889.

Up to the present day, the best uses of it are confined to the interiors of buildings, such as the reading room in the National Library and the inside of the Hippodrome, its role is thus practical and limited, purely internal.

This was the state of architecture when the 1889 Universal Exhibition[3] took place.

It will be curious to see if, as regards the main exhibition pavilion[4] and the Eiffel Tower, ironwork has come out of its tentative phase and, with the help of majolica and tiles, finally invented a new style.

In order to judge the architecture of the pavilion impartially, it is necessary to repeat, at every sudden shock one experiences, that these temporary structures have been erected to satisfy the tastes of rustics from the provinces and foreign upstarts lured here from their country by our advertisements.

From this point of view, the architects have fully achieved their goal; they have created a transoceanic art, an art suitable for Americans and the native inhabitants of New Caledonia.[5]

Indeed, how else could one account for those two squat domes, gaudy, craquelured like Japanese ashtrays, glazed with turquoise enamel, and highlighted in gold; or those long galleries fronted by cast-iron verandas, with metal columns painted sky-blue and encrusted with broken pottery; and especially how else could one account for that third dome surmounted by a winged god in gold, the dome that covers the monumental entrance, wrought with massive sculptures, covered with statues and heads, and emblazoned with the coats of arms of various cities? It looks like half a pear, its stalk in the air, or the giant helmet of a deep-sea diving suit, enamelled, perforated with glass panels, plated in gold, patched in azure and glazed in brown. And everywhere, around the galleries, in niches, amid furling banners, are naked gods brandishing the staff of Hermes and palm leaves; there are chubby cherubs, motifs of tin-coloured bunches of chicory with

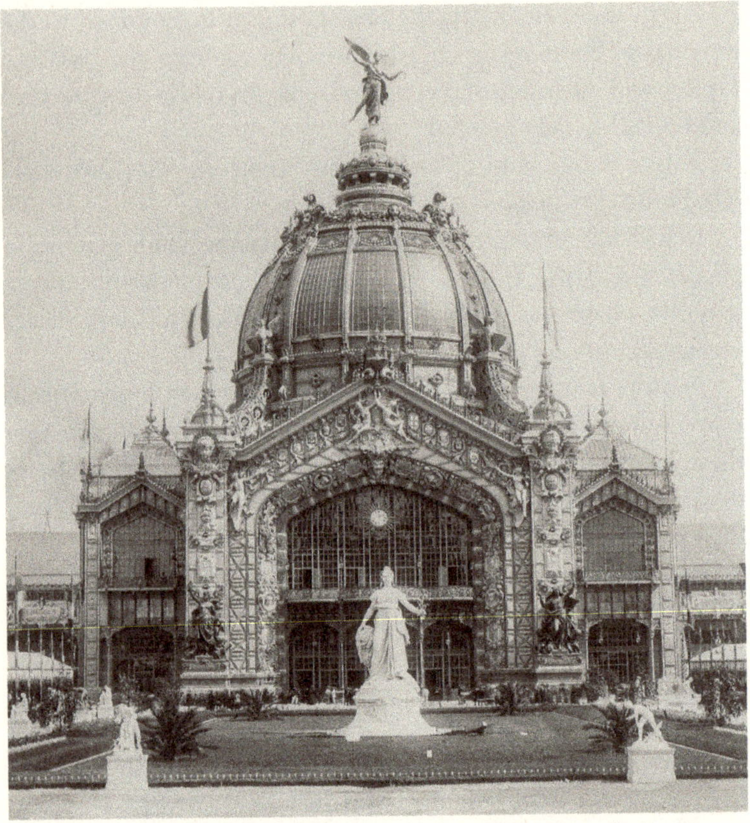

The Grand Dome over the entrace to the Universal Exposition, Paris, 1889.

a jewel in the centre like the nose-stud of a savage, all mixed up with city coats of arms topped by mural crowns[6] with golden crenellations.

It is a triumph of mosaic, of faience, of enamelled brickwork, of iron painted chocolate cream and blue; it's the most passionate affirmation of polychromy; it's ponderous and garish, pompous and cheap; it evokes, in a different art form, the theatrical painting of Hans Makart, so dear to Hamburg amid the superfluous splendour of its brothels!

It has to be admitted that, in a stroke, the bad taste of the stonemasons has been surpassed; but it is also worth repeating, these temporary constructions are wonderfully adapted to the spirit of the crowds going round them. In the evening, while the Exhibition becomes a monstrous and charming thing, with its consensual truce of the day's cares, its casino-like air of good humour, its exasperating festive mood, the central dome, lit from within, looks like a night light with a paper shade in a Celtic stained-glass pattern, but the irritating excess of its facade subsides; despite the strings of lights that run around the dome, the harsh, blaring glare of its bronzes and golds dies down and, in front of this monumental entrance and the pavillion it dominates, one thinks of a church dedicated to the religion of gold, sanctified by an altar onto which, to the sound of a steam organ, ascends the richest man in the world, the American pope, Jay Gould,[7] who celebrates a golden Mass, and in front of the kneeling crowd, to the repeated peals of an electric bell, lifts the communion host – a cheque ripped from a chequebook!

In front of this temple stands the infamous tower, about which the entire world has gone mad.

All the panegyrics have been trotted out. In fact, the Eiffel Tower hasn't, as was feared, acted as a lightning conductor, but rather as the most formidable conductor of clichés: "an Arc de Triomphe of industry", "a Tower of Babel", "a work from the forges of Vulcan", "a Cyclopean thunderbolt",[8] "a spider's web of metal", "a piece of lace made from cast-iron". In a touching unanimity – no doubt paid for – the entire press has prostrated itself, exalting the genius of Monsieur Eiffel.

And yet his tower looks like a factory chimney under construction, a structural carcass waiting to be filled with dressed stone or bricks. One would never have guessed that this infundibuliform piece of grating was actually finished, that this singular suppository riddled with holes will stay just as it is.

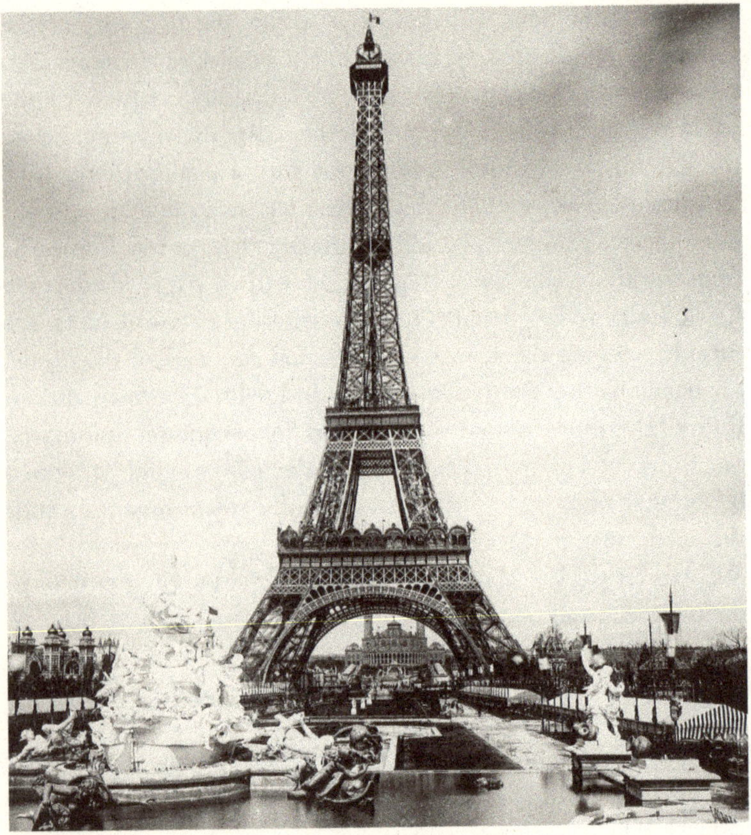

The Tour Eiffel, during the Universal Exhibition, Paris 1889.

This appearance of scaffolding, this pose of incompleteness, co-opted onto a now complete building show the absolute meaninglessness of art. And what, moreover, is one to think of this ironworker who had his work enamelled in Barbedienne bronze,[9] who made it look as if it was soaked in congealed meat juice? In effect, it's the colour of the jellied veal you get in restaurants; it's the jelly beneath which you glimpse, as you do in the first stage of the Tower, that disgusting shade of yellow grease.

The Eiffel Tower is truly of a disconcerting ugliness – and it's not even that big! Seen from below, it doesn't seem as high as they keep telling us it is. You need to have some point of reference, but if you imagine the Panthéon, the Invalides, the Vendome column and Notre-Dame all stacked on top of one another, it's impossible to convince yourself that the viewing platform of the Tower outclimbs the summit attained by that unbelievable pile. Seen from a distance, it's even worse. This shaft barely surpasses the tops of the monuments just named. From the Esplanade des Invalides, for instance, it's scarcely higher than a five-storey house; from the Quai d'Orleans, one can see it at the same time as the delicate, tiny bell-tower of Saint-Séverin – and both appear to be on the same level.

From near or far, from the centre of Paris or the depths of the suburbs, the effect is identical. The emptiness of this cage diminishes it; the latticework and mesh make this iron trophy look like a hideous birdcage.

Ultimately, whether drawn or engraved, it looks pathetic. And how could it be otherwise, this bottle covered in a wickerwork of painted straw and stoppered by its viewing gallery like a cork with a pouring spout, when compared to the powerful constructions dreamed up by Piranesi, not to mention those monuments imagined by the Englishman John Martin?

Whichever way one turns, this work is a lie. It is three hundred metres tall but seems to be a hundred; it's finished but it barely seems to have been started.

In the absence of artistic form, difficult to find perhaps with that latticework which is in effect nothing more than an accumulation of bridge pilings, they should at least have tried to produce something gigantic, to suggest the sensation of enormity; this Tower should have been immense, it should have sprung up to insane heights, it should have punctured space, it should have stood at more than two thousand metres, with its dome serving as an incredible milestone amid the ever-shifting roadway of the clouds!

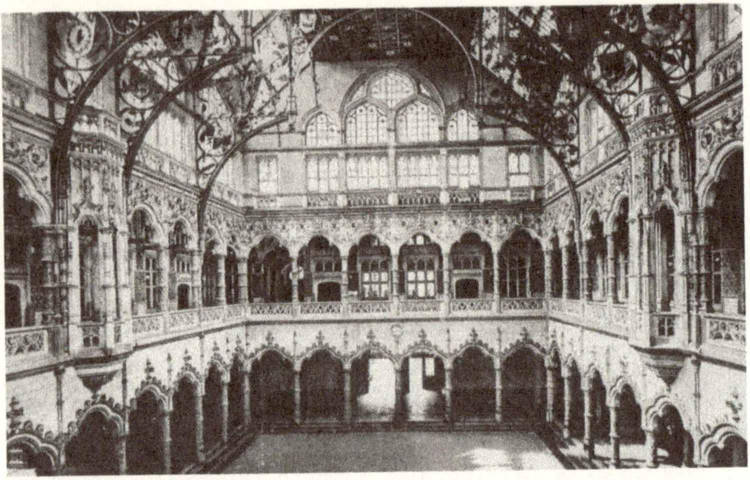

Stock Exchange, Antwerp.

But that was unachievable; so what good was it erecting a hollow obelisk on an empty pedestal? It will no doubt seduce foreigners, but it will not disappear with them, at the same time as the temporary Exhibition galleries, as the blue domes whose metallic sections were bought by the yard.

If now, leaving aside the whole, we concern ourselves with the detail, we continue to be amazed at the crudity of each element. You tell yourself that ironworkers in antiquity nevertheless managed to create powerful works, that the art of the old blacksmiths of the sixteenth century hasn't been completely lost, that a few modern artists have also sculpted in iron, that they've bent it into the snouts of wild beasts, the visages of women, the faces of men; we tell ourselves that they have also cultivated, in the hothouse of the forge, an iron flora, and that in Antwerp, for example, the pillars of the Stock Exchange are entwined at the top with creepers and stems that curl round each other, blending, blooming up in the air into supple flowers whose metal bouquets serve to lighten, to atomise as it were, the ceiling of this heraldic hall.

But here, nothing; no adornment, however tentative it might be, no caprice, no trace of artistry. When you enter the Tower, you find yourself in front of a chaos of criss-crossing beams, riveted by bolts, hammered with nails. You can't help but think of props holding up an invisible building that is falling down. You can't help but shrug your shoulders in front of this glorification of wire and sheet metal, in front of this apotheosis of viaduct pilings and bridge supports.

Ultimately, one has to ask oneself what the purpose of this Tower is. If we consider it separately, isolated from other buildings, abstracted from the Palais d'Industrie in front of it, it offers no meaning, it's absurd. If, on the contrary, one looks at it as part of a whole, as belonging to the other constructions erected on the Champ de Mars, one might speculate that it was the steeple of a new church in which, as I said above, the divine service of the most holy Bank was celebrated. This would make it the belfry, only separated from the transept and the choir – similar to the cathedral in Utrecht – by a vast public square.

If this were the case, then its bank-vault material, its beef-casserole colour, its factory-chimney form, its oil-well shape, its framework of a large mineshaft able to extract gold-bearing sludge from the stock exchange, would make sense. It would be the spire of a Notre-Dame of Trade, a steeple deprived of bells, but armed with a cannon that announces the opening and closing of financial services, that summons the faithful to a financial mass, to a vespers of bankers' fees, a cannon that, with its puffs of smoke, marks the liturgical holy days of capitalism!

It would, like the gallery of the monumental dome that it complements, be the symbol of an era dominated by the passion for profit; but the unthinking architect who built it didn't know how to find the ferocious, hypocritical style, the demonic character, that this allegory demands. Truly this perforated pylon is enough to make you despise a metal that allows itself to be confected into such a work, if its incomparable power didn't shine forth in the prodigious nave of the Machine Hall.

The interior of this hall is indeed superb. Imagine a colossal gallery, wider than anything you have ever seen, higher than the highest nave, a gallery soaring up on arching shoots that describe broken-backed semicircles in the air, extravagant ogives whose vertiginous tips join together beneath an infinite sky of glass, and in this formidable space, in this complete void, are enormous machines that seem to have shrunk, are almost dwarfed, machines that are unfortunately all-too banal, with their lubricious pistons and whirling flywheels.

The form of this hall is borrowed from Gothic art, but insanely expanded and enlarged, impossible to achieve in stone, and, with its great arches on calyx-form feet, original.

In the evening, as the Edison lamps come on, the gallery seems to stretch out into infinity; the lighthouse[10] at the centre seems like a glass beehive dotted with fires; stars abound, pricking the crystal whose cut edges burn with sulphur-blue and vine-shoot red flames, with the lilac and orange of gaslight, and with the

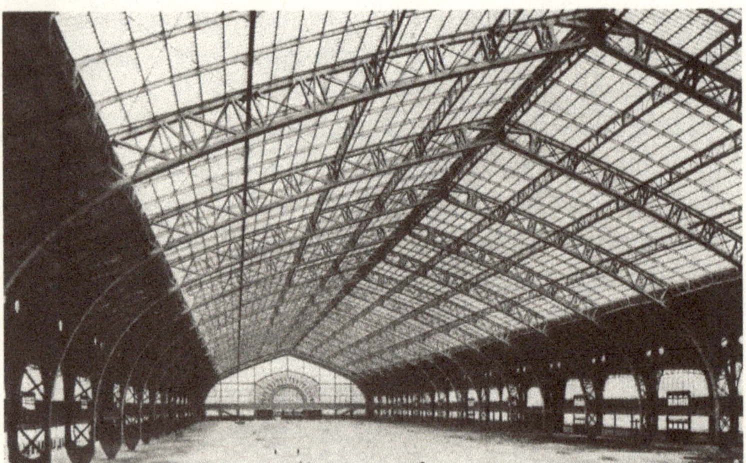

Machine Hall, Paris, during construction.

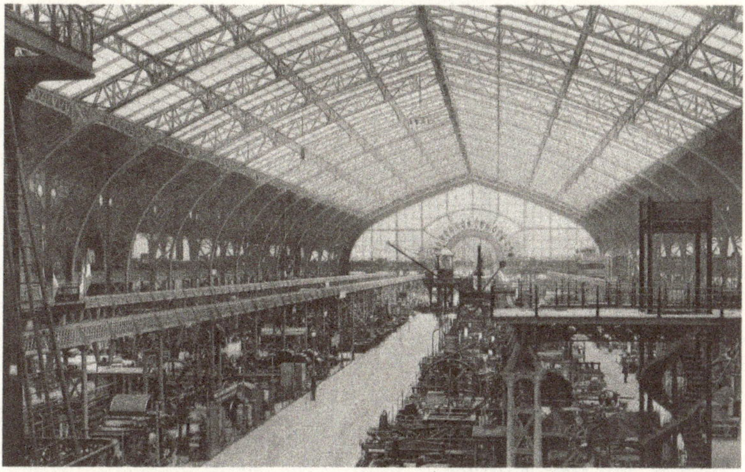

The Machine Hall at the Universal Exhibition, Paris, 1889. The lighthouse can be seen in the middle distance.

green of vigil-lights around a catafalque; the electrician aims his lenses, shoots beams of luminous dust beneath a glazed sky that transforms into a sheet of water. A stream of fine jewels seems to flow in a moonbeam and prism gleams appear, wandering in procession around the room like regimented automata, they pass slowly along the walls, sometimes shapeless or like smears of light, sometimes flaring out into tulips of fire, teeming with the hitherto unknown vegetation of flames.

The sovereign grandeur of this hall becomes fantastical; one has to admit that, from the point of view of art, this gallery constitutes the most admirable effort that metallurgy has ever attempted.

Except that – and I must repeat it again – as with the Hippodrome, as with the National Library, this effort is completely internal. The Machine Hall is grandiose – as a nave, as a building interior, but as an exterior, as a facade seen from the outside, it is nothing.

Architecture has not, therefore, made any new advances in this direction; for want of a man of genius, iron is still incapable of creating an entirely personal work, a true work of art.

*

MILLET

Each time the Beaux-Arts clinic exhibits the work of a dead painter in its hospital on the Quai Malaquais, I am gripped by fear. The experiment is always a failure. Even Delacroix and Manet didn't escape intact from that zealous free-for-all of canvases. For Corot, it was a disaster; the vague aroma of his pipe smoke evaporated and the nothingness of his pictures was revealed behind the dispersed fog of identical skies, from which could determine neither its latitude nor time of day; twilight or daybreak, heat-haze or clouds of rain, it was all the same; from the grey wash of a preliminary sketch, to a grey relieved only by the dashes of vermilion slapped on any random figure wearing a red beret; as for Courbet, it was the complete revelation of working-class ideas served up by the brush of an out-of-date classicist; it was the definitive demolition of that great lout, whose brain was in his belly.

I was put in mind of these lamentable predecessors, when the owners of works by Jean-François Millet exhibited them in the obscure hangars of the Quai Malaquais. Was the experience deplorable or favourable? Did the anticipated disappointment have to be endured? Is Millet really the great painter that the whole press is lauding to the skies at the present moment?

No – if you consider the dreary imposture of his dressed-up peasants, who conform to La Bruyère's inflexible theories,[11] or if you only take into account his oils, which are monotonous and inflexible, banal and stale, fake and fraudulent. Yes – up to a certain point – if you only look at two or three of his pastels.

But it has to be said first of all that his peasants are, as a type, as conventional and as fictitious as 'François the Foundling' and 'Little Fadette',[12] as all the comic-opera yokels invented by that old chorus-line dancer, that old spinning-jenny of stupid idealism they call George Sand. While she was transforming the filthy rustics of her native Berri into incorporeal Céladons,[13] Millet was remoulding the peasants around Fontainebleau, the people of Brie, into innocent convicts, into inept orators.

So when he represents a peasant, exhausted, leaning on his hoe, staring ahead with his dead eyes, he is lying – and it's really time to say it, finally! The peasant annihilated by incessant toil, the peasant dying in need, screaming in poverty on the land, doesn't exist. To maintain that he's happy? Of course not, for he must plough and sow, harvest and thresh; but if you put next to this man, who owns or rents a cottage for a few sous, who sometimes raises cows or pigs, always chickens, and often geese, and who harvests potatoes and cabbages from a small garden – if you put this man next to a Parisian worker, then you'll see the difference. And that's without trying to find the most miserable or the most downtrodden artisan in the city, without mentioning the composters of sarsaparilla with their uncontrollable vomiting, or the crushers of white lead and the distillers of mercury with their rotting guts and soft bones; no, take a printer whose profession is pretty mild. Getting up, like the peasant, at dawn, he slaves away in a workshop, without stopping, without a break, until the evening, then he returns to a flea-ridden bedsit, inhales the noxious stench of a communal drain, drinks fiery beverages and, if he's still single, satisfies his need for love in a perilous brothel; however unfortunate he might be, the peasant at least works in the open air, he gets drunk on unadulterated wine, satisfies himself with a strapping country wench, returns to an airy room, and, if he fancies, inhales the bracing evening breeze from his back garden. Does the Parisian worker have these things, the long chats walking along the road, the impromptu snacks on the way, the endless loafing around, all the distracting excuses of the rustic? – And it's the same for women. Like a beast of burden, the peasant's wife brings in the hay, chops wood and cooks, digs and gives birth. Yes, but a working woman in Paris, cloistered from early morning in the airless atmosphere of a Bon Marché or a Louvre, a woman always on her feet and attentive to the demands of the public, is weaker and suffers more, is more painfully steamrollered by life, and is more truly to be pitied.

And keep in mind that when it's freezing, the farmer rests and warms his legs in front of a log fire that costs nothing, while in the same situation the ordinary housewife has to sift through the embers, make briquettes out of half-burned coke moulded in a terrine, and try to warm herself and her kids with this random detritus as best she can; at the end of the day, the peasant is not to be pitied when you compare his fate to that of the manual worker, or even to that of most employees in a city.

It is, therefore, supremely unjust to provoke our pity, and to claim in favour of these lazy brutes a compassion that only the suffering mercenaries of fixed labour deserve.

But it also has to be said that Millet understood them well, his brothers of the plough, his parents of the stable. Read his biographers. Mantz,[14] who provided the preface to the catalogue sold at the Quai Malaquais asylum,[15] reports that Millet attended his village school, and then came to Paris to study painting under Delaroche; it's always the same thing; we are in the presence of a peasant's son, of someone poorly educated, whose ignorance is superficially plastered over by a pedant, then let loose in the capital, in the midst of painters who are no less ignorant but whose populist spirit is ameliorated in bars and restaurants. As far as reading goes, Millet undoubtedly knew La Bruyere's hackneyed clichés which I spoke about earlier; he'd also groped around in scenes from the Bible, which he was already neither simple

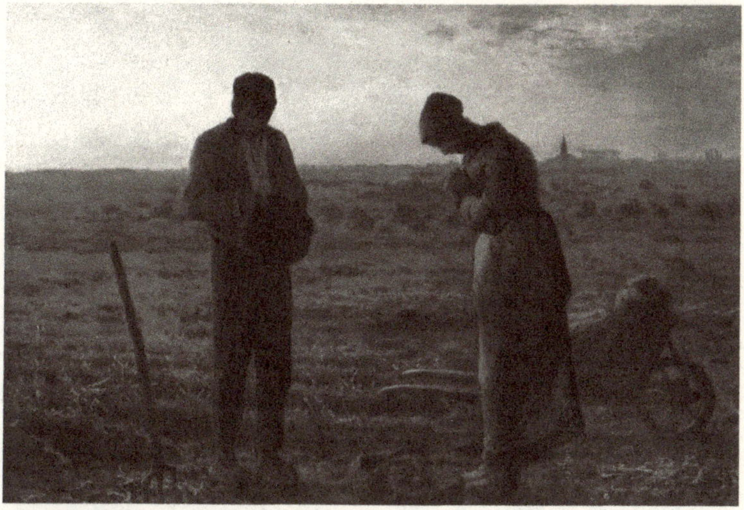

The Angelus by Jean-François Millet.

enough, nor refined enough to understand. He transferred these poorly digested readings onto his canvases pell-mell, and instead of actual Brie peasants, petty and devious, greedy and whining, he served us up with exiled slaves who beg for mercy and spout tirades like Jean Valjean. Instead of rustics who have never prayed in their life, he depicted men who stand in silent prayer at the Angelus, idyllic and pious herdsmen – as if for a shepherd working in the fields the sound of a church bell wasn't just a simple signal indicating the right moment for a snack, or marking the usual time to go home.

No, Millet was a painter, that is to say, a man endowed with a commendable manual dexterity and a certain agility of the eye, but he was a rustic without a proper education, a workman led astray by the polemic of arty cafés, a peasant spoiled by the company of other painters who were born in Paris and whose only schooling was music hall songs and restaurant gossip.

Leaving aside Millet's conception of the country peasant,

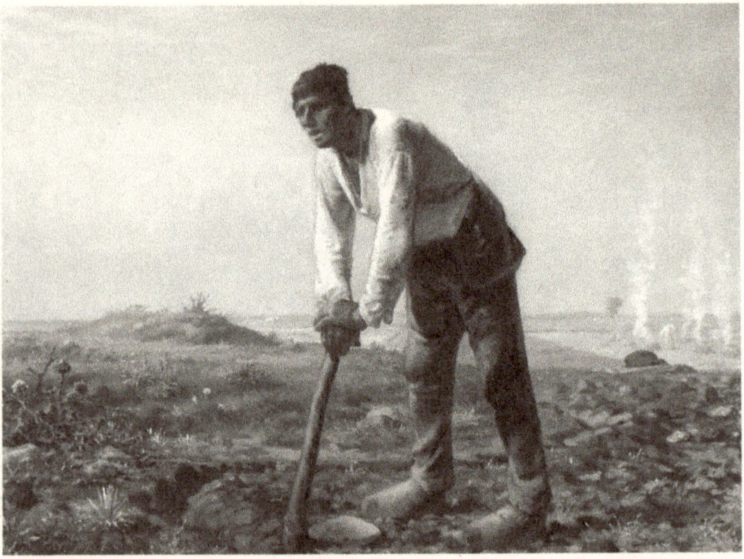

Man with a Hoe by Jean-François Millet.

eloquent in look and expression, mercilessly martyred to an ungrateful society and a harsh environment, we come to the actual exhibition of his pastels and his oils.

His paintings, so vigorously celebrated since his death, are – and one really has to say it – rough and a bit shabby, old-fashioned and dull. Take *Man with a Hoe, The Angelus,* or *The Gleaners.* What do we find here? In a landscape that has neither clarity nor air, monotonous reddish-brown figures, seasoned with a bit of mud on their clogs, standing beneath a harsh sky. These works in oil betray the labour that went into them, the sweaty exertion of his big arms. All of the old masters of landscape – because he paints in their tradition – painted canvases that were more candid; and none of their paintings have, after just a few years, become so superficial and arid in this way. As an oil painter, he is mediocre and of a clumsiness that makes you despair.

But fortunately he is not entirely represented by these

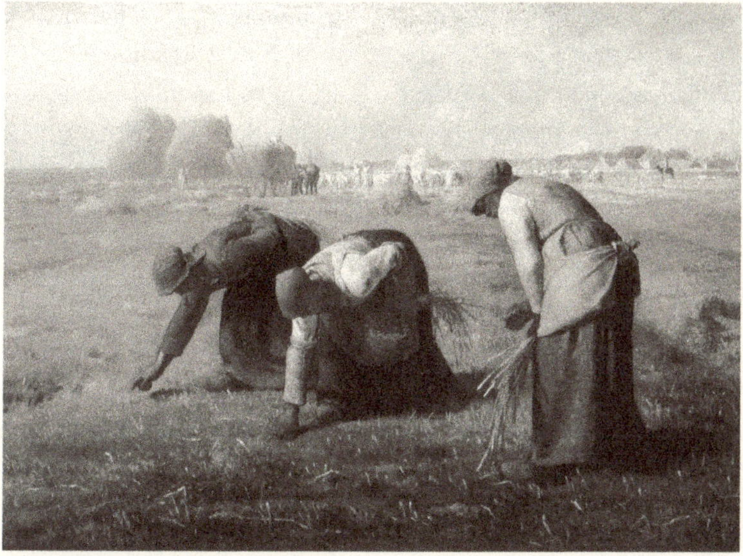

The Gleaners by Jean-François Millet.

paintings. A very real artist is now emerging from his least praised works, from his pencil sketches highlighted with pastel.

Among this series of works, those in which the painter's temperament is most clearly marked are, without any doubt, his scenes of a sunrise in a still sleeping countryside, from which the human figure is banished or barely visible on the horizon.

Here, he reveals a wholly unique emotion when confronted by the 'dawn of the day', which has such a singular effect on man. For sensitive types, it's typically a kind of unease or confusion; there's a vague sense of expectation, of a new day, of the threshold of morning, of something known only in a dream; there's an unsettling surprise at seeing this silent birth of the light, emerging gradually from the spreading matrix of the sky; there's a frisson of the spirit, a chill in the soul, a desire for this transience of nature to cease, that these shadow pass. But the rising of the sun doesn't have this effect on Millet, whose nerves remain calm, rather a strange impression comes to him and he renders it with an energy that grips you. The dawn for him is in some sense an armistice concluded between the earth and man. Look at his *Sunrise on the Plain*, a deserted plain, with a harrow lying in a piece of fallow land and a single plough standing straight up in the furrows, while a flock of swirling crows punctuate the pale and slowly brightening sky with dark commas. It looks as if this earth, churned up and torn apart the day before by the march of the ploughshare, belonged to a region devastated by murderous conflict. Night has necessarily put an end to the struggle; the truce holds, but it seems that the dead are now going to be removed and that as soon as the sun has fully risen, the mute battle between the tenacious peasant and the harsh land will resume.

Another pastel, *The Plain*, gives the same distressing and lofty impression; it's an immense plain, lying under a sky slashed with blades of pale fire at the horizon, and already in the distance, man enters on the scene, because one can glimpse a woolly flock followed by a shepherd, whose tall silhouette has an inexplicably unfriendly aspect. Deep down, it's still the same idea of the starving everyman who wages war to gain his crust of bread; but, expressed in this way, without the special pleading of a human face – in other words without being directly described, and just being simply suggested – it makes an impression.

But then the pastellist is something other than the painter. The shrunken horizons of the canvases are gone; now the sky stretches as far as the eye can see, fresh air bathes the fields and a quality that Millet possesses, perhaps more than any other, appears. Raw matter, the very soil, seeps from his frames, lush and full of life. You sense its thickness and heaviness; you sense that beneath its clods and its grass, it always goes deeper. You breathe its odour, you could crumble it between your fingers or bury your feet in it. With most landscape artists, the earth is shallow; with Millet, it is profound.

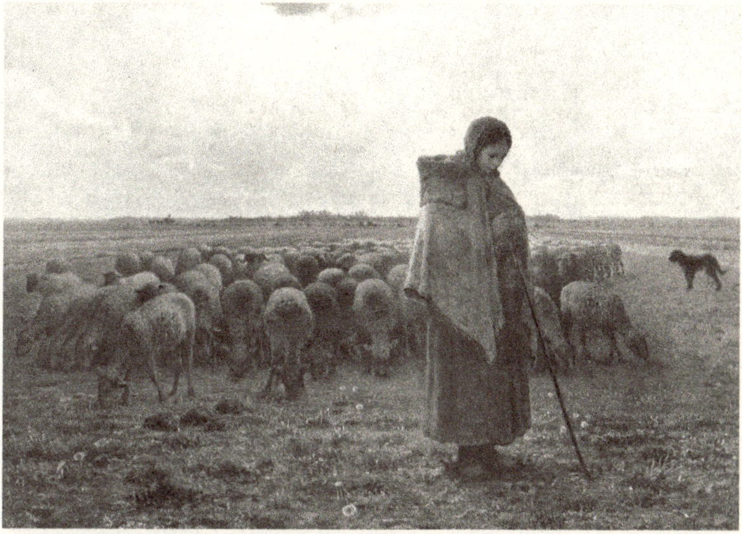

The Shepherdess (oil) by Jean-François Millet.

Ultimately this man, whose methods are so second-rate and whose execution is so commonplace when it comes to painting, suddenly reveals himself as possessing an individual craft, an original technique in his pastels. His works in pencil, their filiform lines, their needle-like streaks, their borders with their deft blend of coloured pastels, are truly convincing and forceful.

Where before he was hesitant and ponderous, he shows himself to be determined, almost agile; even his figures seem more sophisticated in the powder of his pastels, become less pompous and more lively, and the comparison is very easy to establish, because the same subjects are often treated in both mediums. *The Shepherdess*, knitting in front of her flock of sheep which a dog guards, is, when painted in linseed oil, like an image for a First Communion card, a silly and feeble illustration. Sketched in pastel, she is purified of her lifeless and insipid cuteness, and approaches reality; and her surrounding environment also changes. The soggy coffee grounds she seems to be standing on in the painting are

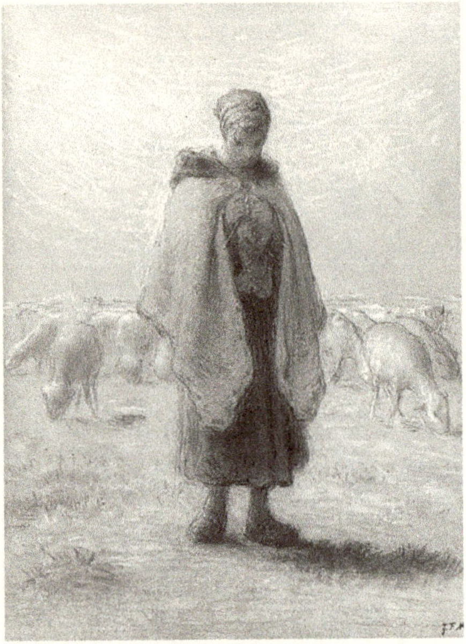

The Shepherdess (pastel) by Jean-François Millet.

transformed into real earth, the heavens have expanded, air circulates, animals are panting, because a breath of life animates them, and almost quivers beneath the girl's red cap and hood.

If you gather together the discrepancies that I spoke about, you eventually manage to synthesise into a strange whole this work formerly so denigrated and now so inordinately vaunted. In the man, you discover someone who is both not enough, and too much of a rustic; in the painter, a ponderous panel beater, imbued with the outdated scruples and outdated conventions of the palette painter; in the pastellist, representing solitude, you find a suggestive and suffering artist, a master landscapist who has experienced nature at certain hours of the day, and who has, in a style of his own, gravely and eloquently rendered it.

VIII

Goya – Turner – The State Hall at the Louvre – Bianchi

GOYA – TURNER

At an exhibition of old masters which took place in 1887, at the Quai Malaquais galleries, for the benefit of flood victims in the Midi, two really beautiful canvases. One, a bullfight by Goya;[1] the other, a landscape by Turner.

The Goya: a crush of red, blue and yellow, commas of white, a paté of vibrant tones, plastered pell-mell, applied with a palette knife, smeared, rubbed with a thumb, the whole thing spreading out in uneven rough patches from top to bottom of the canvas. You study it. Vaguely you can make out, amid the hustle and bustle of these solar flares, a wooden toy in the shape of a cow, covered in round white stickers and black stripes, and topped by a brown umlaut; then, further up, inverted commas and full stops, a whole array of coloured punctuation marks spreading out on a sheet of fawn paper. You step back, and it becomes extraordinary; as if by magic, everything resolves and falls into place, everything comes alive. The paté is a crowd of people, the commas are neighing horses, bullfighters appear, brandishing their red capes, striving, jostling, shouting beneath a biting sun. The little cow transforms into a formidable bull that rushes, furious, its horns thrust forward, into a group in disarray. At the bottom of the bullring, horses are stamping their feet, and those blobs applied with a palette knife, smeared with a rag, those thumb-prints become a seething crowd, working themselves up, swearing, threatening, letting out deafening *Olés*. It's all simply superb. And from this confused mess, distinct details emerge: those umlauts are sparkling eyes; those black stripes, gaping mouths; those inverted commas, clenched hands. It's the most frantic uproar that has ever been thrown onto a canvas, the most intense ruckus that an artist's palette has ever created.

Goya's etchings are of an incredible liveliness, with their madly slashing strokes, but even they can't fully convey an idea of this ferocious, turbulent painting, this sudden burst of design, this frenzy of Impressionism, moulding life with its bare hands, this furious cry, this intense rearing up of art.

As for the Turner, it also amazes you at first sight. You find yourself faced with an absolute effervescence of rose and burnt sienna, of blue and white, scumbled with a rag, sometimes turning

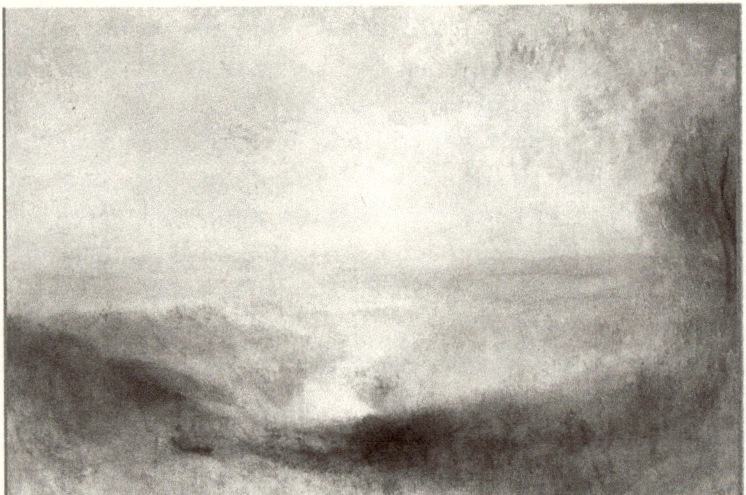

Landscape by J.M.W. Turner.

in a circle, sometimes dragging in a straight line or splitting into long zigzags. The print looks like a sheet of paper that's been rubbed with breadcrumbs, or with a mass of muted pigments diluted in water, that you fold and then scrape, violently, with a brush; it produces a play of amazing nuances, especially if, before folding the sheet, you sprinkles it with a few spots of white gouache.

Seen very close up, that's what it looks like, and then from a distance, just as with the Goya, everything falls into place. Before your unbelieving eyes, a marvellous landscape emerges, a fantastical scene, a radiating river flowing beneath the iridescent rays of the sun. A pale sky disappears into the distance, drowns in a mother-of-pearl horizon, is reflected and runs in water that shimmers, as if with soapy bubbles, in all the colours of the spectrum. Where, in what country, in what Eldorado, in what Eden, do such deliriums of light, such torrents of daylight, refracted by milky clouds stained with red fire and furrowed with violet like the depths of a precious opal, burn? And yet these scenes are real; these are autumnal landscapes, russet-coloured woods, flowing streams, windswept forests, but they are also volatilised landscapes, wide-open skies at dawn; they are celestial and fluvial celebrations of a transformed, distilled nature, rendered in a wholly fluid fashion by a great poet.

*

THE STATE ROOM IN THE LOUVRE

In this State Room,[2] recently inaugurated in the Louvre, I found a large number of pictures which I hope never to see again. I had thought they were mislaid in the crypt of the Luxembourg Museum or buried in some other sepulchre of art, but not a bit of it, here they are, exhumed and spread out in broad daylight, from top to bottom of the newly-painted walls of this opulent room.

Gerard and Pagnest, Scheffer and Delaberge, Gleyre and Heim, Vernet and Gros, Léopold Robert and Devéria, Regnault and Daubigny all reappear, embalmed in frames touched up in gold. A few had remained for years without a proper burial, abandoned in some lost hall near the Senate; others had been laid in open graves, relegated to a room in the Louvre, watched over by a recumbent guard, stupefied with boredom on his new bench; and lastly, some had been interred no one knew where, and one might have hoped that no obituaries had preserved their names.

But bureaucratic ambition has rediscovered them, and the hour of injustice tolls for them, because people will pay their respects, and the public is already visiting with a reverential air this gallows of hanging canvases, full of wooden Romans and scenes of families who seem to be made of hair. But in the promiscuity of this morgue, one work shines forth, the terrible comicality of which gets to you, a painting by Guérin, *An Offering to Aesculapius*, which is composed in this fashion: a plinth, topped by that bust so dear to pharmacies, in front of which an old man is scratching his frizzy head, while two statues of young men each advance a leg and extend an arm. It goes without saying that these young men are naked as can be, and that a young girl is squatting in front of them, in a dress with pleats that go up from her waist,

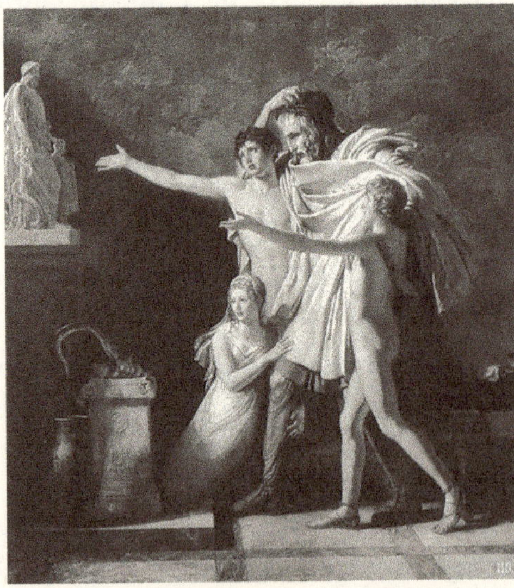

An Offering to Aesculapius by Pierre Guérin.

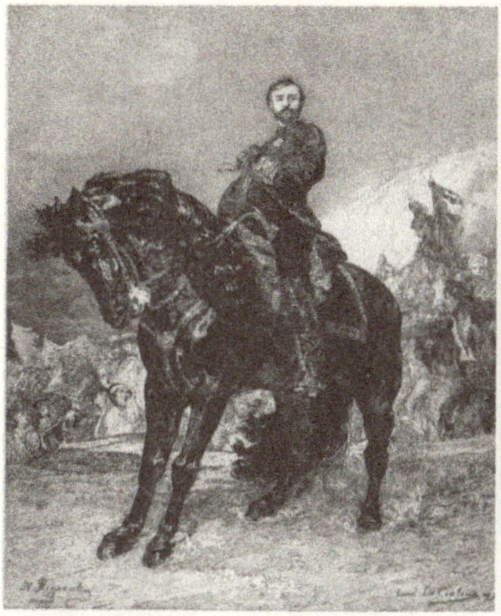

Marshal Prim by Henri Regnault.

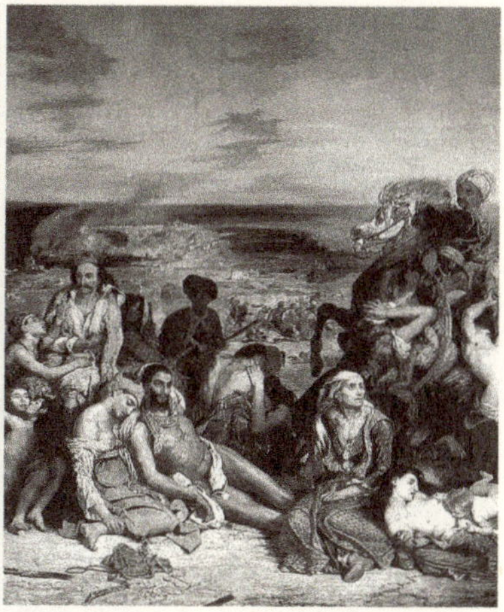

Massacre at Chios by Eugène Delacaroix.

beneath her arms, and up her chin by way of her breasts. This dreary, cold, over-the-top, clichéd painting disconcerts us, and yet, is it not superior to the portrait of Marshal Prim,[3] the rambling design and hammy ineffectual colours of which are truly painful?

In short, there's nothing of real interest in this public hanging of frames, apart from the Delacroix and the Ingres.[4]

Delacroix has some of his great pictures here: *The Massacre of Chios, Dante's Barque, The Women of Algiers in their Apartment.* These works are too contaminated by constant viewing for me to describe them; they have figured since time immemorial in museums, and again, recently, as a result of the Quai Malaquais exhibition, they were reproduced in all the illustrated magazines and done to death in the press.

I will deal particularly with the *Entry of the Crusaders in Constantinople*, which, having been buried for years in some forgotten necropolis in the provinces, ended up being acquired by the Louvre.

This painting is the centrepiece of the new hall and it is, of all

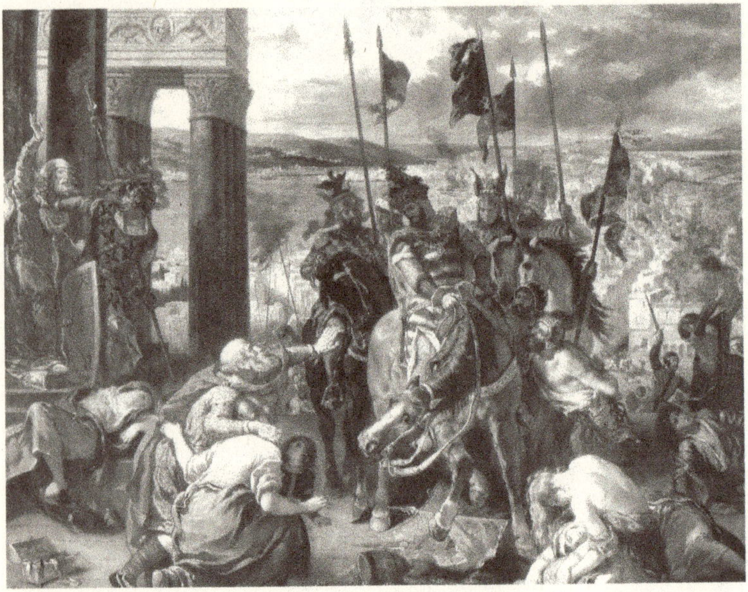

Entry of the Crusaders in Constantinople by Eugène Delacroix.

the works of Delacroix, his most personal canvas, and perhaps the most perfect.

For the first time, the entry of victorious troops into a city that they are putting to the sword has not been laid out as a storm of cheers, triumphant fanfares, salvos of gunfire and a blaze of glory. Here, the Crusaders arrive exhausted, almost dead on their feet; the knights are slumped in their saddles, and their subdued eyes, as if glazed over by fever, scarcely see the vanquished populace being trampled by their horses. An immense overwhelming fatigue furrows their faces and slashes their sagging mouths, now that victory has relaxed a nervous system exasperated by so much effort. And yet, on those faces whose lassitude is such that no other feeling should seem be able to further alter their features, hints of emotion pass: a ferocity not yet extinguished in some, a vague pity in others who watch an ordinary old man kneeling, holding his wife in his arms and crying for mercy. This triumph, so melancholy and so true, is at the same time a spiritual delight, a feast for the eyes. It is one of the painter's most distinct images, an admirable harmony of tones, a bonfire of pigments, sonorous and clear, a 'Tally-ho!' of flaming colours against a backdrop of the sea and a splendid blue sky.

It has to be said, especially after the inopportune exhibition of the all-too copious batch of Delacroix paintings they served up to us, pell-mell, in the gallery of the Beaux Arts, that this painter wasn't always so vibrant and so vigorous. An uneven and inconsistent artist, a Rubens made leaner and more refined by neuroses, who was purged of the coarser side of populist art and fleshy painting[5] that held the sanguine diplomat of Antwerp in its sway despite his prodigious talent, Delacroix was graced with ailments that gave way to returning bouts of good health. There is nothing in him of humdrum routine, of sedentary life, of the sage withdrawn from the commerce of art, his work is all somersaults and exultations, the rearing up of poorly-dominated nerves leaping over his consumption and mastering it; on the other hand, he was also perennially impulsive; a random migraine, a fitful sleep, and – particularly if you add the misfortune of a periodic loss of visual acuity – he spoils everything, he becomes singularly inferior; his enthusiasm, which he tries to whip up, rebels, and then the tones thicken and the unfinished design strays and falters. A strange man, almost always imperfect, bad-tempered and indolent, superb when his fever flares, hammy and schmaltzy when it smoulders, he was like a powerful shock delivered to a comatose art, like a dose of strychnine that electrified the old syrupy concoction that had been prescribed by the conventional colourists of grand art. In short, he infused into the painting of his time, not so much good health as a determined bravery, a nervous energy, an intermittent force of anger, a pulsation of love; in short, before the advent of Manet, he began to sweep the

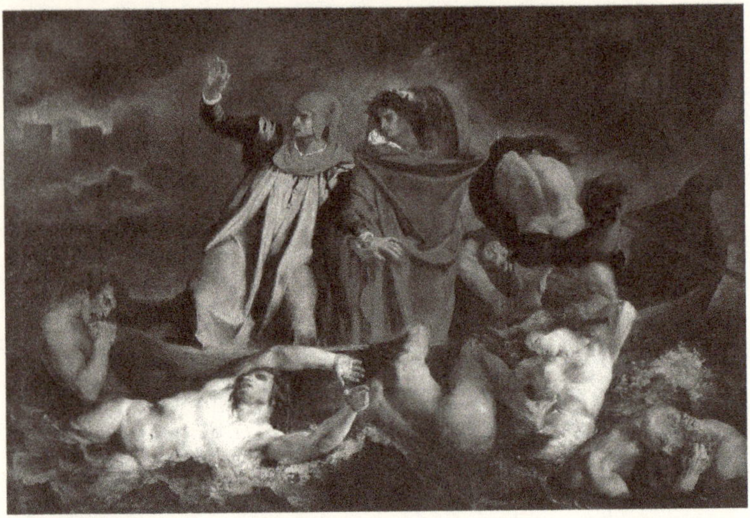

Dante's Barque by Eugène Delacroix.

chimney and clear out the old stove of art; he rejected the old black and brown shadows, making them derive from the same colour as the object that gave them form; he paved the way for the Impressionists of the present period. Despite the distance that seems to separate the painter of *Dante's Barque* from the painters of contemporary modernity, Delacroix has bequeathed them the hereditary traces of a powerful ancestor. One of the advocates of the new movement, Paul Cézanne, descends directly from him, and it is to the school of Delacroix that Degas owes that science of colours which he handles like a master.

Next to Delacroix, a single painter installed in that same room in the Louvre manages not to falter too much – old Ingres. I'm not talking here about his *Apotheosis of Homer*, that glacial transposition into paint of an already mediocre bas-relief. I also leave aside his blimp in human form, which he calls *Angelique at her Bath*, so stiffly boring, with its naked woman wearing a headscarf, turning her back to us, while behind the tubular folds

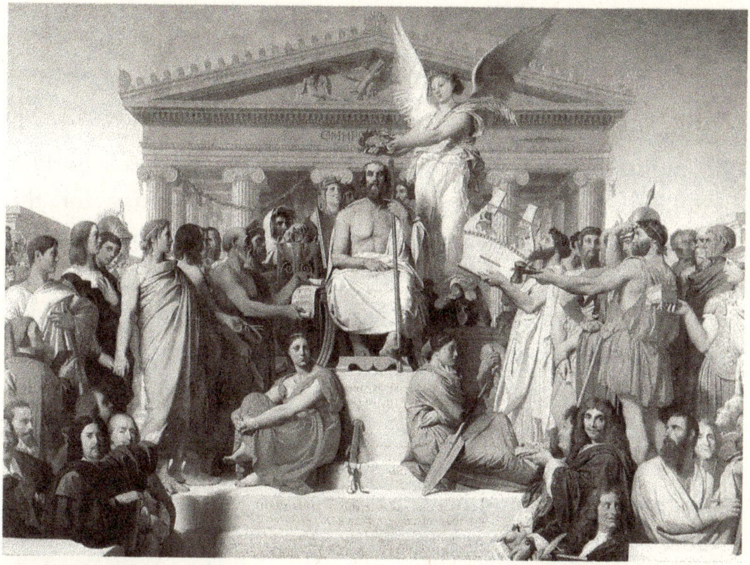

Apotheosis of Homer by Jean-Auguste-Dominique Ingres.

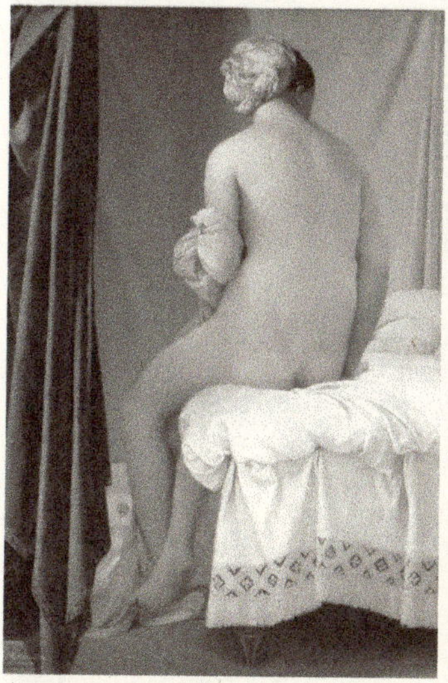

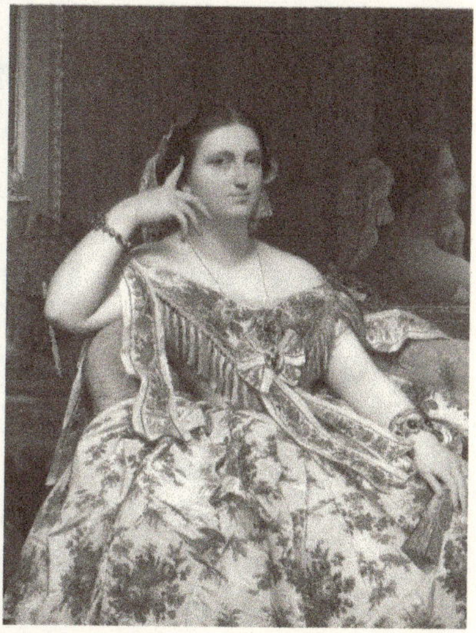

Angelique at Her Bath (left)and *Portrait of Madame Moitessier* by Jean-Auguste-Dominique Ingres.

of a sheet-metal curtain a lion's head – stolen from a legionary's belt, for which it no doubt served as a buckle – can just be made out, spitting water into an unseen pool.

Outside of portraiture, Ingres is nothing; he's a patient calligrapher, a Chouilloux de Radrets[6] of painting, a laborious disciplinarian, a departmental head at the Ministry for the Arts, and even in portraiture he's double-edged, being, by turn, obnoxiously clumsy and curiously subtle.

Clumsy, in his portrait of Madame Moitessier, a woman with flesh preserved in the refrigeration unit of a morgue, a frozen mannequin sitting in a flowery white dress on a pink ottoman, her back reflected in a mirror. And what a reflection – porcelain on sheet metal! And that souvenir-locket pose, the head of a dummy supported by an arm, with a finger resting on its temple and the eyes of a dead fish. It's wallpaper in all its glory. It's garish, arid and harsh, with its pretentious simulation of a fabric stitched in *petit point* that's been lapidified in the same way as the flesh, and then polished like a parquet floor with wax.

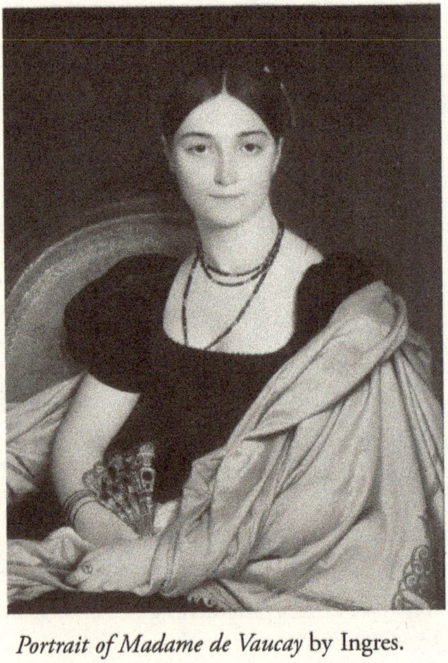

Portrait of Madame de Vaucay by Ingres.

Subtle, in the portrait of Madame de Vaucay whose mysterious life grips you to the core; a portrait painted flat, it doesn't come out at you like usual portraits, nor does it recede like those by Whistler. It's fixed, as if glued to a board, ghostly and mute. Madame de Vaucay is posed against a green background in this fashion: seated, in a low-cut dress of black velvet, she has a cloak carelessly thrown over her arm, a sort of cachou-brown toga, edged with a pattern like that of sticks of ordinary sealing wax; and the fabrics are painted in a similar fashion to those in Ingres' Persian watercolours, precise and painstaking; but beneath her flat, centre-parted, chestnut-brown hair, her pale face springs out and stares at you with such a fascinating and bizarre look that one is captivated by the enigma of that countenance, which makes one think of Edgar Allan Poe's Ligeia[7] – a Ligeia who has settled in France after undergoing a bromide cure.

This portrait is truly strange, truly subtle; by dint of hard work and good faith, the old aphasic has managed to cry out and light the tiny flame that burns in this canvas, so different from his usual crabby and dreary work.

This portrait has also influenced the present-day art movement; the attention to detail, the arduous work, the brutal honesty, the painter's willingness to be real and exact have succeeded. The Impressionist school remembered this Japanese-style veneer, this almost ferocious simplicity of tone, this deliberate pictural awkwardness, this sincerity of a Flemish Primitive. One of them was even inspired by this portrait a few years ago: Forain, who painted Madame M***, alleviated of unnecessary fabrics,

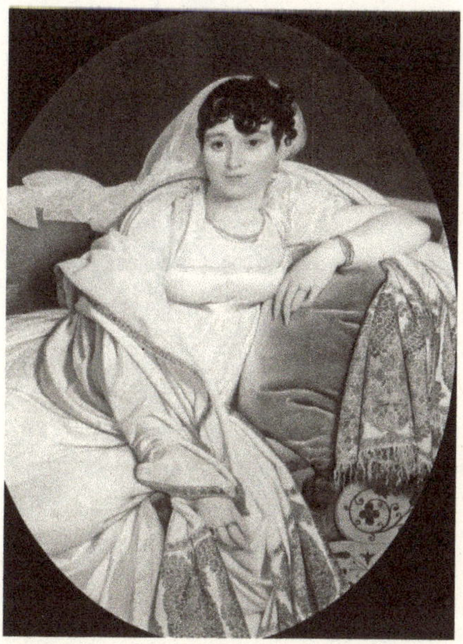

Portrait of Madame Rivière by Ingres.

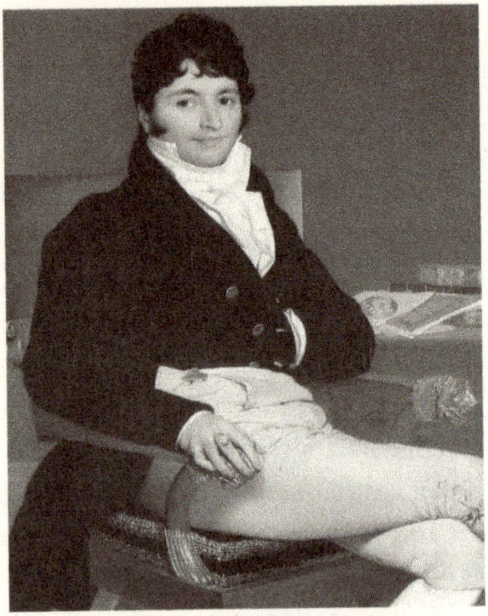
Portrait of Monsieur Rivière by Ingres.

but also deprived of the older painter's complete sincerity.

Unfortunately, the portrait of Madame de Vaucay does not belong to the Louvre, though another one can be found there which recalls it a little, and justifies the wall of the deplorable hall it honours: the portrait of Madame Rivière, sitting on an azure couch and staring at you, motionless, from beneath her curls of brown hair. Here again, the artist's fidelity sollicits us. The flesh is like mother-of-pearl, without flaw, smooth; the shawl which is next to her is stippled like an Indian watercolour; but this woman breathes and her eyes are disquieting; she lives a frozen life, so to speak, like Madame de Vaucay; she's been brought back from the dead and is still a little cold: it's by the magic of the eye that Ingres animates his figurines and infuses them with a mysteriousness that one modern artist, Odilon Redon, also obtains, frequently through clever distortions of the pupil.

One could also take note, in the State Room, of the portrait of Monsieur Rivière, painted dab by dab, a trifle fanciful, moreover, but already relapsing a little into the class of those works produced in his studio, by means of which Ingres so often got business.

In short, five or six canvases by Delacroix and one by Ingres might justify the baying clamour that the opening of the new gallery has given rise to. As for me, I am especially glad to see it reinaugurated because its shininess and its gold frames attract the tramping mass of visitors who pile in there, and leave the corridors, in which admirable Italian and Flemish Primitives are crammed, empty, and which now makes it possible for me to contemplate them at my leisure, without being disturbed.

*

BIANCHI

Never have I seen a copyist setting up his easel in front of this painting. No one, out of the few stray visitors to the gallery of Italian Primitives in the Louvre, stops in front of this work hoisted onto a partition wall, in a corner by the door. The very artist who created it, Francesco Bianchi, is unknown. According to Lancilotti,[8] he is supposed to have been born in 1447 and died in 1510. Vasari, who buries him in just four lines, states that he was active as a painter in 1481. Even his name remains uncertain. Some call him 'Bianchi Ferrara', others 'il Frare', others 'Brother Francesco'. All agree to confirm that he was Correggio's teacher, but if we accept the date of his death as being authentic, he would have died when his disciple was just sixteen![9] Biographies are silent about his works, which are now lost. Although all the artistic scribblers[10] go into ecstacies over Raphael's dull mediocrities, none of them even seems to suspect that Bianchi was a unique personality. Where did he come from? What was his life like? Nobody knows. What school did he belong to? School of Modena, says Vasari; School of Lombardy, says a catalogue; School of Ferrara, claims another. And then everyone passes on, happy to get back to the well-trodden path and rediscover the time-worn praises devoted to the triumphant Correggio, his hesitant pupil.

The Louvre possesses a single picture by Bianchi,[11] and for me this canvas gives off some delightful emanations, those of doleful

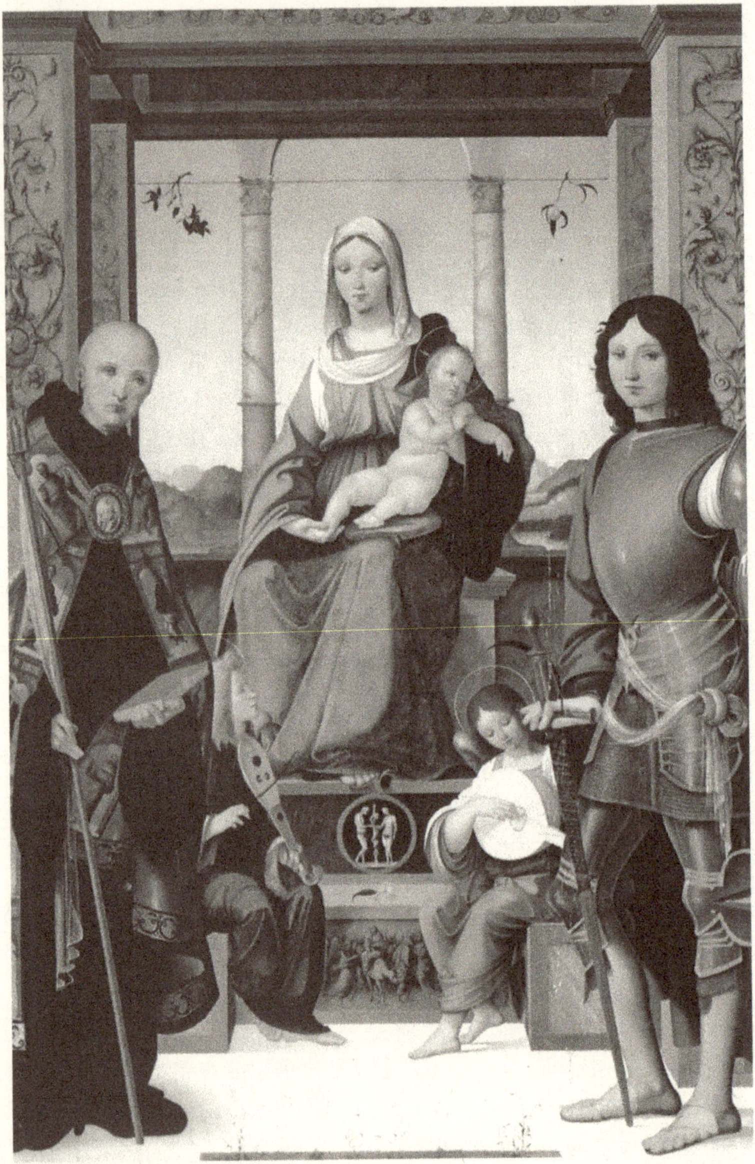

The Virgin and Child, Surrounded by Saint Benedict, Saint Quentin and Two Angels, now attributed to Francesco Marmitta.

obsessions, of surreptitious sacrilege, of troubled prayer.

The layout of this work is this: the Virgin, seated on a throne, holds in her arms an infant Jesus adorned with slender bracelets, his naked flesh squeezed under his chin by the chain of a gold necklace. Behind her, between two pilasters on which spiralling golden stems climb, is a distant landscape, traversed by a river and scattered with the rounded summits of mountains in a calm sky; at the foot of the throne, a seraph in a green dress plays the theorbo, another, in a pink dress, plays the viol. On each side of the frame, standing, are two extraordinary faces: that of an old man dressed in an abbot's habit, holding in his hand a book with a clasp, bound in red; and that of a young man dressed in knight's armour, staring out, his hand resting on a sword with a handle in the shape of a cross.

According to tradition, confirmed by the opinion of hagiographers, the old man is Saint Benedict, and the young man Saint Quentin.

The imposing appearance of the old man, livid and bald with a rigid face, his staring eyes, his priestly and princely appearance, is, indeed, appropriate to that formidable saint, the patient sower who ploughed fallow souls and germinated in them the monastic harvests of his great Order. The book he holds in his slender fingers, in his methodical hands, contains the rules that he promulgated, rules that, whether reformed or unchanged, still weigh heavily on thousands of people throughout the West, under the discipline of the cloisters.

The look on his face, so sad, so profound, so clear, and across which passes the recurring memory of terrible struggles, could be that of the man who took refuge in the desert of Subiaco,[12] and who, groaning with anguish and consumed by carnal temptation, rolled around in the green embers of nettles and brambles.

We can equally understand his haughty, despondent smile. Indeed, the line of his hard mouth hints at the overwhelming task assumed by this Director of divine disputations, this Caretaker of heavenly dependencies on earth, this Steward of the estates of the soul. The dead smile on his lips can also be explained when one recalls the hatred that was directed towards him, especially the attacks by that priest who wanted to poison him and who tried to pervert his monks as they prayed, with the sight of girls whose pale nudities were revealed through seductive dances in the garden of the very monastery he had founded.

The complex expression on this face is therefore understandable; but how is one to characterise the disturbing figure of Saint Quentin, an ephebe of indeterminate sex, a hybrid of mysterious beauty, with long brown hair parted down the middle of his forehead and flowing in waves over his iron-clad throat? If it weren't for his feet – which rather than being inserted in armoured sabatons are bare and wearing sandals attached by straps to the bottom of his feet – one would think it was the traditional uniform of Ariosto's heroine, Bradamante,[13] or of Saint George.

What is one to think of that adorable head, whose features are veiled by an inextinguishable melancholy? What is one to think of those clear eyes, whose faded blue is as impenetrable as the depths of a muddy pool? These aren't the despondent eyes, the pure eyes, the eyes like spring water, limpid and cold, of Saint Benedict, they are eyes burned by temptations succumbed to, these are pupils like agitated waters that reflect, when they become still again, the autumnal red of the sky, these are belligerent eyes ill-pacified by an act of penance after committing a sin. And the saint's whole appearance makes one dream. That boyish form, those immature hips, that girl's neck, with its flesh as white as the pith of an elder tree, that mouth with lips that sabotage, that slender waist, those furtive fingers straying over a weapon, that swell of the breastplate which bulges in the place of breasts and hides the plunging neckline of the bust, that undershirt which one glimpses under the armpit, open between the shoulder and the gorget, even that little girl's blue ribbon tied under the chin, obsess. All the frantic compromises of Sodom seem to have been consented to by this androgyne, whose insinuating beauty, now a cause of pain, reveals itself already purified, as if transfigured by the slow approach of God.

Because it hasn't yet happened for him, that burning of the soul that melts and flows into the Lord; that perfect state of ecstasy, in which the mind intoxicates itself with the delights of quintessential existence, has not been experienced by this androgyne, whose lack of restraint has doubtless not been sufficiently restrained by remorse. The inconsolable distress of his countenance attests to it. It seems that the Renaissance is born in this attitude, which displays an intermediate stage of the soul which the Middle Ages, more absolute, had suppressed.

But all these comprehensible ideas, while they can be applied to saints who, after being imprisoned in that exquisite lepers' colony of the flesh, were suddenly illuminated by grace, become meaningless when you try to apply them to St. Quentin. Neither the martyrologies, nor the monograph by Abbé Mathieu[14] discuss a hermaphrodite in iron armour, a knight who, after having been plagued by lustful desires, dies under the weight of his grief. Legend simply represents him as the son of a Roman senator who came to Amiens[15] to proclaim his God, and who Varus, the prefect of Gaul under Diocletian, had tortured.

Tillemont[16] relates the successive stages of his torture. He was first hanged on pulleys and stretched in such a way that his dislocated knees hung loose; he was then flogged with short chains, then his back was prodded with flaming torches kindled with pitch, and his mouth filled with a paste mixed with quicklime.

These preludes over, the executioner wanted to revive him, so he put him in a cellar. Assuaged by the cold darkness, he recovered, and so the torturer pierced him from the neck to the thighs with two sharpened iron bars, then he hammered nails under his fingernails, and, finally, he pierced him with long spikes, one of which, poorly directed, penetrated his brain and put an end to his martyrdom.

Now nothing either in the face or the attributes of the saint recalls the circumstances of this torture. The subject of the painting thus remains mysterious, and what adds still more to the enigma of the scene is the sorrowful and noble face of the Virgin, with her downcast eyes, eyes that one senses are like those of Saint Quentin, limpid on the surface but troubled in their depths. What's more, none of the individual figures helps to provide an explanation of the group as a whole. Indifferent to the Madonna and the infant Jesus, who smiles and plays, the saints stare sadly in front of them and no link seems to connect these two noble figures, whose lives haunt and torment you.

And then you realise that they all resemble each other. One might say of Saint Benedict that he was the father of Mary and of Saint Quentin, sister and brother, and that the little angel dressed in pink playing the *viola d'amore*, is the child of the diabolical coupling of these saints. The old man is a father who has resisted the lure of an unspeakable debauchery, but whose son and daughter have yielded to the temptations of incest, and deem life too short to expiate the terrifying delights of their crime; the child implores forgiveness for his origins, and sings mournful litanies to divert the sovereign wrath of the Most High.

Such is the meaning, perhaps, of this painting, in which the red-haired and sinuous perversity of the Renaissance is already starting to spring from the rigid innocence of the Middle Ages. No doubt Bianchi, like most artists of his time, has simply painted the family of the donor who had commissioned this work to adorn a chapel; he has dressed up in religious costume city councillors worn down by the disappointments of happiness and the pleasures of vice; if one accepts this presumption of a simple series of portraits, what a superhuman feeling, what a subtle and imperious skill Bianchi has managed to imbue his work with! Art collectors endlessly praise the wavering smile of the *Mona Lisa*; but how much more mysterious, more commanding, are those closed lips, august and heartbroken, sweet and wicked, vivid and dead; how empty the predictable, certain eyes in da Vinci's painting seem if one compares them to these pupils, which like the waters of a rock pool or a stream struck by lightning are purified after a storm.

Inexplicable, in spite of everything, this canvas with its flat and bruised colour, its solemn and elegant design, its infinite sadness, its inexpressible pleasure of art, drags you out of your present life and insinuates disturbing reveries in your mind, as, driven away from that solitary room by the lateness of the hour, you descend again onto the Place du Carrousel and return to the crushing hustle and bustle of a public street.

Notes

I

1 In the original Huysmans refers to the now defunct card game, '*bouillote*', which involved betting on, and typically bluffing about, the strength of the cards in your hand. Many see it as a forerunner of poker.

2 Georges Ohnet (1848-1918) was a prolific French novelist. An admirer of George Sand, he was firmly in the idealist camp and against the realism of the Naturalists. Albert Delpit (1849-1893) was another prolific, popular novelist and dramatist whose work first appeared in a review established by the Romantic novelist Alexandre Dumas.

3 Huysmans had written a laudatory article about Émile Zola's controversial novel, *L'Assommoir* (*The Drinking Den*) when it first appeared in serial form in 1876.

4 Francisque Sarcey (1827-1899) was the drama critic for *Le Temps* for thirty-two years, from 1867 until his death, his reviews being printed every Monday. He was hostile to Naturalism and was seen by many of the younger writers as a defender of bourgeois ideals. The nuances of Huysmans' insult is hard to capture in translation, the final phrase reads '*…les éjaculations théâtrales de ses Lundis*' (literally: 'the theatrical ejaculations of his Mondays').

5 In the original Huysmans uses the untranslatable term '*fouille-au-pot*', which was slang for a man who was more involved in household duties, such as cleaning and cooking, than was considered manly. The perjorative implication here, as elsewhere, is of a kind of effeminacy. The term can be found in Alfred Delvau's 1866 *Dictionnaire de langue verte* (*Dictionary of Slang*).

6 The Delacroix exhibition at the École des Beaux Arts, and the Bastien-Lepage exhibition at the Hôtel de Chimay ran concurrently in 1885. The Hôtel de Chimay was a former townhouse which, due to its

proximity, served as an extension of the École des Beaux Arts.

7 Paul Siraudin (1813-1883) was a prolific author of vaudevilles and also the owner of confectionery shop. He concocted the pastille that inspired des Esseintes' erotic flashback in *À rebours* (*Against Nature*).

8 In the original, Huysmans feminises the two men's names in order to emphasise the 'lightweight' nature of their work.

9 In the original, Huysmans writes '*baladiner avec des thèses soumises et des idées en carte*', a difficult phrase to translate literally. There is a strong overtone here of venery, '*baladine*' was slang for a woman of easy virtue, and '*une fille soumise*' and '*filles en carte*' were common descriptions for types of women involved in prostitution, the former being a kept women and the latter, a licensed prostitute.

10 Ernest Renan (1823-1892) was a writer and historian of religion who was perhaps best known for his 1863 book *La Vie de Jesus* (*The Life of Jesus*) which caused controversy not just because it attempted to humanise Jesus – Renan denied the truth of miracles – but also because he claimed that Jesus had purified himself of Jewish traits.

11 Between 1874 and 1878 Puvis de Chavannes painted six murals for the Parisian church of Sainte Geneviève, today known as the Panthéon, located in the fifth arrondissement of Paris.

12 i.e. The annual Salon. The Palais de l'Industrie et des Beaux Arts on the Avenue des Champs-Élysées was built for the Exposition Universelle of 1855. It was demolished in 1896 and is now the site of the Petit Palais and the Grand Palais.

13 Goupil & Cie, founded by Adolphe Goupil, was one of the leading art dealers of the nineteenth century. Moreau's show was the first and only exhibition that was devoted solely to his work in his lifetime.

14 One of the unique – and some people would say attractive – features of Parisian urban planning was the way in which trees lining the roads were encircled by a cast-iron grate, thus allowing the earth surrounding the tree to be watered naturally.

15 Hippolyte Taine (1828-1893) was a French critic and historian, closely associated with sociological theories of positivism and naturalism. His view that a work of literature was a product of the times – the 'environment' or the 'social milieu' – in which it was written, was a major influence Zola's literary Naturalism and his conception of sociological positivism.

16 A reference to the eighth and last 'Impressionist' exhibition held between 15 May to 15 June 1886 in rooms above the restaurant La Maison Dorée, situated at the corner of the Rue Laffitte and the

Boulevard des Italiens in Paris. Degas exhibited fifteen works, ten of which constituted the series of pictures of women at their *toilette*.

17 '*sabouleuse*' in the original, a neologism coined by Huysmans from the verb *sabouler*, to beat.

18 '*cul-de-jatte*' in the original, an expression Huysmans used frequently but which doesn't have an exact English equivalent. Essentially *cul-de-jatte* (*cul* meaning arse, *jatte* meaning bowl) referred to those, usually ex-soldiers, who had lost both legs and who consequently were forced to wheel themselves around in a small trolley or cart in order to beg.

19 A type of decorative pattern consisting of a white background on which a pastoral theme or an arrangement of flowers is repeated.

20 The collection of paintings that Louis La Caze bequeathed to the Louvre in 1869 constituted one of the most important collections of eighteenth-century French art received by the Museum. Jean-Baptiste Regnault's *Les Trois Grâces* (*The Three Graces*) was seen as one of the exemplars of neoclassical art.

II

1 Paul Albert Bartholomé's 1884 painting, *La Récréation dans la cour d'une école* (*Playtime in a School Courtyard*), is a companion piece to the more well-known *Jeu de furet* (*Find the Ring*), a game in which players form a circle and pass a ring from hand to hand, usually along a string, while the player in the centre has to guess which hand the ring is in.

2 From the Latin *candor* ('whiteness').

3 Georges Petit (1856-1920) opened his large gallery in the Rue de Sèze in 1882. Raffaëlli was among a number of Independent artists favoured by Petit, and his series of landscapes based on successive trips to Jersey were exhibited at the gallery in 1886 and 1887.

4 Issue No. 50 of *Paris-Illustré* (1 August 1886) included seventeen illustrations by Raffaëlli, of which Huysmans refers to just one: '*Quadrille naturaliste aux Ambassadeurs*'. I have corrected Huysmans rendition of the title of the series, which he gives as '*Paris-Café-Concert*'.

5 A type of flat iron. It had a police badge and the words '*Le Gendarme*' (policeman) cast into its top.

6 In the 1903 edition '*mouillé*' (damp) appears as '*moulé*' (moulded).

7 Huysmans uses the word '*déshérences*', the legal term for an escheat or the reversion of a property to the state when the owner dies without a legal heir.

8 In the original, Huysmans uses the term '*la peche muet*' (literally 'the mute sin'). In one of his notebooks, he elaborated that '*masturbation:*

peche muet', which Jean-Marie Seillan allies to a reference to Durtal and Madame Chantelouve in *Là-bas*. However, the term has a broader and longer history as a veiled reference to sodomy, perhaps its most famous locution in this regard being 'the love that dare not speak its name'. Either way, whether Huysmans is hinting at the woman's self-absorbtion or her lesbian tendency, the use of the term shows his methodology of imagining a narrative from the picture he is looking at, a narrative which is not something inherent to the picture but which is brought to the picture by the viewer.

9 Charles Sedelmeyer (1837-1925) was an Austrian art dealer, collector, and publisher active in Paris from 1866, with a gallery at 6 Rue de la Rochefoucauld. The Tissot exhibition, entitled *Quinze tableaux sur la femme à Paris* ('Fifteen paintings of women in Paris') ran from 19 April to 15 June 1885.

10 The reference to Savoyard may be to Tissot's ancestry. Although the painter was born in Nantes, his father was from the Franche Compté region, close to the Swiss border. The female counterpart to the stereotypical British male, John Bull, was not commonly used at this period but it would become so as the feminist movement gathered pace towards the end of the nineteenth century.

11 In the original, Huysmans uses the phrase '*Madame Pète-sec*' (literally 'Madame Dry-Fart'), *pète-sec* being used to refer to people who were too bossy or abrupt.

12 Théophile Pierre Wagner, his painting, *Cirque* (*Circus*) is now lost. Wagner was a circus acrobat as well as a painter, and formed a double act with the aristocratic trapeze-artist Comte Hubert de la Rochefoucauld, who performed at the Cirque Molier in Paris. Somewhat coincidentally, a painting by James Tissot which included a portait of Rochefoucauld – and presumably Wagner – sitting on their trapeze bars in a crowded circus appeared in Tissot's 1885 exhibition, which Huysmans saw and wrote about. When Huysmans originally wrote his piece about Wagner – who had studied at the École des Beaux Arts but was an Impressionist in style – which was published in *La Cravache Parisienne* (4 August 1888), he claims he did not know the painter's identity, but by the time *Certains* was published he had discovered who Wagner was. Nevertheless, he seemed to prefer to maintain the fiction of the unknown artist, partly perhaps to emphasise the critic's role as someone who could identify genuine works of art that were overlooked by the ignorant crowd. Ironically, Wagner's name doesn't feature in the *Catalogue raisonée du Salon des Indépendants, 1884-2000*.

13 The first Salon des Artistes Indépendants opened on 1 December 1884 at the Pavillion de la Ville de Paris (near the Palais de l'Industrie) on the Champs Elysées. The exhibition featured works by Georges Seurat, Paul Signac, Odilon Redon and Albert Dubois-Pillet – all of whom were among the original founders of the Société des Artistes Indépendants – as well as by Armand Guillaumin, Charles Angrand, Paul Cézanne, Paul Gauguin, Henri de Toulouse-Lautrec, and Vincent van Gogh.

14 Chevet's was a high-quality food shop and caterer near the Palais-Royal ('Suppliers to Her Majesty the Queen of England' as the company boasted on its advertisements). The chef Auguste Escoffier worked as a general manager there for eight months.

15 Huysmans was not alone in attributing the unconventional use of colour in the work of Cézanne and the Impressionists to diseases of the eye. Although it is easy now to ridicule these views, at the time they were given at least some credence by the latest scientific research in ophthalmology. In *L'Art moderne,* for example, Huysmans' referenced Charcot's studies on colour perception and aberrations in the brain as well as other scientific papers on the subject. Recent studies have shown that some of the Impressionists did indeed suffer from problems with their eysight – Cézanne, Pissarro and Renoir from myopia, Degas from retinopathy, and Mary Cassatt and Monet from cataracts in later life, although obviously the impact this may have had on their painting remains highly debatable.

16 This was the third Impressionist exhibition, which ran from 1 to 30 April 1877 at 6, Rue Le Peletier. Among the 241 works on show, Cézanne exhibited fives still lifes, four landscapes, two portraits, a study and three watercolours. Many critics took the opportunity to make fun of the work on display. Roger Ballu, in *La Chronique des arts et de la curiosité* (No. 15, 14 April 1877), wrote of Monet and Cézanne's canvases that 'They are laughable and yet also lamentable. They reveal a profound ignorance of design, of composition, and of colour. When children amuse themselves with paper and coloured pencils they do better.'

17 The statue, *Gloria victis,* 'glory to the vanquished', by Antonin Mercié, was a tribute to the soldiers who died in the Franco-Prussian war, and won a medal at the 1874 Paris Salon.

18 In the original, Huysmans uses the word '*maraudeuse*' (a woman who steals or pilfers). This would later became a slang word for a prostitute, though it's not absolutely clear if it had acquired this meaning when Huysmans was writing.

19 A character from Balzac's novel *La Cousine Bette* (*Cousin Bette*), Baron

Hector Hulot sacrifices his family fortune and his reputation for the sake of the mercenary widow Valérie Marneff, a courtesan who subsequently discards him for a richer merchant, Célestin Crevel.

III

1 Jean-Charles Adolphe Alphand (1817-1891), a French civil engineer. In 1854, Baron Haussmann hired Alphand as chief engineer for the Bois de Boulogne, a role that expanded into director of the newly-formed parks department, and subsequently led to Alphand becoming the director of public works in Paris.

2 Huysmans' reference is a little disingenuous, as the black-suited Pierrot appeared in a pantomime he and Léon Hennique published in 1881, *Pierrot sceptique*, and which Chéret had illustrated.

3 Henri Agoust (1840-1901), a French juggler and mime artist. He met the Hanlon-Lees during their tour of America in 1865, and gave them the idea of adapting the pantomimes of the famous mime, Jean-Gaspard Deburau. Agoust, who wrote pantomimes himself, would become a leading member of the Hanlon-Lees and was influential in the development of the inventive, knockabout comedies which the Hanlon-Lees became famous for. See note below.

4 Perhaps the best-known troupe of English acrobats of the nineteenth century, the Hanlons comprised the six Hanlon brothers and their mentor, the celebrated acrobat John Lees. After the death of Lees in 1855, the troupe adopted the name Hanlon-Lees in his honour. Huysmans had written enthusiastically about them ten years previously in 'Les Folies-Bergère en 1879' in his book *Croquis parisiennes* (*Parisian Sketches*), published in 1880.

5 Georges Duval (1847-1919) was a French journalist and playwright. His *Paris qui rit* was published in 1886, but copies with Chéret's distinctive cover intact are now hard to find.

6 Huysmans was always derogatory about people from the south of France and southern Europe in general, here using the word '*gnaff*', meaning a stunted object, to belittle them.

7 In the original, Huysmans uses the word '*trottin*', slang for a young girl working in a milliner's.

8 The Paris Hippodrome, or the Hippodrome de l'Alma, was an immense building, much of it in iron, capable of holding 6,000 spectators. It was used for horse racing, as well as other mass events. It opened in 1877, but was forced to close in 1892 because the owner of the land refused to renew the lease.

9 Guillaume Joseph Rousselle (1743-1807), also known as 'Cadet Rousselle', was a French bailiff from Auxerre who became celebrated for his eccentricity in an eponymous popular song.

10 Les Frères Bozza (The Bozza Brothers) were an Italian burlesque troupe – or 'musical clowns' as they were described in the press of the time – consisting of five brothers who found unusual ways to make music. *The Music of the Future* made use of kitchen utensils and equipment, and played during 1881 at the Folies-Bergère. The troupe's subsequent show, which ran in 1882 at the Cirque d'Été on the Champs-Élysses, was entitled *The Diabolical Orchestra.*

11 Huysmans uses the term '*parisianisme*', a concept which has no real counterpart in English. Huysmans is perhaps influenced here by Balzac

12 *Les Mystères de Paris* by Euguene Sue was originally published in 1842-43, but the edition with Chéret's illustration was that published by Jules Rouff in 1885. The same publisher also put out *Le Drame de Pontcharra* by Paul Saunière in 1886.

13 Théodore Duret (1838-1927) was a French journalist, author and art critic. He was one of the first advocates of Courbet, Manet, and the Impressionists. The book Huysmans mentions, *Critique d'Avant Garde* (Paris: Charpentier, 1885), has a section on Whistler in which Duret states – incorrectly – that Whistler was born in Baltimore, rather than Lowell, Massachusetts. But Huysmans must have had another source of information as the details about Whistler's father and West-Point don't appear in Duret.

14 Huysmans wasn't always careful in the spelling of people's names, but his consistent misspelling of Whistler's name is quite extraordinary. Not only does the artist's name appear as 'Wisthler' throughout *Certains*, when Huysmans dedicated a copy of *À rebours* to him, he misspelled it in exactly the same way.

15 'Edgard Poe' in the original.

16 Fernand Desnoyers (1826-1869) was a French critic. The passage quoted comes from *Salon des Refusés* (Paris: Dutil, 1863), pp 27-8.

17 Pseudonym used by the art critic Théophile Thoré (1807-1869).

18 *Fors Clavigera* (spelled '*Fors Clovigera*' in the original) was not a review as such, but a series of 'letters' which Ruskin addressed to the 'workmen and labourers of Great Britain', and published in the form of pamphlets during the 1870s.

19 Author's original footnote: "At exhibitions in London a register is open in which the painter writes down the price he would like to charge for the work."

20 After the lawsuit, Whistler went bankrupt. In 1881, Lady Meux offered Whistler his first significant commission after the bankruptcy for a full-length portrait, known as *Arrangement in Black, No. 5* (*Portrait of Lady Meux*). Meux was a former prostitute who became a Victorian socialite after marrying the London brewer, Sir Henry Meux.

21 i.e. the Georges Petit gallery, see note 3 on page 223.

22 The full text of Thomas Carlyle's *Sartor Resartus* had not been translated into French at the time Huysmans was writing, so his quotation is not particularly accurate. The actual sentence in English runs: 'Silence and Secrecy! Altars might still be raised to them.' I have adapted the version that Huysmans most likely read, that contained in Émile Montégut's 'Thomas Carlyle, sa vie et ses écrits', in *Revue des Deux Mondes* (vol. 2, 1849). 'Des autels devraient être élevés encore aujourd'hui au silence et à la solitude, et un culte universel devrait être institué pour leur rendre hommage.'

23 Dr William Crookes (1832-1919) was a British chemist and physicist who made genuine advances in the field of spectroscopy. For a time he was also interested in spiritualism and attempted to investigate it scientifically, though in this he was less successful. Despite his claims to scientific rigour he was somewhat gullible – and possibly also short-sighted – which led him to proclaim as genuine mediums who were subsequently proved to be fraudulent.

24 It is difficult to identify the exact paintings being referred to here as Whistler did so many with similar titles and Huysmans was not always accurate in his French transcriptions of them. I have used the actual titles of Whistler's work that most closely correspond to Huysmans' French versions.

25 Whistler's lecture was first delivered at Prince's Hall, Piccadilly, on 20 February 1885 and published as 'Mr Whistler's 'Ten O'Clock'" in 1888. Stéphane Mallarmé's translation was published in *La Revue indépendante*, May 1888, under the title 'Le "Ten o'clock" de M. Whistler'.

IV

1 This seems to be a reference to a case that was making the news in the 1880s. W. T. Stead had exposed a child prostitution scandal in a series of articles entitled 'The Maiden Tribute of Modern Babylon', published in *The Pall Mall Gazette* in July 1885. The articles, which detailed the abduction, procurement and sale of young English virgins to Continental brothels, caused a huge outcry. Villiers de l'Isle Adam

subsequently wrote a story based on the affair called 'Le Sadisme anglais', which he dedicated to Huysmans when it was reprinted in *Histoires insolites* ('Strange Stories') in 1888. Villiers made a specific point about English hypocrisy, referring to the thousands of people who had mentioned the victims of 'the lubricious hypocrisy of their compatriots', but that 'the strange thing was, it was only this hypocrisy that seemed to outrage them!'

2 Huysmans refers specifically to 'lupulin' and 'camphore' in the original, but as their medical properties are not commonly known now I have substituted more comprehensible terms.

3 '*Délectation morose*' in the original. The Latin concept on which it is based, *delectatio morosa*, is found in Thomas Aquinas' *Summa theologica* and can be defined as 'the habit of dwelling with enjoyment on evil thoughts'.

4 Huysmans takes his definition of *delectatio morosa* not from Aquinas but from Léo Taxil's *Les Pornographes Sacres: la confession et les confesseurs* ('The Holy Pornographers: Confession and Confessors'), published in 1882. Léo Taxil was the pseudonym of Gabriel Jogand-Pagès (1854-1907) a writer who, after spending his childhood in a Jesuit seminary, became disillusiond with Catholicism which he saw as socially harmful. Taxil's book included extracts from a treatise on lust called *Moechialogie, ou traite des peches contre le sixième et neuvième commandements* (1845) written by a priest and Trappist monk, Pierre-Jean-Corneille Debreyne (1786-1867). Debreyne also has a section on 'morose delectation', but unlike Taxil's his definition is in Latin. Huysmans had already referred to Debreyne's book and the notion of 'morose delectation' in Chapters III and IX of *Against Nature*.

5 Huysmans frequently uses the word '*hennissement*' (literally the sound of a horse neighing) as a synonym for the carnal act. As it is literally untranslatable, I have used the term 'ejaculate' which has both a sexual meaning and an old-fashioned meaning of an irrepressible cry.

6 In French the part of the library reserved for such works is popularly know as '*l'enfer*' (hell).

7 Giulio Romano (1499-1546), was an Italian painter and architect, the pupil of Raphael, who help define the Mannerist style. Huysmans refers to him on account of his suite of erotic drawings, *I modi* ('The Way' also sometimes known in English as 'The Sixteen Pleasures'). Although Romano's work was destroyed, Marcantonio Raimondi (c.1470-1534), an Italian engraver, produced copies of them in two editions published in the 1520s, the first of which was also destroyed by the Catholic

church. Copies of the originals were also made by Agostino Carracci (1557-1602) whose versions survived.

8 Johannes Torrentius was the pseudonym of the Dutch painter Johannes Symonsz van der Beeck (1589-1644). Charles I was an admirer of his work and offered him exile in England when the artist was imprisoned and tortured after he was accused of being a Rosicrucian and an atheist. Charles refers to van der Beeck's 'bawdy pictures' but none of these survive, as almost all of his work was burned.

9 '*Place de Grève*' in the original. This was a public square in the 4th arrondissement of Paris, now called the Place de l'Hôtel de Ville. It was the site of many public executions.

10 'Adamite' refers to an obscure religious sect that believed it had recovered Adam's original innocence. In its thirteen-century incarnation in the Netherlands followers advocated free love and, as the historian Norman Cohn put it, 'declared that the chaste were unworthy to enter the Messianic kingdom'.

11 There seems to be some confusion about Huysmans' reference in the original to 'Carême' here. In his critical edition, *Félicien Rops* (Le Livre et l'estampe, No.128, 1987), André Guyaux states that it refers to Marie-Antoine Carême (1784-1833) who was famous as a chef, but who doesn't seem to have painted or illustrated anything that could be termed licentious. In her translation of Huysmans' article on Rops, Rosemary Lloyd states that it refers to Claude-François Carême (1709-96), but this latter is so little known and his work so rare, it is difficult to believe Huysmans was referring to him – and in any case there is no indication that his work was pornographic. Volume IV of the new *Oeuvres complètes* (Classiques Garnier, 2019), which includes an incredibly thorough critical edition of *Certains*, plays it safe and doesn't give any information about Carême at all. In fact, critics seem to have been thrown off the scent by Huysmans' carelessness in orthography, in that 'Carême' was a variant name for Jacques-Philippe Caresme (1734-1796), a French painter and copperplate engraver. Unlike the two previous candidates, Caresme (or Carême) did indeed paint a number of lightly licentious works with eroticised subject matter. As he is contemporaneous with Baudouin (1723-1769) it is almost certain that Caresme is the painter Huysmans is referring to, so I have inserted his name here.

12 The print is titled '*Carnival at Venice*'.

13 Auguste Poulet-Malassis (1825-1878) was a French publisher and printer. His name is frequently linked to that of Charles Baudelaire, whose

work he published. After being prosecuted for debt, Poulet-Malassis fled to Belgium where he published a number of licentious or erotic literary works.

14 *Le Théâtre gaillard* (*Bawdy Plays*) was a collection of erotic and scatalogical plays that dated from the eighteenth century, edited and published by Poulet-Malassis in 1865, and for which Rops did the frontispiece.

15 Dominique Vivant, Baron Denon (1747-1825) was a French artist, writer, diplomat, author, and archaeologist. *Point de lendemain* (1777) was a short novella emblematic of libertine literature. Poulet-Malassis published a version in 1867 with a frontispiece by Rops.

16 *Le Parnasse satyrique* was a collection of poems dating from the seventeenth century. It is best known in the edition by Poulet-Malassis of 1864, with its frontispiece by Rops.

17 In Greek mythology Bacchantes were the female worshippers of Dionysus or Bacchus, the god of wine and fertility.

18 Joseph-Albert-Alexandre Glatigny, known as Albert Glatigny (1839-73), was a French poet, writer, actor and playwright who died at the age of 33, hence Huysmans' use of the word 'poor'. His collection of erotic poems, *Joyeusetés galantes et autres* (*Galant Joys and Other Pleasures*), was published by Poulet-Malassis in 1866 under the pseudonym Vidame Bonaventure de la Braguette (*braguette* being French for codpiece).

19 Alfred Delvau (1825-67) was a French journalist and writer. Delvau also worked as a lexicographer and his *Dictionnaire érotique moderne* (1864), for which he was prosecuted, was published in Brussels by Jean Gay.

20 Curiously, the otherwise thorough critical edition of *Certains* contained in Volume IV of *Oeuvres complètes* (Classiques Garnier, 2019) gives no explanation for this sequence of titles, which in fact aren't titles at all. The 'books' that Huysmans gives here are actually part of the pseudonymous publishing information used by Poulet-Malassis on the books' title pages to protect himself and their authors from prosecution. So '*Partout et nulle part*' ('Everywhere and nowhere') figured instead of the place of publication on four titles that Rops illustrated, including *Les Quatre petits poèmes libertines* by Louis Protat; '*Eleuthéropolis*' (effectively a pseudonym for Brussels) was used on two books, including *H.B. par un des quarante* by Prosper Merimée (1864); while '*Lampasque*' served a similar function on the title page of *Amours et Priapées* by Henri Cantel. In the original, after the first 'title' Huysmans included the initials '*S.L.N.D.*', a French bookseller's shorthand for '*sans lieu ni date*' (i.e. neither the place or the date of publication appear in the book), which usually signalled that it had been produced illegally, or

was seeking to evade laws governing the publication of material deemed to be obscene. But since none of the books Huysmans is alluding to used these initials, it is curious why they appear. It is possible that Huysmans wrote, or meant to write, the initials that do feature on the books mentioned, '*S.P.Q.R.*', which served as Rops' pseudonym, and that '*S.L.N.D.*' was simply a slip of the pen by Huysmans or by the printer. I have used '*S.P.Q.R.*' here as that is consistent with the other references. I have also slightly clarified the text.

21 Théodore Hannon (1851-1916), a Belgian poet and painter. Huysmans had contributed a preface to the first edition of Hannon's *Les Rimes de joie* in 1881, but the preface was removed in subsequent editions, perhaps because Huysmans made too much of Baudelaire's influence on Hannon for the younger poet's taste. Although the engraving Huysmans referred to was withheld, the book nevertheless carried a frontispiece by Rops.

22 *Les Sonnets du docteur*, published anonymously in 1884 by Georges Camuset (1840-1885), an opthalmologist who becamse better known for his poems. The book's frontispiece by Rops is also known as '*La Jolie fille en chemise*'.

23 Henriette Doucé was an editor who, with the publisher Jean Gay, formed Gay et Doucé, a publishing house based in Brussels that specialised in erotic literature. Jean Gay had published Huysmans' first novel, *Marthe, histoire d'une fille*, in 1876.

24 Rops maintained a *ménage à trois* with two sisters, Aurélie and Léontine Duluc, who ran a successful fashion house in Paris, Maison Duluc, in the 1880s and 1890s. They each bore him a child (one died at an early age) and they lived together for over twenty-five years, until his death in 1898.

25 '*Ephialtes*' in the original, from the Greek meaning 'nightmare', typically one in which the sleeper is attacked by a demon.

26 Jean Bodin (1530–1596) was a French jurist and political philosopher, but also an influential writer on demonology. His *De la démonomanie des sorciers* (*On Demonmania and Sorcerers*) appeared in 1580.

27 Martin Delrio (1551-1608), a Jesuit theologian. His *Disquisitiones Magicae* (*Magical Investigations*) first appeaered in Leuven in 1599.

28 Johann Joseph von Görres (1776–1848) was a German writer and theologian. His *Die christliche Mystik* (*Christian Mysticism*) was published in five volumes between 1836 and 1842, with the last two volumes being devoted to diabolical mysticism. It was translated into French as *La mystique divine, naturelle et diabolique* in 1854.

29 *Les Sataniques* (*Satanics*) comprised a series of five heliogravures by Rops produced in 1882.

30 *Les Diaboliques* (*The She-Devils*) was a collection of short stories by Jules Barbey d'Aurévilly (1808-1889), published in 1874. Each story centred on a woman who commits a crime or an act of violence.

31 Joséphin 'Sâr' Péladan (1858-1918) was a French novelist, a devout Catholic drawn to the occult and alchemy. He was interested in Rosicrucianism and in 1884, along with the esoteric poet and occultist Stanislas de Guaita (1861-1897), tried to resurrect the Rosicrucian Brotherhood.

32 A rogation was a solemn supplication consisting of the litany of the saints chanted on the three days before Ascension Day. Its use shows Huysmans' familiarity with some of the obscurer aspects of Catholic observance even before his conversion.

33 This was the frontispiece to Péladan's *L'Initiation sentimentale* (1887). I have used the title that figures on the engraving itself, rather than the form which Huysmans gives: *In lombis Diaboli virtus*.

34 Péladan's novel *La Vice suprême* was published in 1884, the same year as Huysmans' *À rebours*. The book blends romance and occultism, depicting the struggle of occult forces to destroy humanity.

35 This print seems to be '*La Femme et la Folie dominant la monde*'.

36 Although the title of the short story was published as '*La Dessous de cartes d'une partie de whist*', Huysmans gives the title as '*La Dessous d'une partie de wisth*'. As Rops himself gave the title in this form in a letter to Léon Evely in 1885 it is possible that Huysmans got the title directly from Rops. The story concerns the secret affair of a lady and an expert whist player, which leads to an horrific act.

V

1 Some of the irony of Huysmans' title is lost in translation as the French word '*prix*' can mean both 'prices' and 'prizes'. Here, he combines his sarcasm on these two targets – the prizes awarded by the State to painters he considered unworthy of merit, and the inflated prices of art bought by collectors he considered had no taste – which he considered were ruining art.

2 During the 1870-71 civil war, a hospital was established by the French War Department in the Jardin du Luxembourg. The wards were comprised of 22 wooden pavillions, each of which held 20 beds. A Senate report in 1884 authorised the use of funds to create a museum of contemporary art. It was built perpendicular to the Orangerie in the

Luxembourg (built by Alphonse de Gisors in 1839). The new wing was opened on 1 April 1886.

3 See Section II, Note 1.

4 The sons of the banker James de Rothschild (1792-1868), Alphonse, Gustave and Edmond were known for their financial support of artists, museums and art schools. The Camondo family was a prominent European family of Jewish financiers and philanthropists who amassed a large collection of art which would subsequently become a Museum of Decorative Arts. Maurice de Hirsch (1831-96) was a German Jewish financier and philanthropist who set up charitable foundations to promote Jewish education and improve the lot of European Jewry. The inclusion of the name 'Judas' in the list is indicative of the era's growing tide of antisemitism.

5 In the original, Huysmans refers only to the name 'Morgan', but this was not, as one might assume – and as the notes to the new *Oeuvres Complètes* (Classiques Garnier, 2019) state – a reference to John Pierpont Morgan (1837-1913), the rich financier. Huysmans was actually referring to Edwin Denison Morgan (1811-1883), a successful wholesale grocer and bond merchant who became governor of New York and a United States senator. Morgan aquired an impressive collection of work by Europe artists such as Bouguereau, Vibert and Breton – all painters Huysmans detested – which was sold off when Morgan's estate was auctioned in 1886.

6 Henry Hilton (1824-1899), an American jurist and businessman who paid $66,000 for Meissonier's painting.

7 John Wanamaker (1838-1922) an American merchant who opened his first department store in 1861. He bought two paintings by Munkácsy – *Christ in Front of Pilate* for $150,000 and *Golgotha* for $175,000 – from the dealer Charles Sedelmeyer in 1886, making him the highest-paid artist in Europe at the time.

8 The massacre began in the night of 23–24 August 1572 (the eve of the feast of Bartholomew the Apostle), two days after King Charles IX's attempted assassination of Admiral Gaspard de Coligny, the military and political leader of the Huguenots. The massacre lasted for several weeks, spreading from Paris to other urban centres and the countryside. Estimates of the number of people killed vary from 5,000 to 30,000.

9 Théodore-Agrippa d'Aubigné (1552-1630), 'the epic poet of the Protestant cause', was a French poet, soldier, propagandist and chronicler. His poem *Les Tragiques* (1616) is regarded as his masterpiece.

10 Author's original footnote: "*Mosaize historie der Hebreeuwse kerke*,

Amsterdam, in-folios, undated."

11 Author's original footnote: "*Het Leerzaam Huisraad, etc,* Amsterdam, by de Erven van F. Houttuyn, in-18, 1771." The book was a practical, religiously-inspired manual for housewives. Luyken added moralistic verses to each of his images.

12 Luyken's *Des menschen begin, midden en einde* was published in 1754.

13 Berossus, a Hellenistic-era writer active in the third century BC. His most influential work was a history of Babylonia.

14 The *garuda* is a legendary bird or bird-like creature in Hindu, Buddhist and Jain mythology; *yali* is a mythical creature seen in many South Indian temples, often sculpted onto the pillars. It can be portrayed as part lion, part elephant and part horse. It has also been described as a leogryph (part lion and part griffin) with some bird-like features.

15 Typhon, the son of Gaia and Tartarus, was a monstrous serpentine giant, one of the deadliest creatures in Greek mythology. Typhon and his mate Echidna were the progenitors of many famous monsters of Greek mythology.

16 The Tarasque is a fearsome legendary dragon-like mythological hybrid from Provence, in southern France. It was tamed in a story about Saint Martha.

17 In the original, Huysmans uses the phrase '*Logeurs du bon Dieu*' ('the Good Lord's lodgers'), to refer to the masons who built the cathedrals, probably because itinerant artisans would be housed by monks during the period of the work.

18 In Greek mythology Stymphalian birds were man-eaters with beaks of bronze and sharp metallic feathers which they could launch at their victims.

19 Filariasis is a disease caused by several species of parasitic roundworms. It is spread by blood-feeding insects such as black flies and mosquitoes.

20 Moritz Wagner (1813-1887) was a German explorer, collector, geographer and natural historian. At the time Huysmans was writing only one of his books had been translated into French, *De la formation des espèces* (Paris: Doin, 1882), which dealt with the influence of geographical separation on evolution.

VI

1 The Grande salle du Conseil d'État was begun by Napoléon I and burnt down by the Communards on the 23 May 1871. The ruins were eventually demolished and a new train station was built in their place, the Gare d'Orsay. In the 1980s the station was converted into the

Musée d'Orsay, the French national museum for art created between 1848 and 1914.

2 The Musée de Cluny in Paris is the French national museum of the Middle Ages. It holds a large collection of objects, such as tapestries, ceramics and furniture, as well as sculptures and paintings spanning the Roman period to the Renaissance.

3 *Estelle et Némorin* was a pastoral written in 1788 by Jean-Pierre Claris de Florain (1755-1794). In 1876 it was turned into a popular opéra-comique by Louis-Auguste-Florimond Ronger (1825-1892), a composer more popularly known under the pseudonym Hervé, who was both friends with and a rival of Jacques Offenbach.

4 A *chaufferette*, a form of portable heater, was typically a rectangular box, either of metal or wood lined with metal, that included vents or holes so that the hot coals or embers it contained would radiate heat.

VII

1 The Palais du Trocadéro was built for the 1878 World's Fair. The Palace was comprised of a large concert hall with two wings and two towers. It's blending of different historical styles was not to Huysmans' taste. It was partly demolished and renovated in 1937.

2 Louis Philippe Napoléon, also referred to as 'Napoléon the Small'.

3 The 1889 Exposition Universelle (Universal Exhibition) ran in Paris from 6 May to 31 October.

4 Galerie des machines, or the Palais des machines ('Machine Hall'), was built for the Universal Exposition of 1889 at the foot of the Champ de Mars, in front of the École Militaire. Its architect was Ferdinand Dutert, and the iron structure was built by the Société des Forges de Fives-Lille and the Cail factory. The building was comprised of a huge glass and metal hall with an area of 115 by 420 metres (377 by 1,378 ft) and a height of 48.3 metres (160 ft). It was free of internal supports, with the framework consisting of twenty trusses that incorporated hinged arches, originally developed for bridge building.

5 '*Kanaks*' in the original. A reference to the indigenous inhabitants of the French colony New Caledonia. During the 1889 Universal Exhibition a Kanak village was reconstructed on the Esplanade des Invalides, and served as an ethnographic display. The 'native villages' were installed behind tall fences that effectively caged in the 'natives' and turned them into a kind of human zoo.

6 A mural crown (Latin: *corona muralis*) is a crown or headpiece representing city walls or towers. In classical antiquity, it was an

emblem of tutelary deities who watched over a city. Later the mural crown developed into a symbol of European heraldry.

7 Jason Gould (1836-1892) was an American railroad magnate and financial speculator. He was one of the wealthiest men of the late nineteenth century, but his unscrupulous and often dubious business practices made him a controversial and unpopular figure. He is widely regarded as one of the era's great 'robber barons'.

8 I have expanded these allusions to make them easier to comprehend. In the original Huysmans uses only the words '*Vulcan*' and '*cyclopes*'.

9 Ferdinand Barbedienne (1810-1892) was a French metalworker and bronze founder. As well as helping to democratise art through the development of a process of producing bronze sculptures on a small scale, Barbedienne, along with his partner Achille Collas, helped create a new process of colouration and patination for bronze sculptures.

10 The firm Sautter-Lemonnier had installed a revolving lighthouse in the middle of the Palais des Machines, opposite the entrance hall. It contained a light with an intensity of 30,000 candela, and a projector that was 1.50 m in diameter with an intensity of 100,000 candela.

11 Jean de La Bruyère (1645-96) was a French philosopher and moralist, perhaps best known for his 1688 book, *Les Caractères ou les moeurs de ce siècle* (*Characters, or the Manners of the Age*). La Bruyère, a precursor of the Romantics, contrasted the artificial world of Parisian society with that of the natural world: 'If I compare the two most opposite conditions of men, I mean the great and the common people, the latter appear satisfied if they only have the necessities of life, and the former fretful and poor amidst superfluities. A man of the people can do no harm; a great man will do no good, and is capable of doing great mischief; the first only plans and practises useful things, the second adds to them what is hurtful. Here, rusticity and frankness show themselves ingenuously; there, a malignant and corrupt disposition lies hidden under a veneer of politeness. If the common people have scarcely any culture, the great have no soul; the first have a good foundation and no outward appearances; the latter are all outward appearance and but a mere superstratum. Were I to choose between the two, I should select, without hesitation, being a plebeian.' (*The 'Characters' of Jean de La Bruyère*, translated by Henri van Laun, London: Nimmo, 1885, p.230.)

12 *François le Champi* (1848) and *La Petite Fadette* (1849) were rural-themed novels by George Sand, which, along with *La Mare au Diable* (1846), made up what is referred to as her 'pastoral trilogy'.

13 Céladon was one of the main protagonists in Honoré d'Urfé's classic pastoral novel, *L'Astrée* (1607), which told the story, at great length, of the love affair between a young shepherdess, Astrée, and her suitor, Céladon, a shepherd. The novel formed the basis of the 1691 opera, *Astrée*, with a libretto by Jean de la Fontaine.

14 Paul Mantz (1821-1895) was a historian of French art and the administrative director of the École des Beaux-Arts. He organised the retrospective exhibitions of Eugène Delacroix (1885) and Jean-François Millet (1887).

15 In the original, Huysmans makes an allusive reference to '*la maison du quai*' meaning the École des Beaux-Arts. Given the health metaphor given at the start of the article I have used '*maison*' in the sense of '*maison d'aliénés*' ('insane asylum') rather than 'business' or 'firm'.

VIII

1 Goya painted numerous bullfighting scenes so it is not easy to determine which painting Huysmans is talking about here.

2 The State Room, which was built during the reign of Napoléon III (1852-70), was inaugurated on 27 October 1886.

3 A portrait by Henri Regnault. Juan Prim (1814-1870) was a Spanish general and statesman who was briefly Prime Minister of Spain until his assassination.

4 The works of Ingres and Delacroix were moved to the Louvre from the Musée du Luxembourg at the beginning of the Third Republic.

5 Huysmans uses the term *peinture bouchère* in the original, playing with the French word *boucher*, 'butcher shop', and the bare flesh often on display in Rubens' paintings.

6 A rare instance of Huysmans making a private joke, as Pierre-Vincent Chouilloux was the professor of calligraphy at the Lycée Saint-Louis, the school in the sixth arrondissement of Paris which Huysmans had attended when he was fourteen. The name Chouilloux des Radrets would have been unfamiliar to the majority of the readers of *Certains*.

7 'Ligeia' is an early short story by Edgar Allan Poe, first published in 1838. The story follows an unnamed narrator and his wife Ligeia, a beautiful and intelligent raven-haired woman who falls ill and dies. After her death, the narrator marries the Lady Rowena, who also falls ill and dies. The narrator stays with her body overnight and watches as Rowena slowly comes back from the dead, but she has transformed into Ligeia.

8 Francesco Lancilotti (1472- ?) a painter about whom little is known.

His *Tractato di pictura* ('Treatise on Painting') was published in Rome in 1509.

9 Correggio was born in 1489, which would have made him 21 at the time of Bianchi's death. Most experts today accept that he became Bianchi's apprentice at the age of fourteen, as it was not uncommon for boys to be apprenticed to an artist at a very early age.

10 In the original, Huysmans uses the neologism '*peinturlographes*', a combination of '*peinturlurer*' (to daub) with '*graphe*' (from the Latin, to write).

11 Although at the time Huysmans was writing the painting was attributed to the Italian Renaissance artist Francesco Bianchi (c.1447-1510), it was later reattributed to Francesco Marmitta (c.1472-c.1505), an Italian painter from Parma.

12 The Abbey of Saint Scholastica, also known as Subiaco Abbey (Abbazia di Santa Scolastica), is located just outside the town of Subiaco in the Province of Rome, Italy. It is still an active Benedictine order. It was in one of the Subiaco caves that Benedict made his first hermitage. Legend has it that an envious priest, Florentius, tried to poison him with poisoned bread, but his plan was foiled when Benedict blessed the loaf and a raven swooped down and flew off with it. Having failed with poison, Florentius tried to seduce Benedict's monks with prostitutes.

13 Bradamante is a fictional female knight who appears in two epic poems of the Renaissance: *Orlando Innamorato* by Matteo Maria Boiardo and *Orlando Furioso* by Ludovico Ariosto.

14 *Saint-Quentin: sa vie, son culte, restauration de son pèlerinage* (1878) by Abbé Adolphe Mathieu.

15 '*Vermandois*' in the original, the name of a French region during the Merovingian period (fifth to seventh centuries), roughly situated in the Picardy region of northern France.

16 Sébastien le Nain de Tillemont (1637-1698), a French ecclesiastic and historian. Volume IV of his *Memoires pour servir a l'histoire ecclésiastique* (1696) contains a chapter on St. Quentin.

Glossary of Artists

Pierre-Antoine Baudouin (1723-1769), a French painter and illustrator who was a pupil of Boucher. He is perhaps best know for his lightly erotic genre paintings. **96**, 97, 230

Paul Albert Bartholomé (1848-1928), a French painter (and subsequently a sculptor) who studied at the École des Beaux Arts under Gérôme. He was a close friend of Degas who persuaded him to take up sculpture. 12, 19, 25, 55, **56**, 137, 223

Jules Bastien-Lepage (1848-1884), a French painter who studied at the École des Beaux Arts under Cabanel. He was considered by many to be part of the Naturalist school in painting, though Huysmans always felt he didn't go far enough and that he pandered to his audience by making his pictures too idealistic and romantic. 20-1, 27, 37, 38, 221

Auguste Delaberge (1807-1842), a French landscape painter. 204

Rosa Bonheur (1822-1899) a French painter and sculptor who specialised in genre scenes featuring animals. 140

Léon Bonnat (1833-1922), a French painter who taught at the École des Beaux Arts. He was especially known for his portraits, and was a frequent target of Huysmans' scorn. 38

François Bonvin (1817-1887), a French realist painter influenced by the Dutch old masters and by Chardin. 138, **139**

Hieronymus Bosch (c.1440-1516) one of the early Flemish Primitives perhaps best known for the bizarre images in his work, such as in *The Garden of Earthly Delights*. 156

François Boucher (1703-1770) was a French painter, draughtsman and etcher, who worked in the Rococo style. Known for his idyllic, voluptuous paintings on classical themes, for allegories and pastoral scenes, he was perhaps the most celebrated decorative artist of his time. 97

Glossary

William Bouguereau (1825-1905), a French academic painter, perhaps the most well-known of the artists who specialised in the bland desexualised idealisation of the female form. One of his most famous works, *Naissance de Venus* was shown at the 1879 Salon. Huysmans frequently ridiculed his work. 7, 139, 140, 142, 234

Gustave Boulanger (1824-1888), a French Academic painter whose work often featured classical and oriental subjects. He taught at the Institut de France and was noted for his hostility to Impressionism. 39

Félix Bracquemond (1833-1914) a French painter, engraver and ceramicist. A founding member of the Society of Watercolourists, he was one of the first French artists to express an interest in Japanese art. **137**, **138**

Rodolphe Bresdin (1822-1885) a French engraver whose work, which often had a strange, fantastical quality, was a huge influence on Odilon Redon. 138

Jules Breton (1827-1906), a French painter of the Realist school who was renowned for his paintings of peasants and of rustic life. 130, 234

Alexandre Cabanel (1823-1889), a French painter of historical, classical and religious subjects in the Academic style. He represented the epitome of all the things Huysmans hated about official art. 7, 39

Jacques Callot (c. 1592-1635) was a baroque printmaker and draftsman from the Lorraine region. His stylised engravings have a certain bizarre quality about them. **158**

Jacques-Philippe Caresme (1734-1796), a French painter and copperplate engraver. Caresme (or Carême) painted a number of lightly licentious works with eroticised subject matter. **97**, 230

Jean-Baptiste Carpeaux (1827-1875), a French sculptor and painter. 67

Jules Chéret (1836-1932), a French painter and lithographer, was a master of poster art during the Belle Époque period. In 1881 Huysmans used Chéret to illustrate the pantomime he wrote with Léon Hennique, *Pierrot sceptique*. This was a beautifully produced book – in a limited edition print run that included five copies printed on deluxe pink paper – and featured a distinctive cover and illustrations by Chéret. 12, 13, 16, 19, 23, 24, 25, 27, 73-9, **75**, **76**, **77**, **79**

Benjamin Constant (1845-1902), a French painter best known for his Oriental subjects. He was a pupil of Cabanel. 140

Jean-Baptiste Corot (1796-1875), a French painter and illustrator mostly known for his landscapes. He was one of the founders of the Barbizon school, a group of landscape artists who, in reaction against

Romantism, drew their inspiration directly from nature which they tried to capture in a more realistic fashion. 188

ANTONIO ALLEGRI DA CORREGGIO (1489-1534), was the foremost painter of the Parma school during the High Italian Renaissance. In 1503-05 he was apprenticed to Francesco Bianchi.

GUSTAVE COURBET (1819-1877), a French painter and sculptor considered to be the head of the realist school, as opposed to the Academic tradition. His work often challenged conventions – such as in his more realistic treatment of peasants and workmen – and consequently provoked a scandalised response. 51, 188, 227

KARL DAUBIGNY (1846-1886) was a French landscape painter. He was the pupil of his father, Charles-François Daubigny (1817-1878), an influential figure in the Barbizon school, whose talents as a painter Huysmans rated even less than his son's. 204

EDGAR DEGAS (1834-1917), a French painter, engraver, sculptor and photographer who is recognised as one of the most influential artists of the period. He helped to organise what would become known as the Impressionist exhibitions, the first of which took place in 1874. At the time Huysmans was writing, Degas was not the universally admired artist he would later become. 7, 9, 10, 12, 16, 21, 23-5, 38, 46-51, **47**, **48**, **49**, 67, 68, 112, 137, 208, 222

EUGÈNE DELACROIX (1798-1863), one of the emblematic figures of nineteenth-century French art, and perhaps its foremost exponent of Romanticism. For Baudelaire, Delacroix was 'the most original painter either of modern or ancient times'. 20-1, 25, 27, 37, 38, 66, 188, **205**, **206**, 207, **208**, 212, 221, 237

ACHILLE JACQUES-JEAN-MARIE DEVÉRIA (1800-1857) was a French painter and lithographer. He exhibited at the Salon from an early age, but became better known for his illustrations, many of which had an erotic content. In 1876 his illustrations were used for an edition of Alfred de Musset's erotic novel *Gamiani*, for which Huysmans provided an anonymous preface. **98**, 204

GUSTAVE DORÉ (1832-1883) was a French artist who is now best known for his distinctive woodcut illustrations and engravings, though he produced a number of paintings earlier in his career. 146

ÉDOUARD DUBUFE (1819-1893) a French portrait painter. 140

TONY ROBERT-FLEURY (1837-1911), a painter and art teacher best known for his history paintings. 39

JEAN-LOUIS FORAIN (1852-1931), a French painter and illustrator who was closely associated with the Impressionists. He exhibited at four of the Impressionist exhibitions between 1879 and 1886. Huysmans knew Forain, who painted his portrait, and used his engravings in *Marthe* (1879 edition) and *Croquis parisiens* (1880). 7, 24, 25, 67-9, **68**, 112, 137, 212

FRA ANGELICO (c.1395-1455), an Italian painter of the early Renaissance. Huysmans would write about his *Coronation of the Virgin* in *La Cathédrale* (1898). 104

JEAN-HONORÉ FRAGONARD (1732-1806) was a French painter and printmaker of the late Rococo period. Among his most popular works are genre paintings conveying an atmosphere of intimacy and veiled eroticism. 97

PAUL GAVARNI was the *nom-de-plume* of Sulpice Guillaume Chevalier (1804-66), a French illustrator born in Paris, whose erotic series *Scènes de la vie intime* dates from 1837. In these 'twelve not-so-chaste lithographs', as Goncourt called them, there was was 'more passion, more sensual ardour, more libidinous voluptuousness, than pure obscenity'. **98**

FRANÇOIS GERARD (1770-1837) a French painter who studied under David. He is perhaps best known for his portraits. 204

JEAN-LÉON GÉRÔME (1824-1904), a French painter and sculptor whose work included historical painting, Greek mythology, Orientalism, and portraits. Huysmans rarely has a good word to say about Gérôme, who embodied the Academic style he hated so much. 7, 39, 140, 142

HENRI GERVEX (1852-1929) was a French painter who studied under Cabanel and Fromentin. He is perhaps best known for his painting, *Rolla,* which was exluded from the 1878 Salon a month before it opened on the grounds of immorality. Huysmans wrote favourably about it the same year, but his opinion of Gervex became more critical over the next decade, seeing him as a painter who preferred to paint in a fashionable idealised style, rather than representing true reality. 38

CHARLES GLEYRE (1806-1874), a Swiss painter who was a teacher at the École des Beaux Arts in Paris. His students included Monet, Renoir and Sisley. 80, 204

FRANCISCO GOYA (1746-1828) was perhaps the most influential Spanish painter and printmaker of his time. 15, 25, 158, 201-3, 237

ALFRED GRÉVIN (1827-1892) was a French caricaturist who specialised in drawings of Parisiens. He also founded the Musée Grévin of waxworks in Paris. 21, 37

Antoine-Jean Gros (1771-1835), a French history painter working in the Classical tradition. 204

Matthias Grünewald (c.1470-1528), a German Renaissance painter who rejected Classicism. Only a few of his paintings survive, the largest being the Isenheim altarpiece. Huysmans would write about his *Crucifixion* at more length in his novel, *Là-bas,* and was undoubtedly influential in reviving interest in his work. 11, 15, 104

Pierre-Narcisse Guérin (1774-1833), a neoclassical French painter, who studied under Regnault. 204

François Joseph Heim (1787-1865), a French painter who was appointed President of the Académie des Beaux-Arts in 1853. 204

Jean-Jacques Henner (1829-1905), a French painter in the Academic school. 39, 139

William Hogarth (1697-1764), an English painter, printmaker and cartoonist. 100

Hokusai (1760-1849), a Japanese artist, *ukiyo-e* painter and printmaker of the Edo period, perhaps best known in the West for his print *The Great Wave off Kanagawa.* **102**, 158, **159**

Jean-Auguste-Dominique Ingres (1780-1867), one of the most influential of the French neoclassical painters. 158, 205, 208, **209**, **210**, **211**, **212**, 237

Ludwig Knaus (1829-1910), a German painter of genre scenes and the head of the Dusseldorf school. 140

Alphonse Legros (1837-1911), a French painter, etcher, sculptor, and medallist. 138

Timoléon Marie Lobrichon (1831-1914), a French painter known for his genre work and especially for his paintings of children, which are of an almost nauseating sentimentality. 37

Stefan Lochner (c. 1410-c.1451) was a German painter of the late Gothic period. Perhaps the best known representative of the Cologne school, his work is seen as the most successful visual interpretation of late medieval German mysticism before Grünewald. 155

Hans Makart (1840-84), an Austrian history painter, designer and theatrical decorator. Huysmans mispelled his name 'Mackart' in the the original. Makart's work was an influence on Klimt. 180

Édouard Manet (1832-1883), a French painter who was a key figure in the development of modern painting and considered one of the fathers of Impressionism. In 1863 the Salon refused his *Le Déjeuner sur l'herbe*, which was subsequently shown at the Salon des Refusés, where it caused an enormous scandal. 66, 67, 80, 88, 137, 188, 208, 227

ADRIEN EMMANUEL MARIE (1848-1891), a French engraver and painter. His illustrations for *L'Education de la poupée* ('The Doll's Education') in 1881 were cloyingly sentimental. 37

JOHN MARTIN (1789-1854), an English Romantic painter, engraver and illustrator. His work combined the fantastic and the melodramatic. He was perhaps best known for his triptych, *The Last Judgement*. Huysmans spelled his name 'Martins' in the original. 183

ERNEST MEISSONIER (1815-1891), a French painter particularly known for his pictures of Napoléon and for his battle scenes. His paintings were renowned for their fine detail, and he famously produced a series of miniature paintings in oil. 138, 139, 140, 234

HANS MEMLING (c.1430-1494) a German painter who worked in the Flemish tradition. 104

ANTONIN MERCIÉ (1845-1916), a French sculptor who trained at the Beaux-Arts. His plaster statue of *Gloria victis* won a medal of honour at the 1874 Salon and bronze copies were subsequently produced by the Barbedienne foundry. **68**, 225

JEAN-FRANÇOIS MILLET (1814-1875), a French painter and one of the founders of the Barbizon school. He was the son of a farming family, and his work is noted for its scenes of peasant and rural life. 15, 26, 112, 188-96, **191**, **192**, **193**, **195**, **196**

GUSTAVE MOREAU (1826-1898), a French painter who became a major figure in Symbolist art. Huysmans' descriptions of his work in *À rebours* of 1884 had a huge impact on his reputation and on the way people subsequently regarded his work. 7, 12, 13, 21, 23, 24, 26, 38, 39, 41, 42-6, **43**, **44**

GIUSEPPE DE NITTIS (1846-1884), an Italian painter whose work crossed the borders of the Salon style and Impressionism. In 1880 Huysmans had seen potential in his work, but during the 1880s he grew progressively more disillusioned by it. 62

AMABLE PAGNEST (1790-1819) a French painter whose work was exhibited in 1814 and 1819 at the Salon. He was the pupil of Jacques Louis David. 204

GIOVANNI BATTISTA PIRANESI (1720-1778) was an Italian architect and artist perhaps most famous for his series of etchings of imaginary prisons, the architecture of which was almost impossibly labyrinthine. 171, 183

PIERRE PUVIS DE CHAVANNES (1824-1898), a French painter best known for his mural work and for the flat, fresco-like style of his paintings. 12, 26, 39-42, **39**, **40**, **41**

JEAN-FRANÇOIS RAFFAËLLI (1850-1924), a painter and illustrator closely associated with the Impressionists. Huysmans used some of Raffaëlli's illustrations for the first edition of his *Croquis parisiens* (1880). 7, 12, 14, 19, 57-60, **57**, **59**, 223

ODILON REDON (1840-1916), a French painter, engraver and printmaker whose work is almost unclassifiable, but who is linked with the Symbolist movement. He was relatively unknown when Huysmans first wrote about him in *L'Art moderne* and *À rebours*, and the two subsequently became friends. Huysmans had a considerable impact on his career, not only exposing Redon to a wider audience, but also shaping the public's conception of his work through his interpretation of it, something which Redon disagreed with and which eventually led to a cooling of their friendship. The three albums Huysmans refers to in *Certains* are: *Les Origines*, eight lithographs and a frontispiece (Paris: Lemercier, 1883, edition of 25); *La Tentation de saint Antoine*, ten lithographs and a frontispiece (Bruxelles: Deman, 1888, edition of 58); *À Gustave Flaubert*, six lithographs and a frontispiece (Paris: Becquet, 1889, edition of 60). 7, 12, 16, 18, 19, 22-5, 46, 138, **160**, **161**, **162**, **163**, 212, 225

HENRI REGNAULT (1843-1871), a French painter who trained in the studio of Cabanel and is known mostly as an Orientalist. 204, **205**, 237

JEAN-BAPTISTE REGNAULT (1754-1829), a French Academic painter. 50, **51**, 223

REMBRANDT VAN RIJN (1606-1669) perhaps the most famous painter and printmaker of the Dutch 'Golden Age'. Among his works are a small number of erotic or obscene drawings and engravings. 97

PIERRE-AUGUSTE RENOIR (1841-1919), a French painter, who studied under Gleyre and who first exhibited at the Salon in 1864. Inspired by Pissarro and Manet, Renoir joined forced with the nascent Impressionist movement and exhibited with them in 1874, after a series of refusals by the Salon jury. 137

LOUIS LÉOPOLD ROBERT (1794-1835), a Swiss painter who moved to Paris at the age of sixteen. 204

THOMAS ROWLANDSON (1756-1827), an English artist and caricaturist. Although perhaps best known for his political satires he also produced a number of obscene prints, though their intent seems to be more caricatural or comical than erotic. 98-102, **99**, **100**

PETER PAUL RUBENS (1577-1640), a Flemish painter in the Baroque tradition. His depiction of women as plump and sensuous became such a defining characteristic of his work that the term 'Rubenesque' is often applied to them. 101, 207

ARY SCHEFFER (1795-1858), a French painter of Dutch extraction, considered one of the masters of Romantic painting. 204

MARTIN SCHONGAUER (c. 1450–53 to 1491), an Alsatian engraver and painter, one of the most important Gothic printmakers before Dürer. 156

ALFRED SISLEY (1839-1899), a landscape painter who was born in Paris to Anglo-French parents and spent most of his working life in France, but retained his English nationality. An early associate of the Impressionists, he exhibited at their first show in 1874. 137

NICOLAS FRANÇOIS OCTAVE TASSAERT (1800-1874) a French painter, engraver and illustrator whose work veered beween the sentimental and the lubricious. **98**

HORACE VERNET (1789-1863) a French painter mostly known for his military paintings. 204

ROGER VAN DER WEYDEN (c.1400-1464), an early Flemish Primitive. 104

JAMES MCNEIL WHISTLER (1834-1903), an American painter known for his distinctive portraits. He came to Paris in 1855 where he became acquainted with Fantin-Latour, Carolus-Duran and Manet. 12, 16, 17, 22, 25, 26, 81-9, **81**, **82**, **83** **84**, **86**, 87, **88**, 137, 138, 210, 227-8

ADOLPHE LÉON WILLETTE (1857-1926) was a French painter, illustrator, caricaturist, and lithographer who studied for four years at the École des Beaux-Arts under Cabanel. His work was often satirical, poking fun at the government or at established political or societal norms, and it also had more of an erotic content than Chéret's. His name is closely associated with the image of the Pierrot dressed in black and his illustrations can be found in many publications including *Le Rire, Le Courrier Français,* and his own paper, *Le Pierrot.* 74

Books by J.-K. Huysmans available from Dedalus:

Translated by Brendan King:
Marthe
The Vatard Sisters
Parisian Sketches
Drifting
Against Nature
Stranded
Modern Art
Là-bas: A Journey into the Self

Translated by Clara Bell (revised by Brendan King):
The Cathedral

Translated by W. Fleming:
En Route

Translated by Edward Perceval:
The Oblate of St. Benedict

Dedalus has also published Robert Baldick's *The Life of J.-K. Huysmans*, edited by Brendan King.

Modern Art by J.-K. Huysmans

'Huysmans reviewed the Salons of 1879-82 and the Independent Exhibitions of 1880-82 at considerable length. His articles, collected as *L'Art moderne* (1883), have never before been translated into English, probably because he is the least known of the writer-critics, and his French is often not straightforward. Robert Baldick, biographer of Huysmans (1955) described his style as 'one of the strangest literary idioms in existence'. Brendan King, who has already translated most of Huysmans's fiction, has produced an excellent version. Rarely can it have been such fun to read translated denunciations of so many forgotten French pictures.'

Julian Barnes in *The London Review of Books*

'King displays both considerable knowledge and easy humour in the tone of his introduction. His detailed notes and glossary of artists are useful, but particularly appealing to the reader will be the inclusion, in the main body of the text, of small black-and-white illustrations for a number of paintings referred to, some taken from the original Salon catalogues.'

Nicholas White in *The Times Literary Supplement*

'What a joy this was to read, a superbly translated volume, with excellent footnotes and small inserts of the artwork studied.'

The Guardian

£10.99 ISBN 978 1 910213 99 5 313 p B. Format

Against Nature by J.-K. Huysmans

'Huysmans' study of obsession and aesthetics got up no end of reviewers' noses on its 1884 publication. It's not hard to see why: decadent aristocrat Jean Floressas des Esseintes, afflicted by nerves so grievous they cause his spine to freeze when he sees a servant wringing out washing, takes turns kicking out at classical poets, modern novelists and the church. The poor are grotesque, the rich are decaying and the bourgeoisie simply insufferable. Only Dickens, Baudelaire and the odd enema provide respite. Cloistered in an opulent house in the suburbs of Paris, des Esseintes undertakes a series of experiments in living which prove to be an absolute hoot. He decorates an unfortunate tortoise with precious stones, tries to go to England, but only makes it as far as a nearby pub, and attempts to turn an urchin into a killer by buying him credit at a brothel. This largely plotless mix of bilious satire, broad comedy and literary criticism may have lost some of its immediacy, but it remains a captivating, contradictory work of art.'

James Smart in *The Guardian*

'Perhaps the key book of Decadence, Huysmans's curious novel can be considered many things, though a style manual comes closest to defining it and this sparkling new translation by Brendan King is both overdue and to be warmly welcomed.'

'Books for Christmas' by Peter Burton in *Three Sixty Magazine*

'For a novel about the highs and lows of isolation, I'd choose J.-K. Huysmans' *Against Nature.*'

Will Lloyd's 'Lockdown list' in *The Spectator*

£8.99 ISBN 978 1 903517 65 9 315 p B. Format

Là-Bas by J.-K. Huysmans

'Huysmans' dark masterpiece, published in the same year as *The Picture of Dorian Gray*, is a serious, uncompromisingly learned depiction of the Hell through which the search for spiritual meaning must lead. The protagonist, Durtal, is investigating the life of Gilles de Rais, mass-murderer and unlikely – or not so unlikely – companion-in-arms of Joan of Arc. Long meditations on the nature of art, guilt, the satanic and the divine take him to a black mass. This superb new translation by Brendan King vividly recalls the allusive, proto-expressionist vigour of the original; images snarl and spring at the reader. '

Murrough O'Brien in *The Independent on Sunday*

'This Gothic shocker is not for the faint-hearted.'

Jerome Boyd Maunsell in *The Times*

'As with most of Huysmans' books, the pleasure in reading is not necessarily from its overarching plot-line, but in set pieces, such as the extraordinary sequences in which Gilles de Rais wanders through a wood that suddenly metamorphoses into a series of copulating organic forms, the justly famous word-painting of Matthias Grünewald's Crucifixion altar-piece, or the brutally erotic scenes, crackling with sexual tension, between Durtal and Madame Chantelouve. If it is about anything, *Là-Bas* is about Good and Evil. This enlightening new translation will be especially useful to students of literature. Not only does it contain an introduction that puts Huysmans in context for those who are new to his work, it also includes extensive notes to unlock the mass of obscure words that litter the text, and references to a vast array of scientists, false messiahs and misfits whose ideas went into the concoction of this strangely fascinating book.'

Beryl Bainbridge in *The Spectator*

£9.99 ISBN 912868 41 3 329 p B. Format

Parisian Sketches by J.-K. Huysmans

'This fine new translation by Brendan King not only reprints some of the eaux fortes of Jean-Louis Forain and Jean-François Raffaëlli which illustrated the first edition, but also reproductions of Forain's excessively glamorous image of 'The Streetwalker'. Which was suppressed in 1880, and of Odilon Redon's 'Hommage a Goya' series which inspired Huysmans's 'Nightmare' (one of the seven pieces added to the new Léon Vanier edition of 1886, all of which are included here).'

Nicholas White in *The Times Literary Supplement*

'Sharing a common milieu that of the Impressionist circle, writer J.-K. Huysmans' effervescent portrait of Parisian life in the 1880s captures a moment in time with vivid, sensory precision. Here is the world of the flamboyant Folies-Bergère and the Opéra Garnier, showgirls and streetwalkers all filtered through the consciousness of a shrewd observer who paints Paris' vibrant hues with both affection and candour.'

The Good Book Guide

'An enthusiastic flaneur (if that's not too much of a contradiction). Huysmans created evocative prose-pictures of Parisian life – a visit to the barber, a gloomy railway café, a chestnut-seller – that merit comparison with the pictures of Caillebotte, Degas and Atget.'

Christopher Hirst in *The Independent*

£8.99 ISBN 978 1 903517 24 6 196 p B. Format

Drifting by J.-K. Huysmans

'Huysmans's protagonist here, M Jean Folantin, is an ageing bachelor employed at the Ministry of the Interior... Wandering the streets of Paris, wallowing in antipathy towards the encroaching Americanization of European manners and modernizing construction works that are ruining his once-familiar city, he seeks refuge in taprooms and chop-houses, hoping only for the fleeting satisfaction offered by a savoury meal. Alas, in attempting to achieve even this modest goal he is repeatedly thwarted... but his condemnation of the world around him are ultimately comic and inspiriting, and are given piquancy by Brendan King's new translation, which preserves the sheer delectability of the language even when it's describing something disgusting. That, along with King's introduction, notes, with their intelligence on everything from lead oxide used to adulterate nineteenth-century wines to the ubiquity of syphilis in the French capital, makes *À Vau-l'eau* a good place in which to consort with Huysmans's miserable creations.'

Matt Sturrock in *The Times Literary Supplement*

'[The] *Iliad* of indigestion.'

James Huneker, *Unicorns*

£7.99 ISBN 978 1 910213 63 6 109 p B. Format

Stranded by J.-K. Huysmans

'Jacques and his ailing wife, Louise, have lost nearly everything. Desperate for a refuge, they abandon Paris in search of something simpler and cheaper, accepting the one barely habitable room of a decrepit chateau of which Louise's uncle is the negligent caretaker. They soon learn that the family is no protection from their problems, however, and that leaving the city may not lead to savings: the harsh life of the peasant produces only selfishness and cruelty , while the constant thieving they suffer at the hands of even their relations risks ruining them. With their future dependent on the collection of promissory notes, they can only wait and hope.

Like Huysmans's best-known novel, *Against Nature, Stranded* offers little plot, emphasizing instead subjective experience, atmosphere, symbol, and an unorthodox morality that prizes the artificial above all. Contemporary criticism was divided over the work veering between scenes of unflinching naturalism – including a graphic description of the birth of a calf – and a series of long dream sequences with little immediate relationship to the story: Jacques imagines himself a witness to the life of Esther; later he and his wife take a walk on the moon. Modern readers will have to decide for themselves if Huysmans's quest for symbolism wasn't better served by the more conventional means he also deployed: the ruined castle representing unguarded civilization eroded by the cold indifference of the natural world, and the dying kitten at the story's end – an embodiment of the hope and compassion the couple risk losing.

King has written an excellent introduction in which he relates the critical history of this unusual work and highlights the contrasts and creativity that made the era of its publication such a rich one to revisit. His translation is scrupulously accurate.'

Tadzio Koelb in *The Times Literary Supplement*

£9.99 ISBN 978 1 903517 84 0 251 p B. Format

The Cathedral by J.-K. Huysmans

'Durtal extols the flaming raptures of the mystical Gothic, tries to comprehend the stone text of Chartres and is extremely funny about the horrors of living in the provinces, although equally viperish on the subject of Parisian literary life. These books mark a 19th century spiritual journey undertaken by a very modern sensibility; Durtal's wicked, witty, self-lacerating voice could be that of a contemporary medieval scholar with a bad case of mystical anomie.'

Elizabeth Young in *City Limits*

'To get at that truth which is...the deepest meaning of beauty, to find that symbol which is its most adequate expression, is in itself a kind of creation; and that is what Huysmans does for us in *The Cathedral.* More and more he has put aside all the profane and accessible and outward pomp of writing, for an inner and more severe beauty of perfect truth. He has come to realise that truth can be reached and revealed only by symbol.'

Arthur Symons in *The Saturday Review*,

£9.99 ISBN 978 1 903517 90 1 364 p B. Format